PRAISE FOR TIF MARCELO

"Marcelo loads their darling romance with touching drama and sweet moments while seamlessly weaving in Filipino culture, language, and food, adding depth and authenticity to the plot. The endearing protagonists, dramatic sibling rivalry, and idyllic coastal setting make for a feel-good romance that readers won't want to miss."

—*Publishers Weekly*

"Readers will yearn for more stories about these compelling characters."

—*Booklist*

Know You by Heart

OTHER TITLES BY TIF MARCELO

Heart Resort

It Takes Heart

Contemporary Fiction

In a Book Club Far Away
Once Upon a Sunset
The Key to Happily Ever After

Journey to the Heart Series

North to You
East in Paradise
West Coast Love

Anthology

Christmas Actually

Young Adult

The Holiday Switch

Know You by Heart

Heart Resort Book 2

TIF MARCELO

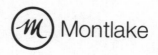 Montlake

Published by Montlake, Seattle

www.apub.com

Amazon, the Amazon logo, and Montlake are trademarks of Amazon.com, Inc., or its affiliates.

ISBN-13: 9781542034142
ISBN-10: 1542034140

Cover design by Hang Le

Printed in the United States of America

To my #5amwritersclub UCIJ retreat cohort,
who helped me through the toughest and most
rewarding parts of this book

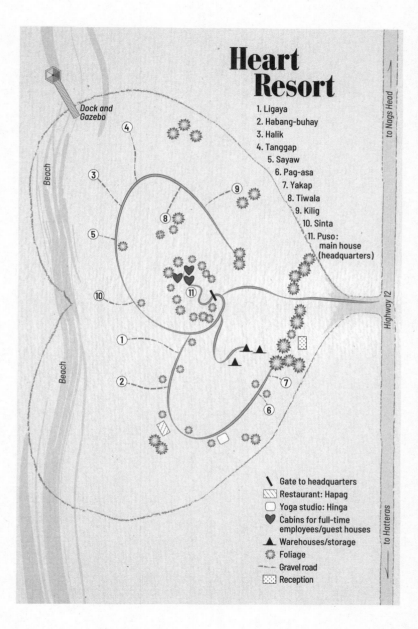

Heart
Resort

1. Ligaya
2. Habang-buhay
3. Halik
4. Tanggap
5. Sayaw
6. Pag-asa
7. Yakap
8. Tiwala
9. Kilig
10. Sinta
11. Puso:
    main house
    (headquarters)

Dock and
Gazebo

Beach

Beach

to Nags Head

Highway 12

to Hatteras

🖊 Gate to headquarters
🔲 Restaurant: Hapag
⬜ Yoga studio: Hinga
💜 Cabins for full-time
   employees/guest houses
▲ Warehouses/storage
✳ Foliage
--- Gravel road
▦ Reception

CHAPTER ONE

Las Vegas, Nevada
Four years and seven months ago
Word of the day: nuptials

Romance author Eden Chan never thought she would become a romance trope, much less one of the hardest tropes to write: a marriage of convenience. But here she was, in an exquisite princess-cut wedding gown made of lace, satin, and tulle, wearing makeup precisely applied by a bona fide makeup artist, holding a pen poised over a stapled contract, hands shaking.

C'mon, this is a no-brainer. It's only five years, the devil on her shoulder said.

But the angel on her other shoulder was ready with his rebuttal. *That's five years of your wonderful life.*

It's not all the way wonderful, the devil reminded her. *And think of the payoff.*

"Eden?" Seated in a luxurious love seat across a cherrywood coffee table, Christopher Puso, her soon-to-be husband—if and when she finally signed the document—startled her out of her apprehension with a frown, looking very much like the alpha hero she'd written in her books. Sexy in a slim-cut barong tagalog with a smoldering gaze, exuding pride through his pores, he was beautiful. To some, his current expression could be intimidating, but Eden had come to the conclusion that he was more of a softy than he let on. In the years she'd watched him (he was a great character study), she'd catalogued his nuanced mannerisms. For example, when he lifted an eyebrow, he was being sarcastic. His crooked grin signified a jovial mood. When he bit his bottom lip, that meant he was deep in thought.

And right now, Chris was concerned. "Are you okay?" His voice cracked with worry.

"Yeah. I think?" Her answer came out like a wheeze. She inhaled a long and steady breath and imagined her alveoli blossoming, turning blue from oxygen. This was fine. Everything was fine.

A simple signature would be the difference between working as a respiratory therapist super part time and finally writing all the books waiting their turn in her head or succumbing to a full-time job with benefits and writing in the wee hours of the morning or night. The second option sounded to her like the worst-case scenario; those hospital shifts were both backbreaking and emotion-depleting work. But the pain of not writing superseded all that.

Eden *had* to write. When her day job took her energy and her inspiration, Eden felt herself withering away, like a plant whose soil was being siphoned of water.

This chance was what she wanted. What she needed.

But the corset-style bodice fought against her breath. Marrying Chris meant there would be pretending. Lots of pretending: to her family, to his three siblings and their families, and to everyone else in the world. She was already pretending with her current, unsuccessful pen name, Malia James. "I just can't . . ."

Breathe. She couldn't breathe.

"That's it. This is *over*." From Eden's right side flashed an apparition in peach, and her best friend's face cut through the haze of her nervousness. Paige Miller, with her blonde hair in a coif so dutifully sprayed that Eden guessed it was as stiff as cardboard, held her by the shoulders. From behind her, Chris's best man said something, to which Paige yelled, "You shut up, Max Aguilar."

"Eden," she continued, blue eyes blinking in earnest. "You don't have to do this. You can say no. I can go in there and tell everyone to go home, and I'm not afraid to do so. You're not obligated. You have choices."

Eden's head bobbed like a buoy, most likely because she was still holding her breath. So after she instructed her lungs to work, she focused on Paige's face. On how pretty her friend was in peach, and how six months ago Paige had challenged her and Chris's engagement. Last night, Paige had even attempted a one-person intervention at an all-you-can-eat twenty-four-hour breakfast buffet, saying this exact same thing.

Now, in what Eden could describe only as a slow climb to awareness, she arrived back in the bridal suite, to this contract that would be more important than the marriage certificate she and Chris would sign later on.

All this *was* her choice.

"I still say yes. Even if in five years, we're going to d—" She choked out the word. "Divorce. I never thought I'd divorce. Heck, I never thought I'd marry."

Christopher stood and rounded the desk and politely gestured for Paige to step aside. After a protracted silent argument between them, he took a knee in front of Eden. The sight of him doing so, when he didn't even do that when they decided to marry, made her giggle. It was official. This was a fever dream, like a scene she'd conjured after eating too much spicy food and then falling asleep on the couch. "Oh my God. This is so freaking weird."

"Eden, I know this is scary and unconventional." Chris held her hand—caressed it, even—dulling some of her jitters. His hands were rough from the hours he'd worked in the garden, his complexion darker than hers from sun exposure. While he was stoic around everyone else, to his indoor and outdoor plants he was a nurturing father. The entire combination thereof was off-the-charts sexy.

And yet . . .

"It's all going to be a lie." And oh God, she was going to cry. She was going to cry and mess up this runway-worthy makeup that had cost hundreds of dollars. "And it was my idea too. I think I'm going to be sick . . ."

"Wait." He leapt in, halting her tirade and her tears. "It's true. This marriage will be a lie. But what's on this contract *won't* be. What's written plainly and simply is that you and I will become partners. A relationship built on friendship and an agreement. It says that what I have is yours." His words cajoled her; he had such a way with them. "And this plan *was* a great idea, Eden, because when we sign this document, you'll always have a place to call home. You don't even have to work your respiratory therapy job if you don't want to; you can be who you want to be. You can write. You can travel to see your family anytime. And after five years, when we receive my parents' inheritance, we can part ways. We split the inheritance fifty-fifty; you and I will be that much richer. All we need is to somewhat look like a couple." He smiled up at her.

It was a sincere smile, making it all the way up to his eyes. Chris really *was* handsome. She could look at that smile for five years, right? "It's always about the numbers. Book sales, percentage of oxygenation, rent money, cost of insurance. Why?"

"I wish it wasn't so, but it is. There is a bright side to this. I'm the best partner you can have for all these numbers. Except for the oxygenation part." His lips twisted into an adorable grin. "But I know how to manage money. I'm a professional, and you and I and what we'll build in five years will be so wonderful and enormous. And honestly." He pressed his lips together so a dimple appeared. This was Chris being pensive and vulnerable—Eden's heart squeezed with affection for him. His gaze dropped down a beat. "I need you."

Eden's breathing steadied. She and Chris, indeed, were in the same boat. The Puso siblings had put all they had into Heart Resort, and her family counted on her financially. She'd also endeared herself to Brandon, Chris's youngest brother, when she'd first met him as his dorm resident advisor when he was a freshman undergrad, and since then she had been a part of their spiral-tight, though fragile, circle.

From beyond came a child's cry and the laughter of people. The chapel was filling. Their wedding, planned by Chris's only sister, Beatrice, would be attended by an intimate group of fifty people and promised to be impressive and classic. Some guests had traveled across the country. Eden's own immediate family had driven from Austin to be there today despite their initial shock that Eden and Chris were marrying in Vegas.

It hadn't been what Eden's mom and dad had hoped for their eldest daughter—they'd expected a wedding in their parish church or, at the very least, for the groom to have asked her father for Eden's hand in marriage. But she and Chris had agreed Vegas was most appropriate because it was a place they had the least attachment to. At the heart of it, this was a transaction. A transaction that would bode best for her in the end. All that was required of her was time.

Eden looked down at their clasped fingers. At her engagement ring, a sparkling circle-cut diamond surrounded by baguettes. It was too large on her finger, not quite her style, but Chris had picked it with care.

So, too—she was sure—Chris would treat her with care. And she would do the same.

And wasn't that all anyone really wanted in the world?

"Eden?" He searched her face.

"Five years," she said again, more to herself.

He nodded. "Then we go our separate ways."

"I'll only be thirty-seven, and you forty-one."

"And until then, you can write to your heart's content."

It always came down to this: the writing, her dream. Scratch that. Her family took priority, but her dream took the rest of her heart, her soul. Marrying Chris would satisfy both.

And what would one do to secure the life they'd always wanted? These five years would be a reprieve—she would work enough just to maintain her RT licensure and skills. But the rest of her days would be spent writing and editing stories without risking her contribution to her home.

Plus, she'd be on the shores of the Outer Banks.

She nodded then.

Chris lifted her hand to his lips and kissed it, seeming to exhale into her knuckles. From the warmth of his ragged breath, she realized: he was as desperate as she was. Which meant that maybe this would work out after all.

♡

Christopher Puso hovered over the porcelain goddess, eyes shut as tears streaked down his face. After he caught his breath and was sure he was done dry heaving, he sat on the ground and leaned against the cool tile wall. Through his white undershirt the practice chords from the chapel's organ vibrated against his spine.

It's for real.

This is really happening.

It wasn't supposed to be like this. Chris had a clear sense of what he'd wanted to accomplish on the other side of thirty. He'd created lifetime, yearly, and quarterly goals, all for the sake of the betterment of his career. He'd painstakingly arranged his entire life plan from the moment he was a freshman in high school to make sure that he'd gone to the right colleges, acquired the correct degrees, attended recommended internships, and networked with the most awful people so he could be in the highest realm in finance.

And then Mom and Dad . . .

Nausea bubbled inside of him. He couldn't even think about it, not one more time today. It was bad enough that every day, for a brief moment, despite them being gone for three years, Chris would forget that his parents had died. He'd dial up his dad to ask him some sage advice—his father had never needed to know the entire context of a situation to dispense counsel—only for the call to go straight to his cell phone's voice mail.

No, Chris had never turned the service off. He was still paying his parents' cell phone bill just to keep all their texts, messages, and voice mail greetings.

A pounding sounded on the door. Then came a voice: "Chris."

Max.

"You've been in there fifteen minutes. Beatrice is about to lose it, and I can't do a thing if she decides to come in here and murder you."

Maybe if Chris said nothing, he would just go.

"Let me in, man," Max pleaded. "I can't be there for you if you don't let me in."

Max's tone and the accompanying guilt nudged Chris off the wall. "Give me a sec."

Chris hefted himself to his feet and made his way to the sink. He braved a look at his tearstained face and bloodshot eyes in the mirror, then washed his hands and rinsed his mouth out with a cupped palm of water. He wet a paper towel and pressed it against his cheeks and closed eyelids.

Chill. He had to chill.

Then he grabbed his barong hanging on the doorknob, threw it on, and buttoned it up, glancing once more at his reflection, remembering the times his father had worn this shirt.

Its design was simple: sheer with one delicate detail of stitched hearts that ran vertically on both the left and right shirt panels. Just like Joseph Puso, the shirt was unassuming but displayed a streak of an unyielding pride that one couldn't miss.

Would his prideful dad have married for money?

"It was you who made that completely ridiculous rule in your freaking will. Who does that? Who adds an extra trust for a spouse?" he whisper argued at . . . whatever or wherever his father was. "And you always told me to look for creative solutions. Well, *she* found *me*, Dad. She found me."

"Who are you talking to, my dude?" Max asked.

"No one." Finally, after a breath, Chris opened the door.

Max Aguilar was across the threshold, hands stuffed in the pockets of his slacks. Chris had given all his groomsmen the choice between a barong and a gray tux, and his best friend had opted for the latter. His dark eyes widened. "Finally. Thank God. Are you okay?"

Chris winced. He couldn't pretend, not with him. They'd known each other too long, and much more, they knew each other's family history. Max also understood some of the cultural nuances of being eldest born in a tight-knit immigrant family, though his from Dominican and Puerto Rican roots. "No."

He *had* been all right. He and Eden had both been logical up till today, despite this heist they were trying to pull. After they'd shaken hands to their agreement months ago, Chris had spared no expense because everything was going to be perfect. Everyone was going to believe them; it would be the wedding of the year.

But seeing Eden crack minutes before had brought on a slew of doubts. Chris hadn't realized how much he'd relied on her stoicism. He'd known he was marrying up—Eden had all the qualities he had hoped for in a wife: beautiful, caring, loyal, ambitious, and more—and her strength had been the quality he had most admired. When that strength had wavered, he'd felt himself begin to crumble, and nausea had invaded every pore in his body.

Max dragged him back to the groom's anteroom. He poured still water into a beveled glass and handed it to Chris. "Not quite whiskey, but this might help."

Chris offered him an almost smile—it was the best he could do. Behind Max was a charcuterie board layered with all his favorite cheeses and meats, but right then, even the smell was too much. He went to the solitary window, which overlooked the horizon of downtown Las Vegas, the very last city he'd ever thought of marrying in, and his gaze locked on a small piece of green space. He imagined himself lying on the grass, his face to the sun.

He hadn't had a drink since his parents' accident. He hadn't been tempted either, not till now.

Christopher blurted out, "My mother's probably turning in her grave. She was a romantic."

"Not sure if *romantic* is the right description. She and your father had agreed to this stipulation in their will, after all." Max was as straightforward as ever. When Chris had gone to him with their marriage-for-money plan, Max had all but refused to help him draft the contract. *It's against everything I stand for,* he'd said. "But your plan might actually work."

"As soon as Eden hinted at the idea, I thought the same thing. With Eden, I know it'll be easy. She understands my family. She can keep a secret. And I can do what's needed to make it work. Is that messed up or what? Am I that superficial? Some people know when it's love at first sight—"

"And you knew that it was secret contract at first sight?"

Chris half laughed, though it transformed into a choke. He took a sip of the water, and it brought a second of relief. "But now."

"Now you must follow through." Max approached him and took the glass; from his pocket he retrieved a small package of mints. He handed Chris a mint, then straightened his barong, dark eyebrows furrowed in concentration. Like a father would have done to his child. Like Joe had done for Chris time and again for homecoming, prom, and graduation.

Dammit, it should have been his father who was preparing him for his wedding. How much crap had Joe given him about not settling down and having a family? Joe had wanted to be a grandfather—not that Chris's marriage to Eden would lead to children. It had been a line item on their contract: *Both parties agree that there will be no children, born or adopted, during the marriage.*

Then again, if his father had not died, Chris would've not been in this mess at all. He would have been with Max at God knows where, making money and participating in shenanigans. Chris had been a man who worked hard and played hard, with the latter taking the greatest precedence.

But playtime was over.

A squeeze on both his shoulders woke him up.

"Five years will be done before you know it," Max said. "And after that, it's back to you, and me, and travel, and—"

Their conversation was interrupted with the door slamming open.

Beatrice was at the doorway, wearing a peach dress. Her hair was in a fancy pile on her head, with curled tendrils framing her temples. She looked ethereal, and Chris did a double take. His only sister looked so much like their mother, with light-brown skin, high cheekbones, and, not to mention, a stern expression on her face.

Because she was also the wedding planner.

"Oh my God. What the heck is going on with you two? The ceremony starts in five minutes. You should already be at the front of the chapel." Her voice had taken its highest octave. After a beat, her eyebrows plunged with suspicion. "What's going on?"

"I . . . ," Chris started but could not finish. Where would he start? In all cases, it was too late. He and Eden were committed to this now.

Five years committed. Not quite the happily ever afters Eden wrote about but perhaps a happy temporarily. Was that such a thing?

"He got a little sick," Max said pointedly. "He misses your dad."

All truths. His best friend was so good at that. And it worked. Beatrice softened, approaching Chris with her arms opened wide. She embraced him. "Oh, Kuya. I miss them too."

And by God, Beatrice was also wearing their mother's perfume. Lauren by Ralph Lauren, in the amber bottle, had been the most prominent on her vanity.

The scent conjured his mother and, specifically, her straightforwardness, kindness, and fortitude.

Eden is just as strong, his gut reminded him.

Beatrice stepped back, a hand on each of his shoulders. "They're around."

"You think?"

"I know." She nodded, her expression serious. "They wouldn't miss this. You were their favorite first son, after all."

He laughed. That was a title he carried with as much pride as all the awards and accolades he'd received.

"Are you ready?" she asked, gently this time.

"I am now. Thank you."

She dropped her arms and shrugged. "Eh, that's what we wedding planners do." She looked at the phone in her hand, then turned to Max. "I expect you to lead him to the altar. There will be no runaway grooms on my watch. I'm holding you accountable."

"Yes, ma'am," Max answered with sincere obedience.

She stepped out of the room. Max and Chris followed the clack of her heels to the double doors of the chapel. As Beatrice stepped in, the low murmurs of conversation wafted into the hallway until the doors shut.

Alone once more, Max turned and blocked the door. "Not to sound like I'm copying off that maid of honor, who is a pill by the way, but . . . if you're having second thoughts, we can call off this whole thing. We can find money for the resort another way."

Chris thought back on the last three years, on the whiplash of events, from the death of his parents and then finding out about their sizable inheritance; to Beatrice's discovering a heart-shaped peninsula, purchasing it for a bargain, and realizing it was a money pit; and then to the discovery of the additional trust.

To stop right now would be sealing their fate. They would drown in a business that could actually bring them together as a family.

The other option was to live a lie, but they'd see Heart Resort to its full potential, a true Puso legacy. "There's no choice but forward, Max," Chris said, a hand on the chapel door. "And right now, it's for me to tie this knot."

CHAPTER TWO

Heart Resort, North Carolina
128 days until the Chan-Puso contract expiration
Word of the day: disrupt

It was still all about numbers. Never mind that her work was in words, language, and expression, Eden Chan Puso, also known as *USA Today* bestselling romance author Everly Heart, dealt with numbers each and every day. With words dictated into her phone and typed by her fingers, she created worlds, developed characters, and challenged the status quo through kissing books built by the number. While writing the heart-wrenching push and pull of couples finding their way through love, Eden tackled both her thesaurus *and* spreadsheets. With the second book of her first contemporary romance series, *The Time between Us*, she'd grappled with identity and a timeline she couldn't get right (what was it with dates that beguiled her?). With her seventh novel, a paranormal romance stand-alone titled *Awake*, she'd questioned the meaning of life and contended with dismal preorder sales that she had been convinced meant the end of her career.

Today's number? Ten thousand six hundred thirty-two.

Certainly not the leftover amount of student loans she had yet to pay off (if only!) or her print book sales the week prior (ditto!) but her ghastly word count.

With sixteen books in four years and eight months as Everly Heart, and six other romance novels under another pen name that never got off the ground premarriage, Eden's well of stories and words had seemed to have no limit. Sentences had appeared like conjured spells. Solutions to plot points had unfolded while she was in the shower. At times, after a long writing sprint, she'd startle to the present, realizing she'd written a thousand words without remembering a single word. Storytelling was as simple as falling into her mattress after a long workday with patients.

But these days, and especially right now, Eden wanted to chuck her computer out of this tiny beach house's window. For despite her expensive ergonomic chair—and sitting in the most peaceful office she had ever imagined creating in, with the warm wind blowing against her face through the open window, in front of the most beautiful sunset—she was stuck.

She had the dreaded writer's block.

Eden reread her last painstakingly written passage—from yesterday, goodness—once more, then looked down at her detailed outline next to the keyboard. An outline she had typed out with enthusiasm, approved by her editor with confetti-bomb emojis. An outline that, in the past, would have unfailingly led her down the winding road of a story.

But she couldn't seem to get past the parking lot.

What the hell.

Her document had the same number of words as it had over three hours ago. Three hours of sitting in the chair, in position, ready for whatever magic had compelled her in the past. Three hours of switching out candles, because sandalwood had been too spicy and vanilla had reminded her too much of Christmas, and this book was supposed to be published in the spring. One hundred eighty minutes of gazing out said window into the gleaming ocean. Six Pomodoro timers of glancing at her phone whenever it lit up from her social media accounts.

She'd even chosen the beach house named Tiwala, *Faith*, which she'd moved her office to from the main house (vacancy at Heart Resort was at 75 percent this early in the spring) to get away from distraction—a.k.a. her husband—convinced it would give her good luck. She wasn't into the woo-woo, but at this point, she was welcoming it to slap her in the face.

What more did her muse want?

"Where are you, words?" she said aloud. Because she wasn't above talking to herself. In fact, she talked not only to herself, but she spoke to her characters. Not the visual representation of her characters—but to their spirits or what have you. Their vibes.

She would've preferred to speak to them now, but they were too elusive, hiding underneath the behemoth book contract she'd signed, the large advance like a brick tied at her ankles.

A knock at the door startled her from her thoughts, and she sighed. Though she wasn't doing any actual writing, her brain was at least thinking of writing, and her body was poised for it. She hefted herself to standing and padded on bare feet to the door.

The distance wasn't far. Five steps, if that. Tiwala was 225 square feet, and the loft was a hundred square feet, but it had recently been remodeled and decorated to the nines. It showcased a plush carpet in the living room, a geometric tapestry on a painted accent wall, and patterned, sheer curtains.

She opened the door to a handsome man with dark skin and silver-streaked dark hair wearing linen pants and a white button-down shirt. He was rubbing a palm against his cheek, his fingers running through his short beard. The sight of him prompted her body to take a slow, deep breath.

Her first thought: *How did I get so lucky to have married such a specimen of a man?*

Her second: *Why, oh why, is he here?*

Christopher Puso—the CEO of Heart Resort, a prominent couples resort in the United States; head of household of the Puso family; and her partner-husband—stepped in.

"Is this a good time?" he grumbled without preamble. But from the way he started to pace while cradling his iPad, which meant he had likely been reading the news, Eden knew she didn't really have a choice but to make time.

So she plopped on the plush cushion of her love seat. With a quick glance at her laptop clock, she confirmed that they had only ten more minutes before their features interview with ABN, so what the hey. Not like she could bring five thousand words into existence before then. She sighed. "Sure."

He slid the iPad onto her lap. On the screen was CNN Malaysia. "They're at it again."

Whenever her husband said *they* in a way that dripped sarcasm and vitriol, it meant only one person or, in this case, business. And by the grace of whatever was keeping her words hostage, she somehow kept herself from rolling her eyes when she answered with, "Let me guess. Willow Tree Inc.?"

He nodded, then shoved his hands in his pockets. "The gall of that Dillon McCauley the *third*." He snorted. "The gall for him to say that Willow Tree's programming is groundbreaking. Can you believe it? They modeled their programming after us. Us!"

Eden didn't bother to read the article. This conversation was par for the course. At least once a week Chris took offense at something Willow Tree put out into the world and vented to her because she was the only one who was contractually obligated to listen to him. She loved listening to his voice, but sometimes, his messages got a little old. "I don't get why this matters. They're not even running a couples resort but an adult summer camp. You're being paranoid."

All right, so that was mean, but her patience was onionskin transparent because of her own tangible deadline, not some supposed rivalry. "Chris," she started once more with what she hoped sounded like empathy, "when people say these things, they don't necessarily mean to attack you. They're simply making a statement about their own capability. If I took offense every time someone said they preferred Jacky Hallan's books over mine, I would be curled up in a corner."

"From the beginning, you remember," he continued as if Eden hadn't spoken, a hurricane at its beginnings. "And last summer? They tried to poach our contractor Mike. Who knows if they've sent spies, if any one of our guests now"—he meandered to the window, which showed only the view of the sound—"are actually here to take notes. That's what money does. It buys partnerships."

She snickered. If there was anyone who was aware of this, it was her.

Still, she stood from the love seat and went to Chris. He sought the view—or the garden if it was within reach—only when he had to calm himself. She sat on the wide windowsill, facing him. She pulled on his shirt.

He looked down, and when the dark pool of his irises met hers, his face softened. "I shouldn't care, but I do." Then he slid down to sit next to her, though their bodies didn't touch. He rested his elbows on his knees and cradled his forehead.

Eden's heart squeezed. She wished she could wrap her arms around him; she wanted to ease his worry. Perhaps it could knock her out of her funk too. It had in the past, among the other ways his touch affected her.

She shook herself to reality. Nope. Not allowed, since they had this thing called a *contract* that she had every intention of following. This time.

To get her mind out of her lonely gutter, she opted for words of encouragement. "Hey, you're doing all the right things. And *if* Willow Tree did say it as a dig, you know by now that haters come with the territory. But you can't let it get to you. What you've built here is something great. Better than great, and you should be proud."

He shook his head. "I feel like we could do more. Promote internationally, sell across markets, offer better amenities."

"Technically, you could." Eden smiled, then bumped him by the shoulders. "And you will, if it's truly right for Heart Resort, whether or not Willow Tree is around. That's just you. You go big, better. You work your butt off, Chris." Then, with the reminder of her book due in three months, short by at least sixty thousand words and lacking a plot, for God's sake, she grimaced. "At least your efforts are showing rewards. Mine, on the other hand . . ."

He groaned, realization blooming on his face. "Dammit. You were in the middle of a sprint, weren't you?"

"Yeah." Eden shook her head. "Actually no. A writing sprint technically means words are actually happening. These sessions are more like a writing think, or a writing lament. There's no sprinting happening. Not even a jog. I think I need . . . I've been ho . . ."—she recalibrated her speech, a breath away from calling Heart Resort *home*, and gave words to a nagging thought—"here the last six months. I think I need a change of scenery."

It had been a while since Eden had accepted a traveling respiratory therapist gig because of her writing deadlines and Heart Resort's needs. When she'd become Everly Heart almost five years ago—taking on the English translation of her new husband's last name—she'd wholeheartedly jumped into hashtag wife life. And it had gone well for the most part, but now she was struggling with the very reason she had become a wife in the first place.

And in four months, at their contract's end, she wouldn't even have the right to be here.

The thought made her wince.

Stupid numbers.

"I think it's time for me to go back to Austin," she added. "I haven't seen Josie and my dad in a while. They miss me. It's Josie's last semester of high school, and prom's around the corner. There's a lot going on, and I want to be there for all that."

"So it's not about the writing." Chris's voice dropped.

"I mean, it is." She pressed her lips together to reset, wishing she had her own edit button. "Something's not working here. I'm distracted, even being out here close to the water. And all of these things we're doing, like this features interview, just cuts into my vibe."

"But we've RSVP'd to a slew of events to attend. Together. If you want a change, why not switch houses? It's the slow season, and . . ."

"But . . ." She shook her head. Chris wasn't understanding.

"Look, this was the deal. It was part of the contract."

Her gaze dropped to the floor alongside her patience. Their marriage *contract*. That c-word was a card they'd kept in their pockets and, in the last six months, had been the first card each of them played. It had rules that they had both dutifully tended and adhered to but these days fought and negotiated over.

But Eden knew her rights. "Inherent to that contract was me being able to seek my own career, right?"

"Yes."

"And I can't finish this book in this house, even with that view. I need a change."

He pressed his hands against his forehead, one of his tells of frustration. "I get that, but you've been making changes all along. Like moving out to this beach house to work when we have ample office space in the main house. Sometimes you even end up sleeping here—"

"I told you, when I work into the night—"

"I know, Eden. You've explained, and of course I understand. But someone is bound to notice. Including Mortimer."

She rolled her eyes. *Kyle Mortimer Esq.* The judge and jury and the purse strings holder of the trust, and a nosy one at that.

"My siblings haven't said anything, but they notice," Chris continued. "Which means you can't up and go now. We're a couples resort. For me to show up without my own wife—that's unacceptable." The lines on his forehead deepened, and she felt her insides relent. This was her problem, her weakness—it was her affection toward Chris. For all that everyone assumed, he was a man who loved the limelight, who blazed his own trail, but Chris also was a creature of comfort, highly attached, and was hardest on himself. She loved both of these sides, as much as they drove her bonkers.

Hence why she'd had to move her office to Tiwala and find ways so she could sleep there, using her (non) writing as an excuse. She couldn't focus. *Torn* was her middle name, and Chris sleeping across the room was causing her as much insomnia as her unfinished book. And having to split her time between Austin and the Outer Banks filled her with guilt when she was in either one place or another; it certainly wasn't doing anything for her inspiration.

Eden pushed her wayward feelings away. At the moment, it all came down to her next book, which she needed to draft. She opened her mouth to begin another round of negotiations so she could make time for said book, when her iPad alarmed. It was followed by her Pomodoro timer. Then a knock on her door.

Work over, she guessed. She blew out the air in her chest.

Chris straightened and pressed a hand against the back of his head. He shut his eyes for a beat. "Ready?"

"This conversation isn't over." She stood from the windowsill. "But yes, ready."

He held out his hand, and she took it. His skin was softer these days—she'd given him a tub of goat's-milk lotion that he'd dutifully used at night—and she entwined her fingers with his. He tugged her closer so they were a breath apart, and his chest rose in a deep inhale. "Eden."

She knew what was coming next.

"We'll figure this out," he said.

She treasured his predictability. They were, after all, linked by the same goal. They were partners, and she trusted him. Their life was strange, but one thing remained true: for all the tension they'd had lately, when she walked into a room with Chris, she felt part of a whole. "I know," she answered.

"Here we go," he whispered and opened the door to Tammy Dirks, the resort's publicist. She pushed her sunglasses off her face to hold back her light-brown hair and gestured them out. She introduced them to a photographer and Vera Menaj, a prim Brown woman in a pantsuit—another journalist wanting yet another interview to cover the rise of Heart Resort. That kind of public attention should have normally given Eden the shivers—she hated the spotlight. But none of this was about her; it was about the man standing beside her and their supposed inspirational story.

And with the way Chris wrapped his arm around her waist—their agreed-upon go-to method of showing their public affection—she could barely keep abreast of the small talk. What she was aware of were the tingles that ran up and down her spine that reminded her of the last time they'd succumbed to their married-though-forbidden pleasure. For although she and Chris had a contractual marriage, she couldn't deny that over the course of their topsy-turvy relationship, she had fallen in love with him.

Even if they had only 128 days till their marriage was set to end.

Damn numbers.

♡

At the main house and Heart Resort's headquarters, aptly named Puso because it was situated in the heart of the resort peninsula, Eden sat by Chris's side on the leather tufted couch. Behind them were the office's bookcases (they'd pre-rearranged the furniture to get the perfect shot), and with Chris's arm behind her, she spied the outline of their reflection against the camera's lens trained on them. They looked like two humps of a camel's back.

They began the interview with some basic questions. How did they meet? What was their love story? The topic swiftly moved on to Chris's goals for the resort. All the while Chris drew lazy circles against Eden's exposed shoulder, and she found herself snuggling into the crook of his arm. Every once in a while, he'd look down upon her with a gleam in his eye, and while she knew it was from the zeal he had for work, she imagined it was for her.

Relaxed, Eden forgot about the lights against her face and the clicking of the camera. Everything hazed around her as she relished this public intimacy. Admittedly, their marriage of convenience had its perks, one of which was moments like these. Not the part of being under the microscope but the occasions where she felt safe and comforted. Where she, for a few minutes, *belonged*.

What person didn't want that? Certainly, it was what her book protagonists desired. From Melinda in *Stars in the Sky* to Lucille of *Kiss Me Now*, her heroines sought home and family in addition to their happily ever afters.

Eden tumbled down the rabbit hole of her imagination, and what came was an image of a woman in her forties unearthing a tattered quilt from a trunk in her attic.

Oh my gosh. Her breath hitched. It was a new character. For another book. Not quite the inspiration she had been hoping for, but it was *something*.

"Second chances. I need my phone." Eden startled herself along with everyone else. Chris had been midsentence; he raised an eyebrow. *Whoops.* But she couldn't bother with how she must've appeared right then. If she didn't write this thought down, it would go poof.

Eyes darting around the room, she scanned for her phone. She patted her back pockets and realized she was wearing a dress with no pockets. Curses!

"I was holding it for you. Here, babe." Chris pressed the phone into Eden's hand.

"Thank goodness." Relief spilled out of her—*thank everything!* Maybe her story well wasn't dry after all! Maybe this would be the beginning of a waterfall of words for her first draft.

Eden was so grateful that she did the unthinkable before she caught herself. She cupped Chris's face in her hands and kissed him.

The cameras clicked, and she froze, still lips to lips with her husband, and her would-be idea went kaput. Replacing it was the heat of embarrassment that she had lost track of her faculties.

Heat, because his lips felt so good against hers. And it had been too long since their last kiss.

"Gosh you guys are cute," Vera said, berry-stained lips parting into a smile as Eden eased into a more proper sitting position. "What was that about? What did you mean by second chances?"

"I . . ." Eden scrambled for an excuse, when the only thing running through her head was: *I want to kiss my husband more.*

"Eden's always doing continuing education," Chris chimed in, eyebrows raised, lobbing the cue.

It still took Eden a beat, but she caught it. "Oh, right, and . . . I have this paper, um, about . . ." She looked to Chris.

"Second chances when patients . . ." He stalled, with a lift at the end of the phrase.

"Yes!" She nodded, still not quite knowing what to say. *You make stuff up for a living, Heart. Yeesh.* "Second chances . . . patients have when they're seen by a specialist and not a generalist in the emergency room." She swallowed the lie. "A paper I was stuck on but now am . . . unstuck."

23

"Well, nothing like a kiss to stir up the inspiration." Vera sighed. "Honestly. The both of you have such chemistry."

At the change in topic, Eden thought the cliché that she avoided writing: *she released a breath she didn't know she was holding.* Chris's lips quirked upward, which meant he'd done the same too. "We are definitely a team," she said.

"You married after you opened Heart Resort. Does it help to be in the business of love when you are in love, Mr. Puso?" Vera asked.

Chris shot a glance at Eden. She read his thoughts: it was silly to assign causation that the success in their marriage was due to the success of Heart Resort and vice versa. Surely they didn't assume that hospital CEOs were in the best of health or that murder-mystery authors had firsthand experience. (She hoped not, anyway.)

And love, after all, was a tricky thing. It was a tricky thing to write and to decipher in real life. Love encompassed the gamut of emotions; the gamut thereof wasn't the same for everyone. And, bottom line, what she and Chris had was not textbook love or marriage.

"We've never claimed to be in the business of love, Vera," Chris started. "We're in the business of giving people their happily ever after, and that is defined by the individual. It's about connection and what that means to the couple. Connection is what's most important to us here at Heart Resort."

Eden nodded appreciatively at her husband. This was why each one of her book heroes was inspired in small part by him. For all his faults, he had glimmers of empathy and understanding that she wanted her characters to have.

"That's interesting. But if I'm hearing you correctly, if we apply the inverse to that statement, you're saying that people could be paying for a breakup at Heart Resort." Vera leaned forward in her chair, and at that moment, the air crackled around them. It was innocuous enough that if Eden hadn't spent her days writing nuance, it would have passed her by.

Vera was implying that the resort was a waste of money. And by the look on Chris's face, he hadn't noticed. He was grinning, swept up in the banter. "It's not like we can control what people feel and do, Vera. Our goal is to give these couples the time and space to figure out their relationship's next step."

Eden jumped in, awash with protectiveness. Vera was all but showing her incisors, ready to make a meal out of Chris. "To emphasize, if I may . . . it boils down to how a couple defines *their* happily ever after. The resort can't tell them what that is. They have to discover that on their own. Sort of like how we discovered our own, right, babe?" She fluttered her eyelashes at him and laid a hand on his thigh.

Chris's eyes rounded in wonder.

Just go with it, Eden tried to emit with her imaginary thought bubble. "Have we mentioned how we met?" She slid her gaze to Vera.

With a belated sideways glance, Vera took the bait. "You haven't. Tell me all about it."

"We met on Christmas. I was a guest at the Puso home—a stray, I guess."

"Far from a stray, and I'm just glad that she gave me a chance." Chris shook his head. "She was so out of my league." He looked straight into Eden's eyes. "The truth, though? It wasn't love at first sight, but I felt a connection to her."

"I felt a connection to you too." Eden was caught off guard by this reveal—he'd never mentioned it. "When did that happen for you?"

"The moment I met you in my parents' kitchen. You were wearing that hideous Christmas sweater, but you . . . you were beautiful. Still are."

Eden's heart clenched. "It was the same moment for me, except you were wearing a cozy cable-knit sweater." Her memory flipped through the reel of that first meeting; back then she'd hoped that they would exchange numbers, though they hadn't. But in seeing Vera's inquisitive reaction, she refocused. She released a grin for her sake. "But Vera, it was me who asked him out years later."

"Oh wow! That's so . . . sweet. And interesting. From what I can tell just from today, can I assume you're the introvert of the two?"

"It doesn't mean she's quiet by any means." Chris raised a finger. "My wife is not only evocative but decisive."

Eden squeezed his thigh in a quiet thanks. She'd told him time and again that she hated the stereotype that Asian women were meek; she abhorred it when people had assumed she was a pushover because she was introverted.

"And she keeps me on my toes still," Chris added, voice hinting at humor. The corners of his mouth curled upward.

She pressed her lips into a smile. Their pretend relationship required the both of them to pay attention. Though these days, in nearing the end of their contract, their lives had felt even more complicated. She formed her thoughts and said, "I mean, there's no choice but to keep up. Marriages aren't . . . supposed to be a perfect cruise, you know? We're both super busy; as with everyone, there've been rough waters."

Their beginnings might have started like a historical romance novel with a marriage-of-convenience trope, but they had yet to make it to their own happily ever after.

"You travel for work; is that right?" Vera asked.

"I do. Just as he has his goals for this resort, I have my career goals too. Couplehood is about two lives, of two arcs converging."

"That's an interesting way to describe it."

Eden smiled, though to herself she thought, *It's romance 101.*

"I think we have enough photos with you both sitting," Tammy suggested, unintentionally saving the moment. "Now for a few photos of just Mr. Puso. Perhaps behind his desk? A CEO at work."

Eden giggled. That massive antique desk was rarely used by her husband. He might have liked to sit behind it during meetings, but Chris preferred to work on the bed with his legs up. She'd also occasionally invaded that desk with all her notebooks, pens, and snacks to pound out her words.

Which she wished she was doing at the moment.

Chris posed, perched on a desk corner, while Eden watched him from behind the group. The last four and a half years had put some gray in her husband's hair and a few wrinkles on his forehead. But right then, Eden imagined Chris with more salt than pepper, with a slight hunch on his back, and envisioned her right next to him, at a point in her life when she no longer decided to keep dyeing her hair.

Of them growing old together.

Eden shut the image down just as her heart began to ache—it was her romantic side plowing through. Everly Heart and her insistence on looking for love in all corners of everyday life. But in Eden Puso's case, there would be no happily ever after—not in the way that she wrote in her books.

Her vision cleared to Chris looking at her from his seated position. He was clearly uncomfortable, his shoulders lifted in tension. And though his expression was unreadable to everyone else, Eden understood his mood. Chris loved work but hated the hoopla, though it was a necessary evil of business. She herself hadn't known that being his wife would turn into this. That everything would revolve around the resort, him, and this constant push and pull of making herself invisible but being too important to this family unit.

Eden's phone buzzed in her hand, and the picture of her literary agent shone on the screen. Her heart rocketed to her throat.

Paloma Wright never called straight out. She usually scheduled a call, understanding that Eden needed the emotional prep. Introvert problems.

She excused herself from the room and jogged through the front doors, to the flagstone walkway, where she accepted the call. Her destination was the driveway, to get as far away from the house and from prying ears. "Hey, Paloma?" She was breathless.

"Everly?" Paloma's voice sounded frantic, high, and squeaky.

"Yes?"

"Ivy Montana is on the line."

Ivy Montana was Eden's film agent, a woman who she knew only by name, with her messages passed on secondhand through Paloma. Eden had certainly never heard her voice.

"Hi, Eden." Ivy's voice was distinctly alto, and she spoke with an American southern accent.

"Um . . . hi."

"Are you sitting down?"

"No . . ." She slowed to a halt, though her thoughts continued to jog down the winding road that would take her out of the Pusos' privacy gate. "Just . . . just tell me." This was her caregiving side coming out. She preferred the full-on truth rather than wading through the false positives, ending only with bad news.

"*One Plus One Equals Me and You?*" Ivy prompted.

Her rom-com, published two years ago, about a down-on-his-luck manny hired by a socialite as a fake fiancé in order for her to be taken seriously at her inherited business. It was a hardworking book, published to mediocre acclaim. The first month, Eden had thought her career was over because the book's sales had been so low. But as the months had passed, word of mouth had grown.

Thank God for readers.

"What about *One?*"

"Goldstein Productions would like to option the film rights."

"Um . . ." She shook her head. Paloma had informed her over the years whenever one of her books was being read by the film agent and when the agent pitched it to production companies. With *One*, there had been a few production companies interested, and her book had once ascended another rung in the film and TV rights ladder. Then it had all gone quiet. Eden's saving grace was Paloma—her agent was adept at putting everything in perspective so that Eden's focus remained on her next book, her front list.

So this thing Ivy was saying felt far fetched. And she waited for the magic word. "But . . ."

"There's no *but*. They want to option your book for film. They want to chat with you. They want to make a deal."

"A deal." The breath left her body. Logically, this was great news, but it wasn't sinking in. Because it wasn't possible. It was unreal. Stuff like that didn't happen to her. *Work twice as hard; expect half as much* had been her father's motto—an immigrant's mantra.

"A deal, Eden. A bona fide deal!" Paloma's voice resonated through the phone.

It was only when a line of birds flew in a V across the sky, with one just askew from the formation, that Eden fully understood the message.

Then Eden Chan Puso, a.k.a. Everly Heart, screamed her head off.

CHAPTER THREE

118 days until Chan-Puso contract expiration
Word of the day: revelation

Chris raised a tumbler of sweet iced tea. "To Everly Heart!"

"To Everly!" his family echoed back.

"To Tita Eden," Kitty and Izzy, his seven- and five-year-old nieces, chimed in at the end, punctuating their sweet voices with giggles.

To Chris's right, Eden pressed her lips together, into what he knew was her attempt to stifle a cry, before saying, "Thank you, everyone. Tonight has been perfect. I just can't believe it."

He kissed her on the cheek with all the reservation he could muster when what he was tempted to do was wrap her into him. It was more than perfect on this Friday night. They'd just ordered at their mainstay restaurant, Salt & Sugar, in Rodanthe, a few miles south of the resort on Highway 12. And in attendance for this specific Puso Friday dinner was everyone who knew Eden as Everly Heart: Three out of his three siblings, along with Geneva Harris, Brandon's fiancée—which was a weird thing to say, since Geneva had once simply been Beatrice's best friend—and Beatrice's office manager, Giselle. The last couple, though not least, were his nieces.

The vibe was electric this evening; it had been a banner week. Eden had officially signed her contract with Goldstein Productions, and Chris had been given a report that Heart Resort's reservations starting late May would be at 80 percent capacity until early fall, their highest numbers on record.

And the weather—the weather was perfect. They were seated outside on the balcony, with the Pamlico Sound just a stone's throw away, and the water was like a mirror for the moon—the sight was breathtaking.

So few were these moments, where nothing was foreboding, that he wanted this one to last.

"So what's next?" Beatrice asked after setting down her sparkling cider. "When do we get to see the movie?"

"Oh my gosh, not for a while." Eden sipped her drink. "These things take forever. We won't even go public until the contract finalizes, whenever that is. But when it announces, the book's going to get a little buzz." Eden slid Chris a look. "My agent asked me if I would be willing to go out on a book tour when my next book comes out."

Chris raised an eyebrow. A lot was in that sentence: Everly's next book's release was after their marriage contract ended. And Eden coming out of anonymity? That was . . . startling. He couldn't believe she hadn't run the idea by him.

And now that he thought of it, he couldn't imagine not being there for the next Everly Heart book.

The table quieted, as if reading his thoughts.

"It makes sense, you know?" she continued. "I've showed myself a handful of times on social media but not completely. And it's been almost five years since my debut as Everly Heart. It's time, right?"

Discomfort pricked through Chris. The irony wasn't lost on him. Everly Heart had been born the day they had gotten married; she'd switched from a previous pen name. To go public just as their marriage would end . . .

But this moving on, this idea of new beginnings after something ended, continued to prove to Chris that life wasn't a trajectory but a period of stops and starts.

Still, the idea was disconcerting—it was written all over Eden's face. "Do you have to step out?" Chris asked. "You don't have to do what they say. You can stay anonymous."

Gil spoke up from across the table. "I get what Eden means, Kuya. She wants to feel the recognition too. She wants to be able to meet her fans, and to speak to them. Is that right?"

"It's exactly right," his wife said. "Thank you."

Chris snorted at his brother's hypocrisy, seeing that Gil had since ducked out from the Hollywood limelight.

"What?" Gil said. "It's true. At some point, Everly Heart has to get out there. Authors are no longer obscure. I took the girls"—he gestured to his daughters, currently on their devices—"to see Desiree Hui. You know, that picture book author? And they all but passed out fangirling over her. The bookstore was packed."

"She even signed my book." Izzy, sitting on the other side of Eden, looked up from her iPad screen.

"Did you like that, sweetheart?" Eden turned her direction.

"Uh-huh." Izzy recounted the play-by-play of the book signing and started in on her suggestions on how to plan Everly's first event. And while the rest of the table moved on to their side conversations, Eden gave Izzy her full attention. Her eyes lit with interest at every tiny detail Izzy imparted, and Chris couldn't take his eyes off her. He was absorbed with the joy so evident on his wife's face.

She was so good with kids, so caring and attentive. For a beat, he wished . . .

"I love all of these ideas, Izzy," Eden finally said with eyebrows furrowed, snapping him out of his thoughts. "I'll give it all some thought."

Chef Pris Castillo arrived along with one of the waitstaff. They filled the middle of the long table with large platters of food. Their

Friday dinners were family-style, this time with pork sisig, laing, shrimp adobo, pinakbet, and garlic fried rice.

Immediately, hands dug into the food. It became the priority, and the conversation turned light, though Chris still mulled over Eden's announcement. He pushed away the foreboding inching into his periphery reminding him of changes up ahead that would be precarious at best. At times he chose not to think about the future—work was his best distraction—but if he was being honest, things were moving too quickly.

The conversation veered to Brandon and Geneva's upcoming wedding in six months, and Chris was glad for it.

"I don't have great news, though," Geneva said, glancing a beat at Brandon. "The wedding planner we'd initially hired is pregnant. Which is the best thing ever, though not for us."

"Oh bummer," Eden said. "Surely there's someone else that can plan it. In fact, I can help you look."

"But aren't you under deadline?" Chris whispered.

Eden sighed and said loud enough for only him to hear, "Are you my keeper or something?"

"I mean, no . . . I just thought . . . anyway, sorry," he said, flummoxed, now wondering what else he had done wrong. He took back what he'd thought earlier—*precarious* did not fully describe the stage they were in. Sometimes their interactions were damn near contentious.

If there was anyone who could knock out a deadline, it was Eden. She'd rise like a phoenix from under the heap of paper and snacks. Chris had full confidence in his wife; he looked up to her, even. What was wrong with reminding her of something she'd kept hammering into him?

Sometimes he just couldn't win.

"Helloooo! How about me?" Beatrice pointed at herself. "*I* can plan your wedding."

Beatrice, who could never keep still, was not only the director of guest relations for Heart Resort but also ran a subscription clothing-and-housewares business on the side with Geneva.

Beatrice was only six years younger, but she had the energy of a twenty-something, which boggled Chris. He was a man who needed his sleep.

"Oh, oh no. No, no," Brandon chimed in; his youngest brother had been quiet all this time, and he was midchew. He drank down half his glass of water. "Absolutely not. You will drive me up the wall, Ate Bea."

"Hey!" Beatrice whined. "I don't drive your fiancée up the wall."

Geneva took a long sip of her glass of water with a pinkie up, as if drinking tea. The entire table erupted in a laugh.

"The banter," Eden whispered. From under the table, she tugged on Chris's khakis, and with the hint at their inside joke—that Beatrice was a nag in a motherly way, and Brandon could never say no to Beatrice, and that there was no such thing as quiet when it came to the Puso family—the tension between them passed.

How many times had he and Eden commiserated in their bedroom, with her under the covers in the bed and him under his on the pullout love seat, where he'd soak in her impressions of the day. Chris hadn't understood anything before they'd married—he hadn't noticed the dynamic of their family until Eden had walked into his life. Then suddenly, his eyes had been opened. He didn't know what made her so wise—scratch that; it was probably all those character books she read, along with the Myers-Briggs and Enneagram worksheets and podcasts about human behavior she listened to.

He turned to her. "Can you even imagine?" Meaning with Beatrice taking over as wedding planner. Beatrice was a go-getter but also quite pushy. Beatrice had been *their* wedding planner, after all.

"But you made it down the aisle because of her." Eden leaned in to whisper in his ear. Close enough that he could kiss her just below her earlobe, her favorite spot.

Chris held his breath. Since the posed pictures a couple of weeks ago, he had been increasingly tempted to break all their rules. He had missed her. Things between them had become tense the last six months. He knew it wasn't just from the stress of her increasing deadlines—he, too, had dug himself knee deep in work. It was from the chasm their affair had caused.

It had served them right for having broken their rules the first time, but God, it had been good while it had lasted.

So, he dared an arm around her chair. It was on their approved list of PDA. Their rules had boiled down to the criteria that they could show the same affection that good friends would, which they were. They were the best of friends, in fact, even through their ups and downs. And right then, he yearned for some comfort that everything wasn't changing after all. He smirked. "Best decision I made, to walk down the aisle."

"I guess it hasn't been so bad," she quipped back and settled into the crook of his arm, sitting close, leg touching his. "I have the best pen name because of it." She laughed, and her voice vibrated through him like the midrange notes of the saxophone. It put him at ease.

"Aw, you guys are so cute," Geneva said from across the table. She wrapped her arm around Brandon. "Right, Bran? Will we be like that in five years?"

Were they cute? Or was it pretend? Years Chris and Eden had been practicing, from the moment they'd decided in his bedroom that they would take this on. That night, they'd kissed under the mistletoe, in front of everyone, to mark the beginning of their whirlwind romance. All their public interactions had been scripted, discussed, and plotted out like one of her books.

Chris took it back. It wasn't so much now. Perhaps it was like most marriages, where they'd fallen into a kind of routine. Like lines in a book known by heart.

"I don't know. These two probably talk each other to death," Brandon said sardonically. "Ate Eden and her books, and Kuya Chris and his meeting notes and speech rehearsals?"

"They're made for one another," Geneva protested. Then she bumped shoulders with him, a signal. Brandon stared down at her, as if asking permission. She nodded.

Chris scanned the table. It had gone silent, and 100 percent of them had this crap-eating grin. When he got to Eden, she, too, had mischief in her eyes. "What?"

"Kuya Chris."

Chris turned to the sound of his name. Brandon had leaned closer to him, face serious, almost somber. Okay, this was enough. He hated angst with a passion. He hadn't realized it was angst, until Eden had schooled him on it—all he knew was that it felt like his shirt collar was tightening with this undeniable sensation of being strangled.

He preferred to be placed out of his misery—in Eden's world, it meant characters hashing out every fight to the teeth. In his world, it meant none of these serious looks. "Jesus, Bran. What?"

Brandon cleared his throat. "Will you be my best man?"

It was absolutely the last thing Chris had expected. Gil had chosen Bran to be his best man; Chris had chosen Max. He'd guessed that Brandon would have chosen his best friend, Garrett. And eight months ago . . . eight months ago they'd had this huge fight that was the epitome of angst that he'd never wanted to repeat again and . . .

Eden nudged him with tears in her eyes.

"I . . ." He hiccupped. Except it wasn't a hiccup more than it was a cough. Because he had a ball of rubber bands in his throat.

"Oh, dang, here we go," Gil said to their baby brother, though his eyes were watery too. "You did it now, Bunso."

"Is that a yes?" Brandon's eyes rounded in cautious concern. "I know you're busy with Heart Resort everything, but I can't think of anyone who . . ."

Chris didn't want to hear any more. "You . . . you had me at *will you*."

Brandon's lips wiggled into a grin. "Was that . . . a *Jerry Maguire* reference?"

"Yes, yes, f you, okay. Romance-writer-husband problems. I can't help it that I have to stay on top of all the pop-culture stuff. Come here." He gestured Brandon over for a hug. "It's an honor."

Brandon clapped him on the back. "I want you to know that the only thing you'll be responsible for is to show up the day of the wedding and be our witness. No need for any special prep. And there will be no bachelor party."

"As if you have a choice," Gil said with a thick paste of sarcasm, waving the notion away, and with a sly look at Chris. "We're taking you away for the weekend at least. For like . . . a camping trip."

Brandon grimaced.

"Spa weekend!" Chris joined in.

"Book club weekend." Gil waggled his eyebrows.

"Oh yeah. Book club with knitting lessons." Chris snickered, because *hello*. He wasn't going to let any of his brothers get away with a quiet night after the ruckus they'd thrown for his own bachelor party. They'd hit Vegas, gambling at the cheap tables and eating horrible buffet food and staying up for almost two days, the whole time with heartburn. "Wait a sec, wasn't there a book about that?" He turned to Eden.

"Close," she said, amused. "There's *Real Men Knit* and *The Bromance Book Club*."

"See? So in tune," Geneva said, refocusing the conversation and pressing her cheek against Brandon's arm. "Even when things get tough, you two always seem to talk it out."

"You mean she talks to me about what I need to do," Chris quipped, comfortable now.

"It's true, what Brandon said," Eden redirected the banter. "We do talk a lot . . . but there are *more* things that happen." She sipped her drink, and her pinkie flashed up.

His siblings made hacking noises, and laughter skittered through their group. The conversation segued to something about the last rom-com they'd watched, and the attention veered away from the two of them.

It was the perfect delivery by Eden, and she knew it too. She lifted her gaze to him with a smirk.

Chris wanted to kiss it off her lips, because Eden was just so . . . genius. And he could get away with it too. A peck was allowed, and they'd done their share of kissing in front of people. He was still having withdrawal from that accidental kiss at their last interview.

Eden's eyes flashed, reading his intentions. Her face neared, and her eyes darted down to his lips—*yes*, she was thinking of it too. When she wrapped her arm around his, a signal of consent, his body temperature rose by a zillion degrees.

Yes, he had problems with hyperbolic speech, but who cared? He was going to kiss his wife.

But a buzz took her attention, and her focus swept away from his face and onto the table, to his phone. She exhaled minutely and settled back into her chair. "That phone," she whispered with a curl to her lip.

Dammit.

Whatever was simmering between them was extinguished, and with the continued buzzing came Chris's defensiveness. Yes, it had interrupted the moment, but he didn't understand her disdain for his phone. After all, his work was what made Heart Resort go.

Eden had known this from the start.

He picked up the phone and stood from the table, then walked to an empty corner of the deck. It was only then that he looked at the phone ID. Max. He swiped the answer button without hesitation. "Max. It's been a minute! Where the hell are you?"

"In probably an equally relaxing place as you're in, except I'm not working. I'm in Italy, man."

"What's up?" The last he'd heard from Max was a check-in after Tropical Storm Oscar. He leaned his elbows against the railing and gazed upon the calm water. To his right, a group of teenagers sat at the edge of a dock, cackling and smoking. He bit his lip and rubbed his beard with a hand, craving a cigarette—he'd been nicotine-free six months now, since . . . "You didn't just call me from Italy to say hello."

"Well, I was sitting here with a drink, looking out over the piazza, and checked in on the news, and guess whose picture came up on ABN online? You and Eden."

"For real? It's up already?" Chris hadn't been expecting the feature to post for another couple of weeks. He placed Max on speaker and thumbed through the screen.

"So, you haven't read it."

"Nope." Chris was distracted as he tapped on links. The pop-ups were always a bear. "Can you text me the direct link to this article?"

"Yeah, sure. But hey, the write-up had more than you and Eden. It had stuff about the resort."

"Okay?"

"Just be prepared. And before you go headlong into reading it, I wanted to mention that I met someone."

Chris inadvertently misclicked a link, and it took him to Buzzfeed. He harrumphed. "That's not new."

"I asked her to marry me."

Chris's fingers halted against the screen. Married? Max? "No lie?"

"Nope. Vanessa—that's her name—she's pretty amazing. And I'm planning on bringing her home. To meet the parentals. And, of course, I want her to meet you and Eden."

"Wow. Yeah, of course. Sorry, I guess I'm just surprised."

"I hadn't mentioned her because . . . I wasn't sure if you and Eden were doing okay . . . if, um, the contract was still on or not. But the article had only good things about you as a couple. Congrats, man. Honestly, I wasn't sure if the both of you were going to last a year, and look at you now. Anyway, I never thought it would happen to me too, but yeah, I'm in love."

"I'm happy for you." Chris was taken aback at Max's declaration. At the freedom with which his friend said his feelings. The two of them had been two peas in a pod since grad school. They'd tackled single living with this smorgasbord attitude, believing that their futures were theirs for the taking. For Max to fall in love—that was huge, so Chris refrained from correcting Max's assumptions about him and Eden. Mentioning the word *divorce* seemed inappropriate. "I can't wait to meet Vanessa."

"Thank you. Well . . . I need to run, but I'll send you more details about us visiting soon. Tell Eden I say hi."

"Will do." Chris looked over at the full table roaring with laughter. "Talk soon?"

"Talk soon," Max said and hung up.

A beat later, a text came in from Max. It was the direct link to the ABN online article. He read the title, though just barely, seeing red.

He thumbed through the screen as he bounded toward their family table. "Let's grab the check. Emergency meeting at Puso."

♡

"Heart Resort promises a happily ever after, but is it all just lip service?" Back at Puso, Chris read the headline on the ABN online article to his siblings—Geneva and Eden had put his nieces to bed—as they stared at their own devices. Irritated, and unable to sit still, he stood from his office chair and strode to the window, where his orchids were perched.

Having a garden outside hadn't been enough for Chris these days; he'd slowly brought home an indoor plant every few months—orchids mostly. As one of the hardest flowers to raise, it was a reminder that nothing that was easy was worth it. And certainly, if these flowers could grow under his care, then everything would be all right.

"This is ridiculous." Beatrice scrolled through the article with a thumb. "I thought this was supposed to be a feature on you and Ate Eden."

Chris growled, shaking his head at the memory of the interview, when Vera had asked him about the happily ever after. "I was too relaxed. I didn't pay enough attention to what she was really asking."

"The rest of the article questions the validity of our programming." Gil frowned against his phone screen. "This is libel, right? We need an attorney."

"I already texted Max," Chris said. "He's reaching out to ABN."

Tammy walked into the office. She was in pajamas and a robe. "No comments about my fit, please. I was already in bed when your text came through. I got in the car and didn't even think about what I was wearing until I drove over the land bridge."

"I think you look marvelous, Tammy," Beatrice said.

"Thank you, Bea."

"Thank you for coming. We were just discussing how to handle this," Chris said, only to catch sight of Eden hovering by the door.

How long had she been listening?

On the way back to the resort, Chris had asked her for space amid all her questions. Eden had signed up for a marriage of convenience, not business drama. He knew exactly what she had given up to be a part of this charade. Hearing Max on the phone, and that even he had found commitment and love, had been like a double-edged sword.

And this had ruined her celebration dinner, to boot.

"Eden, we're having a meeting right now," he said.

Silence descended in the office, presumably due to his tone, which had come out like a boom. He inwardly cringed at how harsh his words sounded.

Eden stepped in—of course she ignored him. "Since I was part of this interview, I should be here, shouldn't I?"

"I agree that Eden stays because . . ." Tammy heaved a breath. "They've tagged you both directly on social media. And they want a response."

"Who the hell are *they*?"

"People."

"And so what?" Chris lifted his hands up and shrugged. "*They* can tag all they want, and we don't have to play the game. *They*'re trying to bait us."

"True. But if this blows up, you'll need to make a professional statement. Something heartfelt, to let them know that you're not taking the bait. To be silent might indicate agreement."

"I agree." Gil was still scrolling through his phone. "Ah . . . I see it, on Twitter. Here's what one person says: 'A sham. All that expertise, the studies—it all doesn't work. Call it a vacation and end it at that.'" He looked up at Chris.

This was asinine. Chris ran a hand through his hair. "Fine, let's make a statement and post it tomorrow." With a glance at Tammy, who readied to take notes, he said, "Here's the message: 'Heart Resort believes in transparency, and we stand by our mission statement.' Good enough? What do you think, Eden? You're the writer."

"It's fine, though I think you should explain what the mission is."

"I don't want to give them more than that."

She scowled. "Then why even ask?"

Chris winced at her public comeback, though he pushed away his unease. He'd have to chat with her later about their bickering. "We go with the original message," Chris decided. The more concise, the better.

"All right. I'll post tomorrow, though hopefully this will die down overnight. My big ask, for each of you—stay off the feed." Tammy looked at them pointedly. "Don't respond, don't rebut, don't double down. Call one another; complain to each other if you have to. And please, don't do anything to inflame. It might not be a big deal to the people at large, since travel Twitter is niche. But any kind of conflict out there makes everyone salivate."

Chris raised his hands in surrender, though what he wanted to do was tell that person who called them a scam where to stick his—

"I'll keep him in line," Eden said, halting his train of thought.

"Good." Tammy heaved to standing. His siblings milled around aimlessly and eventually made their way out of the office.

It left Chris alone with Eden. After a quick glance at the door, she took a seat in his office chair. With steepled fingers under her chin, her face fell into a frown. "That was . . . this is all . . . not good." Her voice was soft but serious.

It made him want to gloss over the problem. He'd promised her on their wedding day that he'd protect her from this kind of stress. She hadn't signed up for this. "It's going to be fine. Tammy and I'll take care of it, and it will all blow over. But I think you should move your office back. I feel like we have a spotlight on us."

She shook her head. "That's the thing. I've got a book to write, and I can't seem to do it here. And now with this thing going on. It might be best for me to head back to Austin."

"But I need you."

CHAPTER FOUR

Eden exhaled at the word *need*.

It was both her fuel and kryptonite, the thing inside her that allowed her to work on her feet for hours at a time. The same thing that also, sometimes, rendered her a pushover. For some reason, when someone said they needed her, it motivated her to want to fulfill their wishes.

And whenever Chris said it, she wanted to throw herself into his arms.

Eden opened her mouth to relent, but his phone buzzed on the windowsill. When he stood to retrieve the phone, the opposite emotion spewed forth from her lips. "Do you know how many times your phone buzzed at dinner today?"

Chris scrolled and didn't spare her a glance. "We've talked about this."

"I know we have. But it was a dinner to celebrate me. And we were having a good time, finally, and—"

"Eden, this isn't the time to pick a fight."

"I'm not trying to pick a fight." She shut her eyes briefly to recenter herself and dig deeper like her editors sometimes nudged her to do. "I'm asking for you to give me some respect, especially in front of your family. Some lo—I mean." She stifled the l-word just in time. *Get thee behind me, Everly Heart.* "I mean, some care. Care, for me and my accomplishments."

"I don't understand what you're getting at. I'm like your number one fan. I read your books."

"And so by doing that, then you're excused from everything else? Like this incessant ambition that doesn't know how to ease up so we can talk about this."

"We *are* talking about this. And this is not about ambition. I'm trying to keep away an internet fire."

"Right." Whenever they bickered, Chris was precise and curt while she became this runaway train of words that made her want to clam up and retreat. So she heaved a breath. "And just as you have needs, I have needs too. I need to finish my book, but I can't do it here. Especially not now, with this other new thing."

He looked up from his phone with a frown, and Eden instantly regretted her flippant response. "*Other* new thing?" he asked. "What do you think I'm doing here? This isn't Monopoly. This is our family business. It's the most important thing we should be focusing on right now, not whether or not my phone's buzzing."

"Most important?" Forget relenting. Eden took her last thought back and punctuated it with a cackle. "So all that talk about connection being the most important thing in that feature article was just bull?"

His phone buzzed once more, and his eyes darted toward it.

"Go. Answer it. I'm heading back to Tiwala."

"Seriously?" And as she walked out the door, she heard him say, "Eden. Don't walk away."

"I'm already doing it."

Once in the living room Eden inhaled a deep breath of air.

How had their once logical discussions evolved to train wrecks of conversation where they'd started with one thing and ended up with mangled metal and random electrical wires that screamed *hot mess*?

Her point . . . God, what had been her point? She didn't even remember. But she'd wanted to remind him that more existed outside of Heart Resort. Heck, that more existed within the resort aside from the business itself. And she was just tired of everything . . .

She stepped out of the house and hopped into her golf cart and spun it around. The driveway was illuminated by solar lights, and she navigated the cart out the gate. She hung a right on the main drive that would lead her up to the north side of the peninsula.

Eden took her time, easing her foot on the gas. Some folks avoided driving around the resort at night. Objectively, it could feel a little creepy.

Eden loved it, though. It reminded her of the Texas Hill Country, with its massive sky that seemed to start and end as far as the eyes could see. Tonight, the moon was high—glorious, waning, and gibbous.

As if conjured, Eden's phone rang with the instrumental ringtone of "Thank U, Next" picked specifically by her baby sister, Josie. Her sister, who nerded out on anything space related, including the moon phases, which she'd learned about and had been engrossed with since preschool.

Eden sped down the gravel road to her beach house so she could take the call properly.

Josie was Everly Heart's media maven. A senior in high school, Josie was a whiz, an influencer, a brand ambassador. It only made sense for Eden to hire her—paying her with gift cards to her favorite skin-care stores—and her social media had flourished. Since Eden had sent Josie a few snaps at a time, access to a graphics program, and a book of inspirational quotes by famous authors, Everly's Instagram had been curated to the nines.

But Josie was so present on the net that she could have also read the article from ABN. As much as she seemed mature, she didn't need to see this kind of drama imploding in real time. Though, if Max would do his job well enough, then that article could disappear in the next few hours. Eden answered the phone after she parked the golf cart. "Heyyy, Jojo."

"Ate Eden. I just wanted to see if you had any pictures for me to post."

"Is that all?" Eden exited the cart, then walked around to the front door.

"Yeah. Why?" Her voice tilted upward in suspicion.

"No reason." Eden flipped on the lights and turned to her dreaded desk of incomplete work.

"Oookay." Josie chuckled. "Anyway, I was thinking that it's time to do something different with your Instagram feed. I want more photos of you and Kuya Chris, since you guys are so cute. What do you think?"

"Hmm, we'll see. Not sure if your kuya will want his picture out there." She sat in her office chair and pressed the space bar of her laptop. The screen lit to life. Her work in progress came to view, the Word document now at 20,457 words. Ten thousand in about eighteen days, which was unacceptable.

"Kuya Chris is everywhere online. I don't think it's him that has the issue."

Instinctively, and now with concern nipping at her heels about the business of her career, she clicked through to her social media and then to Twitter. She had a slew of DMs to contend with, especially from her critique group. There was so much to do with so little time, and especially with lagging motivation.

And now with this crisis . . .

Dammit. She couldn't skip town.

"Speaking of getting out there. Um, I think I'm going to have to postpone my next trip out." Eden winced. She had discussed this trip in her last conversation with Josie, and now she was caving to Chris's request. For once, she wished it wasn't always about the resort.

"What? Why?"

"There's just stuff." Eden halted. Yes, Josie was technically an adult, but she didn't have to know everything that was going on.

"But I wanted to shop early for prom dresses."

"You can start looking to narrow down styles, and I'll schedule a flight as soon as I can."

"Fine." Josie's discontent oozed through the phone.

"How's everything at home?"

"Same-o. Dad's at work. And there's still a hole in the ceiling."

Eden startled. "A what?"

"Oh, Dad didn't mention? The upstairs tub leaked onto the ceiling. Someone tried to fix it, and then they were supposed to come back but didn't."

"He called someone else, right?"

"I guess?"

Eden jotted down a note to call a plumber. The Chan family was a houseful of adults with no center of gravity—Josie; her father, Paul, who worked nonstop as a master electrician; and, occasionally, Eden—and their home suffered the fate of no one caring for it.

It was because the person who'd used to care for it was there even less than Eden.

Irritation laced up her spine, but she pushed it away. Their mother, currently living in the Philippines with her family, was doing her duty, and there was no solution to that problem. In Eden's point of view, her only course of action was to be the glue they were desperately missing, even if she wasn't quite the right kind. Like regular glue on felt—she wasn't enough in the ways where she could make things stick. Especially because her attentions were split, with one path toward her own career and one to the Outer Banks, North Carolina.

She would keep trying, though; she saved every bit she could from her travel RT positions and the initial inheritance payment when she had married Chris. And in less than four months, she would have enough to move her family to a home that wasn't on the verge of collapse, and she would be there to be the glue, for real.

But then you won't be in the Outer Banks.

"So have you heard anything from UT?" Eden asked to knock some sense into her silly running thoughts. She knew that missing the Pusos would be a thing, but her family—her blood family—had to come first. Josie would be entering the next phase of her life—college—and Eden wanted to make sure she was there to usher and guide, because she hadn't had quite the same help.

Josie grumbled. "Still languishing on the wait list. My inbox and the mailbox is empty. What if I don't get in?"

"Then you can make your own luck in another school you got accepted to."

"But I want UT."

She sighed. "Sometimes we don't get everything we want."

"You did—you have everything: the career, the life. You even have the guy. You write about the happily ever after, and you have one too. Even if I don't subscribe to that all the way, it's still a bonus."

If she only knew. Eden formed the words carefully, grateful that this conversation wasn't on video chat. "It's not a perfect life by any means, Josie. It's a life I worked hard for and continue to. And yes, there's a little bit of luck thrown in there and especially the unexpected. But decision day is coming, and you have to be open to perhaps making a life elsewhere but UT."

"Okay, Ate."

"Good." Then Eden turned back to her computer screen and started a new list in her notes app. "Now tell me what else is going on with the house."

♡

Eden was dreaming that she was being given a microcurrent facial massage when she was startled awake by the phone under her cheek. While sitting at her desk. And still in her daytime clothes.

She groaned, lifting her face, only to feel stabbing pains from strained neck muscles.

After hanging up with her sister, Eden had given herself a pep talk and then committed to buckle down and write. She'd checked in with her critique group for accountability, and she'd rolled up her proverbial sleeves, only to feel hungry. So she'd eaten a small snack and then realized that her book couple needed to go horseback riding, and she hadn't had any idea what that entailed. So she'd become like Alice in Wonderland, falling down the research hole and ending up on a wiki page on how sinkholes occurred, which then led her down another tunnel of which states had the most sinkholes, with the intent of avoiding them.

So basically: work.

The buzzing that woke her up were text messages from the Puso family group chat. It was a little after midnight, and notifications were flying in like publishing on a Monday, as if everyone scheduled all their mail from the weekend for eight in the morning.

Facial recognition worked after the third time, and as she attempted to massage her neck, she caught up on the chatter.

Beatrice:

I thought Tammy was going to wait to post that note until tomorrow.

I'm seeing it up now.

Gil:

Crap. Lemme see if I can text her.

Chris:

I just did. She scheduled it on the wrong day.

Are you guys reading this crap?

Brandon:

Everyone back away.

Geneva:

Nothing good can come of social media I swear.

Gil:

Kuya don't take the bait.

Don't take the bait? Eden's senses rushed back to her as if someone had called a code blue. On her computer, she logged on to Twitter and checked out the Heart Resort account.

Sure enough, Tammy had posted a graphic with the company message: *Heart Resort believes in transparency, and we stand by our mission statement.*

Below it were responses.

@ColeRicci—Transparency? How about proof?

@ColeRicci—@HeartResort is charging luxury prices for a sham. @WillowTree doesn't make such claims.

Eden felt heat rushing through her. Her first thought: whoever this troll Cole Ricci was, if his job was to get a rise out of people, it was working. Her second thought: if she was feeling angry at this, her husband must have been livid. Third: Proof? What kind of proof was he talking about?

"Don't post," she said aloud, in hopes that Chris felt her vibe somehow. Still she started to text him separately. This was a flame that needed to fizzle out, and it would over time. But Eden was distracted by other tweets flying in, refreshing the page to see the next comment and question. Some inquired as to how much Heart Resort charged.

@ColeRicci—And I got it on good info. The CEO's marriage is in trouble, one of the brother's divorced, the sister's single, and the youngest? He once slept with a resort client. A mess.

Eden shot to her feet. Oh no. No, they didn't.

Where did he get this information?

How did he know?

She began to pace the short distance from the front door to the kitchen. Twitter drags often started like a slow burn, then became a massive fire that engulfed everyone and everything in sight.

She scrambled back to her chair and set the phone down so she could see the upcoming texts as she clicked on this Cole Ricci's profile, noted his info, and then headed to her best friend Google on her laptop and put her author power of research to work.

Her screen refreshed.

@ColeRicci—Why trust a CEO that doesn't show his endorsement of his own system?

Eden's fingers took a life of their own. She'd repeatedly counseled Josie about social media bullying in the same way she was taught about stranger danger. In this case, she would have told Josie: Leave it. Do not engage. Block and move on. Report if needed.

But in that moment, she couldn't *not* say something. After all, when did silence become complicit? One should be able to defend oneself. And one should be able to defend one's family.

Attacking the business was one thing. But going after her siblings . . . going after her family. Her marriage, despite the fact that it was true. And Brandon.

Oh, hell no. That was unacceptable.

"Yes," she whispered in triumph while piecing together Cole's identity and finding he worked for Willow Tree. And with another quick search, she discovered that he'd filed his own divorce. It was enough information to make something up. But when she refreshed the feed, Chris's rarely used handle was on the screen. "Oh my God."

@ChrisPuso—I would suggest halting right there @ColeRicci. You're out of line

@ColeRicci—Oh, there he is! Finally. Now we can get some answers. How do you sleep at night, shamming people out of their money @ChrisPuso

@ChrisPuso—You're speaking lies. Who are you anyway?

And was it just her? But seeing Chris stand against this Cole Ricci was giving her feelings, familiar ones that she knew better than to act on.

But her thumbs had a different idea.

@EdenPuso—@ChrisPuso I'll tell you who he is. He works in @WillowTree's marketing department. This is not the way to clients, Willow Tree

@EdenPuso—@ColeRicci doesn't have his own life so he has to disparage others

The Puso group text message lit up with someone encouraging her to keep going and someone saying to stop. Obviously, that person didn't understand that once you unleashed the mama bear, it took a whole hell of a lot more than a text to rein her back in.

A giggle bubbled from her lips.

@EdenPuso—So worried about people's marriages @ColeRicci. How's yours? Oh wait!

@WillowTree this is your mess. He opened this can

Pounding from the front door grabbed her attention. Eden, still in the throes of the Twitter moment, answered without checking who it was.

It was Tammy with her under-eye masks still attached to her face, hair in a sagging bun. "Stop. Stop it now."

CHAPTER FIVE

Chris knew that he needed to put the phone away. He should have put it away long before now and not responded to this Cole Ricci because he had this tendency to jump into fights. This was also why he'd hired a PR person and wasn't on social media on any regular basis. He was a better person to deal with in real life. There were so many nuances to his sarcasm and what Eden called his "rough around the edges." What might've sounded to him as clever just made him look like a jerk. And he had to face it—his grammar was crap, and one had to be exact with 280 characters.

But he couldn't put away the phone now, because his jaw was on the floor.

Eden had jumped into the ring with him, and this time, her ire was directed at a common enemy.

Dang.

Was it wrong for him to think the way she'd clapped back on Twitter was sexy?

It didn't help that he—they—hadn't had sex in months.

Footsteps came from all over the house. Doors slammed. His siblings skidded in, deer-in-headlights expressions on their faces. Gil and Beatrice were silent, alternately watching their phones and him. Brandon was laughing.

Another buzz.

"Get off the damn phone, Chris!" Tammy charged into the room and made a beeline toward him with a hand out. "Gimme."

As Chris handed Tammy his phone (because his publicist looked like she was going to combust), he noticed another phone already in her hand.

It was then that Eden entered, arms crossed in defiance. He felt his heart expand; with it, emotions filled the extra space. He'd dug this woman from the very start exactly for this, this fire.

So he crossed the room to show solidarity.

To his pure relief, she met him halfway and hugged him. "You are freaking amazing," he whispered into her hair. And God he wished he could do more than just hug. Because those emotions rushing through him? One was this primal urge to make love to her as he'd done before. The second was this maniacal satisfaction that made him want to scream inside his chest. Because this was wild. "We're so in trouble."

Eden busted out a cackle and stepped back, looking up at him. "You started it."

"This isn't funny. Not. At. All." Tammy raised the two phones in her hand, swiveling their attention. "We're going to have to remedy this."

"There's nothing to remedy," Chris said.

"Right. He had it coming," Eden declared, causing a lump to form in Chris's throat. That at the heart of it, it wasn't about them individually but this collective thing they called a *partnership*.

"Whether or not he had it coming, we still have to fix it. *I* still have to fix it. It's my fault. If I hadn't rescheduled accidentally . . . dammit." Tammy bit at her thumbnail.

"I think they're out to get us, Tammy, so it probably wouldn't have mattered when you posted it," Gil reassured.

"I dunno, but that was pretty impressive. Dang, Ate Eden. You went after him," Beatrice said.

"I had to . . . he made it personal."

"And you raised the ante." Tammy had begun to pace.

"Well, people have opinions apparently." Brandon scrolled his phone with a finger overtly, rubbing it in with a foreboding whistle. "Crap. He really called us out. Me, especially."

"Not just you, Bran. How do they even have this information?" Beatrice asked. A beat later, her jaw dropped. "Twitter knows I'm single. That's just great."

"We can still fix this," Gil said. "Kuya, I think you should go with what Ate Eden suggested earlier. Explain the mission. And add on that no one has any right to our personal information. My divorce is public knowledge. But Bran and Bea's private life should be off limits. As for the both of you, Kuya and Eden . . . well . . ."

A hush settled around them, and in the silence, it became perfectly clear that as much as he and Eden had tried to keep their problems to themselves, their issues had spilled over to the rest of the family. Darting his gaze across the room, Chris found that his siblings refused to meet his eyes.

Chris wondered if this was how parents felt, being seen all the way through. Growing up, he'd come to a point in which he'd realized his parents weren't perfect. And now, for all his effort to be the person that his siblings could look up to, especially after their parents had died, it dawned on him for the first time that maybe, he wasn't actually measuring up.

What other faults had his siblings picked up on? Had they been able to tell that he was always waiting for the other shoe to drop? Or that he really didn't know what he was doing, even if he was the so-called head of the family?

Humility washed over him like the tide.

"Okay. Let's send out another collective note." He looked to Tammy, ready to dictate. She was shaking her head, eyes on her iPad screen. "What's up?"

"Cole Ricci again." Tammy paled. "He said, 'I did open this can. So let's dump out all the worms. How about you'"—her eyes lifted to Eden—"'and @ChrisPuso take up one of your programs. Prove to us that Heart Resort is legit and you're not scamming your clients.'"

Chris shook with anger. "That mother—"

"Kuya, wait," Gil interrupted. "That . . . there might be something to this."

"No. Absolutely not. We aren't negotiating."

"Oh wow. Give me a sec." Tammy bit her lip. "You're right, Gil. This might be a way to shut them up for good."

"No!" Chris cut Tammy off. He'd hired her for her out-of-the-box thinking, and last summer, when she'd convinced the family that Geneva and Brandon should appear like a couple on their social media, it had paid off. But this idea was wild.

"Wait. Let her speak." Eden said, leaving his side and taking a seat.

"Am I in an alternate universe? Why am I the only one who thinks this idea is horrendous? Bea?" He turned toward his sister, who was the most levelheaded out of all of them. "Please talk some sense into them."

Except his sister was in a contemplative silence, arms crossed. And when he darted his gaze to Brandon, his brother simply shrugged and said, "I'm on your side, for once."

Chris heaved a breath. "Thank you."

"How long are the retreats?" Eden said above the standoff.

Tammy lit up. "Our five-day retreat is our most popular. It's the same course that Brandon and Geneva did a few months ago. You'd fill out a questionnaire and a program would be picked for you that combines your interests. It's the retreat with the best ratings, called Sorpresa."

"Surprise. Makes sense," Eden said.

"Yep. It employs all the best things that make it our bestseller: a combination of outdoor and indoor activities, therapy, and time alone."

"But how do we prove that it is or isn't working?" Eden asked.

"Am I just speaking to the void?" Chris lifted both arms. "I am literally an apparition with no voice."

"We can stream it," Gil said.

Brandon snickered and adjusted his ball cap so it covered his face. His shoulders shook from laughter.

"Live video?" Eden whispered, then shook her head. "I don't know."

"Snippets, then," Tammy offered.

Chris's control over this whole situation was slipping through his fingers. If he couldn't get their attention now, then everything would be decided with or without him. Wasn't he the CEO? "I don't like it. I don't agree."

"Can we control the messaging?" Eden spoke as if still not hearing him.

"If we have the right director. And I know the perfect one," Gil said.

"And who might that be?" Beatrice frowned.

With a deadpan expression, he said, "Jessie."

At the mention of Gil's ex-wife's name, the room fell silent, and with a glance at Beatrice, Chris saw that, sure enough, a scowl was plastered on her face, like a wild cat on the prowl.

Jessie Puso was a director of photography with a small production company based in Los Angeles.

"We can trust her," Gil said.

Beatrice made a *pfft* noise. "Right. Trust. Do you hear yourself, Kuya Gil? That woman broke your heart. She broke everyone's hearts. And beyond that problematic trait of hers that can never be redeemed, ever"— she heaved a breath—"she's in LA."

"She's not in LA." Gil's voice remained even and strong. "I mean, she is in LA, but she's coming out to spend some time with the girls. She has a condo in Nags Head."

The entire room erupted in chatter, the conversation about the Twitter dumpster tabled for the moment. Chris attempted to listen to his siblings; in this situation, he would have to be the one to mediate before it became a family war.

"You cannot possibly allow that woman on Heart Resort. She doesn't deserve to be in our home," Beatrice said.

"I don't get it. What's going on?" Tammy interrupted.

Among the continued yelling, Eden explained. "Gil and Jessie were married about eight years before they split up . . ."

Bottom line: they'd fallen apart. Their roads had diverged, and they had gone from honeymooners with two kids at Eden and Chris's wedding to two people who fought over everything.

"She has a right to be here. She's the mother of my children." Gil stood, crossing his arms.

"No, absolutely not. Kuya Chris!" Beatrice was now yelling at him. "You will not allow this to happen."

Brandon shook his head, muttering to himself. Gil argued back. Tammy scrolled through her phone, relaying what else was being said.

Allow? As if Chris ever had the power in the first place.

Then, as suddenly as her earlier tweets had appeared on the screen, Eden stood. She grabbed Chris by the forearm. Her warm grip was grounding, and his focus narrowed on her face, as it had many times in the past when things had felt overwhelming. She was probably the only person, besides his father, who understood when he needed a moment to think.

So when Eden gestured for him to follow her out of the room, he did just that.

CHAPTER SIX

Eden pulled Chris out of the office, looking back one last time at a family that was now in the midst of the fight.

"Where are we going?" Chris's voice shook, as she'd expected it would. Her husband was amazing when it came to the boardroom, when doing business, but with matters of the family, he was out of his league. She could see the trepidation on his face, the uncertainty of how to navigate this situation with his siblings at odds with one another.

But this wasn't the time for either one of them to be hesitant. They had to refocus and make a decision as a united front. Because this was a bigger crisis than Chris or she had ever imagined.

"Someplace where we can be alone." She entered the four-seasons dining room with Chris behind her and shut the french doors. She leaned her back against them, and in the silence Eden pressed her hand against her heart. It beat like a bass drum.

Because, God, she and Chris hadn't thought this far ahead, to the almost-five-year mark when they would have to face the true consequences of their actions.

"Hey." Chris rubbed her arms, as if she was cold. His face dipped down to look at her. "Eden, speak to me."

She nodded, composing her thoughts. "I think we have to do this . . . dare, whatever it is. We have to go through what is claimed to be the best couples program in the United States."

"Wh . . . what? Why?"

"Your siblings. Our family . . . they're all caught up in this. They're caught up in *us*. We didn't think about this part, Chris. Our contract spelled everything out. Terms of payment. Contract length. How we act in public. We debated the pet names we would call one another. Our sleeping arrangements, even. No kids. No sex. Supposedly." She braved a glance up, and his lips quirked minutely. "But we didn't think about those people in the other room, or my family in Texas. Do you see how Gil's marriage has affected the dynamic? And you know how my sister is so angry at my mother. When you and I go our separate ways, it will be traumatic for all of them."

His hands dropped, and his gaze followed. "I've thought about it. It's going to wreck them."

Eden waited for more, for an acknowledgment that it would wreck him too; then she admonished herself for such foolish thoughts. They couldn't be wrecked about a plan they'd both engineered. That train had already left the station toward the destination, and they were copilots.

Instead, what flashed in his eyes was confusion. "But giving this guy Ricci any of our attention is pointless. And putting ourselves in front of media like that . . . buh-bye, privacy."

"Yeah, the lack of privacy would suck, but if we can control the messaging . . . you've seen my sister curate Everly Heart's account. This can work if we have control over what's being portrayed." Eden shook her head, her mind already on act two when they were still at the inciting incident of this caper in a caper. She reeled herself back. "Hear me out. If they—your family and mine—know that we did everything we could to save our marriage, then when it comes time to make the announcement . . ." Eden's sentence wouldn't finish itself. Sometimes she had to see the words in order to discern what they meant. Sometimes, she needed an editor to push the message along.

And thank goodness, Chris became that, at that moment. "This retreat would be more their closure for when . . . it happens."

"They'll know that we at least tried." She nodded. "I don't want them to hate me, Chris."

"They won't hate you. They'll hate me." Resignation flitted across his face.

"Hey, I don't want that either." She knew how important his siblings were to Chris, how important their opinions of him were.

He pressed his fingers against the bridge of his nose. "Argh. This is . . . this is so complicated. If we agree to this, we risk everyone finding out about our secret. Mortimer's still suspicious."

Throughout their marriage Kyle Mortimer had continued to check on her and Chris. As Joe Puso's former longtime confidant and best friend, he'd taken his job seriously and scrutinized their marriage from the jump. He'd insisted on attending the wedding and followed the resort's business closely. He was the reason why Chris insisted Eden was at every couples' function and present at every media event. Mortimer would ensure before he loosened the rest of the purse strings that the five years were completed to the second.

"That Mortimer never did like me." She scrunched her nose.

His face eased, reflecting back on the memory. "I sure as heck don't know why. You all but rolled your eyes at him when he asked for his turn with you at the money dance."

"He can keep his personal dollars." She smarted, shivering. "It was the way he looked at me. Like I wasn't good enough for you."

"He was being protective over the trust. And he's a fool—if he only knew how much you changed my life for the better."

Though her husband's tone was casual, Eden's face warmed, adding to her topsy-turvy feelings.

"Anyway." He ran his hands through his hair. "I don't like the idea of opening up our marriage for everyone to analyze."

"Look, I don't like it either. I have a book to write. I don't have the headspace for any of this. But if Mortimer hears about this whole accusation, he might wonder if we'll split up too, so doing this retreat may quell his suspicions. It would shut Willow Tree up because we would prove your program works. Doing the retreat would bring promo to the resort. And it'll prepare our family. The only downside . . ." Eden dropped her gaze to the floor.

He picked up where she left off. "Is that when we split up, it might prove Willow Tree right that the programs don't work after all."

She shrugged with the swirling unease in her belly. "Maybe not? What if we can say that splitting up was our happily ever after? It's something you've said all along—that HEAs are different for everyone."

He shut his eyes for a beat in concentration. "The other option is to not do the challenge and deal with Willow's Tree's accusations and Mortimer when he hears about all of this. And the family will wonder why we just didn't do it. And in the end they'll be shocked when we split up. It's a lose-lose."

"What's better of the two?" Eden blinked up at him.

He growled in indecision. Then he gazed over her shoulder and snorted. "Aaand we have an audience."

She looked into his eyes and stepped closer. They were *on* once more. "Who is it?"

"Everyone."

"Okay. We should hug."

He nodded and enveloped her, and as soon as their bodies touched, they both seemed to sigh into one another. Chris *did* give such great hugs. He was perfectly proportioned to her frame, and he wasn't afraid to take her all the way in. In his hugs she was cocooned and safe, if only for the moment. She breathed in his scent, undeniably him: a mixture of clean laundry, the outdoors, and a hint of his patchouli-scented lotion.

His face dipped low as he whispered in her ear, beard brushing against her cheek, and at the intimacy of it all, of his nose grazing her earlobe, his breath caressing her skin, Eden's knees buckled ever so imperceptibly. "You're right. We have to do this, even if I don't want to."

"You make it sound like you don't want to be in close quarters with me for five days," Eden said wryly to push herself out of her lazy hormonal reactions. "Afraid of me busting your chops all that time?"

"I mean, if we're being honest about it . . ." He half laughed, but she heard his trepidation. They'd just agreed to a ruse within a ruse where they had to act perfectly, knowing full well that they weren't perfect.

It wasn't about her giving him a hard time. It had everything to do with whether they could resist one another.

God knew they couldn't do it once before.

CHAPTER SEVEN

Annapolis, Maryland
Christmas, eleven years and four months ago
Word of the day: reminisce

Chris entered the Annapolis town house, dragging his hard-shell suitcase behind him. He stomped down on the mat in the front foyer to loosen the snow off his shoes and ruffled his hair. Snowflakes sprinkled down toward the wood floors. He shivered reflexively—it was freezing.

"Ma? Dad?" He unwound his scarf and took off his peacoat, then hung both on the oak coat-tree that had reliably stood in that same corner for years. He kicked off his shoes and arranged them with the several pairs lined up to the side of the rug. It was a full house by the count, with him the last to arrive.

The house smelled like Christmas. Like coffee and cinnamon and pine, and the living room was replete with all the trappings of his mother's favorite holiday. It had been a discussion every year—his mother wanted to decorate for Christmas starting in September, as was her childhood tradition in the Philippines, but his father, as well as the rest of the family, argued that it was hard to celebrate Halloween and Thanksgiving with tinsel and candy canes.

So Marilyn had responded by being extra about all of it. Greenery was hung over every doorway and was wrapped around the banister. There was a tree in every first-floor room. Their original fifteen-foot plastic tree blinked white lights, with gifts overflowing from underneath. And the thing that set their decor apart from any other place Chris had attended in his almost ten years since leaving home were the parols that hung at every common-room doorway. Some of these star-shaped lanterns had been especially mailed from the Philippines; others had been handmade by him and his siblings using long bamboo sticks and cellophane and tissue paper. They shimmered with every slight bit of wind, bathing the house in colorful light.

The house also sounded like Christmas. Sitting on a bookshelf in the corner of the living room was his dad's record player, spinning another cherished LP. Barry Manilow piped through the speakers. The above-the-stove vent grumbled in the kitchen. From upstairs came voices and the thuds of someone walking. It was just after four o'clock, which meant that his siblings were hiding out and waiting on the start of dinner. Because whenever they all came home, they'd all revert back to their childlike selves. Chris was no exception. He was days away from thirty, but as he parked his suitcase next to the bookcase that still shelved some of his favorite books, he was back to being fifteen. He'd left his professional life at the door, to include all the stress and the expectations from strangers.

Chris followed his nose; something was cooking. He bounded through the house and entered the light-filled kitchen, cluttered and cheerful, where his parents had their backs turned to him. Joe Puso was at the stove, and Marilyn stood at the sink. They were singing along to the music while Dad stirred and Mom set another rinsed bowl onto the lower rack of the dishwasher. Because they never used the dishwasher for its intended function.

Chris leaned against the doorway, arms crossed. His life had been on the go—his work as a financial analyst had taken him to all corners of the world. He'd stayed in fancy hotels where he'd had to lift nary a finger, as well as hostels where he'd had to go without a shower for a couple of days. But coming home to this was irreplaceable; the reliability of his parents was comfort.

Chris just wanted to soak it in. This was goals. Though he wasn't quite sure about the wife part, this feeling, right here . . . that was what he wanted at their age.

Then his dad started to sing into the ladle, his mother started swinging her hips, and Chris couldn't let it go further. He might have been nostalgic, but he had his limits. He couldn't watch *American Idol* without being completely mortified for some of their contestants' auditions.

He cleared his throat.

The two turned with a quickness.

"Anak!" Marilyn threw her hands in the air and rushed toward him, then wrapped wet hands around his torso. He kissed her on top of her head, and his father stood behind to wait his turn, hands on his hips. Joseph had this stance, a hunched-over, serious look that would intimidate Chris when he'd been a kid. Chris's friends and coworkers had told him he stood in the same way, in a contemplative silence that made it tough to figure out which Chris they were dealing with. The fun-loving, sarcastic guy or the serious businessperson who gave no cares to feelings.

He wasn't sure if he was a fan of this dichotomy for himself, but it fit his father's persona perfectly.

After his mother stepped back, Chris slapped his hand into his father's. Then came the one-arm hug that wrangled him in his place. It was a feeling that Chris understood undeniably that in that house, he was somebody's son.

And some days, he just really needed that.

"We didn't think you'd be here until later. And"—she pushed him out of the way and peeked down the hallway—"where's Jenny?"

"No, mahal, it's *Janie*." His father snickered.

"*Janine*." Chris winced, sighing. "She's not here. And anyway, what am I, chopped liver?"

Janine was his . . . he didn't know now. But they'd been together for three months, the longest relationship with a woman since his college girlfriend, and his parents had insisted on meeting her.

Except . . .

"Not here? She's coming for Christmas dinner, right?"

His father was watching this interaction. Chris felt it in his stare. "Nope, Ma, she's not."

"I don't understand?"

To his parents, it was unheard of for friends not to come and meet the family. Their town house had been a catchall for acquaintances, for friends of friends, for neighbors who needed company, for the parish priest for good luck. Their crowded table could always fit another body. Every couch was a pullout, and every kid bed was a trundle. Immigrants understood the struggle to find family, and their parents opened their homes so others felt that they had a place to go. They made and kept family wherever they moved.

"No, that's not it." Chris rested a hand behind his head. "I didn't want . . ."

His mother's face slacked. "Iho. What is it now about this one? What's your complaint?"

"It just wasn't right." He looked to his dad for help; Joe remained stoic.

"What has to be right? You said she was nice. Smart. Employed. What more do you want? You're thirty, son."

"Not yet. I still have six days." He smirked.

His mother clucked. "Ha ha. You joke. But you can't navigate the world by yourself, iho. Nor are you getting any younger. I don't understand this need to wait." She lifted a finger, and a lecture was foisted upon him like a bag of mulch at the gardening store.

So Chris zoned in to the coffee corner of the kitchen. It was literally in the corner, where the carafe was always filled with hot java. Next to it was a blue-and-white container of sugar. He grabbed his favorite coffee mug, still where he had left it last time, and poured himself a cup, and his mother grabbed the milk from the fridge to cut the tar. She was still speaking, and his father was humming in agreement, but Chris had learned to fine-tune his selective hearing because there would be no talking back tolerated. He leaned against the counter and blew into his cup.

"Ma," he said gently, when he was sure that she was done. "I can't just be with anyone. I need to be with the *one*."

"That's the thing, son. No one really knows who the *one* is. There is love, and care, and friendship, and time," his father added.

Chris sipped his coffee. It was easy for them to say, now married thirty-two years. He'd held up their marriage against all the relationships—hell, all the nonrelationships—he'd had, and none had come remotely close.

What sounded like charging elephants echoed through the house. It was followed by banter and cackling. Chris smiled into his coffee. Saved by his siblings.

"Kuya Chris! How long have you been here?" Beatrice rushed at him and threw her arms around his torso, with just enough time to set his cup down on the counter.

"Oy, it's the man," Gil said with a hand raised for a high five.

"What's up, bro." He slapped him five, then moved in to hug Brandon, the youngest, in his last year in undergrad. He was going to school in Texas, and Chris hadn't seen him in forever. "Dang, you got bigger. You're working out?"

"Sort of." He dipped his chin, shy.

Chris continued down the line, hugging Gil's longtime girlfriend, Jessie, and Geneva, Beatrice's best friend.

But there was an extra person, a stranger in their midst. A pretty one wearing a hideous pine-tree-green Christmas sweater.

"Oh, Kuya Chris, this is Eden Chan. She was my RA at my dorms for like two years. She's in town for work," Brandon said.

This Eden Chan had dark-brown hair and dark eyes, with a heart-shaped face and full lips. Kissable lips, in fact.

He shook himself awake. That was . . . inappropriate. "Hi, uh . . ." He wasn't sure how to greet her—hugs usually ran aplenty in the Puso house.

"I wouldn't mind a hug too." She read his mind with a smile. "Your parents were nice enough to invite me over. I'm a travel respiratory therapist out of Georgetown Medical. It would have been a lonely Christmas."

Chris felt his entire body exhale with her sincerity. He leaned down for a polite hug. "Well, welcome."

"Okay, everyone in the dining room." His mother clapped and directed the crew to set the table. It was a production, and Chris fell right into step with everyone, and right next to Eden. She had an easy laugh, a bright smile. Throughout dinner, she wasn't intimidated by the chaos of their family, which Chris was always aware of. There was no keeping the volume at a respectable noise, from the occasional curse word, either in Tagalog or in English.

And he couldn't stop looking at her while they ate, at how she fit right in. He could swear, too, that at times she was sneaking glances at him.

Chris's curiosity was on overload by the time the family converged to set up Pictionary after dinner. As Brandon was leaving the guest bath, Chris ambushed him.

"Holy crap. You scared the living daylights out of me," Brandon said. Then he did a double take. "What do you want, Kuya?"

It would have been a good opportunity to give Brandon a hard time about something. He was graduating in the spring but had yet to figure out what he was going to be when he grew up. But Chris was keenly aware of their vast age difference, and sometimes his jokes and gentle jabs didn't land quite right with Brandon. So he opted for a straightforward approach. "You and Eden—are the both of you . . ."

"What? No." He cackled. "She's like a big sister . . . whoa, wait a sec. Are you asking because . . ." His face slipped into a frown. "No no no no. Kuya, she's *nice*. She's like super nice and has a heart of gold. And you go through women like . . ."

He eyed his brother. "Please. Don't call the kettle black."

His cheeks darkened. "Fine, yeah, but I mean. Okay. But listen, please, be good to her. She's . . . she's really cool."

It was enough of a blessing.

♡

Eden sipped her warm apple cider and reveled in the comfort of this Christmas night. She had her legs pulled up underneath her and wished, for the tenth time since she'd arrived in the Puso home, that she could spend the night instead of heading back out to her short-term apartment rental. Being in this family circle, though sans parents—they'd retreated to their bedroom after dessert—was familiar, comfortable, and relaxing.

Alas, she had work in the morning.

At the moment, she was the only one sober. Wine, spiked eggnog, and beer flowed in excess. Bodies were stretched out around the coffee table like languid cats, and their voices undulated in a singsong that could be accomplished only around a group who knew each other's core.

But the person who she couldn't get her eyes off of was Chris, the eldest of this crew. He was four years older, but she felt most akin to him, possibly because they were both eldest born. He was beguiling, like a shell of a character that intrigued her. She wanted to take the time to sketch him out on paper. She wanted to know what was inside him that made him tick. The other Puso siblings each had their quirks, but they all watched Chris and his reactions. They listened to him.

Eden had heard about Chris through Brandon, of course. Brandon, once one got him settled, talked incessantly about little things, and it had been clear that he was in awe of his oldest sibling. It made sense now, seeing everyone in one room.

"Let's play Never Have I Ever instead of Pictionary," Gil piped up. When he was answered with a resounding *noooo*, he lifted his drink. "Look, we're hardly ever in the same room. With me and Jessie in LA, Bran in Texas, Kuya Chris in Philly, Bea in Virginia. And then Geneva." His face screwed into a question. "Where the hell are you these days, Geneva?"

"Also in Virginia for grad school." She laughed.

"Right, and then Eden, who's new to the crew. This is a good way to catch up."

"All right, I'm down," Beatrice said with a sly smile.

"Yeah!" Gil launched to his feet and grabbed the last two bottles of wine from the dining room table. "Who needs a refill or a new cup?" He made quick work of doing the honors. When he came to Eden, she covered her cup. "Not for me. I'm driving."

"Okay, lemme go grab you a . . ." But as he turned, Chris was already handing her a soda. "Thanks, Kuya. Okay, everyone, hear me out. Drink if you've done the things? Get it? Brandon, do you understand the directions?"

Brandon pressed his lips together and rolled his eyes.

Laughter skittered through the group, and Chris sat down next to Eden, though closer this time. She stilled her body; it was starting to hum. "Don't feel pressured, okay?" he said just loud enough for her to hear. "It's easy to get caught up with us."

She found it sweet. "Eh, this is pretty much on par with how it is in my family. I've only one sister, and she might be louder than all of you."

72

"Is your family in Texas?"

"Yeah." She braved another glance at him, and holy Christmas, he was still as cute as he was five minutes ago. "I spoke to them earlier today. They're celebrating with our neighbors and probably in the middle of karaoke."

"Kind of crappy you have to work during Christmas, and far away from home."

"It's not crappy. It's good money," she said, straight to the fact, because she didn't want him to feel sorry for her. This had been her decision, and she was proud of it. She would be more thrilled when she got her paycheck. "Patients need to celebrate the holidays, too, and I don't mind being there for them. Besides, I feel like I get to have my Christmas after all."

He turned to look at her then, and she dragged her eyes away.

Gah. It was official. She had a crush on him. It was so silly. Maybe her best friend, Paige, was right—she was lonely. But it wasn't as if she hadn't been trying to date. Her social card was full by her standards. And there were nice guys out there, just not *the one* she'd wanted to stick it out with. And definitely none she would bring back to her sister and dad. It was a whole different thing entirely to bring friends back home to chill, but a significant other? They'd get the third degree.

Never Have I Ever commenced with easy questions. *I've never done something I would never tell my parents.* (They all drank.) *I've never thought about quitting my job.* (They all drank.) *I never want more money.* (They all drank.) And Gil was right—the questions, innocuous as they were, stirred up conversation. Geneva talked about wanting to start her own business. Brandon revealed he was scared about grad school. The mood turned thoughtful quickly, and Eden found herself opening up, still with Chris's question in her mind.

"I help my family out a lot," Eden admitted, though she didn't feel a lick ashamed or shy about it, unlike when she'd told other people. "My mom went back to live in the Philippines to take care of my lola. And I've always worked, I guess. I always knew where my money was going."

They all nodded without pity. They understood. Their parents were immigrants too—what came with that was this inherent allegiance to family, even across the world.

"Is there something else you want to do?" Chris asked.

She bit her lip and braved a glance at Brandon; he'd lit up. There were few who knew what she did, or was *trying* to do, on the side.

"You can tell them," Brandon said. "If there are people you can trust, it's them."

She looked down at her soda and wished that it was filled with a little bit of alcohol to fuel her strength.

At her silence, the rest of the siblings weighed in. "You don't have to say," Chris said as Beatrice declared, "Bran, don't put pressure."

Eden could have scripted their reactions—she was so in tune. So she went with her instinct, much like how she trusted it to detect distress in a patient's breathing patterns at rest. "I write on the side. Romance."

"As in, books?" Chris leaned forward.

She nodded, feeling herself lighten. "I'm what you call an indie author. I self-publish my books under the name Malia James."

"Oh my God, I'm going to look it up right now." Beatrice thumbed her phone.

"You don't have to, I . . ." Eden bit her cheek. It was entirely one thing to publish a book and somewhat bury her head in the ground and another to have a real live person looking up her books in front of her.

"Ooooh." Jessie leaned to peek at the phone. "Sexy cover."

"Hey, hey!" Gil said. "You've got your own personal set of abs right here."

Pride filled her at their sincere interest.

"You've got three books here." Beatrice gawked. "This isn't on the side. This is a start of a career."

Her words were like a poke of a sharpened pencil over skin. Eden hadn't thought of it that way—not in the slightest. Writing was something she loved to do, her passion. But it was far from a career. "Nah, the money I make isn't close. It's . . . a hobby, really."

"Well, I support you," Brandon said.

"Hell yeah. I'm downloading one right now," Chris added, swiping on his phone.

Heat rushed to her cheeks. "Oh my God." Her eyes dropped to the ground now, in full realization. There were only a handful of people who knew about her writing: her sister and dad, Paige, and her critique group.

And now, these people.

"Speaking of romance." Beatrice peered at all of them and then leveled a knowing smile at them. Like she knew Eden needed the subject changed. "Never have I ever kissed someone recently that I regretted."

Everyone drank except for Jessie and Gil; it was followed by conversation on who they'd just recently broken up with. It brought Eden back to the ease that she'd felt before she'd told them of her dreams, which she'd kept so close to her heart.

That night, in the shuffle of the cleanup, and with a couple of people in the group too drunk to help, it was Chris who ended up walking Eden to her car, carrying leftovers nestled in Tupperware and tied in a grocery bag. She popped the rear passenger door of her rental, and he set it down on the floorboard so it wouldn't spill.

She opened the driver's-side door and set her purse in the middle console. "Thanks for bringing that out."

"My pleasure. It was good to meet you."

"Same." Mist left her mouth when she answered. The snow had stopped, but the wind blew snowflakes in the air. Chris hadn't turned right away to go, and the moment was so easy, so she ventured another question. "When do you head up to Philly?"

"On the twenty-seventh. You? How long are you in town?"

"Fifteenth of January. I've been here since Halloween. They needed coverage for the holidays, and then back to Texas I go."

"Sounds like an exciting life."

"It is." She smiled up at him. He was backlit by the streetlight, and for all book purposes, it was the perfect scene for a first kiss.

"Will you be coming back east at some point?" His gaze dropped to her lips, or she swore it did, and she tingled with anticipation. With how confident he was, she could guess he was a good kisser, among other things.

Her cheeks heated by a degree. "I . . . don't know. Maybe. It depends."

"So this could be the last time?"

She hadn't thought of it that way. "I guess . . . so."

With her answer, the facts lined up, and awkwardness bloomed, and whatever romantic thoughts she'd had withered. She was simply a guest in his home. "Well," she said, to move the moment forward. "Merry Christmas. And happy early birthday." Then she got up on her tiptoes, and they shared a hug.

"Thanks. Merry Christmas to you."

He held the door for her as she climbed into her rental, and with a protracted look where she thought for sure he'd say something—about what, she had no idea—he raised a hand goodbye.

The door closed with a thunk. As Eden backed out of her parking space and glanced back at that handsome man waving goodbye, she sighed.

Well, she could at least go to bed with a book boyfriend.

CHAPTER EIGHT

105 days until Chan-Puso contract expiration
Word of the day: fathom

Chris was on the move in the golf cart with Sal Medina, their security lead, bright and early at seven o'clock. It had been their weekday routine since Heart Resort opened, a standing appointment when the two of them discussed pending security and maintenance issues. Chris wanted to be kept abreast of everything. Heart Resort was only a hundred square miles, with, at most, ten sets of guests, but little problems could become unwieldy if ignored.

Sal was driving—and going the speed limit, of course—and he was giving a recap of last night's happenings. "The Kristoffs arrived late since their flight was delayed. They checked in at about eleven. I took them straight to Yakap."

Chris frowned. "Chet didn't meet them?"

"No, the Kristoffs declined the half-hour wait for Mr. Seiko or Miss Beatrice to arrive. They said they were tired."

Chris increased his grip on the golf cart's bars. This was the third time late-arrival clients had been checked in by Sal. Sal was great; Sal understood the inner workings of how the resort worked, as humbly as he appeared to everyone. But clients expected a level of service, and at check-in, it was imperative that a director greet them, even if it ended up with a simple escort to their beach house. Chet, as the director of programming, would have been the ideal person, followed second by Bea as the director of guest relations.

"I don't understand why those two can't get it together," Chris mumbled.

"Perhaps they need extra help?" Sal shrugged. "We've gotten quite busy. Mr. Seiko and Miss Bea could do with an assistant. To think of it, Mike with maintenance as well."

He looked at Sal—the man's expression was easy, almost unfazed. But there was something more in his words. "Are you hearing complaints?"

"Not complaints. Just . . . suggestions for a better Heart Resort experience for employees."

Chris grumbled. It was always so easy to say *hire more people*, but it wasn't that simple. The resort wasn't liquid in the financials and wouldn't be until he and Eden received the second half of the inheritance.

He'd need to find a solution.

Right then, however, no idea came to mind. He blinked against something that caught in his eyelashes, against his brain fog, unable to focus.

His sleep had been sporadic the last few days; he was so entrenched in what was going to be Heart Resort Exposé. *The name makes it sound more professional* was what Beatrice had suggested. It was all hands on deck. Even Max, all the way from Italy.

Yes, there were amateur creators filming their lives and uploading them on YouTube. These days, what was privacy? Society had evolved since the late nineties, when *The Real World* was novel and shocking. It shouldn't be a big deal for Heart Resort to film Chris and Eden, especially since they both consented to it. But Chris wanted to make sure they were protected—he wanted everything in writing. He wanted staff members to be aware. He wanted no surprises.

His lack of sleep was also due to the fact that Eden had slid into their bedroom well past midnight last night—she'd moved her office back into their apartment after their decision to do the exposé—and then, after getting into bed, sat up thumbing into her phone, writing, he supposed, and he'd been able to detect the pads of her fingers hitting the screen, even if her volume was turned off.

"Sir?" Sal asked, jarring Chris from his thoughts.

"Ah, I'm sorry, Sal. Say that again?"

"I was suggesting that perhaps we turn one of the cabins behind the gate into temporary quarters for Mr. Seiko for those times we're expecting a client."

Three tiny houses existed behind the gate, one of which was used full time by Sal. The two others, however, were used by family visitors. "I'll bring it up to the team." Still, it didn't feel like a straightforward solution. It never was; he was fully aware that the resort took so much of his life, of the lives of his employees' families. Chet had a wife and kids. Chris didn't want to burn the guy out by keeping him on the resort longer than he should. Nor did he want to ask Beatrice for more of her time; he knew how hard his sister worked, not just in Heart Resort but in being the mother his brothers sorely needed.

They buzzed down the main road toward Hapag, the resort restaurant. As they neared and Chris detected the scent of food, he perked up. Heart Resort's chef was Filipino American and the twin sister of the proprietor of Salt & Sugar, their go-to location for their Friday dinners, and the smells that wafted through this part of the resort brought him back to his parents' kitchen. Of his dad making breakfast on Sunday mornings. Of fried eggs, garlic rice, and tocino. When appropriate, Joe Puso had taken the leftovers from the night before and added it in the breakfast repertoire, reviving it somehow so Chris and his siblings were never the wiser.

It reminded Chris that while he knew how to cook, at his age, his father had had a family: a wife who loved him and two sons and a daughter who worshipped him, with a fourth kid on the way.

And here Chris was, on the verge of a legal separation and dealing with an internet dragging.

"Are you all right, sir?"

Chris did a double take at the man who he'd come to know the last six years. Sal had been his first hire, a North Carolinian but with Portuguese roots, who'd done his time with the Secret Service. He was a fatherly figure and calm presence at the resort. "Yeah . . . just lots on my mind, Sal. Willow Tree has screwed around with my head. They seem to know a lot of what goes on around here. Would you know who may be talking?"

He shrugged. "I don't know, sir. If people are making assumptions, it's definitely not out of spite. Everyone who works here is like family. My guess is it might be guests?"

Chris thought back to the countless times Eden had ridden back and forth in her golf cart alone—to how many conversations they'd had outside of Tiwala. That despite the beach houses being sufficiently away from one another that there was privacy, every house was equipped with binoculars. "Those damn binoculars."

Sal shrugged. "Guests love the binoculars. That was a great idea by Ms. Beatrice. Maybe, though I hope you don't find offense with this, instead of taking away what you don't want others to see, it's time to just be okay with what everyone does see."

Chris half laughed at how astute Sal was despite not knowing everything that had gone on in the boardroom the other day. "Were you snooping in on our last meeting?"

Sal smiled. "Believe me, sir. I'm perfectly happy not knowing anything. I like being out here taking in the ocean air."

"Fair enough, though I think I want to take a look at a list of current and recent guests to see if there's any connection with Willow Tree," Chris said to end the conversation, though he continued to mull over Sal's words. Sal didn't know how right he was—everything between him and Eden, between Willow Tree and Heart Resort, was about perception. Chris's chest swirled with unease, and though he and Sal still had the other half of the peninsula to visit, he decided that a little comfort food would do him some good. "Let's stop at Hapag this morning."

Sal grinned. "Do you want me to radio in your order?"

"Nah, we're so close. Might as well walk in."

At Hapag's gravel parking lot, they got out, Chris's belly growling at the prospect of food and another cup of hot coffee. The dining room was still closed, though the guests' custom breakfasts were being made to be delivered to each of the cabins. Custom dining had been one of their perks in their all-inclusive retreats—their menus were tailored to the guests' needs and wants. Meaning, the menu was suggestive but not inclusive of everything that they could offer. If they could think it, Chef Paula Castillo could and would make it.

Sal opened the back door, Chris right behind him, and stepped into the dark hallway, then walked toward the bright overhead lights of the kitchen. Something sizzled in the fry basket; the warming lamps lit a yellow glow on the stainless steel countertops. The oven had its light on, illuminating a dish inside.

But the room was empty.

"Chef Castillo?" Chris called out, confused at the sight. "Hello?" He made his way toward the swinging kitchen door, and it opened inward to Chef, carrying a stack of plates, with Mike Strauss, their contractor, behind her.

Mike? What was he doing here? Chris's antenna detected something amiss. Whenever Mike was here, it added up on their spreadsheets. Resort maintenance was their biggest cost—and a nonstop expense.

"Oh, good morning." Chef Castillo was breathless—those plates must have been heavy. She wore her standard chef's jacket, and her dark hair was in a high bun.

"Morning. We stopped in for breakfast, but, Mike, is everything all right in here? Any issues?"

Mike was also carrying a stack of plates. His cheeks were pink, though he always looked like he was sunburnt. Beatrice was constantly reminding him to put on sunscreen, especially on his face, neck, and bald head. "I was just checking on—"

"The AC." Chef set the plates on the counter. "It acted up this morning. Shut down for a bit, and I texted Mike, and he was on the resort for something else . . ." She scratched something off one of the plates, then picked up another one to inspect it.

Mike cleared his throat. "And she needed help with the plates. Saved her a trip."

"I also needed a taste tester for my newest recipe." She gestured to the oven. "It's almost done, by the way. Would you and Sal like to try too?"

"And the AC?" Chris wanted the bottom line.

"Yes!" Mike's face lit up. "It's good. I . . . we'll just have to keep an eye on it."

"Well, thank goodness." Chris's shoulders slumped in relief. "And I don't blame you for staying on for something to eat. What's on the menu, Chef?"

A smile blossomed on Chef Castillo's face. "You'll taste soon enough." She brushed past them, taking three plates. "Do me a favor and wait in the dining room? There's only room for one chef in the kitchen."

"You don't have to tell me twice." Chris hustled Sal and Mike out of the kitchen, into the soothing dining room. Last summer, Hapag had been a dark space with heavy cherry-stained oak furniture that did nothing but accentuate an intricately designed wallpaper and made one feel that they were under the canopy of a forest. Now, the dining room exuded light and spaciousness with textured beige wallpaper. The furniture remained, though the tabletops had been painted white, and modern light fixtures had replaced the dreary can lights. Chris didn't have an eye for design—that was Brandon and Geneva's deal. But in this room, he felt inspired. He could eat every meal here if he had the chance. Eden had mentioned sneaking in to work in here, too, once or twice.

With his thoughts back on Eden, Chris thought about the exposé and Willow Tree. Now with Mike in front of him, he decided to broach the topic. "Mike, I need your thoughts."

"Yeah, boss?"

"It's about the McCauleys."

His blond eyebrows lifted. "Oh. Wow." His Adam's apple bobbed.

A while back, Willow Tree had propositioned Mike with a director of resort maintenance position at their South Carolina adult summer camp with, Chris assumed, the intention to glean as much information from Heart Resort as possible.

At that time, Chris hadn't pried into the details of Mike and Willow Tree's conversation. He hadn't wanted to intimidate his own employees; ultimatums for loyalty never ended well, and he had learned this in his own personal relationships. With Mike's sister a McCauley, Chris understood that he stood to lose Mike.

The fact that Mike had decided to stay had been good enough. But now, all the gloves were off. Two could play at this game.

"You've seen the tweets, right?"

Mike's gaze dropped to his hands clasped in front of him on the table. He nodded.

"They've gotten pretty personal, and I'm curious how they could have found out so much about our family, especially about me and Eden." He leaned in to catch Mike's gaze. "If you know something . . ."

"I . . . I don't know how to tell you this, boss, but nothing's really a secret on the resort. And you and Miss Eden's business is on everyone's radar. It's a given that she's in Tiwala."

"She's in Tiwala to work," Chris proclaimed.

"Right, boss. But this is the first time she'd done that in all these years." He shook his head. "But I know what you're asking me. Who of the staff would have told Willow Tree, and I guess I could say that anyone could have, accidentally. We're all locals, and the McCauleys are from the Outer Banks, with family scattered throughout. They've got that big vacation home in Corolla. It's a small world. I guess nothing's really a secret."

"There's more, though. I can feel it," Chris said. "And since you have a connection to them—"

Mike raised an eyebrow, discomfort on his face. "Boss, are you asking me . . . well, I had nothing to do with—"

"I know you didn't." Chris raised a hand. "That's not what I mean. I know I'm putting you in a tough situation with your sister, but can you find out why they're doing this? What's their plan? Are they trying to really take me out of business? They're hard charging toward us, and I can't sit around and let it happen."

Mike heaved a breath and looked down at his lap. After a long moment he said, "Can I think about it?"

"Of course. I just . . . I just need a hint. We're here. We're staying. Heart Resort is our home, and I don't understand their beef with us."

The kitchen door swung open, and Chef Castillo entered, deftly balancing a tray of fragrant dishes that flipped the mood on its head. All three men stood, though Mike beat Chris to the punch by lifting the tray from her hands. "Sit, Paula."

Paula? Chris stole a glance toward Sal, who was promptly ignoring it by looking up at the ceiling.

Was there something personal brewing between the two? It wasn't prohibited. But the reminder of what seemed like a blooming connection meant that Heart Resort was doing its job for all people involved. That was, except for his own love life.

That afternoon, with Mike and Chef Castillo on the brain, among everything else, Chris walked into his office with the intent of taking care of his orchids. Today was watering day, and he had not once missed it in months. It said a lot about his life now that he hadn't missed a watering day; he hadn't been on vacation despite living in a destination spot.

His office wasn't empty when he entered it. Gil was perched on his desk.

And Jessie was sitting on the leather tufted love seat.

Chris froze, midstride, a step into the office, and for a moment, he wondered if this was exactly the thing his parents had meant with *there's always a crisis in a big family.* That when one kid's drama was in an ebb, another flowed like a wave during high tide.

Nonstop, they'd said. *We can't let our guard down, not for a second.*

Now, seeing Gil's ex-wife, his ex-sister-in-law (was that a real term?), Chris understood that the crisis that they were in—him and Eden, and this thing with Willow Tree—might be overshadowed by this.

"Kuya Chris." The woman stood. Jessica Puso looked not a day older than the last time he'd seen her over a year ago. She was White American of Irish descent, fair skinned with jet-black curly hair. She walked up to him and gave him a kiss on the cheek.

It was a respectful gesture, so Chris obliged, even if he knew her presence was going to cause World War III in their household, with the opposition by the name of Beatrice Puso.

"Jessie. What a surprise."

The polite smile on her face faded, and she looked back at Gil, sighing. "You didn't say I was coming."

Gil piped up. "I thought it was a good time for me to, I dunno, bring the both of you together first. Kuya, since we have yet to hire a film crew for this exposé . . ."

Why was his brother making moves without checking with him? Chris winced. "Ah, Jessie, I'm not sure what Gil told you, but—"

Jessie groaned.

"It's okay, Jess. Kuya, can you hear me out?" Gil asked, frowning now. "Jessie's perfect. She's *here*. She knows that Eden is Everly—she has been and will be discreet about it. She needs a job."

And there it was. Gil's landing spot. Nepotism. Which wasn't unheard of. All industries, right up to the presidency, rode on nepotism. But it wasn't only that. There was more to this relationship and how it would affect the rest of the family. This wasn't just another director of photography. This was Jessie, Gil's first love. The woman who'd had an emotional affair with someone else and admitted to it. The woman who had all but broken Gil.

Chris shook his head. "I don't know if this is a good idea. And the both of you know why."

"What if I make it all right. I'll . . ." Jessie's voice rose to what sounded like a desperate soprano. "I'll talk to Beatrice, get her blessing."

This was all too much for Chris. His orchids would have to wait. He raised a hand to stop Jessie's words from flowing forth. "You know? Sometimes I wonder why I left finance. Dealing with strangers and their money was so much easier than this . . . I'll be back." Then he shot his brother a look. "Gil, I'll talk to you later."

Chris turned and hightailed it out of the house and up the stairs to his apartment to Eden to talk through this situation. She knew how to manage emotions and compartmentalize. Chris was good about compartmentalizing, too, but it was more for business. The rest just made him uneasy, and oftentimes he lashed out inappropriately, loudly, and roughly, even if he tried not to.

The door opened, and Eden was on the other side of the threshold with a notebook in her hand. A pencil stuck out from a bun in her hair, and another was perched behind her ear. She looked comfy in her pajamas and was midstride. Pacing, as she did whenever she was rereading her chapters.

At seeing her, he felt immediate relief. That she was here, in their apartment, doing her thing. That maybe the vibe was good between them once more.

Then he realized: she was pacing because she was working, and he'd interrupted her. Again.

It was a forehead-slap moment of regret.

She stepped aside without a greeting, a confirmation.

"How are things going?" he tested, grimacing on the inside.

She crossed her arms and grunted and led the way to the kitchen table, where her laptop and printer were set up; the printer was spitting out paper. On the floor were haphazard stacks of paper. "I've got thirty thousand words, so not even halfway. I thought laying things out on the floor would give me more ideas. Hopefully there'll be enough floor space. Ugh."

Chris nodded. He knew just to nod.

"But I did want your help in something. The first chapter, if you can take a read." She grabbed a stapled stack from atop her iPad. The screen woke, flashing a picture of a house.

He absentmindedly accepted the papers, eyes drawn to the screen. "Yeah, sure." He'd become her default first-draft reader. Apparently she liked his point of view, whereas Chris had always been just in awe that she could make things up.

Right then, however, curiosity about the house had overtaken his brain. "What's that?"

"Oh, that. Um . . ." She picked up the iPad and handed it to him.

The picture righted. The home was a two-story colonial-style with dormer windows, the exterior made of both siding and brick. The city: Austin. The heading read, "Four bedroom stunner with a forest view." A red banner at the top read, "Upcoming."

"Are you making an offer?"

"I'm thinking about it."

His tummy flipped. "It looks nice." He cleared his throat. He was unsure how to react. Should he cheer? Encourage? What was he supposed to say when a part of him absolutely and positively wanted to tell her, *No, absolutely not. You can't go.* After all, he had no hold over her. So he shoved his errant thoughts away.

Her eyes darted to the iPad. "I thought I'd buy now in prep for . . . you know? Dad's house is falling apart. I figured, why not get a big enough place for all of us."

"Oh." Chris felt his lungs constrict. Eden *had* been making plans. She had plans for *after* them.

With the sound of the printer beeping for more paper, his logic kicked in. With it, admonishment that he'd expected less. Eden thought of others, always.

Her words belatedly caught up. "Your dad's house is falling apart?"

She sighed while loading more paper into the machine. "Yeah. The plumbing is finicky. And Josie spilled yesterday that there might be some issues with the foundation. But my dad. Well, you know my dad. It's the 'cobbler's children have no shoes' syndrome. A master electrician surely has contacts in contracting, and yet. Oh." She picked up a sheet of paper on the floor and scanned it, then pulled the pencil from her bun. Her hair cascaded down, and for a beat Chris flashed back to a memory of him burying his hands in her hair as he made love to her.

His heart rate tripled, and what followed was a series of reactions: tingly fingers, a warmth spreading throughout his chest, and a growing need to undress her.

"Chris?"

He blinked back to the present. Eden was recoiling her hair up into a bun. "What?"

"You mumbled something."

"Oh, it's nothing." No, no, that wasn't all truth; he'd totally lost track of the conversation.

She rolled her eyes. "Anyway, my Realtor thinks this house is going to go pretty quickly. So I need to have a clear idea of how much I want to spend."

Chris refocused and once more scanned the iPad in his hand. The house was a new build, unlike the Chan home in Tarrytown with a storybook stone facade. "This house is so different than the one your family lives in now. Do you think your dad will be willing to move?"

She shrugged. "I'm thinking of Josie." Her gaze dropped a beat. "I want her to live in and come back to a home with a solid foundation, you know? I know I do."

He nodded, though his heart was speared by the double meaning in those words. Despite their married years, he hadn't been able to give that to her. Yes, their marriage was for convenience, and because of his parents' inheritance, it had been a privileged one, but solid? The thought of it didn't sit well. Still, Chris stayed on course. "We have a contractor in the family. A designer, too, and you have full access to them. We can help fix your dad's house. Upgrade, whatever you need."

"Yeah but . . ." She walked to the open window. Facing away, she added, "I didn't want there to be lingering ties."

Ouch.

"I respect that," he said after a protracted silence. She wanted a clean break; what had he expected? For her to call on him as she did today?

She spun around. "A brand-new start, you know? It's also a good location for Everly Heart Inc.'s first office."

"Inc.? Incorporated?"

"That's the plan." She crossed her arms. "You didn't think you were the only one with a vision board, did you? It's just that mine is on my iPad. Take a look at the home screen."

Chris pressed the button, and a nine-grid photo came into view. An office, a map, money, a house by the water. A house in the mountains.

"I *was* hoping you could help me with that part. Incorporation. Since you're the expert on that," she said.

"Of course." He was stunned, still looking at the photos and finding neither him nor his family in them. He and Eden had never talked about incorporating, hadn't discussed her vision boards. Then again, was she in his? "I'll help you with everything you need."

"Great!" A smile bloomed on her face. "So? What do you think? Is the house a good Everly Heart investment?"

"Well." Chris wandered to the love seat as he swiped through the photos. "For starters the four-seasons room looking out over the trees— that's your office right there."

She beamed. "That's exactly what I thought."

As they discussed the rest of the house, Chris had a sudden realization that Eden *would* have a life beyond him, and beyond Heart Resort. And that he wouldn't be taking part in it. His stomach bottomed out, but he swallowed against the rising nausea. "Pending the house inspection, I think this is a good buy."

She sighed. "Thank you. Your opinion means a lot. But anyway." She shook her head and checked her watch. "I'm sorry, why are you here? You never come home midday."

Chris had truly forgotten, so he clamored for the first topic that came to mind. "I . . . I wanted to follow up with the . . . timing of the exposé."

"Ah."

"I think we need to talk about dates to film. Tammy and Gil seem to think the sooner the better."

"Oh gosh. I have to prep. If I'm putting my book down for a week, then I need at least a week to take hold of my word count."

Deadlines manifested differently between them. When Chris had a deadline, the entire staff ran amok. It was a flurry of activity with him at the helm. With Eden, it became that much more quiet. She retreated into herself, into the story. He winced, understanding what this would mean for her. "I'm sorry. I know this isn't a good time."

"It isn't, but when is ever a good time to take a vacation? I don't even know what that means." She shrugged. "And it's for our family, right?"

He nodded, heart squeezing at the term. "Our family." Then, remembering why he was there in the first place, he said, "Speaking of, Jessie is on the resort."

She covered her mouth with a hand. "Does Beatrice know?"

"Not yet." He dragged a hand down his face. "Or maybe she does, I don't know, but I didn't stick around long enough to find out."

She giggled. "You walked out? Like, actually?"

"Yep." Thinking back, he now felt a little foolish. He snickered. "I couldn't do it. Be in the middle? Because that was what Gil wanted— my approval—and I couldn't give it. Don't judge me."

"You're not getting any from me. We are definitely not even in the realm to." She grinned. "You will have to talk to Gil, you know."

He nodded. "I know . . ."

"But I don't mind if Jessie's part of the exposé. She's kept my secret all these years. I trust her."

"Okay. So it's just Beatrice. We are really dysfunctional, aren't we?"

"But what family isn't?"

"You're right. Well . . ." He rested a hand behind his head, unsure how to proceed. This conversation had been easy, a reminder of how it had been in the past. He wanted more of it. But . . . "I know you're busy. I'll get on out of here, and I'll follow up with dates."

"Sounds good. And you're reading for me, right?" She gestured to the document he'd since put down on the desk.

He snatched it up, grateful for the reminder and that despite everything, he was still her first reader. "Of course. I'll have my thoughts for you by tonight."

She looked off into the middle distance, as she did routinely. "If I can put in about five thousand words today and get enough momentum to add ten thousand on the weekend, I'll be in good shape. But I'll need to hide out for a while."

His wife was scouring her mental calendar. It was the cutest but also most badass thing she did, and was it wrong for him to put those two things in one docket? Eden had full control of her intentions, which was something he wished he possessed.

"I'll make sure no one bothers you."

She nodded.

Silence descended between them, and it was apparent, with the printer humming in the background, that it was time for him to go. He stood, and she walked him to the door.

As he stepped out, she grabbed him by the arm. "Oh, wait."

"Yes?" He relished her bare hand on his arm. The rest of him warmed with the contact.

"Pick the house well."

It took a second, but her meaning dawned on him. "Ah, the beach house." Each of the beach houses and buildings were named, a tradition taken after their parents naming their own homes.

She nodded. "Let's do this right. Pick the house that represents us and where we are today."

"I will. And good idea. You and your themes."

She lowered her hand—though to his surprise, she tackled him with a hug around his waist.

This unscripted PDA was something she hadn't done in a while. He wasn't sure what to do with his hands but eventually settled them around her in a hug.

"Sorry, I . . . ," she said, then backed away. "Everything seems to be coming so fast."

"I know." He mourned the loss of the close contact of her body, so he stuffed his hands in his pockets.

"Keep me posted on plans, okay?"

He nodded, then stepped outside.

"And hey," she called after him. "It's going to be all right. We've been through worse tests."

But that was the thing. Chris had had a hand in creating these retreat programs. They were meant to be difficult.

CHAPTER NINE

Twitter Feed

@HeartResort—Want to know what happens in a Heart Resort retreat? Tune in soon to Heart Resort Exposé, where our own Christopher and Eden Puso tackle their marital issues using their trademarked 5-day retreat program. #HRExpose

@ColeRicci—@HeartResort are you kidding me right now? Talk about a desperate plea for publicity.

@HeartResort—@ColeRicci you and @WillowTree asked for it, and you're getting it. You need proof of concept? You've got it.

@ColeRicci—@HeartResort you can't pay me enough to watch

@HeartResort—@ColeRicci we bet your boss @DillonMcCauleyIII will beg to differ

♡

100 days until Chan-Puso contract expiration
Word of the day: felicitate

"It won't be too hard, right? We've gone almost five years fooling everyone." Eden twirled spaghetti against her spoon, then paused. She looked across the table to her best friend, Paige, who lifted the top noodle of lasagna with a curl of her lip. "What? What's wrong?"

They were at a beachside mom-and-pop Italian restaurant south of Currituck. Halfway between Heart Resort and Norfolk, Virginia, where Paige worked as an occupational therapist and lived with her wife, who was in the navy and stationed at Naval Station Norfolk, it was their go-to for their once-a-month meetups.

Except her friend always had a thing to say about the food.

"There's nothing in these layers. Literally. Where is the cheese? The spinach, even?" Still, as if giving up the fight, she cut it with a fork and put it into her mouth. Then she shrugged. "It's fine enough. Anyway. You were saying?"

But by then, Eden had a mouthful of carbonara.

Paige blotted the side of her lips with a napkin. "I'll go first. I think that Val and I are ready to adopt."

Eden choked on her pasta. She brought her water to her lips. "Oh my God. What?" Tears sprang to her eyes, courtesy of the choking and of the revelation that her friend, *the* Paige Miller, her undergrad roommate who could not be held down by any person, wanted a baby. "Where did this come from? I thought . . . I thought you didn't want kids."

"I know. I thought so too. But every time someone puts a baby in Val's arms—oh, my ovaries. I can see her as a mom, and honestly, she makes me believe that *I* can be a good mom. I was also scared of the adoption process. It could be long and disappointing, especially being a same-sex couple. Val is the strongest woman I know, though, and I'm ready to fight for us."

Welp, there went Eden's tears. They leaked out of her eyes, and she dabbed her face with a napkin. It was wonderful news, and she was so happy for Paige. It was beautiful how families continued to evolve; her sister and nieces were growing up, Brandon and Geneva were getting married, Gil and Jessie were attempting to get along, and Eden and Chris . . . Eden and Chris were months away from a divorce.

Her happy tears turned to a sob.

"Oh my God, Eden." Paige dragged her chair next to Eden and wrapped an arm around her.

"I'm awful and selfish. This is your moment, and I'm ruining it. I can't wait to see you become a mom. You're going to be so great, Paige. And I'd better be a godmother. Ninang Eden has a ring to it, right?"

Eden was hiccupping now. Being a Puso was steeped in her identity. Her pen name was Everly *Heart*, for heaven's sake. What had she done? What was she going to do when she had to walk away? She would be starting over empty handed when it came to love.

"Of course you'll be the godmother. You're going to be the one sending all the noisy toys and telling them all about our party days. Only the PG stories, though." She grinned.

"But I won't be in North Carolina . . ."

Her friend's face registered the message Eden was trying to communicate, what Eden had been feeling for months.

Paige pulled her dish to her new place setting, so they were now side by side. Having Paige closer, so Eden didn't have to shout across the table, comforted her. "Tell me what's on your mind. Catch me up."

Eden updated her about the Twitter exchange, the exposé, the countdown. About the dichotomy of making plans after the divorce as if it was a simple next step. "You should have heard me the other day with Chris—we talked about houses in Austin like it wasn't a big deal. He didn't even flinch. In fact he kind of just . . . I don't know . . . became his whole logical self."

"How did you want for him to react?"

"I don't even know." Eden felt foolish now that she was saying this all aloud. If he'd gotten emotional, she would have felt pressured.

"Have you made an offer on the house?"

"I tried. It went above asking, and I was too slow to move." She shook her head. "Chris and I are in the position where we're damned either way. The resort was called out, so if we don't do something about it, it'll be a cloud over everyone's heads. There's no choice but to, quote, pass this retreat program and then turn around and split up after the five-year mark. We're going to look bad either way, but at least with the second choice, we can hope that some other scandal will take people's attentions." She sighed. "There's more."

Paige halted midchew and raised her eyebrows.

"After our dinner, I'm helping Geneva find a wedding dress with Beatrice. Geneva and Brandon are getting married in about six months. After the divorce. Will I be disinvited? It's a whole mess."

Her lips turned downward. "Oh, E, that sucks."

"See, so it's lies upon lies for the last five years, and now that the term's coming to an end, was it worth it?"

She set down her fork. "Are you kidding? You are Everly Heart! You agreed because you wanted a career, and you have it. And honestly, Eden, your relationship hasn't all been a lie. Sometimes I forget that this relationship was just an arrangement. It has felt so . . . organic. I was vehemently against it. I thought Chris was rough, and selfish, and too ambitious, and I thought that you deserved someone who would cherish you. But what I've seen on this end is a lot of respect between the two of you, which many marriages don't have. The longer I'm married, the more I'm starting to feel that that's the basis of a good relationship."

"Not love?" Eden asked. That didn't make sense. Her entire career was built around romantic love.

"I mean, yeah, love too. But love isn't everything. The everyday thing is respect. And who's to say you don't love Chris. In my opinion, you do."

Eden neither confirmed nor denied, because if she said the truth aloud to anyone—that yes, she loved him—it would break her heart. Because Chris had been transparent from the start: that when he chose love (which itself was a long shot because work was his first love), he wanted that person to be by his side, always, at Heart Resort.

And Eden belonged to her family, who needed her: Dad and Josie.

"But." Paige filled in the silence. "If this divorce has to happen—"

"When," Eden insisted.

"Okay then, when." She pointed her fork at Eden. "You do what you have to do. You have to act your butt off so that you're given everything you were promised from the start. You made it all this way for this inheritance, and you're not going to walk away empty handed. And most of all, you've got to take care of yourself."

"I'm trying." She thought of her list in her notes app labeled "Future plans." It covered everything from *buy a house* to *finish the book.* "I'm even thinking of taking a pottery class when I move back to Austin. I want to make sure I stay busy, to keep my mind off things . . ."

Paige snickered. "Oh my friend, that's all great and lovely. Believe me; self-care is paramount, but do you have a good divorce attorney?"

Eden's face snapped to her friend. "I . . . no. Max is taking care of everything."

"Max Aguilar? That guy?" She snorted. "You mean Chris's best friend who insinuated you were a gold digger? Now don't look at me like that; I can infer even if he didn't say it out loud."

"I mean, it's kind of true if you think about it." Eden snorted.

"Still. This guy has *Chris*'s interest at heart."

Eden released a breath at the thought.

Paige raised her hands as if in surrender. "Just saying. The contract might be straightforward, but what if Chris doesn't pay up? Who takes care of you? And a thought for later, but what happens to that Instagram feed?" She raised an eyebrow. "It's basically a love letter to your husband, that Mr. Heart. You gonna divorce that too? Trust me when I say the process brings out the worst in people." She lifted her soda to her lips and raised an eyebrow. "Marcus and I were married only fourteen months, but getting divorced took twice as long with the way he jerked me around. Remember?"

"I do." Marcus and Paige had married a short month after their first date. Their romance had been a whirlwind, but soon after the excitement had died down, so had all the reasons why they should stay together. "I feel like this is different, though. We agreed to this arrangement together."

"Call me jaded, but I'm cautiously optimistic. When you're ready, I can float over a name."

♡

"Eden? Is this a good time?" Paloma, Eden's literary agent, asked through the car's Bluetooth speakers.

"Yes, it is. Perfect timing." Eden buckled her seat belt and waved to Paige in the adjacent car. Behind her, the sky was an orange ombré, and scattered across the parking lot were gulls hovering for scraps. Eden and Paige had spent two hours at the Italian restaurant, and the sun was just starting to set.

She thought of Paige's sage advice. After she and Chris split up, what could she salvage of herself? Who would she be if she was no longer a Puso? Who would take care of her?

"Eden?"

"Oh, yes, I am. Sorry, I just got into the car." Eden pulled herself from her thoughts and programmed Kitty Hawk Bridal into the GPS. "I'm on my way to help with wedding-dress shopping. What's going on?" She'd been in constant email communication with Paloma since the film-rights announcement, so this had to be important.

"I thought it would be easier to call than type this all up in an email. All good news—no worries."

"Oh, good," Eden breathed out.

"We'll be able to announce the movie deal soon. I had anticipated that it would take months before we could make the announcement, but I think with the need for rom-coms, things are moving quicker. Now, we can't be sure how fast after we announce when production will begin, but your publisher wants to make a coordinated effort for max promo. They're planning on putting *One Plus One Equals Me and You* on sale." Paloma went on to relay her last conversation with Eden's publisher, which included news that they'd been able to sell additional foreign rights.

All of the information swirled in Eden's head. "That's great."

"Eden, this is an amazing time for you. I thought that you'd be jumping for joy."

"I am jumping for joy, but things here at home have been a little bit of a mess."

"Can I help? Though you don't have to say a thing if you prefer not to. I'm on a need-to-know situation, so if I don't need to know . . . it's fine."

Eden smiled into the phone. She and Paloma had built a relationship that had gradually moved from being purely professional to a friendly one. Paloma could read in between Eden's lines, literally and theoretically. She knew just enough about Eden to send her official contracts and tax documents but somehow was an invisible fishing line that Eden could grab on to for a moment's breath of fresh air. Paloma knew Everly Heart's real identity.

Paloma was also a third party who could give her a fresh perspective, so Eden also caught her up on the dilemma she faced, though shy of telling her that she and Chris had a contractual relationship.

Eden was met with seconds of silence, then, "So, you and your Mr. Heart run a couples resort on the Outer Banks? This is, like, a series in itself." The click-clack of her keyboard sounded from her side of the world. "Wow. I'm on the website now, and it looks so luxurious."

"There's definitely enough conflict to fuel it," Eden said under her breath.

Paloma hummed, a sign that she was deep in thought. "That is a whole lot to contend with. Whew. I'm just glad it's Eden and not Everly who's caught up in it. That would be the kind of PR you might not want."

There was safety in writing under a pen name. But with her best friend's message in her head, that she had to take care of herself, Eden was revisiting her hesitation in revealing her identity. Doing so could open up a door that could lead to even more income. She could participate in media, maybe attend conferences. "Paloma . . . I'm wondering if now is the time for me to show my face? Especially after the movie-deal announcement?"

"Only you can say. Before finding out about this whole exposé situation, I would have said yes. It doesn't have to be an announcement—you could slowly show yourself on your socials. You could begin to merge your writing identity with your real identity. But now, with the upcoming attention, is that something you want? Do you want to be associated with the resort, and when?"

"I have a lot to think about." Eden nodded. This was why she loved her agent. She didn't mince words. The loss of privacy would be a real thing, but the connection to readers was equally important. And while Eden hadn't mentioned her upcoming divorce, Paloma had intuited a growing worry of a spotlight on her failed marriage, and this time by readers. "I just feel like so many of my childhood author idols didn't have this issue. They just wrote."

"Not to say that you can't remain anonymous, Eden. You can. But no doubt, there's a little bit of pressure to be transparent, though I wish it weren't so. I wish that you could just write, too, because you're pretty dang good at it."

"I needed that. Thank you." Her cheeks warmed, and she lowered her visor to block out the sun's glare. "I still have to turn in my next book, and I'm woefully behind."

"Then let's deal with that, first and foremost. Your deadline. Do you need an extension?"

The e-word. Eden had never asked for an extension in her entire career, and she couldn't start now. Everything she'd done in her life, she'd done to standard and many times early. "No. If I don't make this deadline, that pushes the rest of the edits, which might push release day."

"Then how can I help?"

"I don't think anyone can help me. I just need to get my brain to work."

"What has helped you before?"

"I . . . I've never been here before. I had so much energy, so many ideas. And now . . . I just don't want to look at words for a while," Eden said as Paloma added, "Maybe you need some space from your manuscript."

"Yep," they both said at the same time.

"Maybe this retreat will be a good break?" Paloma offered.

"Maybe."

"Well, I'm here for you to help in any way."

"Thanks, Paloma." Eden entered the Caratoke Highway headed south, and though she was in the slow lane, she felt the pressure of the traffic behind and around her. "I'd better go."

"I'll keep in touch. But, Eden, be gentle on yourself. Yes, these deadlines are important, but they're just things. You as the writer, as the human . . . you are important."

"Thank you. And thank you for everything; I couldn't have done any of this—"

"Hey, I know I'm pretty amazing, but no need for that. You did it."

"Okay." Eden never really knew what to do with compliments, and in her heart, she believed that no one could do it on their own. She was, after all, there because she'd had a husband who had taken care of her every need. She was there because her agent had become her advocate. Life was a series of cascading events, interconnected somehow, fueled by disruptions and catalysts and conflicts.

The hard part was figuring out if and when the forks in the road were heading toward the right direction. And was there such a thing as *right*?

They bid their goodbyes. Eden drove another half hour. She rolled down her windows and breathed in the cool air, taking in the sound and what felt like the never-ending sky.

She rolled into the Kitty Hawk Bridal parking lot right on time. Geneva and Beatrice were sitting on Adirondack chairs on the wide front porch of the shop, with Beatrice on the phone. They stood at her arrival.

"Hey!" Geneva gathered her hair and pulled it over one shoulder. "Perfect timing. How was your dinner?"

"So great. As usual." She kissed Geneva on the cheek.

"Thank you for taking a couple of hours off to help me find a dress. I know you're under deadline and all."

"I wouldn't miss it. I'll get my words later." She glanced at Beatrice, who had meandered to the other end of the porch. "Who's she talking to? She's got that expression. Like she's going to pinch someone."

"She's talking to Gil." Geneva lowered her voice. "I think he's telling her about *you know who*."

Jessie was what Geneva's eyes were communicating. "Oh, yikes. Maybe not perfect timing, just before dress shopping?"

She shrugged. "We have no control over these things, I've learned. Especially with Pusos."

Eden laughed.

"How's writing going?"

"Not going, actually." Eden scrunched her nose. "But I've got to keep trying, even if they're sucky words. I hate to say that I think I might have writer's block."

"It doesn't help that there's all this stuff with the exposé. Aren't you worried about being out there for everyone to criticize your marriage? It's hard enough to get it right without anyone else watching."

Eden treaded carefully with her answer. If there was anyone astute enough to detect any inconsistencies with her and Chris's relationship, it would be Geneva. She was socially aware and objective.

Four more months. Four more months of this charade, and then what? "I *am* worried—I value my privacy too. Chris and I think it's the only way, though. And maybe you're right about my writer's block coming from this busy place. My attention is pulled every which way— then again, I want to be involved. All I know is that I can't seem to get into the zone."

"You know where I had my best two weeks? The two weeks that taught me everything about myself?"

"Where?"

"In Ligaya." She looked off to the distance wistfully. "It helped me capture my joy, exactly as its name intended."

Eden nodded, remembering Geneva coming to town late last summer, and a grin formed on her lips. "And I remember calling that just-one-bed trope."

"You did. I also tried to deny the whole second-chance-romance thing."

"Second chance, close proximity, and just one bed. Oh, and yes, best friend's brother." Eden tapped her chin. The most fun part about writing stories and especially romance novels was the tropes. She even looked for tropes in the films she watched. "Anyway, I tried working out of Tiwala. It should be the perfect setting, but it didn't work. I think I'm just tired."

"I feel you." She grasped Eden's hand. "I hope you find a solution."

Beatrice's voice took their attention. She was grumbling into the phone.

"What do you think's going on?" Eden asked worriedly.

"I think that right now, Beatrice is caving. She can't stay mad—though you know she can hold a grudge like no other."

Eden watched Beatrice hang up and brace her arms against the porch railing. Her eyes were shut.

The scene was a stab to Eden's heart. Gil and Jessie's divorce had been hard on Beatrice. It was the first loss the family had experienced after their parents had died. For the tumultuous years of Jessie and Gil's back-and-forth relationship, the family had swayed in their alliances too.

In four months, Eden would be hurting Beatrice.

Overcome with this foreboding grief, Eden approached her sister-in-law and wrapped both arms around her.

CHAPTER TEN

Annapolis, Maryland
New Year's Eve, six years and four months ago
Word of the day: newfangled

It was a truth universally though silently acknowledged that the first-born of every Filipino family took the responsibility of being in charge. In Eden's family, it was law. Yet, in this New Year's and Chris's birthday eve gathering, neither Eden nor Chris could turn the sullen mood.

Around a marred and well-loved wooden table sat four Puso siblings; Gil's pregnant wife; Gil's first child, Izzy; Geneva; and Eden. They all gazed over a tableful of store-bought and home-cooked food. In the background was Times Square on the television. The tree, sparkling with Christmas ornaments, tipped a bit to its side, and from underneath burgeoned Chris's birthday presents.

But despite everyone's grand attempt, Media Noche was everything but festive. Sure, there were smiles and the occasional laughter, but the air was still heavy with grief.

Eden had become part of the Puso clan and festivities the last few years, with Georgetown Medical becoming a mainstay travel-RT work destination. Eden had even attended Joe and Marilyn Puso's funeral services a little more than a year ago. And she'd been honored to have been invited for New Year's Eve, knowing that the family had been mourning.

"How about we play some cards." Chris's smile was hopeful. "UNO? Poker?"

"Nope, not poker. You count cards." Gil snickered.

"Me? Cheat? Don't give our guest the wrong impression." Chris lifted his eyebrows in Eden's direction.

Her insides thrilled at this bit of attention. Was it wrong to crush on someone while they were in mourning? Eden couldn't help but glom on to Chris, who was a true feast for the eyes as well as for the experience. He had so much to him. She wouldn't dare say that Brandon didn't have something about him, or Gil, or Beatrice. Every person— every character, moreover—was multifaceted, with the devil and the angel and the range thereof living inside themselves.

But Chris, well, he was hot. He was sexy. He was mysterious. He was a playboy, too, from what Brandon had said. But Eden also detected the hallmarks of something more endearing. It was in all the ways he was trying to carry this family.

He was a specimen. And she was mirroring one of her heroes after him. Strong and rough, though tenderhearted.

Brandon interrupted her runaway thoughts. "This isn't her first rodeo, Kuya. She knows all about you, about all of us. Eden, can you guess how much we spent for our ten-dollar-gift Christmas gift exchange?"

Eden tapped her chin with a grin. "Hmm, I bet Chris pushed the budget a few cents over because tax shouldn't count, whereas Brandon shot for the lowest-cost item to be funny. Gil got it right to the dot so that he could get the most bang for his buck. And Beatrice totally blew the rules and spent twice as much."

The table erupted in agreement, except for Chris, who looked at her with this expression of awe.

"Well, am I right?" She tipped her head.

"Impressive," he conceded.

"For that, you get dessert first, Eden." Beatrice stood and started to clear off the dinner dishes. One by one, each main dish was replaced by dessert.

Eden's mouth watered at the scent of sugar. There was everything on this table that she could think of, from brownies to leche flan to a red-velvet rolled cake. It was an overabundance for seven adults and something she hadn't grown up with. Not that the Chans didn't celebrate, but what they didn't have in excess gifts and food, they made up for in lively karaoke and laughter.

As if conjured by her thoughts, her phone buzzed in her pocket. She looked at the screen. It was her dad on FaceTime.

Eden stood and raised her phone. "My family. Do you mind if I take this?"

"Not at all. Take it in my bedroom. I'll save you a plate with a little of everything, since Brandon always steals two helpings." Beatrice looked pointedly at him.

With food in his mouth, Brandon pleaded the Fifth.

Eden waited until she reached the top of the steps before she pressed the accept button, and her father's face materialized on the screen. She eased at seeing him and his smile. Interspersed with Paul Chan's dark hair were slivers of white, though his only wrinkles were the ones right between the eyes, for when he stressed and frowned. He was fair skinned from his Filipino-Chinese roots, and even through the screen she could detect his blushed cheeks, probably from his New Year's Eve libations. "Hi, Dad!"

"Iha! Wait a sec. Josie! Your sister's on the phone." He held up a finger, and a half second later her sister appeared and smooshed herself next to Paul on the sofa.

"Hi, Ate Eden! I got my New Year's present. Thank you!" She lifted an arm, showing the bulky watch. "It has everything!"

"Iha, it's too much," Paul said. "She doesn't need an Apple Watch."

"Shh, Daddy, yes she does." Her lips widened into a grin. "It's more for me than it is for you. Dad, I just want to make sure she's all right." There'd been an uptick of violence with the election coming up, and would the watch help her baby sister in a meaningful way? The jury was still out, but it made Eden feel a ton better.

Josie grinned. "I love it. When do you come home?"

Eden melted at the sound of her sister's pleasure. Josie was her baby. "By Valentine's Day. Then we can go head down to South Padre for President's Day weekend."

"That feels super far away." Her expression fell into a frown.

"February will be here soon enough." Eden smiled sweetly at her, though inside a bubble of negative emotions inflated. She didn't know how to manage the roller coaster of Josie's preteen years, and once more she wished her mother was there to take her rightful role.

A second later, guilt replaced those emotions; it wasn't anyone's fault that Lola needed a caregiver and that their mother was an only child. It especially wasn't Josie's fault that she needed her sister.

"And I'll have a bagful of pasalubong," Eden added because Josie loved gifts in all forms. "I picked up another one of those pens with the floating tourist sites in the upper cap, you know? For your collection."

"Thank you," she said politely. As she always did.

Eden pushed the conversation forward. The fact of the matter was that being a traveling RT was lucrative. And frankly, she didn't mind getting away from the family. She loved them, but being a replacement mother was starting to become overwhelming. Eden couldn't get into the space of writing happily ever afters when she was thinking about Josie and school and whether she was hanging out with the wrong crowd. Or when Eden was exhausted from her night shifts. Yes, she'd chosen those shifts for the night differential, but still.

She'd come to the conclusion when she'd done her last round of yearly taxes that if she couldn't get this pen name off the ground, if she couldn't make enough to pay her investment on being an indie author, then she would have to quit.

Charlie, the Chan Chihuahua rescue, photobombed the camera by leaping onto her father's lap, and it woke Eden from her thoughts. They all exploded in raucous laughter, and the conversation continued about how Eden was celebrating New Year's in Annapolis.

After about ten minutes, she said, "Speaking of, I should go. I need to get back to dessert." As she bid them farewell, her heart felt like a piece of paper folded in half. On one side, her Texas family and responsibility, and on the other side, the Pusos and her writing.

Did all mothers feel this divide? Did her grandmothers feel this way? Or was it just women in the search for both family and career? Lola Olive, her paternal grandmother, had left the Philippines to work in the US as the firstborn and had sent all her money back to help her family. Had she felt the same pull of guilt and duty all at once? And when Lola Olive met and married Lolo Fernando, a Filipino-Chinese American, how had it felt to be tied to two different places?

Did her mother feel this same guilt today?

She shook her head from her repeated ruminations and walked out of Beatrice's room. Eden always had these deep thoughts at the wrong times. Where had these thoughts been when she was at the computer? It would make for a great backstory for one of her characters.

A mumbling sounded from the bedroom two doors down. It was punctuated by a stern expletive. The voice was Chris's.

Eden crept along the hallway, intending to simply pass by the bedroom and slip down the stairs, but her ears perked. One couldn't be a good health-care provider without being a little nosy. And the door was ajar . . . so it was an invitation to peek in, right?

What Eden saw was Chris pacing.

"What do I need to do to get this money?" His voice was gruff and serious. "Married? What? How much are we talking about . . . so a portion in cash upon the nuptials and then the rest in trust?" Another pause ensued and the sound of a mattress giving. "Five years . . . that is . . . forever . . . yes, Mr. Mortimer. Wow. Yes, that is quite a sum. But marriage?"

Eden halted. Could this be? Did this even happen in real life? She could be reaching, but an inheritance with a stipulation of marriage? Yes, she'd written the trope, but with it came the assumption that there would be some suspension of disbelief from readers.

His wife is his work, Brandon had said about his brother when she had asked casually about him after that first Christmas four years ago. Because she hadn't been able to stop thinking of him.

Eden had deduced that he was the classic ambitious character, unable to take down the walls from whatever had hurt him in the past. For a marriage of convenience to work for this archetype, he needed a love interest who was equally detached and who had their own ambitions.

Eden's mind cranked with a characterization of the love interest. Yes, what Chris needed was a woman like her, someone who had her eye on a prize, who had her goals mapped out, who had skin in the game. And to make the relationship believable to everyone else, it had to be someone who was already in his tight circle of friends and therefore supported by the family, which would lend to the relationship's success.

Someone who could keep a secret.

Whoa, this can be a book.

At the thought, Eden fished her phone out of her pocket and logged into her notes app. Her ideas came in the oddest of moments, and thank goodness for her smart phone.

Though it wasn't as if she needed more ideas. She had ideas up the ying-yang; it was the readers she was lacking. There was a flood of romance books on the market, and she was missing the mark somehow. Something wasn't clicking.

Her fingers flew on her keyboard, and a greater idea emerged.

Marriage of convenience, marriage in trouble, close proximity. A triple threat. In her books, it took three tropes for a couple to tango and for a romance to bloom. A character could escape one trope. Two was interesting. But three? It spelled conflict and a full-length, hefty plot.

The rest of her surroundings faded into a white noise. It was her and her notes and an increasing need to write. As her thumbs flew across the screen, she decided that she'd excuse herself from staying until midnight and instead greet the New Year in her apartment, writing her heart out. It was supposed to be auspicious to start the year in the way that you meant to live it.

A creak sounded, though her attention could not be deterred.

Then someone cleared their throat.

Her thumbs froze, heart skipping in turn, and finally, Eden raised her gaze up to Christopher Puso, one hand on the door and another holding the phone against his ear.

♡

"I'll call you right back," Chris said to Kyle Mortimer, Esq., the family trustee, but he didn't wait for a response before pressing the red button, his focus solely on the woman just beyond his childhood bedroom's threshold, holding her own phone in her hand. Looking as guilty as ever. "Hey, Eden."

Nothing left her mouth, which was agape.

If he hadn't just been talking about something so ungodly serious and highly secret, he would have cracked up. This moment was straight out of a movie with an irresistible female lead, except that, of course, she was almost like family.

Which meant she was off limits.

Still, she wasn't family and therefore wasn't privy to what he'd been discussing on the phone. Hell, he wasn't even planning on telling *any* of his siblings about the phone call. Mortimer had called Chris only because the special trust was meant for him and his future wife. Because his parents—rest in peace—could not give up this dream of having him married off. They'd even instructed Mortimer to inform Chris on the eve of his thirty-fifth birthday, as if thirty-five was too old to be single.

It had slipped Chris's mind that Eden was on the third floor.

"Eden?" he asked once more.

"I . . . ," she started.

He peered at her and then glanced down to her phone screen. His mind ran through the possibilities of her taking note of his side of the phone conversation, though she'd never come off to him as a person who was a snoop.

A word jumped out at him from the screen—*smol . . . smell . . .* no, it was *smoldering.*

Smoldering?

"What are you doing?" Chris demanded.

"I—"

"You already said that."

Eden had been coming to their functions for several years now. He'd noticed her, flirted with her at times, but never had it gone beyond that. Their encounters had been too brief, and he'd always been too busy, and after his parents had died, well . . . life had changed. Significantly. Who had time for romance when his brain was cluttered with grief? When along with trying to build a life for himself, he was trying to corral his siblings, who seemed to be dealing with their own grief in all sorts of ways he couldn't handle.

And with buying Heart Resort.

He shook his head to clear it of, what else, business. Friend or otherwise, and dinner guest or otherwise, this situation was weird. And Chris didn't have the space to figure out puzzles.

"Your door was open a crack." Her voice was a peep.

"And you decided to stop and listen. Why?"

"Because you need a marriage of convenience." A beat later, her face reconfigured. "Did I just say that?"

"Yes. You did."

She winced and pushed herself past him. "I was writing."

Chris felt himself deflate, though he couldn't relate to artists and their whims. "You couldn't have written when you got downstairs?"

"Yeah, I guess I could have." A hint of a smile appeared. "But I was doing more than writing. I was, I dunno. Planning. Getting inspired?"

Then she did the oddest thing. While biting her lip, she began to pace, her gaze off in the distance, as if working something out in her head.

Again, if it wasn't so strange, he would have considered this cute.

Chris promptly shoved that thought away. He had bigger issues at hand, and now wasn't the time to get caught up with feelings.

Eden halted abruptly, and something else entirely washed over her expression. Her lips flattened to a wide grin, and her eyes lit up. She bounced on her heels. "Holy crap. Oh my gosh. I *did* hear. I heard everything. From your end, anyway. You need to marry in order to access a trust. Am I right?"

Shoot. His heart rate doubled. Chris chose his words carefully, his mind two steps ahead. He would need to control this information somehow so it wouldn't get out to anyone. Not even to his family. "This is true."

She startled. "Have you thought about it?"

"About what?"

"Marrying, for the inheritance."

"I . . . no!" Chris recoiled. "I would never marry a person for money. And why do I need to marry, anyway?"

Chris didn't know where that last part came from. He loved being single. Being single gave him the freedom to make his own choices. He didn't have to change anything he didn't want to. And every single one of his friends was getting married. It was only him and Max left from his college buddies who were hanging on to singlehood, and the two of them had seen how lives were changed by marriage. Their friends were consumed by marriage. His own brother Gil had to clear his schedule with Jessie before he went out with Chris.

His mother had said it was because he was picky. Chris just had high standards, and when he finally decided to commit, he wanted it to be real and forever. It had to be with someone who could take him as he was and stand by him through his ambition, faults and all.

"You're right. No one should need to marry. But." Eden took two deep breaths. "Will you marry me?"

Chris jumped backward and hit the backs of his legs against the bed, causing him to sit. "W-what?"

"Oh . . . that didn't come out right." She bit her lip and took another breath. "I'm a romance author, Chris."

Chris blinked at Eden, not quite understanding. Then he remembered that this woman was his youngest brother's best friend, and maybe she was drunk, and they were alone, and she was standing above him, and the word *married* was shared in their midst. No matter what she was intending, this scene was a bad look. "Um. I know. I'd . . . we'd better get downstairs. Just please don't breathe a word of this to my siblings. I'm counting on your confidence." Chris stood and walked toward the door. Eden didn't follow, so he turned.

She hadn't moved.

"Let me try this again. I'm a fledgling baby author." Her face crumpled. "And it's because I cannot seem to find time to write. Sometimes I'm so tired that I have to ignore all of these stories trying to come through me because I have to sleep. I have to sleep because I have to go to work because . . . responsibilities. I have contributed to my family household for years now. Don't get me wrong—they're not burdens. I love them more than life itself. But I know I can be more."

Chris's heart squeezed at her mention of responsibility, and he empathized. "I get it."

"Good. Because I know in my heart that I can do more with this authoring thing. That I can be who I dream to be, if I just had more time, more support. Because the words and the stories are in here." She pointed to her head. "And I've got all the drive. And all this." She pressed her hand against her heart.

Her puso.

Chris remembered his mom doing that often—she'd connected their last name to their motivations. All their pep talks had ended with her emphasizing grit and purpose. *Without heart, it's all for nothing,* she'd said.

Then it was as if the pieces of the puzzle clicked into place.

"You're saying that you'd want to marry me for convenience?" he asked.

"I'm saying." Her throat shifted as she swallowed. "I'm saying that I love Brandon. He's like a brother to me. I'm saying that the rest of your siblings are amazing humans. I'm saying that I wouldn't mind scaling down to part time so that I can have more time to write, and I can only do that if I have financial support. And that we would need to negotiate. Because from what I heard, there's an advance payment in addition to the final inheritance, and I want to be compensated fairly from both payouts."

Chris's vision cleared; the room seemed to brighten. Along with shock, he was entranced by Eden's boldness. Kind, caring, determined, *and* enterprising? "Seventy-thirty?"

She snorted. "Please. Fifty-fifty or nothing."

He couldn't help but allow a grin to spill out of him. "Okay. And you're willing to sign a contract?"

She nodded. "But before we do it, *if* we do it, we should really make sure that we can get along. That we can be comfortable acting like a couple." She paused. "That we can live together."

Live together. He hadn't been thinking that far ahead. Then again, he'd never in a hundred years imagined that his own parents would try to set him up even from beyond the grave.

His parents were dead. And oh God, he'd probably made a bad decision to purchase that peninsula last year. Heart Resort was a sinkhole where his money was being swallowed up. It had been an imprudent and emotional decision, and the thought of it now made him woozy. He reached out for his desk and steadied himself. "This is surreal."

He felt the warm touch of skin. Eden was holding him firmly by the elbow, and he relished the strength in it. "Yeah, it's wild all right." She offered him a smile, and it was almost apologetic and casual and yet so sincere.

Steady. Another word to add to the list of things Eden was.

It allowed Chris to think. "My buddy Max—he's an attorney. I can talk to him about drawing up a contract between us." He exhaled and shook his head. "I can't believe we're talking about this. This wasn't how life was supposed to turn out. I'm supposed to be vacationing somewhere, being nagged at by my family that I don't come home enough."

"I don't think anyone really expects what they're handed in life. I think we just do the next right thing and hope that it's good enough."

Chris turned to the woman next to him, surprised at her words. It hit him right in the gut; it was clear she understood his situation. "For a romance writer you seem unemotional about love."

"Well, first and foremost I'm an ate. You know what that means, since you're a kuya."

He nodded. The eldest born had pressure. It was real and unrelenting and often unforgiving.

"We're also children of immigrants. And we do what we have to do," she said.

He half laughed. This was true too.

"And," she continued. "Even if I dream and write about the happily ever after, I also know that it can wait. It will be there for me someday."

He challenged her. "Can it wait five years?"

She waved it away. "*Pfft.* Five years is nothing. And anyway, that's at least a dozen books published—to me that's worth it."

Chris was intrigued. More, he was starting to believe in her idea, encouraged by her ambition and faith that it could work.

And it didn't hurt that the beauty that he'd noticed on the outside seemed to match her goodness on the inside.

At the very least, there was certainly nothing wrong in getting to know this beguiling woman.

He cleared his throat. "Eden Chan, would you like to go out on an official date with me?"

Eden smiled. "I thought you would never ask."

CHAPTER ELEVEN

Publisher's Marketplace Deal Report
Film Rights

Everly Heart's *One Plus One Equals Me and You* about a down-on-his-luck manny hired by a billionairess, only to become the groom for a marriage of convenience that leads to a marriage of love, to Goldstein Productions by Ivy Montana of Montana Agency.

♡

95 days until Chan-Puso contract expiration
Word of the day: belie

Tanggap.

Eden read the hammered wooden sign above the entryway of the bright-yellow beach house, and she breathed out a sigh of appreciation. "Acceptance. You picked the most perfect beach house for us."

From behind came Chris's footsteps climbing up the stairs. He carried up their two suitcases. "Actually it was the only one that wasn't reserved for the week."

"Of course." She rolled her eyes, more to herself and her misplaced expectations.

"Dang." He hefted her suitcase across the threshold. "What's in this thing?"

She counted off on her fingers. "Clothes, toiletries, laptop, thermal travel printer. A ream of paper."

"You're kidding." He looked down at the bag.

"I can't travel without my things."

"Eden, I hate to tell you this, but we're a block away from home."

"It just makes me feel better to have it in *this* house with me." Eden had turned in half her manuscript to her agent with about forty-five thousand words on it, but the pressure of the deadline was real.

"We're also turning in our phones to Chet. And we're going to be filmed. To do this retreat by the book, there's no work to be done during the program."

"Ugh, I know already." She waved his grumblings away because she wasn't going to turn around and return her stuff to the main house. Her stuff would stay, and that would be it.

The AC was a welcome reprieve from the sticky humidity. Eden scanned the eclectic furnishings, a combination of boxy and modern with soft pillows on the love seat, an inviting plush carpet, and a textured wall in the living room. All impressive. Eden had helped some with decorating the homes with Geneva last summer, but she hadn't had a hand in Tanggap.

To the right was an actual stairway—not a ladder—to the loft, where a bed was on a platform, and a transparent safety barrier had been installed so one lying in bed could see out of the wide floor-to-ceiling front windows.

The back door, which was through the modern galley kitchen, slammed open. Gil entered carrying a backpack. "Hey, just getting the cameras set up."

"Cameras. Holy crap. This is real." Eden shot a glance at her husband, and her heart skyrocketed into her throat. The last week had been one filled with intermittent spurts of OMGs. Today, her head was still catching up to reality.

"Yep." Chris's face was stern as he lugged their suitcases up the stairs to the loft. "Don't worry; it's not going to be livestreamed. I made sure."

Gil spun, scanning the house. "I'm thinking of setting up a camera right here at the loft's edge. One in the kitchen above the back door." His eyes landed on Eden. "Nothing in the loft or in the bathroom."

At the thought of the bathroom, she said, "What if there are some . . . noises we don't want other people to hear."

Gil's cheeks reddened. "Uh, you can always turn it off when . . ."

"No." Her face heated. Because nothing of that sort would be happening. (And yet the thought of it stirred the butterflies in her belly.) "That's not what I meant. But I sing . . . in the shower."

"You have absolute control," said a woman's voice, and Jessie entered the living room with a critical eye toward the space. Gone was the shy woman who had been walking on eggshells since she'd arrived. She was all business now, with a neat tight braid and the barest of makeup. While definitely still a fish out of water, she was currently in her element. "You can trust me to maintain your privacy when things get too intimate, in all ways. I will be honest but fair. I promise."

"I trust you," Eden said. Even if the rest of the siblings might've been wary, what Eden had seen in Jessie thus far was comforting. Jessie was a professional; she was serious.

"We plan to post one teaser video each evening and the final compiled work a week after the retreat concludes," Jessie continued. "I'll be at every activity."

"Me too," Gil said. "I'm assisting."

"No, you should really stay with the kids."

"I've asked Bea to take the kids."

Eden had caught only every other word with the rush of white noise from all the information shared; still, she felt tension between the couple.

She climbed up the stairs, leaving the two to rig the cameras; Chris was sitting smack in the middle of the bed, legs out straight. He was typing on his phone. As usual.

All at once, her nervousness about this project gave way to annoyance.

Their romantic couplehood might have been manufactured, but her feelings about his devotion to his job were not. What had been something she'd admired—his ambition—was now nails-to-a-chalkboard irritating. She hated how wholly engrossed he was on his phone, especially at a time when they were about to sacrifice their privacy.

And couldn't he have picked a side of the bed? Or maybe asked her which side was hers?

"Sighing already?" He didn't look up.

Had she sighed?

She opened her mouth to say something, but the reminder that they weren't alone halted her. Instead, she bit her lip and dealt with unloading her suitcase.

"Ate and Kuya, we're leaving!" Gil said after a bit.

"Later!" Chris said without fanfare.

Another frustration. Whatever happened to politeness? Eden approached the clear loft barrier, peeked over, and met Gil's and Jessie's eyes. "Thanks, you guys."

"See you in a few hours?"

"Yep," she cheered and waited for the sound of the back door shutting. Then she turned, leaned against the railing, and lingered as Chris finished up whatever he was doing.

Finally, he set the phone on the bed. "Ready to figure this out?"

"I've *been* ready," she made sure to point out, then picked up the resort folder sitting on the bedside table. It was hefty and glossy, with a stunning photo of Brandon and Geneva printed on the front. "Do you mind scooting over?"

"Oh, yeah." He was nonchalant at the request, though he barely moved. He raised an eyebrow. "What are you waiting for? Come sit."

She did, because fine. She heaved a breath to clear her head and opened the folder. Equally picturesque brochures were tucked into its pockets. She read the captions. "Possible activities include overnight camping, rock climbing. Paddleboarding?" She looked up at her husband, and a bubble of laughter ran through her. Her husband hated water sports, which was a whole other conversation on its own. "Cooking class. That's a little more your speed." Then she came upon the last two line items that had her sitting up. "Zip-lining. Rappelling? Oh hell no."

Chris's lips parted into a Cheshire cat grin. Hands clasped on his lap, he shrugged.

The idea of her feet leaving the ground—or faux ground, as she was on in this loft—superseded her initial worry that they were going to be on camera. "You know I don't do heights."

"I don't do water. And yet."

It wasn't a phobia she had for heights; she simply didn't like it. "But you live around water. It would make sense you should try to do water, but jumping off a perfectly good mountain is ridiculous."

He laughed. "First of all, you won't be jumping anywhere. We wouldn't be insured if we made people jump off of cliffs and go snorkeling if they don't have the capability."

"You're right." She heaved a breath. "And oh God. Couples Talk."

Couples Talk was a couples counseling session with a licensed couples therapist.

"What's wrong with Couples Talk?"

"Nothing's wrong with Couples Talk. Counseling is great. Expression is a necessary part of life, in my opinion. Heck, everyone should be in therapy. It just so happens my personal therapy is writing every gosh dang day. But. *Us* in Couples Talk? You know how this works, right? The counselor's going to ask us about our meet cute, and then you'll start on about the Never Have I Ever game at that first Christmas, and I'll have to go into how I sat in my rental hoping you'd ask me out and . . ."

"Hold up." He tipped his head. "What do you mean sitting in your rental hoping I would ask you out?"

"I . . . did I say that?" She winced. See, this was why she was worried about Couples Talk. Sometimes she didn't have faculties over herself when she was on a roll. "My point is that we're going to accidentally spill that we married for money."

He pressed his lips together and refixed his face back to serious. "We can do this. Look, we actually have had a relationship the last five years. Yes, the marriage is contrived, but I mean, you *know* me. I know you. We have . . . our issues. None of it would be a lie." He pointed to the QR code on one of the brochures. "For them to pick our program, we have to scan this QR code and fill out the questionnaire."

"We're really doing this," she said once more.

"We are. All the way."

"All the way." She set her hands on her lap and sat back against the headboard. "We're going to need a strategy to make sure we don't slip."

"I'll follow your lead." He leaned against her so their shoulders touched. "You're the romance writer and the expert on the human condition. How is the arc supposed to go?"

She loved his sideways compliments. She held them closely in her heart just as she cherished the notes her readers sent her. But this felt greater. Readers were writing to Everly Heart. The fact that Chris continuously trusted her was every heroine's dream.

But this wasn't a story. Their real life was at stake.

So, she rested her head on his shoulder, and he rested his head on hers, and they held hands. This was an approved PDA but had since evolved to whenever they were talking about something serious, when they were at a point of a major team decision. They both found strength in this physical bond.

"The traditional arc of the marriage-in-trouble trope would mean that at the beginning of the five days, we would resist one another," Eden started. "Then something happens, and we're thrust together, to work together perhaps. Our truths would come out; we learn more about each other. Something in the middle challenges us, and we start to doubt. Then we'd have a fight over something that exposes all the things. All of our faults. We retreat into our corners but somehow realize that our lives would not be complete without one another."

"Then we get to make up."

"That's right."

"Then we have our HEAs."

"In truth the HEA should be about choosing ourselves." Eden's voice dipped. When talking about craft she always felt blasphemous. She didn't believe in hard-and-fast rules; writing was personal. And she of all people was not an expert. She knew only what was true for her. She cleared her throat with discomfort at the dissection of their relationship. "But for this purpose, in the end, we should choose one another."

"All right then, we'll follow that arc. In terms of our *issues*, what should we bring up?"

Eden didn't hesitate. "That we're going in separate directions."

"All right. That you want to be in Texas, and I need to be here."

"It's way more than that." She shook her head, confused. "That doesn't work in the twenty-first century, and postpandemic. Lots of relationships survived separation. The idea that we can't make it work for that reason is antiquated."

He nodded and bit his lip. "You're right." His eyes flickered upward. "Then what shall we say?"

"Oh c'mon." She peered at him, and a bubble of laughter threatened to escape. "How about that you're so . . . intent on outdoing

Willow Tree? That your work habits are over the top. That work takes precedence always, and no one can compete with that."

"Interesting." His gaze darkened. "And on that note, that you aren't here a hundred percent either, if not physically, then emotionally. Because of your own allegiances and loyalties."

She heaved a breath, feeling her blood warm at the insinuation that she hadn't been loyal to Chris. "A person shouldn't have to choose between two families."

"I beg to differ. Married people choose their new family."

"Look." She pressed her hands against her thighs. Her blood was now at a full boil, and she imagined turning the knob to bring herself down to a simmer. "At the heart of it, the heart of us—"

"Is a contract. Yes, we've duly reminded one another."

Her eyes stung with the beginning of tears, and she looked away, admonishing herself. Their fights had been exactly like this: conversations about disappointment and expectations and then rounding to the conclusion that they had no right to one another. It was a mind game.

But she couldn't feel bad about this. She gathered her thoughts because they still had to come up with a plan. "How . . . how about I say that I wish you didn't work so much, and it's affecting our marriage."

"Okay." Chris looked off in the distance. "How about I say that since you travel for work, I don't feel like we have enough time together."

"Fine." She nodded. "That'll work."

He nodded gravely, then scanned the QR code. "Keep it simple."

"Keep it simple." She followed suit, though inside, their entire relationship was everything but.

♡

"This is very impractical." Eden looked out into the blue-gray sky, her skirt billowing around her. She brushed her hair out of her eyes just as another grain of sand found its way into her eyeball.

"It's better out here. Trust me." Jessie lifted the camera up to her hip and bent down to peer through the viewfinder. "It's to keep the interest on what you're doing versus what you *could* be doing, if you know what I mean. And you'll feel less claustrophobic." She propped the camera on a stand. "I'm filming in three, two . . ."

Eden swallowed a grumble—she had no right to complain. She had backed out of the planning of the wardrobe choices, the location, and all the little things that created the scene for the exposé. It had been because she was doing her own scene setting in a book that had refused to be written.

Eden was fussing not about the location but more about what she was wearing. The dress was one of Beatrice's picks from Beachy and was made of soft gauzy fabric. It was beautiful—practical, too, with how it concealed her wireless microphone—but the skirt picked up with the wind, and as it flew, it shot sand everywhere.

Her eyeballs teared up as a few more grains of sand lodged themselves in her tear ducts, and she wiped them away. In her periphery, she saw the camera sweep toward Chris and Chet Seiko, the director of programming, walking down from the parked golf cart.

She exhaled with relief at the sight of her husband. Despite their tiff earlier, which had ended with a general apology—because what else could they do but move on?—it didn't fail that with him, she felt a little stronger.

Chris was wearing an off-white linen short-sleeve button-down untucked over cargo shorts. *Cargo shorts.* Not ironed khaki shorts but cargo. This hadn't been what he'd worn when she'd left the beach house this morning to meet up with Beatrice for her first day's wardrobe. And his hair—usually his curls were tamed. Now, they were left loose, as if he'd just stepped out from the shower.

She was brought back to a memory of them showering together, their bodies wet and warm and slick.

The tops of her cheeks heated, and as she tracked his gaze from her toes to the slit that exposed the middle of her left thigh, to the plunge of her neckline, and then up to her eyes, she was suddenly parched.

"Hey. You are . . . wow." He leaned in and wrapped his arms around her. He wore a spicy cologne, reminding her of woodsmoke and forest, and goose bumps flourished wherever the delicate fabric of his shirt brushed against her bare skin. His breath tickled her neck in this sweet way.

She stepped back, steeling herself. She had to stay focused. "You're not so bad yourself."

He ran his hands through his hair, and his shy expression pricked at the corners of her heart. Then he took her hand and led her to the chairs set up under a white tent.

Chet was wearing a Heart Resort polo and khakis, and he perched on the seat across from them stiffly. He had a veil of a smile, though his hands shook as he set them on top of a clipboard.

He was nervous too.

"Hey, Chet, you don't look so bad either," Eden said.

Chet cleared his throat and tugged at his collar, where a microphone was attached. "Um, thanks." Then as if remembering, he looked down at the clipboard in his hand. "Right. So, welcome Mr. and Mrs. Puso to Heart Resort." His Adam's apple bobbed. "The resort that promises a happily ever after, on your terms. I'm Chet S . . . Chet, and I'm your program manager and concierge."

Chet launched into his official spiel, which Eden had heard time and again. He discussed the basic rules of the retreat, such as: No contact with anyone on the resort besides those people who would be involved in their activities. No phones or access to the internet. Don't leave the resort without informing the staff. Please respect other couples' privacy.

Eden was hearing his words but was failing in the focus area, distracted by Chris's sure grip on her hand. He hadn't let go, his thumb gently grazing the top of her knuckle, and with every stroke, she felt lulled into comfort.

"Adventure park excursion . . ."

Eden's gaze snapped to Chet. "E-excuse me, what?"

"From the questionnaire you filled out, we've determined that an adventure park excursion could be an activity that could lead to your retreat goals. There will be some climbing, rope activities, and zip-lining. Tomorrow will be boating on the sound."

Chris stilled next to her. *Oh. Oh no.*

There was more. Overnight camping. Yoga. Three sessions of Couples Talk. By the time Chet finished with his speech, Eden's head was spinning. She and her husband were going to be placed in scenarios that would bring out the worst in each other, at the very least.

Then again, maybe that was the point.

Chet stood and approached them, holding out a hand. "Your phones, please."

CHAPTER TWELVE

Chris felt like someone had cut off one of his limbs as he watched Chet walk away with his phone. He thought about the emails that would be managed by Gil and Beatrice the next five days. Surely they could handle it. And surely, if they had any pressing questions, they would find a way to ask him before they made any foolhardy decisions. Still . . .

"Feels weird to give up my phone," Eden echoed, snapping him out of his thoughts. Worry flashed in her eyes. "Our first Couples Talk is next. Are you nervous?"

"Nope. This is old hat to me." He'd spent many a time in the chair, baring his feelings. It took practice to break him out of his shell, but he no longer feared it. "You?"

She nodded. "I'm afraid she's going to look in my brain and know all my secrets."

He gestured to his microphone, a reminder to Eden that she was miked up. "You don't have to reveal anything you don't want to. This is more about feelings than anything. Besides, it's Francesca. You know her." They were intimate with the staff; the turnover rate at Heart Resort was low. And there was no one he would trust more than Francesca Park, who was thoughtful and caring—

"Wait. Who's that?" Eden nudged him. Chris looked up to where her gaze was directed, to a woman walking toward them who was decidedly not Francesca Park, who was a Korean woman in her thirties. The person walking toward them was a Black woman in her fifties. She was carrying an iPad in one hand and, when she neared, offered the other for Eden to shake.

She looked familiar, but Chris couldn't place her.

"Kit Branch. I'm your Couples Talk counselor. It's a pleasure." Her voice, a smooth tenor, jogged his memory. This woman was famous.

"From *Road Trip Adventures*," Chris mumbled.

Road Trip Adventures was a reality show where six people bunked together in a camper and were given scavenger hunt–type tasks to complete; contestants were kicked off by their peers. They'd had a therapist at every stop to manage the participants' mental health.

Now *that* show was a study in human behavior. At the very least, it was full of drama.

For a beat, Chris was unmoved; then he did what he wasn't supposed to do, which was to look straight at the camera and then back at Kit. "Um. You're not part of the Heart Resort staff."

"No." She smirked. "You didn't know about the change, and that was done on purpose. It was thought that you should experience a therapist you weren't familiar with, just as your guests have had to. So here I am."

"Who arranged for this?" He looked off to the side; he searched for Chet.

"Babe, don't be rude." Eden tugged at him.

He acquiesced, though whatever peace that he had felt earlier escaped him. "Okay."

Kit then embarked, without fanfare, on a question-and-answer session that decidedly involved recounting how he and Eden had met and married and their living situation. Stunned, Chris could give only one-word answers—though Eden filled in the rest, and all with a smile, thank God—fully aware that now, the rest of the world would know his and Eden's romantic history.

"We have three sessions planned in five days," Kit reiterated. "This first session is about exploring what brought the two of you here."

Chris snickered under his breath. If Kit only knew that from the complicated web he and Eden had built, sometimes he himself was in a fog as to how they'd gotten here.

Or perhaps not enough under his breath, because Eden shot him a look.

She answered for the both of them. "We are . . . at an impasse. Or a better description is that we're not on the same road in our marriage. I have family elsewhere, and I need to be with them too."

"Yes," Chris added, falling into step. "We've been married almost five years, and since then the business has grown, and I'm needed at work. I'm needed here."

"Whoa." Kit eyed them intently. "To me that sounds like the both of you have made your decisions about leaving one another. Am I correct in that?"

"No. That's not . . ." Next to him, Eden stiffened.

Crap. The woman was already seeing through them. "No," he interjected. "No decision has been made."

"So, you *do* want to work it out." She peered at them. "Because when you make such unmoving statements like *impasse*, Eden, and that you're needed here, Chris—but without any mention of your emotions, or love, or pain, even—it almost sounds to me that you've detached yourself from this relationship. That this marriage is some kind of a transaction. I just want to make sure that you both want to try to be together; otherwise I'm not the resource you need."

"This is totally not a transaction," Eden squeaked.

"Right. We don't want for us to end. We want for us to work out." Chris was sweating now, and he felt the virtual pressure of his siblings and Mortimer studying their every move.

"All right. In looking at the program, and what's been picked, what do you want from this experience? Eden, what do you want to see from Chris?"

"Um." She bit her bottom lip. "I just want for him to spend time with me. He's a workaholic."

"Chris, how about you?"

"I want her to spend time with me too. She's equally busy."

"Eden, is work demanding?" Kit asked.

Eden nodded. "I'm a health-care worker, and I travel for work, though these days, I . . . have a position where I telecommute, though still very busy. But in traveling I also get to visit my family, who I miss."

"You see why I find it hypocritical when she complains I'm the workaholic. I'm at least right here. She's the one that chooses to leave." But when the words left Chris's mouth, he gasped at how close it was to what felt like truth. He backtracked. "Not to say I don't want for her to have her career."

"Why would I want to hang around and wait for you to mentally be *here* with me." She peered at him.

He opened his mouth to rebut. He couldn't tell if her expression, if her reaction, was for real or for show. They'd fought about this exact same thing earlier today.

"Chris, you look like you have something to say," Kit encouraged.

He exhaled and chose his words wisely. *Keep it simple.* "I just want everything to go the way it's supposed to go."

"What do you mean by that? Do you mean business?"

"Yeah, I guess so."

"And for your marriage?"

"I suppose it's the same. I'm doing everything I should be doing, and I don't understand what's going wrong. When we do the right things to the best of our abilities, it should all work out. But it's not happening with us."

Kit raised a finger. "Interesting. So you feel that you and Eden need to try harder."

"Yes." He looked at Eden then.

"Eden, what do you feel when he says that?"

"Frustrated. Because it lets me know that he's not looking at the reasons *why* we're not getting along. He thinks hard work alone fixes things. It's not that way at all. Relationships aren't built on meritocracy. It's insulting, too, because I wonder if he thinks I haven't been pulling my weight." Eden withdrew her hand from his.

"I never said that," Chris said.

"You didn't have to." She clasped her hands together. "I know how much you demand from others and how critical you can be if people don't live up to your expectations."

"Wow." He sucked in a breath. That . . . that was painful. It was a brief exposure of his faults and a sucker punch right in the sensitive area. He knew he was a tough person to live and work with, but coming from her lips . . .

"I'm sorry," Eden said, looking at her feet.

"Why are you sorry?" Kit asked.

"Because that was out of line." Eden blinked up at Chris. "I don't want either one of us to be hurt."

"But sometimes, don't you agree that talking at and about the real problem is important?" Kit asked. After a long pause in which Chris grappled for something to say, Kit's iPad lit up, and an alarm sounded. "Well, that's the timer."

Chris could have fallen out of his chair, as if the tension keeping him upright was severed in one swoop. "But we were just getting started," he said.

Kit smiled. "We'll see each other again, in two days. My suggestion is to really get down to what's motivating you in this marriage." She stood and leaned in to shake both of their hands, but before she straightened, said, "And perhaps, really listen to one another these next couple of days."

It was almost a warning.

♡

Before Chris jumped into the van at the resort reception area, where Eden was already waiting for him, Chris signaled to Chet, and they met feet away.

Chris turned off his microphone. "What the hell was that about, with Kit? Why didn't you tell me we would have another couples counselor?"

Chet heaved a breath. He hiked his hands on his hips. "Chris, you hired me to give you an authentic experience, and that's what I'm doing."

"You should have told me." Chris reeled back his thoughts as well as his tone. He and Chet were partners in many ways despite him being Chet's boss. Chet was skilled and educated in programming—he wasn't a disposable employee. He also remembered Eden's criticism during Couples Talk. That entire session had lingered in his head even after a short break, and he felt heavy with emotions he couldn't discern. "Look, you and I have been working on these programs since the beginning."

He nodded. "And so you should trust me."

"I do." He avoided Chet's eyes, because they both knew that Chris was incapable of that absolute trust. There wasn't such a thing. A CEO never trusted all the way. They might have faith in the people they employed; they might allow autonomy. But absolute trust? Nope. Because anything could happen.

"With what you're trying to prove to Willow Tree and the rest of the world, the process has to be undoubtedly out of your hands. It has to be in the resort's hands. In fact, you and I shouldn't be speaking to one another right now."

"Now that's ridiculous."

"No, it's not."

Chris detected more in Chet's expression. A bit of wariness. "What's going on? Something else is up."

"Nothing's up, except that we need to get you in that van before day one is over. And . . ." His gaze dropped to the ground for a bit.

"What is it?"

"You need to go along with the retreat in its entirety. You have to allow me and the rest of the staff to give you and Eden what you need in your relationship."

Chris jerked back minutely. Was Chet really talking to him about his personal life? "Look, Eden and I are fine."

"Okay. But whether or not a couple's fine coming into Heart Resort, the point of this is that things should become better. So give us a chance to do it. In the end, it'll show in the exposé. Okay?" He hiked a thumb toward the van. "Yeah?"

"Yeah, that's fine," Chris relented and followed Chet to the van. But he wasn't fine, not one bit.

His instincts were telling him that there was more to Chet's concerns today, and he was going to get to the bottom of it.

CHAPTER THIRTEEN

"Wait a hot minute," Eden said as she climbed down from the Heart Resort van. In front of her was a massive structure that was the adventure park called Into the Sky. "We're going to be doing this at dusk?"

She was still processing their first Couples Talk, so she hadn't paid attention during the fifteen-minute drive north on Highway 12. In fact, she didn't even remember saying a word to Chris the entire trip.

What *did* she want?

I just want for him to spend time with me. She'd said the thing that was easiest to substantiate. After all, she was the wife to a busy entrepreneur. Their families saw Chris as someone who spared nary a second relaxing.

But it was only a part of what she felt. It was the most superficial layer of plot.

"This is going to be so much fun." Chris disembarked behind her, buzzing with excitement. He hiked a hand above his eyes. "This looks epic."

"If you consider an overgrown jungle gym for kids that refuse to grow up *fun*," she mumbled, tracking the rope course that drew her gaze upward. There were rope bridges, nets arranged in a weblike fashion, rings of metal to hang from, raised wooden platforms, and zip lines. Her heart thudded at how flimsy it all looked, at the unavoidable fact that it would be all up to her to hang on. "This looks dangerous."

"It only looks intimidating. But we're going to be hooked up the whole time. C'mon." He offered his hand.

She took it, at first for the camera's sake. Jessie and Gil had gotten there before them, and the lenses were trained on the van as they drove up. But in truth, it was an olive branch, a silent apology for her dig during the Couples Talk. She'd known Chris was trying to corral his rough approach when it came to his business, and she'd decided to stick it to him anyway. It had weighed on her shoulders so much that she'd decided that whenever she got Jessie alone, she would ask for her to edit that part out.

The warmth of his hand comforted her, and the obstacle appeared to be less foreboding.

Her arm lengthened as Chris all but dragged her to the entrance, where they were met by a guy with an Into the Sky T-shirt. The shirt was red, accentuating the man's ruddy cheeks and sunburnt nose. He looked like he hadn't worn sunscreen, ever, and his ball cap did nothing to protect his face, the bill facing the back of his head.

He welcomed them with arms out wide. "Welcome, my name's Mack, and I'm your guide today! Are you ready to catch some air?"

"Yeah!" Chris hooted.

Eden looked at her husband, whose lips were splayed out into a wide grin. Excitement danced in his eyes, and he rocked on his heels like he couldn't contain his energy. Was this the same person she'd partially lived with the last five years? She'd known that he'd been outdoorsy before Heart Resort, and he'd spent a good deal of his time in the garden. But a thrill seeker?

Seeing this enthusiasm encouraged her; she wanted more of that smile. They hadn't had enough fun lately. She would give this a chance.

But they were given another orientation—she had a feeling that it would be five days of orientation—and each additional minute looking at the structure allowed her to mull over the possibility of death or severe injury. Look, she'd chosen health care for her occupation for a reason. When she was fitted into her harness, and it became oh so real that she would be protected solely by rope, it was she who needed a breathing treatment.

"Are we going all the way up there?" Her voice came out like a squeak, but she didn't even care. Even if she did, she wouldn't have been able to fake it.

"Only if you want to and are able," Mack said. "This is a team-building exercise, and all we're working off is time. You have about an hour to get as far as you need to get, together."

"This is going to be a super boring hour for you, Mack," Eden said.

Mack barked out a laugh.

She looked at Chris. "He thinks I'm being funny."

"It's going to be fine," Chris said, though not to her but to the air in front of him. Eden could have been dancing naked, but he wouldn't have noticed. "Ready?"

An hour. An hour of torture, then it was back to Tanggap, and she could lie out on the sand and look at nothing but the sky. She heaved a breath and nodded.

Admittedly, the climb to the first platform was easy enough. The monkey bar rings were pleasantly challenging. She wasn't yet so high up in the structure; she could hear the cars whizzing by on the highway. She could also still smell something cooking from the food truck that was parked in the lot. And Chris was an arm's length away, giving her advice and encouraging her on.

This isn't so bad, she thought, focusing on each wooden plank as she stepped across a rope bridge.

I could totally do this, she cheered as she navigated a climbing net with a sure grip on the rope, with Chris up above her, looking downward.

"You've got this, Eden!" he yelled.

"I know I can," she yelled back up. Because yes, she already was.

Right foot up, left hand reach. Left foot up, right hand reach. No big deal. Besides, she was Eden Chan Puso. She'd never backed down from a challenge. She'd all but put herself through RT school. She traveled for work and sometimes to locations where she hadn't known a soul. She was raising her little sister (and quite possibly a father) without a guidebook. All these things had required an emotional grit. This physical challenge had nothing on her.

That was, until she realized that Chris was no longer in front of her. He'd made it to the next platform. Then an Into the Sky employee clipped him into the zip line, and off he flew.

No.

Adrenaline hustled Eden up the net, to the platform, where she found herself alone with the Into the Sky employee. He had a similar ball cap to Mack's and sunglasses with blue-tinted dark lenses. On his nose was a swipe of sunscreen. He gestured to the line. "Your turn."

Eden looked across to the next platform, to Chris, where another Into the Sky employee unhooked his rope from the zip line. Then the handles were slid back toward her platform.

"I . . . I can't." Eden's gaze was now firmly on the ground well below her. She gauged how high up she was. Twenty feet? Fifty feet? Definitely higher than any of the trees she'd climbed as a kid.

"Eden?" Chris's voice was faint. "What's taking you so long, babe?"

"Ma'am, it's perfectly safe. You'll be attached to the line," the Into the Sky employee said.

She nodded. She'd come so far not to get all the way through.

The employee hooked her harness up to the zip line. "The rope can support you, but hang on to these bars to keep you upright."

"Okay," she said, but her body rebelled. She clung to the platform railing; her knuckles turned white.

"Are you scared of heights, ma'am?"

"No, I . . . I'm not. I just don't want to let go."

Conversation erupted on the other platform, but Eden couldn't pay any mind. She had to focus on not making a wrong move so she wouldn't go crashing below.

You're totally hooked up, her logical mind said.

Her body didn't believe it.

She wasn't sure how long she was standing there. But at some point she decided that sitting was more comfortable, and she did so. With her back firmly against the low barrier, she felt safe in knowing that not only her feet but also her torso were anchored to this structure that was still standing despite the gusting coastal winds.

Like book research gone awry, and now with dozens of tabs open in the file folders of her brain, Eden escaped the moment by deliberating the history of Into the Sky. She thought about building code, and did Into the Sky pass theirs? Were there yearly inspections for these things? How were their employees trained?

From above came a dark shadow. "Miss."

She squinted and looked up to the Into the Sky employee's face. He took a knee next to her and lowered his sunglasses so she could see his eyeballs. He had green eyes, an eye color she had never written into any character, because did everyone know how rare that eye color was in real life? It was a whopping 2 percent.

"I can help you back down," the green-eyed person said.

"Down?"

"Yes, there's stairs on the other side. It's just a short walk. The stairs are steep but—"

"I can do stairs."

He offered her a hand, and she took it. In that connection, the facts dawned on her. She'd failed in doing what she'd set out to do. Chris hadn't waited for her. But at least here was help.

Both relief and embarrassment flushed through her as she stood. She looked across to the other platform, which was now empty.

"I could still try," she said, though her words came out flat. How could she have not gone across? It was unbelievable even to herself.

From somewhere, a whistle blew.

"Ah, time's up anyway, miss."

"Oh okay." Eden felt foolish, heart leaping when they got to the emergency stairs. Those, she didn't have a problem with, though the employee descended slowly and checked up on her every few steps.

That was what Chris was supposed to do—he was supposed to have waited for her. Her mind wandered to this feeling in her chest that she couldn't name, to a time similar to this when she'd experienced a deep pull of disappointment. But what did she realistically expect from Chris anyway that would be above and beyond their arrangement?

Eden realized then that the reason why she didn't know what she wanted from Chris was because he'd come through with all he'd promised in their contract. But apparently, now almost five years down the road, that wasn't enough.

♡

The ride to the resort and the arrival at Tanggap had been a blur. It had been as if Eden herself had written the scene as the author of her life, looking down from above. She'd minimized the moment and had said to everyone that she'd been nervous. She'd even allowed Chris to hold her hand for the camera; he'd unsurprisingly had the time of his life. She, on the other hand, was now contemplating what she'd allowed the last five years of hers.

Through the front windows, Eden looked at the undulating waves shimmering from the moon's reflection. On the beach was a couple strolling side by side, their journey marked by the two spotlights of their flashlights.

She wondered how *they* were doing through their designated activities. And had they shown up for each other, or had they let each other down?

Chris brushed her from behind and presented her with a cup of tea, complete with a slice of lemon.

"Thank you." She took the cup, though she doubted the tea would settle her nerves.

Chris sat on the corner of the sofa. "Want to talk about it?"

"Not really." She blew into her cup. What she wanted right then was a little time alone to sort out her thoughts.

He sighed his impatient sigh, though it sounded more like a har-rumph; he hated when she didn't want to discuss everything down to its last detail. And especially with the camera still running.

But Chris, being Chris, never let things alone. "Look, I know you're upset about not finishing up the obstacle," he said.

She guffawed at his nonchalance. "You *left* me, Chris."

"That's not all the way true. I encouraged you the whole way until we got to the platform. And I don't know, I . . ."

"Just completely forgot about me."

"No. I got excited. Got carried away."

"And left without looking back."

"Here we go again. Why do all of my mistakes become a vicious cycle of me defending myself and you pointing out that I'm the worst person ever? Not everything has to escalate. In this case, you kept saying that you were good, and God help me that I took your word for it."

"Not all mistakes, Chris. But *this* was a team-building exercise. I am your team, and you left me behind. That is fact."

Chris pressed his lips into a line. When he opened his mouth once more, Eden speared him with a pointed look. It was a look that asked him to truly evaluate what had happened.

A second later, he raised both his hands in surrender. "I'm sorry, okay."

"Like you mean it? Or just because you want this subject closed?"

"Like, I'm sorry. But honestly. You should have called out."

"I shouldn't have to."

143

"I can't freaking read your mind, Eden." He raised his voice.

"You should try," Eden yelled, then stood from the couch. The cup in her hand no longer looked appetizing, and she walked the short steps to the kitchen and poured the tea down the sink. Then she thought of the footage those last thirty seconds had provided. If this had been their normal fight, she would have simply walked away and swept it under the rug.

But this interaction would be viewed, so they had to look like they were at least trying. She turned and leaned against the counter. "I'm not only mad about you leaving me behind. I'm also upset because I just feel . . . blocked . . . like I'm constantly blocked. Like with—"

He shushed her gently; then his eyes wandered to the camera above. He was telling her to be mindful. That she was seconds from showing herself as Everly Heart. Yes, Jessie would be the one to edit the footage, but they couldn't take the risk.

She nodded, grateful that Chris was paying attention, because she certainly wasn't. "I just wish today ended up differently."

"Well, the good thing is that the day's over."

"I know, but it still happened." And she didn't know what she would do with that. All her life, she'd taken the lead. Much like Chris, she'd been an old soul. When you were a mother figure to your sibling, there was no other choice but to make scary decisions. "I fully expected being scared and doing it anyway, like every other time in the world."

She hadn't thought about what would happen if she couldn't do it. If she was unable to do it. Frankly, there had never been anything that was insurmountable.

Worry traipsed up her spine. What did this say about her unfinished manuscript? What did this say about the new life she would have to undertake?

At the thought, she pressed her fingers against the bridge of her nose. "It's been a long day. I'm going to bed. I'll take the bathroom

144

first." But with a glance up at the loft, where her pajamas were, Eden came to another truth about their living situation.

She stilled.

Just one bed. The trope that guaranteed the horizontal hokeypokey. Last summer, one bed had brought Geneva and Brandon together. A time before, one bed had brought her and Chris together, too, and look how that had turned out.

Still with them on the verge of divorce.

"When is Gil coming to turn off the cameras?" She started up the stairs.

Chris looked at his watch. "Soon . . . wait, so that's it? Conversation's over?"

She didn't bother turning around. "What else is there to say?"

"Oh, I don't know. But I at least apologized. That maybe, you were wrong to jump down my throat just now. You always do this, Eden."

She raised an eyebrow at this silly statement. Her husband, when pushed to a corner, went from logical to bombastic. "Always?"

"Yes, always. We were just starting to talk it out."

In the loft, she retrieved her clothing from the suitcase. "I'm tired, Chris." And then under her breath she said, "This is not a romance novel where we have to hash out every detail to pieces."

Especially because they weren't supposed to end in a happily ever after anyway.

CHAPTER FOURTEEN

Twitter Feed

@HeartResort—Six days until the Heart Resort Exposé, where our own Christopher and Eden Puso tackle their marital issues using their trademarked 5-day retreat program. Here's a sneak peek from day 1: littlelink.com/HRDay1 #HRExpose

@LittleObsessed—@HeartResort OMG drama already #HRExpose . Sad.

@HoleIntheHeart—Gah, talk about putting all your business out for everyone to see. #HRExpose

@RealityTVjunkie—How does anyone fix anything in five days? #HRExpose

@HoleIntheHeart—@realityTVjunkie true. And how graphic is it going to get @Heart Resort ? I hope a lot! #HRExpose

@Romantic—Honestly why did he get ahead of her when she was obviously scared AF. They've been married almost five years and he didn't know that she was afraid of heights? Look at her face!

@ColeRicci—How do we even know that this isn't all staged? #HRExpose

@RealityTVjunkie—@ColeRicci unless you've been living under a rock, I think we all know that nothing is authentic

@Romantic—Don't say that @RealityTVjunkie. I want to live in my bubble.

♥

94 days until Chan-Puso contract expiration
Word of the day: brusque

Chris hadn't been able to sleep. He was a light sleeper to begin with—his mind was always racing—but last night's insomnia had everything to do with Eden and their activity at Into the Sky.

Each time he'd shut his eyes, he'd relived the way she had looked at him when she'd descended from the ropes course. It was with pure disappointment. She'd put up a good ruse at the time—she'd held her anger until they were back in the house, but it was evident that he'd messed up big-time.

So, this morning, he was exhausted and sore. From climbing, from sleeping on the couch—Eden hadn't offered once to share the bed with him—and from this uneasy feeling of not having any contact with the outside world. Unable to relax, three hours before Gil was dropping by to turn on the cameras and well before Eden woke up, Chris jumped into his clothes and snuck out the door.

The coastal sky was just barely pink. There was a slight bit of chill in the air, and a mild wind blew in. As he walked around the house to the back, where the golf cart was parked, he spotted a couple walking out to the pier. He wondered which couple this was. The firefighter and his influencer wife here to rekindle their twenty-five-year marriage? The congressman and his girlfriend, who were looking for a super private location to determine if marriage was the next step?

So much was going on, on this peninsula—in Tanggap alone, with him and Eden and their issues, which had become more complicated than they'd ever imagined.

He rounded the corner and entered his golf cart. Then he stuck his hand in the glove compartment, grasping the corner of a plastic ziplock bag, then retrieving it.

A burner smart phone.

His heart thumped against his chest. Yes, he knew he was cheating. And yes, he'd officially passed the baton to his siblings to manage the resort. But he couldn't *not* be plugged in. Five days was a long time. He had to make sure that the messaging was working. He also had to keep watch on what Willow Tree was saying about him. Being a CEO didn't allow for lapses in attention.

He took the phone out of the baggie and powered it up. It chimed its familiar tune—he'd charged it to full capacity in secret before they'd checked into Tanggap yesterday, and he had a battery pack incognito in the house charging as well for whenever he needed it.

Okay, so maybe Eden was right. Maybe he was too involved with work. But he couldn't get Willow Tree—Dillon McCauley III, especially—out of his mind. Most of all, he couldn't let go of the thing he'd said the first time they had met: *You can't get ahead of legacy, of roots. Willow Tree's roots are what everyone else stands on.*

Chris bristled.

Social media apps loaded on the screen, some he'd preloaded and set up with fake profiles before he'd moved into the beach house. @WildOrchid was his handle.

Who said he was creative with these things? It just had to be good enough so he could remember who he was.

He scrolled through the Twitter feed, careful not to thumb down on the little red heart. He clicked on the #HRExpose hashtag, one that Tammy had set up, and scrolled, mouth agape.

Opinions about the pending exposé ran amok. Criticisms, too, and especially for him. One person linked the preview of day one. It replayed the part where he was speeding through the obstacle while

Eden struggled to keep up, with what he now realized had been a frightened look on her face.

"I didn't know, I swear. *She* didn't even know," he said to the phone, to the people who couldn't hear him.

He clicked on the full video reel posted by Heart Resort, and soon it became his judge and jury. His heart dropped as he witnessed his past self paying no mind to his wife when he reached the zip line platform. He hadn't hesitated, zipping across the line, grinning and gleeful like he'd just won a race.

No wonder Eden was pissed.

Had he always been this way? Had the thing he was proud of—his ambition and drive—made him a jerk? He'd never minded his reputation as a hard-ass. But to the people he cared about . . .

The thought that he had been insensitive and unfeeling made him squirm in his seat. Had he hurt people in the process?

No—he pushed the thought away. He couldn't allow himself to think this way. He was a good man. He was trying his best.

He clicked to the text app, where a message was waiting for him. Only one person knew this number. The message: I have some info. LMK when you get up.

He texted back, fingers flying: Awake. Meet me at storage area. Bring coffee as excuse.

Technically, as a resort client, he was allowed to pick up coffee for his wife, right? There was no rule saying that it couldn't be from another resort employee who was also going to pass on extra information.

He turned on the golf cart, and it beeped to life. He drove up the path, then south and east, to the last driveway before the resort exit. He came upon three large storage facilities and parked in between the first and second.

Only minutes passed, during which Chris used that time to doom scroll—never a good idea because he felt worse about the zip line situation with every second—before the sound of a golf cart engine took his attention. With the squeal of rubber, a cart jerked to its spot next to Chris.

Mike was sporting a hesitant grin and sunglasses on his face. He held out a beverage carrier with two tall paper cups of coffee. "Morning, boss."

"Morning." Chris slid to the passenger side and took the carrier, then set it down on the seat next to him. "Thanks for the coffee."

"No prob."

Chris considered asking about Chef—because why was Mike at the resort so early?—but thought otherwise. Right now was about the 411. "What were you able to find out?"

He winced. "According to my sister, what they want to do is discredit you."

"I mean, yeah." Chris shook his head. "That's pretty obvious."

"Because the word is that they're trying to build a couples resort too."

"Old news. They said that last summer, before that last storm came through. All talk, no action." Conjuring Dillon's face twisted up his belly—the nerve of that guy. "It's always so easy to talk about wanting to one-up, but guess what? It's hard to find property that's sizable, private, commercial, and accessible."

Mike nodded. "Yeah . . . well, there's more."

"Okay?"

"It's on the DL. You can't put me in the middle of it, boss. Because if you put me in the middle, then you'll throw my sister under the bus and—"

"Hey, I won't say a thing." Chris leaned toward him, his muscles tense from curiosity.

Mike cleared his throat and rubbed a hand over his head. "They want to put Heart Resort undeniably out of business. They want *this* peninsula."

♡

"You okay, Kuya?" Gil whispered as he passed Chris in the resort's pontoon boat. He glanced briefly at the rest of the boat's occupants. "Need water?"

"Hmm?" Chris pulled himself out of his fuzzy thoughts, still stuck on the words *want this peninsula*.

"We can't have you become dehydrated. Believe it or not, just because we're out on the water doesn't mean we're absorbing it."

His brother was trying to be funny—God help him and his dad sense of humor—so Chris gritted his teeth into a smile. "Oh, um, yeah."

He watched his brother take drink requests from everyone else, stopping at Eden's seat up front; moving on to Jessie, who was filming using a smaller camera; and finally reaching Heart Resort's water sports director, Lee Hollinsworth, at the driver's seat. All were in various states of glee. Eden, who had been angry with him the day before, was in great spirits, too—even if she wasn't *exactly* talking to him directly—all in anticipation of today's activity.

Chris, on the other hand, was still stunned from his and Mike's conversation. Willow Tree wasn't just competing with Heart Resort. They *wanted* their resort.

He couldn't understand the level of hate. Or maybe he was out of practice. Investment banking didn't come with pillows and stuffed animals. There were mergers, acquisitions, hirings, layoffs. Success was measured in money, power, and stature. And yes, he knew that Heart Resort was the underdog. They weren't southerners. They certainly weren't North Carolinians. They were the new kids.

But they had a right to be there too.

The attack just felt so . . . personal.

Chris, bothered now, hefted himself to standing. With the engine whirring under his bare feet, he gingerly walked to the front to immerse himself in other conversations besides the incessant one in his head. He took the seat behind Eden's. "Hey."

She turned just enough so he caught her profile. Her hair was in an intricate braid that trailed over her right shoulder. On her cheek was a line of sunscreen that she'd missed while rubbing it into her skin, and he had the inkling to do it for her.

God she was cute, even when she was mad. Since returning with coffee—which she'd accepted without a word—Chris had been trying to find a way to apologize to her, for real, where he didn't sound like a douche after the fact, when he had clearly been one at the ropes course. He'd been waiting for the perfect time, but then Gil and Jessie had come over to plan today; then Lee'd shown up and . . .

Yeah, he knew these were all excuses.

Today's activity was a low-key day of sailing down to Rodanthe to a sandbar, where they would jump out and get in the water.

Get. In. The. Water.

Only a handful of people knew that Chris wasn't a great swimmer. He had full respect for Mother Nature and was perfectly content lounging by the water or jumping in a nice safe swimming pool. Especially after he'd almost found himself a victim of an ocean's undertow when he was a tween.

Yet another reason why he was all right living at Heart Resort—the peninsula was on the sound . . . with the shallow water came the kinder waves.

But still.

"It's been forever since I've gone paddleboarding," he yelled into the wind.

"That's nice," she said, tone flat.

She speaks! Chris threw another Hail Mary: "I'm a little nervous."

She didn't answer.

Damn.

Rodanthe came into view. Jutting from the earth were pastel homes and businesses on stilts, though interspersed were a remnant of a mom-and-pop shop, an abandoned miniature golf course, and a boarded-up restaurant. It was a dichotomy of success and failure down one highway.

Chris pulled his gaze away from the wreckage of one business front to ditch the fear that had found its way into his veins. Like bad luck was contagious somehow, and he didn't want that sickness.

"There's Salt & Sugar," Eden said, above the wind, her voice resetting the moment. But she was talking to Lee. "That's where we have our Friday dinners."

They sailed by the restaurant's tricked-out deck. Unlike the unassuming front facade, this view was a one-eighty. Multicolored table umbrellas could be seen from afar, and festive music echoed so it faintly reached his ears.

It lifted Chris's spirits to see that the Castillos had built a thriving business. Like the Pusos, the Castillos were not from the Outer Banks; yet they had survived, their restaurant establishing them as a local favorite. They were hashtag goals. They gave Chris hope Heart Resort would be accepted too.

Chris had considered the Outer Banks his second home two weeks out of the year, when, with a growing family in tow, Marilyn and Joe Puso had rented a first-row beach house in Rodanthe so it was a few short steps into the sand.

Chris remembered those two weeks as easy. Grilling on the back deck, stopping everything to watch the sunset every night. Nighttime excursions where the beach was deserted except for the sand crabs, sand flies, and brave surfers. It had been days with music and salt water in the air, of thick humidity from which a cold shower was only a brief reprieve.

Those two weeks had been so important that when he could, Chris would join his family in Rodanthe even after he'd graduated college. He'd catch a flight from Philly and leave whatever fling or relationship he'd had, because the Outer Banks were sacred.

Wasn't that enough to call a place *home*? Wasn't this emotional tie enough to substantiate it as permanent? What kind of proof, passport, or license did he need to show to lay claim to a new home?

The hum of the engine quieted, and the boat idled, though the shore was still a ways away. Next to him, Eden shot onto her feet with a squeal.

"But we're not at a pier." Chris stated the obvious as the boat rocked. The waves were lively—it wasn't supposed to be this active, was it? The sound was supposed to be still.

"Who needs a pier?" Eden shaded her eyes with a hand. "We're not even far from the beach."

Lee spoke from the bow, lifting his shades and pushing back his floppy light-brown hair to reveal a distinct sunglasses tan, pale against golden brown. "The timeline's open. If y'all wanted, you can go for a quick swim or fish first. And of course we have the paddleboards."

"What I want is to jump in." Eden took off her life vest—they were all wearing vests according to protocol—slipped out of her cover-up, and unhooked her microphone.

She was wearing a bikini. A halter top tied around the neck with scant triangles covered her breasts and a high-cut bikini bottom. Chris's jaw dropped at the sight of her exposed skin, erasing their interactions earlier, because wow . . . she was gorgeous. The knowledge of what she was capable of in bed—or not in bed, whatever the case had been— invaded his train of thought.

They'd had their moments, the two of them. Moments when they couldn't get enough of one another. When the night was too short. When it pained him to start his day.

It was pain he felt now, about how their relationship had taken a one-eighty.

"Look, fish." Eden buckled her life preserver once more.

And then all Chris's primal feelings went splash. Beach wading, yes. Wave chasing, okay—he could get with that. But fighting for space that creatures called home—nah. They could have it.

But before he could say anything, Eden jumped in the water. "The temperature's perfect. And I can touch the bottom with my toes," she said not to him but to Lee.

What was this, an activity with Lee? This silent treatment was getting ridiculous. Chris had to save this moment somehow.

He did a quick mental calculation. Eden was four inches shorter than him, and if she was bobbing, then he certainly would too. Also, he had a life vest. Worst-case scenario, either Lee, Gil, or Jessie could fish him from the water. Worst worst-case scenario, he had an updated will on file. Surely Max could handle being its executor.

"You know what? I want to paddleboard to shore. That okay, Lee?" Eden asked.

"Absolutely." Lee made quick work of grabbing two boards.

Chris's heart ratcheted to high. He had just wrapped his mind around getting in the water, and now he was going to have to heft himself out of the water and then onto that board?

"But," he started, the rebuttal ready to leap off his tongue. Then he caught sight of Eden, hair slick from water and grinning. Her eyes were lit with inordinate joy—the opposite of how she had been yesterday.

It did make him happy when she was happy—this was what he wanted. Yesterday, when asked by the counselor, Kit, what he wanted, he'd been telling the truth. His family was everything to him, and he wanted the best for them.

The first paddleboard splashed into the water, and Eden grabbed it. With one hand she waved at Lee for the second paddleboard, and he eased it in.

Now with both paddleboards, Eden's gaze slid to Chris.

Then he realized: *he* wasn't in the water yet, and the camera, on the left, was trained on him. Yesterday, the camera was just *it*; but after his quick perusal on social media earlier, it was clear that it was also judge and jury to a test he could not fail. What kind of husband would he look like to everyone else: so eager to leave his wife behind one day and then not participating in an activity he clearly wasn't fond of?

A proverbial fire lit his behind, ramping up the adrenaline. He was going to do something that was unnatural for him and that could potentially lead to his death.

Okay, maybe not death.

After unhooking his mic, Chris jumped in feetfirst, eyes clamped shut as water splashed around him. And he felt the ground under his feet.

He was literally standing.

Chris laughed. The sound was almost maniacal, though he didn't care. He was worried about this?

Eden laughed too and pushed his board with the paddle on top of it toward him. "Here you go, babe!" Then she hefted herself onto her board from the tail and, in one slow motion, slithered onto it with her tummy.

Chris imitated her method, but the buckles of his life jacket caught, pushing him backward. He sputtered a mouthful of water, and Eden laughed.

His face burned with embarrassment, especially as he noted the camera's lens. Then he watched the camera pan over to Eden. She was on her knees and had her face turned to the sun, as if soaking it in. So relaxed, so the opposite of how he was feeling.

She said, "What's taking you so long, babe?"

It had been exactly what he'd asked her yesterday, during the obstacle course. Yesterday, he hadn't understood that she'd been scared. But this was different—she was enjoying this.

Irritation rose in his chest—he hated when Eden did this, when she got him back in the tiniest of ways. She never did really clap back; their fights, like last night, always ended with her walking away. Or the silent treatment, and then after . . . she would get him back by saying something that was as slight and as painful as a paper cut.

But he wasn't going to fall for it; he wasn't going to react in a roar. And he especially wasn't going to do it in front of this camera. No, ma'am. He was going to heft himself up onto the board.

He counted to five and activated all his muscles. Then by the grace of everything holy, he crawled onto the board. He paddled to her side on shaky knees. His entire body was experiencing the beginning of muscle failure, even if he was in great shape. It was as if all the mental effort of the day, from this morning's meeting and then this feeling of being *less than*, weighed on his cells. He was getting it from all sides, and he was just tired of it. "Thanks a lot," he seethed.

"What?" Her tone was sarcastic and nonchalant, which he had learned was sometimes worse than the silent treatment. Because she knew. *She knew.*

"You laughed at me. Back there."

"Oh, now I'm not supposed to laugh? What else am I not allowed to do?"

He frowned. Where was this coming from? "I don't know what you're talking about. You have all the freedom to do whatever the hell you want."

"That's the thing, Chris. I do not. I have not. What you said yesterday got me thinking."

"What did I say yesterday, Eden?" He was getting a headache.

"That you couldn't read my mind. So I thought . . . maybe I just won't hold back."

He snickered. "So what has the last six months been, you being silent? Damn."

"That's hilarious." She got on her feet, a paddle in hand and with a deadpan expression, her body steady and strong, as if she'd been practicing balancing on water every day. "You keeping up or what?"

Chris didn't even have the chance to respond. Eden was already paddling away.

CHAPTER FIFTEEN

Perhaps Eden had been a tad rash. Maybe she should have had a little more compassion for Chris. After all, she'd known about Chris's non-skills in the water. Her high school swim and lifeguarding experience had put her at an advantage. Also, she had been born in water (true story)—her mother had been a crunchy woman who'd believed in water births in the eighties—and she took to water like the air she breathed.

But she couldn't help but stick it to him.

What was the statute of limitations for teaching someone a lesson? Was it the same day, the next week? Six months? Was it still valid four and a half years later? Because hearing her husband say that she'd always had her freedom—especially now on the eve of their divorce, when she was going to emerge from a marriage losing so much—just hurt.

Not to say that her writing career was nothing. But she'd staked her entire life on it. And now, she was going to face it without the Pusos, without Chris. All saddled with writer's block and a book that refused to be written.

And this was why right now, hours after they'd returned from their escapade, Eden was hiding out in the loft. It was well after dinner, which they'd taken in under general silence until the cameras had been turned off. Chris was downstairs, which was dimly lit by lamps, sleeping on the couch, while she was starfished on the comfortable mattress.

It had been months since she'd shared a bed with Chris. Honestly, it was one of the best things about being married but not really married—the bed was all hers. She could choose the type of mattress, the bedding, her position; there were no complaints.

Except for tonight.

Chris was groaning. He'd been groaning. He then twisted and moaned.

Eden knew that the couch was uncomfortable; it was the equivalent of sitting on one foam pillow over a plank of wood. Sleeping on it couldn't have been great.

But she shut her eyes to block him out, as if that would shut down her hearing too. She would not feel sorry for him. She would turn off that empathetic part of her that always seemed to rear its ugly head.

Remember that he left you behind.

He didn't mean to, though.

How can he even sleep when things aren't right between you two?

It's called working his butt off trying to keep up with you.

Now it was her turn to groan.

This required an intervention, a distraction.

Eden slipped her hand between the mattress and frame; she felt for her escape hatch. Her fingers crawled until she touched a smooth surface and pulled it out. Her phone.

Okay, so it wasn't really her phone but a new temporary phone she'd picked up last week. Because did they really think that she would be able to get away from her work or that she couldn't watch her feed? Or at the very least have access to the notes app so she could jot down a few words?

There were two text messages waiting for her.

Josie:

Ate, testing 1 2

Eden:

I'm here

Then to the next message from Paige: How's it going?

Eden:

Not well. Worse maybe? Everything is magnified.

A banner notification scrolled down.

Josie:

OMG! I watched you on the preview yesterday.

Preview? She clapped her forehead. She had forgotten about the previews.

Josie:

We both watched it.

Eden:

Dad too?

Josie:

Yes. With popcorn.

Oh God. This wasn't happening. Her sister needn't watch that.

Correction: they all needed to watch it so they wouldn't be shocked when she and Chris divorced.

Eden sighed mournfully at this fact. It was just that she'd crafted her role with Josie oh so carefully: part mom and definitely the older sister that she should turn to. Eden didn't want her image tainted in any way. They'd already lost a mom.

Eden:

Just let dad know that I'm doing alright.

Josie:

OK. BTW your follower count is up with the deal announcement and sale

Eden:

yay!

Josie:

Ate?

Eden:

Yes?

Josie:

I hope that you and Kuya Chris make up.

Eden's thumbs stilled, and she bit her lip to stifle her sadness. Goodness, she wanted so badly to tell her baby sister that everything was going to be fine after this all shook out. That everything would perfect eventually. This was all part of the plan, right?

And yet, she knew that so much of this wasn't part of the plan. Everyone's emotional involvement, her own attachment. Both she and Chris hadn't anticipated any of this, and on the contrary, things were spiraling out of control.

Eden:

I love you Josie. You should be going to bed. I'm turning in.

Josie:

I'm 18, and it's 10pm

Why are you going to sleep? You never sleep.

Eden groaned. Didn't she know it.

Eden:

Night baby cakes.

Eden clicked her screen off, but it once more lit to life.

Paige:

Night shift life. I'm here. Was just thinking of you

Saw the vid.

Eden:

I totally couldn't zipline

Paige:

Not talking about that. Talking about the preview from today. Paddle boarding.

OMG. Today, you crushed that man.

Eden threw the covers over her head, so the phone was bright against her eyes.

Eden:

I know

Paige:

Well, at least the trajectory is correct

I was wondering how you guys were going to start transitioning out.

Eden:

This is getting hard. Things are coming out

Paige:

Feelings are weird. And marriage is . . . complicated.

Eden inhaled slowly until her lungs expanded, and she wished the knot in her chest would unwind. What was it about this retreat? It was exacerbating all their faults, and their initial plan to keep it simple, made as recently as yesterday, had since disappeared.

Eden:

> I need to compartmentalize. Not let things get to me.

Eden nodded, more to herself. Patients had come and gone. People had come and gone. She'd grieved for them. But she'd also moved on by closing the cupboard of that memory, though understanding that they would be living there forever. She would have to do the same for this marriage. And yet.

Paige:

> You love him.

Eden:

> I mean, of course I do. We know each other best.

Paige:

> I mean, you love him love him. The forever love.

Eden couldn't text back an answer in either support or objection. Because to love him forever when they'd had a plan all along and they'd built up lives that were, inherently, separate was foolish and self-destructive.

And the big question remained: Did he *love* her, and would he be able to put her in a category where he would choose her first?

The pressure in her chest ached. She rubbed at it.

Paige:

> I've got to get to work

Eden:

Miss you

Paige:

Miss you too.

Eden:

I'll check in tomorrow night.

Paige:

OK. And hey. Be a little nicer to the guy

I felt the petty from here.

Eden cackled, turning off her phone and tucking it deep into the cushions of the bed.

The pressure in her chest had eased, and she yawned.

See? Not only do you have your career, but you have your family and Paige.

As if in response, Chris moaned one more time.

Eden shook her head, sympathy worming its way through via her conscience (a.k.a. Paige). She couldn't just let him sleep on that awful couch. If it had been her, she would've been in full complaint mode. Heck, she wouldn't have just complained, but she would've climbed the loft and insisted that they share the bed.

She didn't have to be petty tonight.

Eden threw herself off the bed, went to the edge of the loft, and peered down to the living room. Without curtains on the windows, Chris's outline was lit by the moonlight. A thin sheet covered half of his bottom-pajama-clad body. (She bought him all his pajamas. They were organic, cotton, and pin striped, and he loved them.) He was shirtless, and his usual golden-brown skin was gray in the almost-black-and-white picture below. His sleeping position was picture worthy, a scene right out of one of her stories. An arm was hiked up above his head, the other resting on his abs, ridged with muscle, the effort of his gardening on full display.

Never underestimate the value of taking care of plants to build up a body.

But his face. Her husband's face was contorted into a tortured grimace.

That was enough for Eden. She couldn't bear it any longer.

"Psst," she sounded. It was her call sign, and the call sign of every Filipino she knew. Under the radar but distinct. She and her sister could find each other in a crowded Target with that call sign.

"Psst," she sounded once more, and Chris stirred. Finally his eyes blinked open, straight up at her.

"Hey. Everything okay?" He sat up with a quickness.

"Yeah. Everything's fine. But you're not."

"What do you mean?"

"You're groaning. I can hear you from all the way up here."

"Sorry."

"No, that's not what I meant." Seriously, sometimes Chris was so cute, especially like this, when his defenses were down. Eden swore that if Chris was like this during the day, a little vulnerable and soft, he'd have so many more fans. Most people admired him, sure, but it was for his ability, not for his interpersonal skills.

They didn't get to see him like this, fresh from sleep, even if it hadn't been restful.

"Come up," she said.

"Where?"

"Here, silly. Come up here, and stay in this bed. You're in pain."

"But you're sleeping up there."

"Yeah, so? We're supposed to be married."

He snickered. Then, after a beat, he said, "You sure?"

"Absolutely."

"Okay." When he stood, the thin blanket fell away, and his pajama bottoms sagged so they hung low on his hips. Eden spied the trail of hair that led from his lower abs down below . . .

Her breath hitched, and what followed was this urge to let go of her reservations, of all their rules. As Chris climbed up the stairs and the scent of his bodywash filled the tiny space, Eden was gripped with need.

Oh, she wanted him; there was no doubt about it. When was there ever a time when she didn't? She was a woman, after all, a woman with emotions, with hunger, with imagination. She was a woman who wrote about love, about sex, about a person's deepest desires. And right then, as he came close, already half-naked, she was fully aware that it could be so easy to satiate that need.

"Right side?" Chris asked, voice low and husky.

"Right side," she echoed, though not truly understanding what he was asking.

"Thank you," he said, then brushed past her, skin warm against hers. She inhaled a sharp breath and turned just as Chris got into the bed. "You coming?"

"Yes, I'm coming." She slipped under the blanket on the left side, careful to leave a sliver of space between their bodies while he stayed up above the covers, with the separate thin blanket draped over him. And while she wasn't religious these days, she said a prayer anyway.

Because she was going to need all the help she could get.

CHAPTER SIXTEEN

One year and nine months ago
Word of the day: succor

Eden exited her gate at Norfolk International Airport, dragging her suitcase behind her. Already she could feel the summer humidity, a change from the dry Texas air. She thumbed her phone with one hand and turned it on, hopping onto a moving sidewalk.

As she glided, her notifications populated. Mostly texts, she noted when she glanced down, though she kept her attention on the person inches in front of her. These days, she had to remind herself to focus because she was oftentimes multitasking. Ever since she'd changed her pen name from Malia James to Everly Heart, it was as if a mountain had been cleared with a new path in front of her. Her last name seemed to be a good luck charm, and she was riding on its coattails.

It was absolute perfection that as a romance writer, she had the last name of *Heart*. Readers took to her branding. Her logo was her scrolled name with the *a* shaped like a heart. In the last couple of years, she'd even introduced Mr. Heart (in name only, because she still kept their true identities off social media) with Chris's permission, and her readers glommed on to the idea of him with fervor.

Her stories had flowed like water through a wide-open spigot. From her brain to her fingers and then to the keyboard, words spilled out without the slightest bit of effort. In the last year, she'd published three books to surprisingly open arms, and she was under contract for three more. Somehow, she would have to write while she was at Heart Resort, which was going to be tough. These short trips "home," which had ranged from two to six weeks at a time, were code for "checking in" so no one got suspicious of her and Chris's arrangement.

Eden crossed the threshold of the security area, and the baggage claim was within view. She went to her contacts to call Chris. As she lifted her phone to her ear, her attention snagged on a handsome man near the double door. One hand stuffed in his pocket, he stood formidable among everyone milling about. Dark hair, dark eyes, with a square, solid build. He had full lips.

His other hand held a phone against his ear.

"Hey," the voice through the phone answered.

"Hi," Eden said, breathless. Then her brain connected the dots. That hot guy? That was her husband. "I'm practically in front of you."

His eyes scanned the barrage of people and landed on hers, gaze searing; it was serious, but even from where she was standing, she could see that imperceptible relaxation of his shoulders. He was glad to see her, and with that, she, too, felt the tension leave her body.

How was it to see your handsome fake husband after weeks corresponding long distance? As a hugger she wanted to throw herself at him. Her flight had been grueling and long. Texas was halfway across the country, the cabin had been cramped, and she never could loosen up knowing she was packed with others like sardines in a flying tin can.

As a romance writer, she always dreamed of a little bit of fanfare at their reunions, of story-worthy moments of lovers leaping into one another's arms. It wasn't as if Chris didn't shower her with things and affection. He had. He was caring; they had the best conversations. But they were coming up against their third-year anniversary, and part of her wanted romance. She wanted to be swept off her feet, to fall madly in love and in bed with her husband.

What was the point of being married if she couldn't work out these . . . needs? In all her attempts at dating other people—this was allowed in their contract, so long as they informed one another if it got remotely serious—she hadn't been able to get past the first date or encounter.

She wanted her husband. The man she felt safe with and someone who knew everything about her, except what was under all these clothes.

At this reunion, what Eden received was a chaste kiss on the cheek after a brief beat of hesitation, like Chris had to remember that he'd put a ring on her finger. But her body had a mind of its own. She drew him in by the hips and pulled him closer for a hug. When he wrapped her in his arms, Eden breathed him in. She detected his cologne, muted since it was the end of the day. She shut her eyes and pretended he was *really* her husband and that he'd missed her.

She needed to snap out of it; she was simply writing so much romance but not getting enough of it. So finally, with a great deal of pain, she stepped back.

"I'm glad you're here." He unburdened her of her suitcase and backpack, and it was an unexpected relief. Her insides bloomed with appreciation—she carried a bit of life's weight every day.

It was like he knew.

"Me too," she said. It was weird having only her phone in her hand. Which was probably good considering how fast he was stepping out. "I've been craving the beach." *And so much more,* her libido nagged. As if that would be addressed on this trip.

"The beach misses you right back." He glanced at her with a grin. He said things like this sometimes, though she didn't know what to make of it. Then his smile slipped. "But I think something's up with Bea."

Her heart sped up. "What do you mean?"

"I don't know. She won't talk to any one of us." His steps picked up, and they walked out into the sticky humidity of the aboveground parking lot. They didn't have to go far. After quickly stuffing her things into the back seat, she climbed into his Suburban, his behemoth of a car.

She buckled herself in. "Tell me everything you know."

Chris relayed the sudden arrival of his sister after a weekend away to supposedly see friends—that it wasn't like he'd kept up with her comings and goings. And since then, she'd kept to herself in her apartment. She'd yelled at Mike the other day when he'd been in the middle of construction at headquarters, which was so unlike her.

It must be a heartbreak, Eden thought. She was still getting to know Bea, but she knew that her chipper nature was affected only by family and love. Anything else—stuff—didn't matter to her. So when they arrived at Puso, the southern colonial-style main house of Heart Resort, Eden took the stairs by two. "I'll go check on her."

"Do you want me to—" Chris started, with a gentle pull of her hand. "What do I do?"

She squeezed it. She smiled to ease the worry from his face. "I'll see you at . . . in . . . our apartment."

Yep, it was another thing that she hadn't yet gotten used to. Apartment mates, that was what they were, even if she wished at times . . .

"Thank you," he said, snapping her out of her thoughts. He kissed the back of her hand tenderly, in what she knew was gratitude. Tingles made their way up her arm, and they threatened to snag at Eden's heart, so she simply nodded before she turned to head to Bea's apartment.

Heart Resort was in varying states of construction, to include headquarters. It was livable and large. But all surfaces were blanketed by a film of dust, and a perpetual smell of paint or plaster was everywhere.

She climbed to the third floor, where Brandon's and Bea's apartments were situated. Brandon's lights were off; he came and went like Eden since he lived in the former family home in Annapolis.

From outside of Bea's door, Eden heard music. She knocked. "Bea. It's Eden."

The volume lowered, but Bea didn't respond. Eden hung on—she was a patient woman.

She was about to rap her knuckles against the wood once more when the door finally unlocked and popped open. An eyeball peeked out of the crack. "Ate Eden?"

"Hey."

Beatrice stepped back, and the door fell open, showing her sister-in-law's true distress. Her normally messy and cluttered apartment was positively gleaming and spotless.

Definitely heartbreak.

Eden opened her arms to her sister-in-law, and Beatrice started to cry.

♡

Chris paced his and Eden's bedroom area in their studio apartment, pausing briefly to take in the view through the large windows. The sun had just set, though there was a hint of light in the sky, so he could still see the white peaks of waves.

How long had Eden been up there at Beatrice's? Half hour? The full hour? His world had turned upside down the last two days, with Beatrice under the weather. She was like the sun, and with her in a mood that he couldn't describe, he'd begun to worry. Beatrice hadn't even been like this when their parents had died. If anything, while the rest of the family had fallen apart, she had been a reed in the rushing water.

Thank God Eden was home. Although, if this trip hadn't been previously scheduled for their three-year anniversary weekend, Chris would have begged. He'd already been struggling without her here. In their years of "dating" and marriage, they'd gotten to know each other intimately. Emotionally, that was, and he'd started to have feelings. Feelings that he knew were not in the contract. Feelings that perhaps he was alone in experiencing, which meant bad news, right?

And her arrival today at the airport had proven to him that it wasn't just emotional but physical too.

They were doing everything backward, apparently.

And unfortunately, his timing was wrong. Just as he'd predicted, she'd jumped right into her sisterly role. Which was great for Bea but not for him, for what he'd planned to propose, which was for her to stay longer.

The door clicked open, and Chris spun around with both relief and hesitation. His wife entered—his wife! He really had a wife, he had to keep reminding himself—and her face carried a soft expression.

Chris relaxed minutely. "How is she?"

She kicked off her shoes and, as she walked toward him, said, "Well, without me having to reveal anything I haven't gotten permission for, she is, for the lack of a better term, recovering."

"Recovering? That means she's been hurt. Who's the bastard that hurt her?" His hackles rose. He must have also raised his voice, because she lifted her finger up to her lips.

"The last thing she wants is for you to be alarmed—hence why she hasn't said anything to anyone." She raised an eyebrow. "She told me that you and your brothers cornered an ex-boyfriend once?"

"Yeah, because he deserved it." The thought of the guy—he'd forgotten that jerk's name—made him tense up. "So this is about a guy."

She nodded, lips pressed together.

"I didn't know she was seeing anyone." He frowned. "Who is it?"

"Chris."

He dipped his chin and breathed in. He couldn't push, even if he wished he could. "But she's all right?"

"She will be, eventually. She just needs time to think and do all the things to make herself feel better."

"Thank you, Eden." Appreciation gushed out of him in the form of a hug, but perhaps it was he who needed it, because when she wrapped her arms around his waist, he could feel himself uncoil. With Eden, he didn't have to be this image that he presented to everyone else. She'd gotten to know all his insecurities; with her, he didn't have to have all the answers. "You're the greatest."

"I'll take that compliment." She laughed into his chest. "And it's no problem at all. I'm here."

They were such simple words, and Chris would bet they were what she told her patients. And maybe as a romance writer, those words were what her characters said to one another. But right then, those words were everything, because sometimes it felt like no one had him.

She pulled away, though her arms remained. Her face still bore concern. "Bea and I should go out this weekend, take a drive off the peninsula, maybe to Virginia Beach? Change up the scenery?"

"That's a good idea." He gazed into her dark eyes, hooded with thick lashes, then down to her mouth. She licked her plump lips, and they glistened, drawing in his imagination.

He wondered how those lips tasted and how her tongue would feel on his skin. To distract himself, because his brain was meandering into dangerous territory, he pushed away flyaway strands of her hair and tucked them behind her ear. But in doing so, he caught a glimpse of her earlobe, the gentle line of her jaw; he was tempted more than ever to touch her everywhere. He traced his thumb down the side of her neck, and she shivered, though never taking her eyes off him.

"Chris," her voice rasped. "I was thinking. I've been thinking."

"Me too." These days, he could read her mind, and vice versa; their video chats and emails and texts had honed their communication, so with one brief tonal change in her voice, he understood exactly what she was saying. "Things have changed for me."

Relief played across her features. Her hands climbed in quiet exploration up his torso to his chest. It rooted him in his place, and his heart pounded in response. He held his breath.

He wasn't sure what came first: her getting on her tiptoes or him bending down to take her mouth into his. Their kiss quickly escalated; it was a lit match against lighter fluid, without a hint of shyness or hesitation.

It was three years of anticipation, of Chris's imagination run amok, that Eden met with equal enthusiasm. She moaned against his lips and said, "Oh my gosh. Why did we wait?" Her hands clutched his shirt. Gripping her hips, he walked her backward, sidestepping furniture to their bed.

A bed he'd never slept on when she was in it.

"This is against the contract." He laid her down and hovered above her, a leg in between hers. She pressed herself upward, breathless and beautiful, her hair splayed around her. He kissed her, unable to resist.

"I know." Her fingers dipped into the waistband of his pants, and the warmth of her fingers sent waves of lust through his body. "We have rules."

They *did* have rules, rules that they both had committed to memory. Rules that they referred to time and again to keep things platonic.

Though if Chris were forced to tell the truth, all the rules had done was amp all his emotions. His attraction and respect for her had grown by feet since her proposal in his bedroom.

"We can't do this." The word *respect* echoed in his head, but the other side of him screamed in opposition. "But I've wanted this."

"I want *you*. So bad." Eden unbuttoned his jeans, the slight release both a relief and a warning. That if he didn't say something, they would dive headlong into a decision that they might regret.

"Eden," he groaned into her neck, halting her hand's descent.

"I know." She lifted her hands and buried them in her hair. Her chest rose and lowered with two deep breaths. "We have to think about this."

Maybe he'd just gotten too lonely. Three years of self-pleasure and the occasional hookup were getting old. And frankly, no one could compare, because Eden was everything he could want in a woman. In a wife.

His wife.

Almost three years he'd been married to this woman, and every part of him had belatedly wondered why they hadn't gotten to the part where they were making love.

"Chris?" His name was followed by a gentle pressure on his shoulders.

He propped himself up by the elbows and looked down upon Eden's face, which was as serious as he'd ever seen it. His heart thundered in regret that this had been a mistake.

"Look at me." She cupped his cheek and directed his gaze up. She sported a wry smile. "We're married, you know?"

He let go of a half laugh, and it released the pressure in his chest. "That we are."

"And I don't see why we couldn't see this through. The sex part."

"Things would change, Eden. And I'm not the kind of man . . ." He let his voice trail, stopping short of verbalizing this one bit of insecurity, the X factor that kept him as one of the only people he knew, despite being married, who had not fallen deeply in love. What did that say of him, that he was a man who *could* be in a marriage of convenience in the first place?

"What kind of man? Do you mean the kind of man that has been my friend? Someone who I have confided in when I had issues with work or with my family? The kind of man I trust my first drafts with? The kind of man that made a five-year contract with me?" Her eyes softened. "I guess I'm saying that . . . you are exactly the kind of man

I would want to be with. And I think that one line that addresses sex should be amended. There's no one else that . . ."

"I want more than I want you." He finished her sentence, sensing the rise of heat between them. Her fingers were now resting at the back of his neck, as if welcoming him to more intimacy should he agree. That was it; Chris had officially never ever met a woman like Eden. And he would be a fool not to take this chance to be with a woman who he admired. Still, a sliver of worry niggled at him. "I think we need to talk more about specifics."

"Specifics. Hmm. How about . . . both parties can engage in consensual intimacy," she said in a monotone voice. "Monogamous, consensual intimacy."

"Agreed." He frowned. He couldn't imagine either not existing. He cleared his throat. "Both parties will be honest regarding their intentions to continue the sexual relationship."

"Agreed." She nodded once. "Neither party will hold it against each other should the intimacy end, for the sake of the contract."

He bit his cheek as he thought of how to respond. *This* was the territory that he was afraid of. The uncoupling. "Both parties will do their best to remain friends, because that is what matters the most."

"It *is* what matters most." Her eyes rounded; they glassed over with emotion. "And I agree to all points. What say you?"

"Signed, sealed, delivered," he whispered.

She pulled him down by the shoulders, kissing him fully on the lips, and urged him higher on the bed. Without breaking contact, they worked swiftly to remove each other's clothes. And for the first time, Chris and Eden Puso made love and consummated their marriage.

CHAPTER SEVENTEEN

Of course Eden couldn't sleep.

How could she, when her brain had done her a disservice of traipsing down memory lane to the moment when she and Chris had first made love and then promptly to all the other wonderfully lustful moments until they had figured out that sex only complicated matters, and then had found out that stopping sex only caused more strife between them. This was why she'd been avoiding this only-one-bed scenario—why soon after they had stopped sexual relations, she'd moved out to a beach house for work and, sometimes, nights away from Chris. It had been too hard being around him knowing what could have been.

To make it worse, currently, Chris was half-naked, reminding her what she was missing. Talk about a confounding situation where the man she wanted but couldn't be with was literally right at her disposal.

How the heck could *he* sleep? And soundly, she might add. She bet she could be on the phone and he wouldn't be the wiser.

She wiggled under the sheet and stuck a foot out just so she could get more air. She clamped her eyes shut to block the memories. Still, she couldn't get those heart-stopping kisses out of her head. As intense as Chris was at work, he had been equally a perfectionist in the bedroom. His mission had been to please her, and he'd succeeded. Though now, neither one of them seemed happy.

What's motivating you in this marriage?

Kit's words from their first counseling session returned—though this time, she heard them sung in a different tune. Money had been the motivating factor in the beginning, and it had brought out the best in both of them—they'd wanted the relationship to work. Now, the money no longer felt good enough, when she'd been given a fifteen-month taste of what their relationship could have been.

Chris hummed and shifted, none the wiser that Eden's head was packed with images and words.

"Go to bed," she told her brain. She thought of the waves crashing into the surf, its retreat to gather up reinforcement, and the sand beneath her feet being drawn in. When that image didn't work to settle her nerves, she switched to her backup, of her turning a page of a book, though the words were illegible. Eden allowed her body to go slack, from her toes on up (this was a yoga trick that Beatrice had taught her), and the combination of these two things allowed her to let go of these unresolved, misspent emotions.

And it was starting to work; she felt lighter, the proverbial pages turning in slow, methodical succession, until the words began to come into focus.

She was reading *actual words* in this attempt at lulling herself to sleep, and an idea settled down around her. Her eyes flew open. Oh my God, she had to write these words down before she forgot.

Eden slipped out of the bed—though honestly she could have bounded out, and her husband wouldn't have known. She grabbed her phone from under the mattress and climbed down the loft. She tugged a hoodie over her head, grabbed her running shoes, and went out the front door.

She breathed in the oxygen, and it woke her all the way up.

Then she turned on the notes app of her phone and started to dictate.

Eden let herself go. In the last few weeks, she'd had a kink in the hose. Now with the knowledge that she'd have fallow moments, she padded down to the water so she wouldn't need to whisper and allowed for abundance to flow through.

She skirted the water's edge by the light of the moon with the phone's microphone against her lips while the picture of her story came through, until she realized that she'd reached the end of the beach, and to her left was Hapag, the resort's restaurant, with the patio lights on.

She'd walked almost the entire perimeter of the peninsula, though she hadn't felt it. She looked down at her phone—the words on the screen were indiscernible. Still, Eden grinned. She had something to edit.

Varying levels of soprano voices flittered in the air, and Eden peered toward the patio. Beatrice and Geneva were seated at a high table.

No doubt, they were talking about the wedding.

A pang of sadness ran through Eden. When it came time for her move back to Texas, she'd miss these two women. The idea that there wasn't a perfect scenario tore at her. Why couldn't she clone herself like she'd done with her real and pen names, where both could coexist in equal measure?

"Ate Eden?" Her name reached her ears. Beatrice and Geneva stood flush against the restaurant deck. "That you?"

"Oh no." She wasn't supposed to be milling about, nor was she supposed to have her phone. And she realized the full extent of her state. She was in her pajamas.

So, she did what seemed most logical—she scurried back from the direction she'd come. She was a beach crab frantically scouring for cover with the footsteps of humans nearby.

She was two houses away and had just passed Halik, where a couple was kissing at its front steps (Eden burned that metadetail into her memory), when she spotted two shadows of women scream whispering her name and was promptly bum-rushed by bodies.

"Oh my God." She laughed, coughed, and whispered all at once. "How did you even?"

"I'm the fastest golf cart driver here, don't you know?" Geneva pressed her hand to her chest and heaved. "Dang. You're fast, Eden."

"What are you doing out?" Beatrice whispered. "Oh no. Have you already given up on my brother?"

"No. No!" Oh God, those words speared at her. "I needed some air, to think about the last half of my book."

"Wait a sec. I thought you finished your book."

"I did. Sort of. Just part of it."

Beatrice's eyes rounded into saucers.

"It's no big deal." Eden waved a hand.

"No big deal? You have never not made a deadline."

"And that's why I'm out walking." She pulled the women toward the surf. "I guess today's time out in the water helped a ton. Anyway, let's not talk about me. Let's talk about you. What are you both doing out so late?"

"What else? Weddings," Beatrice said.

Geneva frowned. "I was complaining."

"Uh-oh. Trouble in paradise?" Eden asked.

"Brandon wants us to do our own vows. I know—who knew he even cared? And, well, I might be a designer, but I'm not a great writer."

"Duh! Why did I not even think of this?" Beatrice bumped her palm against her forehead. "We have a writer right here. I'm sure Eden can edit your words, give it some flair."

"Oh, I don't—" Eden started. First of all, vows were special, and secondly, who was she to help with vows when she hadn't really undertaken her own? And third. Third, she didn't want to taint those vows for whenever she and Chris announced their divorce.

"Please, please, please," Geneva said, pressing her hands together in prayer. Her hair flew up almost ninety degrees with a gust of wind.

Her face skewed to that pathetic pleading that Eden could never ever say no to.

"Oh, okay, sure. I mean, what's a little editing here and there." Eden shrugged.

She was tackled with a hug. "I would be so, so honored. In all honesty, I've been stalking your author Instagram, all the way back when you and Chris got married, to get some vow inspiration. The things you wrote about him . . . so sweet."

Eden looked away. She bet that the bulk of what Geneva had read were the posts from the months she and Chris had been together, because Eden hadn't been able to contain herself. Her affection, her happiness, had spilled over to all parts of her life. "Thank you."

"I hope that somehow the both of you . . . well . . . ," Beatrice started, then shook her head. "Never mind. We should get going. There are eyes everywhere. Speaking of. How is she?"

She? Eden frowned at the switch in subject, in Beatrice's demeanor and tone.

"You know." Beatrice leaned in. *"Jessie."*

"Oh." Eden scrambled her thoughts together. "Things are . . . fine. Though I haven't really had any one-on-one time with her."

"Well, good. You don't need any of those bad vibes on you and Kuya Chris. I can't believe her gall coming here with everything she did to Kuya Gil. She broke up our family. Ate Eden, you have to tell me if you see anything going on between those two. Kuya Gil is . . . sensitive, and romantic. We need to protect him."

Silence descended in their circle, and with it came a pang of guilt. Eden wanted to speak up, to say that in her experience, people rarely showed what happened behind closed doors. That maybe Gil was old enough to make his own decisions, and perhaps, he had contributed to the demise of their marriage. But in seeing Geneva's eyes firmly on the sand below, Eden knew it would be no use.

Beatrice's mind could not be changed, and right then? In the dark, beachside, was not the time to broach the topic.

"Well, I should . . ." Eden gestured toward the house.

"You should." Geneva jumped to escape the awkward moment. "And I've got flowers to research—right, Bea?"

"Flowers! Yes. I even made up a Pinterest board for you . . ." And with that, Beatrice was redirected.

After a last round of hugs, Eden watched the women head toward the road. Once they were gone, a momentary peace settled in. Thank goodness for words.

But Beatrice's comment that there were eyes everywhere remained with Eden even as she tucked herself into Tanggap's couch (because she still wasn't going to tempt fate by sleeping next to Chris). The most critical eyes were from the people they loved the most.

CHAPTER EIGHTEEN

WomensRelationshipMag.com

Is a couples retreat worth it?

No doubt many of us have tuned in to Heart Resort's social media feed, where they've teased a forthcoming exposé about their couples resort retreat programs. They promise an inside look on the all-inclusive experience, as undertaken by the CEO, Christopher Puso, and his wife, Eden.

What does this tell us? Some things we know from watching dozens of reality shows and biopics: that even the rich and the fabulous have their issues. Marriage is drama filled. No relationship is perfect. And, removing everyday distraction can bring out all the issues simmering under the surface.

It's an interesting concept, this exposé. As of this writing, Heart Resort has teased two completed days, with three days to go. The full show will go live a week after the last day, presumably for video editing, and so we can assume it will promote a positive spin to the retreat. Only time will tell if it will be scripted, if this is a marketing ploy, as suggested by a competing resort, or a true testament of the efficacy of the resort's programs.

So far, what's to be said about Chris and Eden Puso? That Chris is ambitious, and he's linear thinking to the point of selfishness. But Eden's no pushover. She's quietly strong, but she has walls up, to the point of spitefulness. There's a strange dichotomy with the two, a mutual affection and attraction, yet they appear to be disconnected—we at *Womens Relationship Magazine* are flummoxed. How have they survived this long?

It begs the question. Do people change? Can people make long-lasting change in five days in a meaningful way? And if they can't, we wonder if the high price tag is worth this kind of a program. Better yet, one might save those pennies and hire a reputable divorce attorney so one doesn't get screwed.

♡

93 days until Chan-Puso contract expiration
Word of the day: turnabout

Sitting on a chair beachside with his ankle over his knee, fingers steepled together on his lap, and waiting for his and Eden's second Couples Talk session, Chris silently ruminated. Forty-eight hours into this retreat, his body creaked from being out of shape, and his heart ached from waking up in an empty bed.

Next to him, Eden was staring off into space. She had been largely quiet through breakfast and while packing up for the next activity. He'd assumed that their fight after paddleboarding had been resolved, especially after she'd offered her bed, but there was clearly still something on her mind.

He spied for the location of Jessie and the camera. She was filming Kit, who was walking along the beach in their direction. And though hooked up to the microphone, curiosity clawed at him. "Is everything okay?"

"Oh, me? Yeah, I'm fine." Eden smiled, though it didn't quite make it to her eyes.

Her answer was straightforward, and yet her demeanor was revealing otherwise.

"What's up? Something bothering you?"

She shook her head, then looked up to Kit gliding in.

"Hello, Chris and Eden. Good morning." Kit took the seat in front of them, hands clasped. "Well? How have the last couple of days been?"

"It was fine," Chris said, just as Eden said, "All good."

Kit's eyebrows lifted. "All righty, then. Let's get more specific. Eden, how did you feel about Chris leaving you on that platform?"

Chris reared back. "Don't hold back now," he said under his breath.

Eden's response was matter of fact. "I felt alone."

Chris raised a hand. "Do we really need to discuss this again? I apologized the other night."

Kit gestured to Eden. "And did you accept this apology?"

"I mean, yeah. There isn't a choice but to accept it, right?"

"But I meant my apology," Chris said, defensive now. And as far as he was concerned, once an issue had been tabled, there was no reason to go back to it. "We shouldn't even have to rehash it, especially because she admitted that it wasn't just me who she was upset at." He nodded pointedly at Kit, whose serious face beguiled Chris. It felt like he was saying all the wrong things.

"What else were you upset about, Eden?"

"That I couldn't complete the activity. I guess it showed me that, I dunno, that I was fallible. That I can't do everything."

"And what do you think that means?"

She shook her head. "I don't know."

"Let's tease this out. You were having trouble during the obstacle, and he tried to help . . ."

"Right." She jumped in. "At the time I didn't want his help. Because I wanted to see if I could do it first. I wanted to see where my limits lay, and at some point, when I was on the platform, I figured out that I couldn't go much further. But by then, he was gone."

"Are you admitting that in this specific instance, that perhaps, you might be misdirecting some of your anger, when you were actually upset with yourself?"

"Hey, now wait a minute." Chris should have been happy that he'd won this point. It was unfair that Eden was taking the entire situation out on him. But the tension that teemed off his wife was uncomfortable at best. Chris might have been the kind of person who sometimes relished being right, but it was an entirely different story when it was directed at his family or his wife.

He regretted that he hadn't looked back one more time.

"No, it's okay." Eden's voice was soft, and she laid a hand on his wrist. It was warm, and when she withdrew her hand, what followed was the sting of rejection. He'd felt the same thing this morning when he'd been faced by the empty side of the mattress. "Because I *was* mad at myself."

Kit's expression softened. "I don't advocate for anyone to be mad at themselves, Eden. In fact, granting yourself grace has to be the first step in patching together whatever ills you have with your husband. But that is exactly what I'm asking for you to look at. At yourself. At what *you* wanted and perhaps at the way you communicate that. We can go even deeper. Did you really want his help?"

She looked down at her hands. "I guess I'm used to doing things on my own. So I don't know if I really wanted his help more than just to know I have it. And then I got angry that at almost five years together, he didn't think to just make sure that I was all right."

Chris frowned at this seemingly hypocritical statement.

"You take issue with that, Chris?" Kit asked.

"I . . . think it's interesting for her to say that when she left me out in the middle of the sound."

Eden sighed. "My goodness, Chris, it was not the middle. Anyway, what is this double standard?"

"You were getting me back, Eden. Totally different from me not realizing you were stuck on the platform."

"Chris," Kit redirected him. "Do you feel that intention matters more than the act?"

"Yes, I do." But as he said it, Chris settled back in his chair. *Did* it at the very end of the day, when all that was left were the consequences of the action? That drunk driver didn't set out to sideswipe his parents' car that night. And yet, here he was.

When did intention cease to be important? And with Eden, what had he excused himself from in the guise of his noble intentions?

"I think," Kit interrupted his running thoughts, "that it's interesting that the both of you did the same thing but with different motivations. I also couldn't help but note that each one of you brought up the five-year mark."

Chris's heart thudded as he thought back to when that had been mentioned.

"What is it about the five-year mark," Kit continued, "that makes it a deadline?"

Chris looked to Eden, and she returned a wary gaze. In it he heard her thoughts. *We need to be careful here.*

"I guess," Eden started, "it feels like the first milestone." She dropped her gaze.

"Hmm . . . so let's start there. Milestones. Markers. Though we can't depend on these things to determine success, it's good to examine what you thought you'd accomplish by now. So, on your camping trip, think about this: What had you expected from yourself at the five-year mark? Compare your thoughts with one another."

Discomfort pricked Chris at this line of questioning. He felt as if he was under lights, being interrogated. At five years, what he'd been looking forward to was money, a lot of money, that would solve his problems. Yet, here they were at the four-and-three-quarter-years mark, and he was far from problem-free. In fact, it had been a compounding set of struggles.

Kit's iPad rang the end of the session. Next to him, Eden heaved a breath. Kit bid her goodbye, but what remained was the undeniable conclusion that while they were faking their marriage and this resort experience, they were feeling some real things. Or at least he was, anyway.

"Are you okay?" Chris asked Eden.

"I mean, yeah, I guess." She shook her head. "Are you?"

"It's always a little painful when someone calls you out."

"No kidding."

Chris wanted to say more. They needed to talk about this, but the lens and the microphone were obstacles. They would have to wait until tonight.

Chet's appearance was like a dunk in a cold pool, and his smile was wide and clearly manufactured. "How was that?" he asked.

"Fine," Chris said at the same time as Eden.

"Great! Because it's time for your next activity: overnight camping. One of the resort vans will take you in about an hour."

♡

"The hike to Frisco Campground is about four and a half miles." Chet climbed into the van, shut the driver's-side door, and rested an elbow out the window. "We'll have your gear at your campground lot, which will be set and ready to go. If you need anything, of course we'll be available via phone through Gil or Jessie."

Chris nodded. Next to him, Eden was crouched, rummaging through her backpack. They were an hour south of the resort, at Cape Hatteras, in front of a sign that read OPEN PONDS TRAIL. Beyond it was a wide dirt hiking trail that led into the woods.

"Looks like we have enough water and snacks." Eden zipped up the pack. She waved at Chet. "Thanks. See you tomorrow."

As the van did a quick U-turn, Chris loaded up his backpack, unwieldy from its contents.

"It shouldn't be too bad, right?" Eden grunted and hefted her backpack over one shoulder. "Ugh, the water is heavier than I thought it would be."

"The hike should only take us a couple of hours." He assisted her with adjusting the straps of her pack. But truth be told, it was two hours of straight walking *if* kept at a good clip without any major rests. And without all this gear.

They hadn't yet started filming, nor were Eden and Chris hooked up to microphones after their clothing change.

"What if I need to use the bathroom?" Worry etched a line across Eden's forehead, shaded under her bucket hat that had earflaps that protected even her cheeks. It was adorable, especially since their hike would be under the cover of trees.

"I mean . . . you're going to have to do what you need to do." He chuckled.

She scrunched her face.

Mumbling took his attention, feet away, to Jessie and Gil, who were in deep discussion. Seeing the both of them throughout this project had provided Chris with several déjà vu moments, and this was one of those times. All that was missing were their kids to complete the picture.

"What do you think of them?" Eden asked.

"Who?"

"Jessie and Gil."

He shook his head. "I think they're a complicated matter."

"Does them getting back together worry you?"

"Who are we to judge?"

She tucked her hand under the straps of her backpack. "We don't have to judge to have an opinion. Beatrice is . . . not happy about all this."

He snorted. "I believe we have bigger things to worry about right now, like this hike and this exposé. The family drama will be there in a couple of days."

"Don't you ever consider family drama, as you call it, more important sometimes? Oh, wait . . . I forgot who I was talking to. Mister Runaway."

"It's not about running away. It's putting myself solidly where I belong and not in their business." He rolled his eyes. "We don't have to be involved, nor do we need to jump into every situation where people need help. Especially when we're the ones that need to get it together. We're not looking good right now, I'm sure."

She frowned. "And is that supposed to be my fault?"

"I didn't say that." He gritted his teeth. "I'm saying we are priority."

She half laughed. "*Now* you say so."

"We're ready whenever you are," Jessie called out, interrupting them. Her eyes darted between him and Eden. "I don't plan to film a lot on the hike, so I'll be using my handheld for some scenic and periodic shots. No microphones needed. I think we'll all be focused on getting to the campground."

It sounded great to Chris, because he had a feeling that the footage would feature only him and Eden bickering.

Except when they got on the trail and were swallowed up by the canopy of trees, they hiked in silence. Chris busied himself by taking in the foliage and the meditative sounds of the rustling leaves and the crashing surf just beyond the tree line. Now this, he loved. The simple pleasures of nature. His dad had taught him how to appreciate even their postcard-size backyard of grass and rosebushes; and for the moment he was calmed, transported to a time untouched by stress.

A growl to his left brought him back to the present.

Eden slapped the back of her neck. "Can we stop and spray bug repellent?"

"Yeah, sure." In hindsight, Chris was grateful they'd both opted to wear long hiking pants. Mosquitoes attacked them in full force, hovering over the still puddles of water from the spring rain.

They moved to the side of the trail. Eden sprayed the bottom half of her clothing and offered him the can. He sprayed his clothing, all in continued silence. A ways down, Jessie panned the camera across the foliage.

Then they got on the road once more.

Minutes passed, and Chris could no longer stand it. "Are you planning on not speaking to me this entire camping trip?"

He was met with not a peep.

"You know. You *know* I can't stand it when you don't say anything. You need to speak to me."

Still, nothing.

They hiked in silence the next half hour, with Eden ahead a step, until it got so warm that Chris began to sweat profusely. All around him was stagnant air, mosquitos buzzing, and gone were the meditative and the calm. Behind them, Gil and Jessie were speaking in hushed tones that were, as far as he could deduce, respectful and cordial.

How did this happen? How had his brother somehow been able to reconcile with his ex-wife and Chris couldn't get his current wife to speak to him?

This was going too far. He rushed forward and grabbed Eden by the hand. "Eden. I need you to talk to me."

She slowed a tad to allow him to catch up, and he matched her steady stride. And while she didn't answer right away, she didn't pull her hand from his.

It was better than nothing.

"Maybe she's right?" she said, a second later.

"Who?"

"Kit. That I took things out on you when it's me I need to work on."

Chris thought of his brother Brandon, who he'd had conflict with for most of his life. Of the amount of work they'd both had to put in to repair their relationship. "Eden, I should have turned around and waited for you, and I'm sorry. I need to work on things too. Am I doing something that keeps you from speaking up?"

"No." She shook her head. "I have never felt intimidated by you, or silenced, Chris."

He felt a wave of relief.

"I just feel . . . bothered."

"By what?"

"I can't even put words to it."

He thought of the video teasers the last two days. The teaser that had rolled out yesterday of him scrambling in the water after Eden's paddleboard, which was embarrassing, to say the least, seemed an indication that their relationship's end was near. But it was just the tip of the iceberg of the undercurrent of their relationship. "I'm bothered too."

"Yeah? By what?"

How could he say it without putting pressure on her? "That we've come so far, to have done so much, and leave angry."

"It's against the agreement we had." She spared him a glance. "Neither party will hold it against each other should the intimacy end, for the sake of the contract. Remember?"

"Like it was yesterday."

The sound of their boots on the rocky trail filled the pause in their speech. During that time, they continued to hold hands.

"Chris?" Eden tugged on his hand. "I'm sorry. For getting back at you while paddleboarding. It was immature and petty."

"I appreciate it." He grinned at her. "Though I'm sure it will make for good TV."

She winced, swiping sweat from her cheeks. "The plan wasn't to be a perfect couple."

"But we weren't supposed to be unlikeable."

"Unlikeable." She snorted. "I hate that word. It's so . . . misogynistic, because it's me, as a stubborn woman, or a woman who spoke her mind, who'll be slapped by that descriptor. You? You'll be described as grumpy or serious but somehow still likable."

"You're right, and that's crap." Chris couldn't object. It was true with all the critique Eden had received about some of the heroines she'd written. "I'll rephrase. We wanted people to root for us, right? I fear that maybe we've shown too many of our cards."

"Ugh. You're right." She readjusted her hat and waved away a mosquito. "It's Kit and the way she looks at me and the questions she asks. She's got some magic thing that has me flapping my mouth when I know I should be quiet."

"So you're saying Couples Talk is working?"

She gave him a wry smile. "I never said that it wouldn't work. But with Kit, it's hard to pretend."

"Though we've been pretending for a while now."

She nodded. "I think that's the other problem. Sometimes I can't tell what's real."

The words landed like bricks on Chris's shoulders, and he felt the full weight of his backpack. Their marriage had been an exercise in deciphering what was real and what wasn't. The most confounding time had been when they'd stopped being intimate; he was still trying to untangle what had transpired at the end.

They came upon a muddy section in the trail that extended across the entire path, and through it were sunken footprints.

"Nooo," Eden whined.

"There's no way but through. C'mon." Chris took the first step, and his shoe nestled halfway into the dirt. "Ohhh, nooo."

Eden stepped in behind Chris with a giggle. "This is so gross!"

He let go of her hand. "Hold on to my backpack."

Chris stepped onto something imbedded in the mud and slipped. "Whoa—whoa!" As he fell forward, he took Eden with him. Her body tipped into his from behind, and down he went into the gritty, sticky mud, knees first. He saved himself from face planting at the last minute by throwing his arms out, falling on his elbows. Dirt splattered upward, into his mouth and nose.

"Oh my God!" Eden yelped, laughing. "Oh my God, are you okay?"

Chris hoisted himself up to his knees; his torso was covered in mud. He blinked away chunks that threatened to seep into his eyeballs.

He looked to his left; Eden was sitting on her heels in the same state, though she was shaking with laughter that was so pure, so contagious, that he couldn't help but crack up too.

He felt his body give in to the silliness of the moment. The tension of the last couple of days eased. If he'd allowed it, he would have probably cried.

It had been a rough set of years. Since his parents had died, there hadn't been joy that hadn't been interspersed with some sadness. Chris didn't know if that was normal or if that was the side effect of losing people you loved. Once, his brother Brandon had asked him how he could be unfeeling. *Stone cold* had been the exact words. And Chris had declared, though not proudly, that he buried his feelings deep inside.

Chris was great at compartmentalizing, but Eden, his mirror in every way, was his accountability.

Right now, it was this profound release.

Eden crawled to him, and the sight of it, of her eyes on him like she was looking right into his soul, took him aback. How did she do that? How could she tell that for a beat, he was frozen in thought?

"C'mon, big boy," she teased. "You follow me next time." She stood first and then him, and slowly, with coordinated steps while holding on to one another, they moved to the side of the trail. They unloaded their backpacks.

"You should see." She heaved a breath midgiggle. "You should see your face, and your beard! Just chunks." She swiped a hand against his cheek and showed him. "See?"

He wiped his equally yucky hand against his cheek.

"You're going to make it worse." She untied the bandana around her neck, balled it up, and mopped it across his face. "Let me."

The press of the fabric against his skin, solid and real, grounded his emotions back to earth. He watched Eden and catalogued her eyes, which were lit up with her grin, and the wisps of hair stuck to her shimmering, damp skin. His gaze dropped down to her lips, which were pursed in concentration, similar to when she was trying to sort a plot hole or character arc in her head.

He, on the other hand, couldn't focus.

The air between them was heavy.

The nuance of it was something he'd learned to detect. They had their light moments and their tense moments. But right then, there was so much else between them—the unresolved that he wanted to fix, not for the camera but for each other.

He reached up and encircled her wrist. She stilled, eyes locking on his with this acuteness, like she was trying to read his mind.

His belly stirred with the beginnings of need. If she only knew what he was thinking. What he'd been thinking, and missing. It was always pervasive, this attraction, though he'd kept it in check after their lovemaking phase.

Because this woman. This woman didn't have to do much to make him want her. She just had to *be*—and in any way: in his arms, in bed, over sheets, with the lights on. Yes, in that almost year of sexual abandon, they hadn't been afraid to discover, to experiment, to grow together.

Chris's body simmered as the memories cycled back, but he had to tread carefully. There was a reason why they'd quit being intimate, why they had cycled back to their platonic arrangement.

It was called their contract and the consequences of breaking it.

In response to his hitched breath, Eden brought her hands so they rested at his chest, and tentatively he pulled her by the waist so their torsos touched. She crawled her fingers upward to rest at the base of his neck. That stirring in his belly escalated to a full-on assault of his primal senses when she pressed her fingertips against his skin.

"Eden," he whispered, barely able to get the words out. "Is this—"

"What?"

"Is this real?" He did and didn't want the truth. He didn't want to get his hopes up.

Her gaze sobered. "It's real. I want . . ." Her voice trailed.

"Want what?"

He waited through her silence and kept himself contained somehow. His body was trained to her consent. He would hold it back until she said it was all right.

She whispered, "Your lips. On me."

He didn't think twice. He dipped down and caught her lips in his. They had the hint of lip balm and the bitterness of sunscreen, but it was a relief, a feeling of coming home.

And just like home, he wanted to bask in it. He wanted to lie out like one of his orchids under the sun, where every second his life force was getting renewed.

She was on her tiptoes, and she kissed back with a solid force. Her hands dug into his neck, and with it he remembered the last time they'd made love, with her nails buried in his back. When he'd awoken the next morning undeniably marked in every way.

She groaned against his lips. "I feel you."

"I feel you," he said. He'd untucked her shirt, his fingers grazing the tops of her jeans. Her skin was scorching.

Then, in the same way the kiss had come on, it subsided like the tide. Chris noticed that the camera was trained on them. Eden had fallen back onto her heels; he regained his senses.

Her expression was of remorse. "We shouldn't do that, should we?" She breathed out the words in a whisper.

He licked his lips, savoring it while taking in her flushed cheeks. Logically, he knew that their status, their *real* status, was precarious and could not be decided with one kiss. There was too much to discuss. "Probably not. Though it was just as I remember."

"Did it live up to the memory?"

"It was eh," he said, shrugging.

She shoved him playfully. "Whatever."

He held on to both her wrists before she got away, before they buried this moment. He never wanted to take what they did for granted. "It was perfect."

Her gaze dropped, bashful. "Let's get to the campground. No more falling."

He slung his pack over his back. If only it were that easy.

CHAPTER NINETEEN

Eden spread out both sleeping bags over self-inflating sleeping mats inside the two-person tent. She tested the mat by putting pressure on it with her palms, and dread rose.

Tonight was going to be rough; it had been forever since she'd camped. And she was a mess—head foggy after last night's insomnia, Kit's words that had ricocheted in her head like a pinball, and the long hike up to the campground.

But the biggest cause of her discombobulation was the kiss.

At the thought of those brief seconds where that entire hike had fallen away, from the mud to the bugs to the fact that they were on camera and were out in public—okay, perhaps that had added to her lust—her body tingled. Eden hadn't known how she'd made it to the campsite, with how dizzying Chris had made her feel—the cold shower from the campsite's facilities had been a welcome relief to douse the flames roaring inside her.

The kiss had been a mistake—there was no doubt—but the temptation had been overwhelming. There had been too much tension between them. Her body had been taut with it.

Mother Nature was a conspirator, Eden believed, by literally taking them both down with the mud. It had been like the call to humility, to ground them. In that mud, Eden had returned to herself. Not Everly

Heart, not Mrs. Puso, not Ate Eden. She had simply been a woman trying to figure out how to get her legs underneath her. And Chris had been so adorable, vulnerable, and it had hearkened back to all those tender moments in that true honeymoon year.

"That was *the* best shower, ever." Chris's voice echoed through the thin tent fabric, and he lifted the hatch. Light from the late afternoon streamed in, along with the scent of Chris's bodywash. His hair was tousled, face damp from his shower. He was shirtless and wearing knit pants, which hung low on his hips. There was no sign of a boxers or underwear band.

Was he wearing underwear underneath?

Her mouth went dry.

"Eden?"

Her gaze darted up to his face, to the mischievous curl of his lips and the eyes that said *gotcha*.

"Hmm?" She startled awake and scrambled out from the warmth of the tent. "Why are you half-naked?"

"Um." He gestured to the rest of the campground, which was populated by people in swimsuits. "Is it a problem?"

"No, I guess not," she mumbled and avoided looking at his mud-free and toned body. If she didn't watch it, she'd need another shower. "I guess as long as you don't mind people seeing you half-naked." She eyed the camera Gil and Jessie had set up, though it was barely there, hanging precariously on a tree branch with the lens trained at their tent.

Their tent area was secluded on the eastern overlook, with the deserted beach below. Beyond, as far as the eyes could see, was the light-blue-and-white sky. Around their site was a bank of trees, which broke the strong, warm wind.

"I'm not worried." He crossed his arms and stared at her.

"Why are you looking at me like that?"

His eyebrows lifted, and he tilted his head knowingly.

"What?"

Then he gestured his head to the right, toward a multicolor hammock hanging between two trees.

She squealed at the sight of it, and all at once her body relaxed. "You didn't." She rushed at the hammock and fell into its cocoon. It caught her expertly. Yes, she was definitely going to get to sleep. She reveled in the gentle rocking and the sky and tree leaves that appeared through the slit of her vision.

Fingers pulled at the edge of the fabric, and her husband's face appeared above her. He had a smile that split his face.

Eden was overcome with appreciation, with emotion. "Thank you," she said. Then she pulled him down by the neck with a hug, unable to contain herself. "Thank you, thank you. How did you know?"

Chris laughed as he straightened. "What, that you love your great big beds? This isn't big, but Chet promised it would be at least comfortable. Much more comfortable than a sleeping bag on the ground." He shrugged. "I want you happy. I mean, you *are* my wife."

The way he said it melted Eden's insides into one confusing goo. How could something be true and then false and feel real and be manufactured all at once?

His dark eyebrows furrowed, as if he'd read her mind. "Where'd you go?"

She blinked away her thoughts and rearranged her expression. "I'm literally falling asleep right now."

He laughed. "Have at it. I'll go start the grill." But as he started to walk away, she grabbed for his arm. The thing about being married for show was that they watched each other carefully. They had to be in sync purposely. And if she was feeling this . . . awkwardness, or whatever it was, perhaps he was feeling it too?

"What is it?" he asked.

"I feel like we need to talk about it."

He shook his head. "No, we don't. It was a kiss, Eden."

Was it? Then why had she almost fallen apart in his arms? Why had her knees buckled, and why had she been willing to go find a clear, isolated patch of grass and do the horizontal hokeypokey?

She searched his face then, to find any trace of a lie. And he looked fine. Just fine.

And what was she going to do with that? What *could* she do with that? And for that matter, what was she supposed to do with that? It was obvious from her conversation with their Couples Talk counselor that she had issues with herself. "All right."

A sun flare cut between them, and Chris looked up. "I'm starving. Time to cook."

She let him go then. "Okay."

How she had ended up with a life with more angst than her books, she couldn't figure out. She could write her characters into pure maturity. But here she and Chris were, full-fledged adults, and they couldn't seem to say what they needed to say.

It was because, as Kit had said, she didn't know what she wanted.

"They forgot to pack salt and pepper," she heard him say. "I'll head to the other campsite to pick it up."

"I can grab it. You watch the grill." She hopped out of the hammock, suddenly needing space. "I'll take my wallet in case. They should have it at the camp store." She crawled back into the tent and dug her wallet out of her backpack, seeing the glint of her burner cell phone in the bottom.

Temptation clawed at her and won out. She might as well check in with her sister and Paige, so she stuffed the phone in her front pocket and beelined out and down the path to Gil and Jessie's campsite.

There was no sign of either of them. The tent showed no movement, and the car next to it, which would be their ride back to Heart Resort in the morning, was empty. A Sterilite container sat next to the cooler; she checked it for spices to no avail.

She would need to head to the camp store after all.

On the walk there, Eden ensured the coast was clear and powered up her phone. She'd found a way to charge it this morning at Tanggap while Chris had been in the shower, and it had half a battery's juice. Her texts populated, including one from her Realtor, Carol Nieves. Another one in your target neighborhood, and larger.

A sprawling five-bedroom ranch with two en suites.

One for her dad. One for her.

She texted her Realtor: Wow. Tell me more. She continued down the path, passing tents on the right side and the occasional RV on her left. The campground store was up ahead, lit brightly with warm yellow light. The door opened, and a couple stepped out, each holding a cone of ice cream. They were laughing.

It took a beat for Eden to realize that it was Gil and Jessie. They were cozy and sweet, standing close.

Then Gil leaned in, and their shadows mingled for a moment.

Eden rubbed her eyes. Was that a kiss?

But Eden didn't have time to think; she stepped off the path and ducked behind an RV as they headed her way. Eden held her breath until their footsteps faded.

Her phone buzzed with a series of texts. As she entered the campground store and the food aisle, she read her messages.

Carol:

> It's a foreclosure. So, it may take a little longer to close, probably 3-5 months.

> Perfect for whenever you get here, if it all works in our favor

> Shall I preview the ranch?

Then from the front of the camp store, the register dinged, and she tore her eyes from her phone screen. She spotted the salt and pepper and bent down to grab it from the bottom shelf. When she stood, she was eye to eye with Jessie, who was at the next aisle.

Eden startled and stuffed the phone as slyly as she could into her front pocket. "Oh, hey."

"Hey . . . Eden." Jessie's tone was cautious. She lifted up a box. "Toothpaste."

"Salt and pepper." Eden couldn't meet her smile all the way, with her curiosity on overload and this weird vibe between them.

"Well, gotta go pay."

"Yeah. Me too."

They both got in line, with Jessie facing front. The cashier was moving slowly, making conversation with each and every customer, amplifying the silence between her and Jessie. Eden twisted in discomfort—was it a betrayal to Beatrice if she spoke to Jessie?

Jessie paid for her toothpaste and, with a swift goodbye, walked out of the camp store, the bell above the door ringing her departure.

Eden admonished herself. Jessie had always been decent to Eden. They'd spent many holidays and Friday dinners together. She was the mother to her nieces, whom Eden loved dearly. Finally, Eden knew in her heart that Jessie would protect her and Chris the best way she could with this exposé.

She needed to apologize.

"Miss?"

"What? Oh." She glanced at the red numbers on the register, though she couldn't process the information. She set down a ten. "Keep the change."

She burst out the door. Only to find Jessie just outside, hands tucked in her back pockets. "Oh my gosh. Thank you for not leaving. I'm sorry. That? Me back there? That was so awful and rude."

"It wasn't like I turned around to try to talk to you either." Jessie's gaze dropped. "That was the most uncomfortable thing ever. And I hate it. I hate that it has to be this way. Don't get me wrong; I understand why I'm no longer in the Puso circle. But I wish that my and Gil's problems remained just between us."

"I know exactly what you mean." Eden's vision cleared; soon, she would be in the same situation. Her heart swelled with understanding, with sympathy, and with sadness for Jessie. Here was a woman who was on the other side, and Eden had been so caught up in herself that she couldn't see past, to the people around her who deserved acceptance. "Do you want to . . . walk back together?"

A smile quirked. "That might not be a good idea. You're supposed to be on your retreat. You're so lucky, you know. If me and Gil had the same opportunity. Or willingness. Maybe . . ."

"I saw you," Eden blurted out, compelled by Jessie's show of trust. Knowing that she wasn't alone in this struggle made her want to be honest too. "I saw you and Gil, kissing."

"You did?" Her voice lifted along with the corners of her mouth. "I . . . I'm trying not to get my hopes up. The thing with marriage, or a marriage in trouble, is that unless there's a stark villain, then we have to both admit that we had a hand in it. And the back-and-forth of our divorce—it has been torturous and grueling on the soul. Can we love each other enough to forgive and then forget?" She shrugged. "No matter how many people I confide in or try to get advice from, no one can seem to answer it. It'll be up to me and Gil, and even then, we can always change our mind. Sorry . . . I'm rambling."

"No. You're not. This . . . you . . . are being so great and so honest despite everything. My own marriage . . . this retreat has been confusing."

"Can I give some advice?"

"Yes, please." Eden was committing everything she said to memory.

"Take care of yourself, first and foremost. Not only are you the star of your own show, but you have to be the producer, the director, the stage manager. Piecing a marriage back together is a bumpy ride. But if you're good with yourself, then maybe the marriage will be that much stronger. It's what I hope, anyway. It's what I've been working on." She smiled. "I'll see you in the morning?"

"Yeah, okay. Thank you. So much."

Jessie turned and headed down the path to her tent. As Eden started back to her tent site, she mulled over Jessie's words. They echoed the same message Paige had given her.

Perhaps Eden was upset with herself because she wasn't prepared for the transition. She'd allowed this impending divorce to make her feel like she was being sideswiped, when she'd had five years' notice.

So she went to her texts with her real estate agent: Yes, please preview the house.

Then she opened up a new text message to Paige: You were right. I need to take care of myself.

Paige:

Should I make the connection with my friend Ann Allred?

Eden hovered her thumb over the phone's keyboard. Was she overreacting? Did she really need her own attorney?

This was going to crush Chris. Still, she needed to know her rights, as amicable as this divorce was going to be. She typed Yes and pressed the send button and stuffed the phone in her back pocket before she could change her mind.

♡

Eden was drooling by the time Chris brought their dinner to the picnic table. He'd grilled two steaks and two ears of corn and warmed up baked beans from a can in a small pot. Now wearing a ball cap turned backward and a white V-neck tee, Chris exuded youth and vigor. While he divvied up their food, giving her the choice of steak and corn, she felt her hormones taking a nosedive off the cliff of plain old lust.

Apparently her walk to the camp store and her chat with Jessie hadn't cooled her down. Admittedly, it had always turned her on when Chris cooked, which wasn't often. There was something about catching him in the kitchen, barefoot and chopping veggies or stirring a pot. It was a close second to him out in the garden, shirtless and hands dirty from work. Tonight, it was the combination of Chris wrangling coals and the campfire that had stirred her up.

"So?" Chris woke her from her trance, eyes darting to her plate. Unbeknown to her, she'd already cut up the steak. He was waiting for her to take the first bite.

So she forked a cube and placed it on her tongue. It was perfect. "Delicious."

He grinned. "Good. Honestly sometimes that's all you need—a little salt and pepper. Glad the camp store had it in stock."

And the back-and-forth of our divorce—it has been torturous and grueling on the soul. Jessie's words came back to Eden as they dug into dinner. The last six months had stirred up this pinball of emotions, and sometimes the dichotomy of what Eden had felt had been intense. From love to heartache, and now in this middle ground where they were simply trying to bide time . . .

Chris laid down his utensils, frowning. "Eden, we don't have to discuss the kiss. I'm good. We're good. It was a moment."

"Please, stop talking." She half laughed in exasperation. She didn't need to be reminded that he didn't think the kiss was anything when she was still reeling from it. "It's not about that."

His expression slackened. "Oh. Okay."

"When I was on my way to the camp store—" She leaned in to whisper, to make sure the camera didn't pick up her voice. She should tell Chris about what she'd learned. If anything, it could be a point of discussion.

"Hey, you two." Gil emerged from the shadows.

Eden all but choked on her own spit.

207

"Damn. Talk about sneaking up on us," Chris bellowed. "Where are you coming from?"

"Sorry about that. I was just on a hike. There's a trail just down that direction." Gil pointed to the left.

Eden detected a Cheshire cat smile on his lips. *Interesting.* "Where's Jessie?"

"Oh, um, probably at the campsite." Gil wasn't quite looking at her. "Anyway, from Miss Kit." He took an envelope out of his pocket.

Eden shot Chris a look. "What's in the envelope?"

"Homework. It's for you to open after dinner. And, of course, don't forget these." He plopped down two wireless clip microphones. "For when you discuss the homework."

"Thanks, Gil. We'll . . . um . . . address it."

"Cool. I'm off." Gil sauntered away with a grin.

"Did you hear that?" Chris was still watching his brother. "Cool. He said *cool.* And did you see how he kept smiling? Do you think?" As in, did Eden think that there was something going on?

She nodded.

He raised his eyebrows.

She shrugged, as in *I have no idea what to do with that.*

He laughed, which made her crack up. She loved that they sometimes didn't have to say a word to communicate. If they were like this at almost five years, ten was going to be so much fun.

Eden gasped at the errant thought.

"What?" Chris asked.

"Oh, nothing. The food was delicious. Thank you for making dinner." She stood from the bench, avoiding his eyes. "Let's clean up and do the assignment in front of the fire."

"Oh . . . um . . . okay."

After cleaning up, they hooked up and turned on their microphones. Eden heaved a breath. *Here we go again.*

"Are you in the mood for dessert?" Chris bent over their cooler.

"Dessert? You know I'm always up for dessert."

He straightened, shaking a ziplock bag of chocolate chip cookies. Her favorite—the resort catering was really on point. She reached for the bag. "Gimme."

"I knew you'd say that. I'm in the mood for chocolate too." He dragged two camp chairs next to the fire and opened the bag for her to take the first pick.

She sat, selected a cookie, and bit into it; the sugar rush was instantaneous. "Oh yes, that's good."

"Yep. It is," he said with a mouthful while sinking into the chair. He leaned back and shut his eyes. With the glow of the fire against his face, it was a photograph. More than that, it was an essay. A short story. A novel, of someone who had challenged her in every way for almost five years and who would continue to challenge her until their very last day together.

And then what? Would it truly be a clean break? Would they be like Jessie and Gil, who couldn't quit one another?

An eye opened. "Are you watching me?"

Her cheeks heated, and she answered with the first thing that came to mind. "Not at all. I was thinking about our homework."

"Homework." He sighed. "I guess we should just get this over with."

"Yeah, we should." She stood and grabbed the envelope from the table. When she returned, Chris had arranged their chairs so they faced one another. She dropped the envelope into his lap. "You can do the honors." When she sat, their knees were inches from touching.

"All right. Ready?"

"I think so." This assignment felt ominous and serious.

Chris made quick work of opening the envelope and pulled out a set of photos. His eyebrows furrowed as he flipped through them.

"What is it?" Curiosity pulled at Eden.

Chris answered by repositioning the ball cap on his head, like he was uncomfortable.

"Chris?" Eden didn't like this look.

He turned the photos for her to see. One was of the Puso family, complete with Chris's parents, and the second picture was of her family, with her mother and grandmother included.

Two families when they were still intact.

A note was enclosed, and Eden read it aloud. "Besides discussing what you hoped to accomplish in five years, complete this sentence: In this photo, I see . . ."

Chris rubbed a palm against his beard. "I mean, talk about emotional manipulation."

Her husband didn't like being forced to talk about his parents. He came about their memories from the side or in a roundabout way.

She did the same, too, with her mother. Sometimes, she just ignored the fact that part of her family tree was in the Philippines.

This exercise was going to be a bear. "Yeah, but we still have to do the assignment. Want me to go first?" When Chris nodded, Eden gave it a go. "I thought that in five years, I would have my career. And I do have it."

Paige had said as much at their last dinner, but in saying so, Eden was able to take it in. "You and I talked about this, before we married. That I had all these . . . um . . ."—she noted the microphone clipped onto Chris's shirt—"goals. And I accomplished them." She glanced down at the photograph. "But when I see that photo of my family, I realize that my career isn't all I wanted. Is it selfish to say I want it all?" She looked up into his eyes, and in them she caught a glimpse of his pain. She wasn't enough of a fool to think that it was only her having a hard time with how their relationship had managed to turn out, and she wished she could take that pain from him. But she also had to take care of herself. "When I see that photo, I see a family that loves each other so much that they're willing to be apart. My dad and mom didn't split up because of strife. They aren't together because they're both trying to do the right thing by other family members. But the fact of the matter is that it wasn't me who was chosen." Her breath hitched at the words coming through without a filter. "What I want is *not* that." She conjured a line from one of her books. "What I want is a happily ever after, even if it's hard to be together. I want to be the love that requires presence, attendance, attention. I want to be the one chosen."

She'd been so lost in her words that when she refocused, she noticed that Chris was holding her hands. He rubbed her palms with his thumbs, as he'd done once when her carpal tunnel had flared up. It soothed her, like the fresh ocean air after months landlocked in the city. She shook her head and half laughed to break herself from the moment, then squeezed Chris's hands. "Your turn."

"Sure? You can take my turn. No?"

Eden shook her head.

"Okay, fine." Chris heaved a breath. "I know that sounds really naive, but I thought that in five years, all of the problems I had at the time would have gone poof. That everything would have, quote, gone back to normal. That life would have returned to a place where it had been before Mom and Dad passed. When I looked at life in this carefree manner." He cleared his throat. "When I see this photo, I'm reminded that it can't, and it won't ever. They're never coming back. Even now when I say it, it still feels surreal . . . but what I want is what they had. They had this security that seemed so indestructible even through the rough spots. They were happy and content because they were together. I want exactly that." He paused, and a hint of a smile graced his face. It was so sweet that Eden smiled reflexively. "Kit got us again."

The topic change caught Eden off guard. "What do you mean?"

"Kit wanted us to compare our answers. And what we want . . ."

Eden finished his sentence, understanding. "Is the same in many ways. *I* want to be chosen."

"And I want us to be together," he said.

"I want the career and family."

"And I want to give you everything you want."

"You do?"

"Yes."

She examined his face. Carefully this time. Because that statement meant a whole host of things. They would need to go back, to that honeymoon year, and talk about the details. They would have to discuss this contract. They would need to discuss the future, which they had never done before. "So the kiss earlier . . . ," she tested, to see if these thoughts were hers alone.

"Eden, it wasn't just a kiss."

His answer seemed to turn another page in their marriage's book. They'd been in such a rut, and now, to hear him say that he wanted to give her what she wanted brought hope of . . . something. It gave some validation to their history.

Eden drew toward him, and as their faces neared, the heat rose between them. She couldn't help but reach up and touch his cheek, his soft beard sensuous against the pads of her fingers. And when he tilted his face toward her palm, shutting his eyes briefly, her heart burst with a kind of melancholy.

She scooted forward in the camp chair, and he spread his knees so that she could get closer. When he leaned in, she pressed a chaste kiss on his lips as a test.

His breath hitched. "Eden, is this okay?"

She answered him by kissing him once more and by nipping on his bottom lip. He groaned, and her heart leapt at his reaction. Chris, for all his bluster, submitted. Just as he relished working with other competent people, he was spurred by Eden's want to explore.

And it was exactly what she was doing now, fisting his shirt to keep him close. "I want more," she whispered.

"In the tent."

Standing, she wobbled, like she'd drunk too much champagne chased by a can of Red Bull. As if she'd written eight thousand words that day. She followed Chris, stripping their mics, already boneless with need, to their tent.

Inside, the bright moon beamed down through the mesh skylight.

Chris tugged off his shirt in between kisses, though she struggled to take off her shorts. He grunted; she giggled. A zipper sounded. A shoe thudded to the ground. But finally, finally, they both managed to remove their clothing. Chris hovered above her, positioned perfectly in between her legs, skin to skin, and the intimacy of the moment set Eden off like a rocket. She arched her back in anticipation of pleasure, gasping at how Chris expertly used his lips and fingers.

She'd missed this. Together, in this physical way, she and Chris were absolutely in sync. There were no missteps or misunderstandings. There was only connection and pleasure.

Along with this came the knowledge that no other person could fulfill their desires but each other.

"Chris. I want you," Eden moaned, frenzied and impatient.

"I want you too." And then he said, "Dammit."

Only one thing would stop them. "You don't have . . ."

"No, I don't." He lifted up higher on his elbows. "Dammit," he said once more. "I was so caught up. Tonight, with everything. I didn't even think to—"

"I'm on the pill. I've been on the pill."

He bent down and kissed her on the lips. Then he swept hair away from her face. "I know, but . . ."

There it went, their truth hanging in the air. Their imminent divorce. And if she got pregnant, again . . .

"Okay," she said, though it physically pained her to say so. She inhaled what felt like a lungful of air; it would take her sneaking out to the beach to calm down.

"Hey," he whispered into her ear and nipped at her earlobe. It sent shivers down her spine and wrenched her attention back to him. "But it doesn't mean this needs to stop."

A smile grew on her lips. "No?"

"Nope," he said, then kissed down her sternum, then to her abdomen. "Mrs. Everly Heart." He lifted her leg and hiked it over his shoulders. "I'm going to give your book heroes a run for their money."

"Oh, Mr. Heart . . . ," she said as he dipped down, causing her eyes to shut in bliss.

CHAPTER TWENTY

Austin, Texas
Six months ago
Word of the day: touchstone

Chris white knuckled the steering wheel of the rental and dodged cars through downtown Austin to the Chan family home. It had been a while since he'd driven in heavy traffic. Okay, so it wasn't that heavy, but it certainly wasn't the ten miles an hour speed limit of Heart Resort. He was out of practice.

He turned his GPS to low, now recognizing his surroundings. He was a mile away from the exit, which left him just a few minutes to practice his speech. His eyelids weighed like bricks; he'd caught the earliest flight out of Norfolk by a hair, at five thirty in the morning, and the rest of his body was running on pure adrenaline.

But he was intent on getting to Eden, on proposing to Eden. For real.

At a lull, Chris repositioned the rearview mirror so that he was looking at himself. He cleared his throat to practice his speech. "Eden. I don't know why it's taken me so long to say this . . . no, Puso, you have to sound more decisive and definitive." He tried once more. "Eden, when you told me your . . . I mean our news, I thought we should get married." Chris rolled his eyes. It was obvious who the writer was in the family.

Family. At the word, tears pricked his eyelids. He clicked on his photos on his phone (yes, he knew it was illegal, but he had to see it one more time) and stopped at the last one taken. It was a screenshot from yesterday, of his and Eden's last video chat. Eden was laugh-crying, holding up a pregnancy test, and in the little square in the bottom-right corner, Chris was covering his mouth with a hand in delight.

He was going to be a father.

"Take the exit," the GPS said.

"Oh crap!" Chris swerved to exit. He had to pay attention. That and know what the hell he was going to say. Because he was less than a mile from their house, and how was he going to put everything out there? That the last year had been amazing, and now he knew more than ever that what had been an arrangement between them had become more. "Eden, like Heart Resort, our relationship has grown, and I want to be there one hundred percent for you and our baby. I want to be your husband. Ugh." He shook his head. "How clinical can you be, Puso? Just tell her you love her."

That was the problem, though. They hadn't told each other they loved each other. Sure, they'd said it in front of other people but not intimately. They seemed to be coming at this through the back door.

And speaking of doors . . . Chris came upon Eden's childhood neighborhood. It was close to noon, and parents pushed strollers on the sidewalk; some were walking dogs.

Chris cut the engine when he got to the front of the Chan home. Eden should just be getting up; she had talked about doing some late-night writing.

He looked at himself in the rearview, fixed his hair, and noted another strand of gray. *There is love, and care, and friendship, and time.*

He smiled at his father's words to him all those Christmases ago. He had been right.

"Imagine, Dad. All at once—love, marriage, and baby. I know you had your doubts, but here we are," he whispered.

Girding himself, Chris popped out of the rental and made his way up the walkway. He rang the doorbell; the door opened to Mr. Chan. Chris hadn't yet been able to call him *Dad*, but perhaps after he proposed for real it would feel more comfortable.

"Oh, Christopher. You were fast."

"I got here as soon as I could." He drew the man closer to him and clapped him on the back. "Such great news, am I right? Is Eden upstairs?"

"Eden is . . ." He stepped back and examined Chris's face. "Yes, she is now. We just got home."

"Oh, great. Great." Though, even as he said it, Chris felt his smile diminish. Mr. Chan's face wasn't one of joy, nor was their conversation lining up. There was a disconnect. "I'll head on up?"

"Yes, of course. This is your home too, iho."

A sense of urgency overtook Chris, and he took the steps up by two. The house felt somber and still. His memory cycled back to his never-ending drive from Philly to DC when his parents had had their accident. To how every second had felt like twelve years, and by the time he'd gotten to the hospital, he'd been the last to arrive.

He pushed down his rising dread and infused optimism into his voice, and he reached Eden's open door, the first on the left. Her back was to him. "Surprise!" he announced.

His phone buzzed in his pocket just as Eden turned. She had her phone up to her ear. In her other hand she gripped a set of papers. "Chris." She startled, lowering the phone.

"Is that you in my pocket?" He approached her and inspected her crumpled expression, though he forced the smile to remain on his face. He pulled her into a hug, into an unexpected relief.

She's fine. She's fine. She's fine.

"I . . . I was just calling . . . to tell you that . . ." She covered her face in her hands and cried into his chest.

"Eden?" He tightened his hold.

"It's an ectopic pregnancy."

He held her by the shoulders so he could get a good look at her face. "What . . . what does that mean?"

"It means that the egg's in the fallopian tube. It's in the wrong place. I started spotting late last night, so I went into the ER."

Wrong place? Did pregnancies happen in the wrong place? "But the baby."

"No." She shook her head. "There is no baby. There will be no baby. It can't grow where it is. They gave me a shot. Medicine, so it doesn't grow and my tube won't rupture." She pressed the crumbled papers into his hand, though the words swam on the page. "I didn't have the heart to call from the hospital . . . I . . . I'm sorry. I just wanted to come back home. I couldn't even think."

Rupture. The information coming at Chris was so much, too much, that he couldn't process. "I'm here. You're okay now," were the only words that left his mouth. That was the priority after all—Eden's health. And keeping her safe. Taking care of her like she'd taken care of everyone else. And yet what lingered was the speech that was at the tip of his tongue. Love. Marriage. What had been the prospect of a baby. Of a real family. Of a dark cloud. Of a shoe dropping, as it always did.

It felt wrong to say anything now. The last thing he wanted was to pressure her. He was here to support, for her to lean on. There would be time. "It's going to be fine."

"I guess." She shut her eyes, and tears fell from her cheeks.

He forced a close-lipped smile onto his face. "Not guess. Will. You'll rest up; then you can come back home to the resort and the ocean air. You'll be good as new. And it will all be just like before."

"I guess," she whispered once more.

♡

An ectopic pregnancy.

Eden had been prepared for the possibility of miscarriage, being a health-care worker. Her sister, Josie, had also been a rainbow baby, born to their mother after years of secondary infertility and miscarriages. Eden had even considered not telling Chris she was pregnant until she was further along. Putting this kind of stress on their relationship, which was twisted and in a weird limbo, even if their romance had blossomed, was a risk. After all, they hadn't planned this pregnancy, even if, by using birth control, they knew that there was still a chance.

But they were in that stage in their relationship where the line items of their contract had become fuzzy. And she had been excited, though she hadn't realized how much until the two double lines had shown up on the home pregnancy test the day after her missed period. So much that she'd called Chris as soon as she'd washed her hands. She had, however, asked him not to breathe a word to his family; she'd wanted to wait.

Thank goodness.

Eden looked out the window over the sink as she did the dishes and snorted sardonically. She'd had a fake pregnancy, if one was being honest about it. Sort of like her marriage. Though she was definitely injected with real medication. "You'll be at a higher risk for ectopic in the future," the doctor had said, "but this won't preclude you from having another baby."

It had gotten her thinking: *Would she have another baby? And would it be with Chris?*

In the last four days, she'd had a couple of follow-up appointments with her doctor. She'd stiffened at every twinge in her belly, anticipating . . . something. But it didn't compare to the unease that had grown whenever she and her husband had been caught in a quiet moment.

It was bad enough she had to sit with her own thoughts; she didn't have the headspace for his.

Footsteps rattled the house, and she looked over her shoulder. Chris had just come down the stairs and positioned their suitcases by the door. Their flight back to North Carolina was in three hours, and she had just enough time to jump into the shower and say her goodbyes to her family, scattered someplace in the home. The plan was that she would be followed up by her nurse practitioner in the Outer Banks and simply wait.

"Hey." Chris came up from behind, wrapped his arms around her waist, and kissed her on the back of the neck. She inhaled sharply. It was involuntary, and she hoped that he didn't notice.

She knew she was grieving. And she understood that it was okay to grieve, even if she hadn't expected to—and perhaps grieve more because of that fact alone. What was bothering her more acutely was that her husband wasn't grieving. His Mr. Fix-It attitude had gone overboard, when all she wanted was to wallow, to be silent. To be alone.

"I promised my mom a phone call. Real quick, okay?" She offered him a smile to accompany the lie in her attempt to escape, already taking her phone out of her back pocket, shaking it as evidence, despite his unbelieving smile. "I'll be right back."

She padded up to Josie's room, dark and cluttered. It was a Bath & Body Works meets Sephora experience, with the various scents of her perfumes and lotions lingering in the air. Her sister was on her phone— of course—taking selfies and sending them over Snapchat. Normally Eden would have said something sarcastic about her silly poses, but the relief of being away from Chris was a gift in itself.

"Need something?" Josie asked.

"Um . . . ," Eden started, and the phone in her hand rang. Her jaw dropped at the sight of her mother's face on the caller ID. "God, how did she know?"

"Oh, she didn't," Josie remarked. "I just talked to her and said you were leaving soon."

Eden took the call, slumping into Josie's beanbag chair. "Hi, Mom."

"Eden." Her mother's voice was laced with concern. She'd called more in the last four days than she ever had in one week—in one month, even. "I hear you're going home today."

"Mm . . . hmm."

"How are you feeling?"

This question, too, had been asked too often since returning from the ER, and did anyone really want to know the answer? "I'm fine."

"I wish I could be there with you. I know . . . I know you're upset about the baby. I can hear it in your voice. It's okay to talk about it, anak."

"Okay, Ma."

"You can ask for help. I'm here for you." Her voice croaked.

"All right, talk to you soon. Love you." She couldn't take the angst of it all, the insinuation that she needed help—and needed her mother's help most of all—and she got off the phone. Then she grumbled, immediately remorseful.

If she had written this scene down, she would have lost half her readers. They would have said, *Eden should just say her feelings already.* And to them, she would have only been able to say, *But it's hard.*

Because this wasn't about her being mad about her mother but because she *could* have been a mother. That in those few hours, she had been looking forward to it. And where had that feeling come from? Most of all, what could she do about it now while in a marriage of convenience?

She looked up to Josie peering at her. "What?"

"You're not fine." Her usual baby-sister sarcasm had given way to sincerity. "You haven't even typed into your notes app, not once. That time when you had appendicitis, you were writing longhand on paper on the way to the operating room."

There was a knock on the door; then it popped open. Chris. "Sorry, but we've got to get on the road soon."

His expression was cautious, but Eden knew that below it was anticipation. From the increased buzzing of his phone and his resulting excitement, despite his attempt to not call or email back. Though she bet he still did, on the sly. Sometimes she caught him in a daze, most likely thinking of his newest issue with Willow Tree. The pressure of the resort had followed him all the way to Austin, and he was more than ready to return. At this very moment, he was clutching that damned phone like it was his lifeline.

The thing buzzed again. Of course it did, and it was a reminder of what normal usually was, which was the rigmarole of running a family business. Of looking like a couple. Of being everything to everyone, when she couldn't now sort out who she really was.

And she wasn't sure she could do that, go back to normal so fast. Even the couple part, because even if they had taken it to the next level, they'd never named it. They'd just become this couple who slept together but never declared their love.

There was too much pretending at Heart Resort.

"I'm not going," she said.

Chris's eyebrows plunged.

From behind her, Josie eased out of bed and brushed past them, closing the door. The silence was deafening.

"Eden?"

"I'm not ready to go home." Eden's voice came out with a croak.

"But why?"

"I need to recover here."

"But you can recover just as well on the resort."

She sorted through the reasons in her head, and she tried to dig deep into her motivations. This often happened when she was drafting a story; she'd get to know her characters only after rounds of revisions. Because it took her a long time to figure out what made her characters tick. So she spit the words out, much like how she pounded the keyboard, with a haphazard bang. "We don't want the same things." And in hearing herself speak, she kept going. "When we married, I thought we wanted the same things. And we did, when it came to money and career goals. I thought it would be complicated but not difficult. But now, now that we've slept together and everything is different, now I realize we don't want the same things. And I need some space—a week, maybe, so no one worries—so I can figure this out. But I can't go home with you yet. And you and I can't . . . we can't have sex anymore."

As if she'd punched him, Chris stepped back. "But." He paused and swallowed a breath. "Wait. Eden, the reason why I got here so early was to tell you that I wanted for us to be married. For real. I . . . I love you, Eden."

Eden had been waiting so long for those words. So long that she'd stopped hoping for them. "We've been married four years. And been intimate for a year. I believe you, Chris. I love you too. But would you have tried to make it real with me if I hadn't gotten pregnant?"

He opened his mouth, though he uttered not a peep.

"I don't hold this answer against you, Chris. This wasn't in your plans. And I commend you for coming and wanting to step up. You *are* a good man." She offered him a smile; she meant these words with all her heart. "But that's not good enough for me. Marrying and loving me for real means that you shouldn't have been convinced by some kind of obligation. Just for the record, I would have kept the baby, Chris. With or without you. Because I realize now that I do want babies someday. Maybe sooner than I think. But when I become a wife of love, it won't be because of someone's obligation. But of choice."

She reached out to clutch his hand, because she knew that her words were harsh. "I promise you didn't do anything wrong. This has, however, opened my eyes. We have less than a year left on our contract, and we have to do this right."

"But—"

"Chris. I'm staying."

His body seemed to slump. "What do I tell the others?"

"What reason did you give them for why you're here?"

"I said it had something to do with your family. That it was private."

"Thank you." She nodded. "Tell them I need to stay for the same reason."

Silence followed, while Eden waited. She waited for Chris to insist that he stay or insist that he'd fallen in love with her well beyond the pregnancy. Something to reassure her that they had truly ascended to the next level. Just one thing.

The buzz of his phone answered for him.

"It's our alarm to get on the road." His gaze was rooted to the ground.

She stepped in to hug him, heart breaking. "I'll see you soon."

CHAPTER TWENTY-ONE

Heart Resort's YouTube feed after day 3 teaser

HEA forever 1 day ago

I cannot wait to see the full documentary! I so hope they stay together!

Ashley Jones 1 day ago

Was it just me? Did you hear Eden quote Everly Heart?

Janis Kapur 1 day ago

I caught that too. Swoon. I stan another romance reader. #TeamEden for whatever goes down.

HEA forever 1 day ago

There was also talk about family. I feel like there are baby issues going on.

Ashley Jones 10 hours ago

Oh, you think? I looked through the website.
Only one of the brothers has kids.

HEA forever 8 hours ago

Pure speculation but I've got a feeling!

Lisa Harris 1 day ago

I think it's love. I wish them luck!

Phoebe Myer 12 hours ago

By the way they went into that tent and never
came out, the program might be working.

Best Skin Now 10 hours ago

Click here to achieve wrinkle free and supple
skin bestskinnow.co

♡

92 days until Chan-Puso contract expiration
Word of the day: burgeon

"Home sweet home." Chris entered Tanggap's front door and stepped
out of his shoes at the entrance, dragging his backpack. The tiny house
was a sight for sore eyes, and the AC was a welcome relief. He unloaded
his gear, yearning for a shower. This was the last full day of his and
Eden's couples retreat program. After their couples yoga session—and
he would need it—and their final Couples Talk tomorrow morning, it
would be back to real life.

But when he turned, he realized that Eden hadn't followed him in.
"Eden?"

A beat later, she entered the threshold with her things. She was crying while holding a cell phone up to her ear.

Oh no. His first thought—she was belatedly regretting what had happened last night.

Dammit. They shouldn't have kissed, shouldn't have delved back into being physically intimate. How irresponsible could he have been? Things were already precarious between them, and they'd both been vulnerable.

His second thought—why was she holding a phone?

A laugh threatened to bubble out of him. He wanted to kiss her for breaking the rules as he had.

That was, if she hadn't been crying.

"Is everything okay?" He mouthed.

She pushed the phone into his hand. The screen was dark.

She threw her hands around his neck and kissed him, full and hard on the lips. It stilled all his thoughts and brought him back to this morning's bliss. He had woken up a few minutes before her and hadn't believed, as he'd watched her, that she was in the crook of his arms. That with all that had happened between them—they'd found their way back to one another.

"That was Paloma." She settled back onto her heels.

"Oh." He recalibrated his thoughts. "Your agent."

She nodded and paced, the fingers of her right hand pressed against her lips.

"Eden?"

"Josie was managing everything while I've been out of the net, sort of." She looked up and gritted her teeth.

"Go on."

"And she got a message this morning for me to call Paloma back. We did a three-way-call thing with my editor." Eden halted and faced him. "They'd made the announcement about the movie, you know?"

He nodded.

"They put my book under promotion. And it made the *New York Times*."

"Wait." He shook his head. He was hearing things. They were both exhausted. "*The* list."

"Yes." Her eyes rounded in glee, and she started to scream.

"Oh my God. Oh my God!" He picked her up and spun her around. "This is huge!"

It wasn't just about the *Times*—though that alone was tremendous. But this was a lifetime goal she'd talked about time and again, though with a caveat that it would be an almost impossible endeavor. He set her back down and wiped the tears off her cheeks. They were both dusty from breaking down their campsite, and she smelled like sun. Her cheeks were reddened from their hike yesterday, and wisps of her hair framed her face. She was so beautiful, just like this. He wanted to keep this smile on her face. "I'm so happy for you. You did it."

She looked up at him. "*We* did it. That book. That book was the one. Don't you remember?"

He shook his head. His wife had written so many books in the last five years. And with her publishing schedule, she was churning out books in a way that when one was published, she was already two books down.

Still he thought back to *One Plus One Equals Me and You*. Published about two years ago . . .

She tugged on his hands.

"It was the book I was taking notes on when I was snooping outside your bedroom door that New Year's Eve . . ." Her eyebrows lifted.

Oh. *Oh.* "That was the book?"

"Yeah. Remember? Marriage of convenience, marriage in trouble?" She waved the air in front of her. "Anyway, *we* did it. You and me. And I don't know how to thank you." Eden's gaze was searing.

I know how. His mind took off in what she could do with her hands, in what she'd done with her hands on his body last night. But

Chris swallowed back his sinful thoughts. This was her moment—*get your mind out of the gutter, Puso.* "Eden, this was all you."

"No." She fisted the sides of his shirt. "Without you, without us, I wouldn't have had the time, the ability to write that book."

Her words were like water on embers—they extinguished the lust, and what was left over was truth. She was, in part, correct. He would never presume to take credit for anything she'd accomplished, but logic was king. They'd married out of convenience so she could achieve her aspirations and so he could make Heart Resort into something big and meaningful.

It was sobering. Were all relationships like this in part? Transactional? When his parents used to say that they were partners, had that meant their love had become a series of *what can you do for me* expectations? And now that she'd gotten what she wanted, what did it mean now?

But he shook himself out of his meandering thoughts. "We have to celebrate. We have to get everyone for dinner."

"We can't. We're not supposed to contact anyone." Her expression was sheepish. "Supposed to. Though the news will come out pretty soon. We can celebrate with everyone tomorrow."

"One activity. One Couples Talk. Then it's home."

"Home." She looked down. "Right. And I wanted to say I know we have to talk about last night. But . . . I just want to sit with it a little. You know? Enjoy today. We have time."

He nodded, hope filling him. And while he wasn't sure what exactly that would mean for them, he was fine to sit with things too. To be all right with this moment was good enough. "Whatever you wish, Miss *New York Times* Bestseller."

She kissed him on the cheek. And with a final squeal, she grabbed her toiletry bag from her backpack and slipped into the bathroom.

It was only after her shower started, and when Chris was unpacking in a contented haze, that he belatedly realized the gravity of what had just transpired.

Damn. His wife was a *New York Times* bestseller. He had to do something special. Perhaps a nice dinner. Candlelight beachside, maybe, with her most favorite food?

When he heard Eden singing—it was the cutest thing, really, how she was so out of tune—he dug out his phone from the planter, laughing once more that they'd both bought a burner phone. He pulled up his notes app and started brainstorming, then realized he couldn't do this without outside help.

He bit his bottom lip and texted the only person who could make magic happen.

Chris:

Bea, I need help

Bea:

Who's this?

Chris snapped a selfie.

Bea:

Kuya, what are you doing texting me. This is not allowed

You can't put me in this situation!

Chris:

I need help.

Bea:

I can't be an accessory to any of your antics. Delete delete

Chris:

Eden's a NYT

Bea:

What? What's that? Is she ok?

Chris barked out a laugh.

Chris:

New York Times Bestseller dork

Bea:

OMG! And shut up Kuya Dork

Chris:

I want to do a dinner.

Make it special.

Bea:

Well that's easy.

Dinner for two on the deck, bubbly, view of the water, instrumental 90's r&b

Chris:

How do you know this?

Bea:

Have you never looked at her Instagram?

Good lord. Here's the link

Chris lifted his feet onto the ottoman. He clicked on the link to what Tammy, his PR, would say was a heavily curated feed. It had a distinct color scheme and a similar filter on all the photos, and it was mostly about books. Every once in a while, Eden had posted a faraway shot of herself or a book that she'd held up so that only her eyes showed, so intent on keeping some kind of privacy.

Admittedly, he didn't keep up on her socials because they were Everly Heart's.

231

A photo caught his eye; he recognized it as the view outside their bedroom window, where her desk was situated: *Having a time getting my words in. Wish me luck!* Under the post were dozens of comments. Then, another familiar view, of her sitting on the front porch, with her face turned away, holding peonies. Behind her was the Heart Resort logo next to the doorbell. The caption in this one: *Peonies are my most favorite flowers—they had a rare arrangement in town, and I couldn't resist. Isn't that the best? They were in my wedding bouquet. Maybe these flowers will help me grab words.*

Then, another photo of his garden and him bent over at the waist. The caption: *Here's Mr. Heart. Is there anything more sexy than a man in the garden? Nope.*

His cheeks warmed that she'd been watching him. She thought he was sexy? Or was this just Everly Heart content?

Chris:

I don't remember peonies in her bouquet.

Bea:

Of course you don't Kuya, but I do.

Aaaand I bet I know where to find a stem. And boba.

Chris:

Boba?

Bea:

You're hopeless!

They continued to chat, with Beatrice sending him a link of dresses for him to choose from and the menu for tonight.

A flashing screen kept snagging his attention—it was Eden's phone. She had set it down on the ottoman, and her texts were blowing up. The initials *MLS* jumped out in the notifications.

He did a double take, and all at once, he felt his breath leave his lungs. There would be only one reason for all these emails and notifications. It had to be about a house. And yet Eden had mentioned losing that contract to another buyer. Was this for another home? And was it for an investment, or for her?

Yesterday, Chris had said that he wanted her to have everything she wanted. But now he wished he'd asked exactly what that meant.

♡

"Please be gentle," Chris said as he and Eden crossed over Hinga's threshold. He'd meant for it to be a joke, and Eden had responded with a little laugh, but now, seeing the wide-open area that led out to a balcony, infused with the sounds of instrumental music and the crashing waves outside, it felt intimidating.

First, because he had no idea how to yoga.

Second, because the space was spectacular. The floors, the decor—all the little things that he hadn't put value on in defense of the bottom line had created the most perfect atmosphere. It hearkened back to all the activities of the last three days that had run smoothly, down to Chet's decision to employ Kit despite Chris's reservations. So seamless had the transitions been from day to day that Chris's focus had, truly, been his relationship with Eden.

It was the staff that had been spectacular.

Sal's words returned to him: *Not complaints. Just . . . suggestions, for a better Heart Resort experience for employees.*

"Welcome, Chris and Eden. Are you ready for your session?" Darla Puri, the resort's yoga instructor, padded inside. She was barefoot and carrying two blankets, foam blocks, and straps. She set the gear down and handed them their microphones. Steps behind her were Jessie and Gil with the camera.

On his brother's face was the distinct smile of someone who was clearly going to enjoy watching him struggle.

But Chris couldn't focus on that with all the equipment and now with being recorded. "Whoa. Look at all the gear. Are we using all that?"

"I'm so excited." Eden left his side and stood on the mat. She waved him over. "C'mon, babe."

"Have you practiced yoga in the past, Chris?" Darla asked. Her voice was soothing, though not enough to lull him into thinking that this activity would be easy. He wouldn't be fodder for the camera.

"Um, no."

"I think you'll find that practicing with your wife will be a great experience." She gestured to the mat. When he joined Eden, Darla said, "This session is not meant to challenge you with poses. The purpose here is to deepen your connection. Since you hiked and camped yesterday, my assumption is that you will be able to do these stretching poses without issue. But"—she lifted a finger—"should you feel uncomfortable in any of these poses, by all means, speak up. Let's do some individual stretching first."

The song on the playlist changed on cue, and Darla led them through some stretching, which Chris executed without trouble. Darla was right; with Eden next to him as a guide, he felt less self-conscious. He even allowed his imagination to wander, to the little details that would make their dinner celebration tonight. Then, his thoughts slid to the MLS notification he had inadvertently read, though he pushed it away—Eden had always been transparent about these things; if he needed to know, she would tell him.

"Now, Chris and Eden, sit cross-legged and back-to-back . . . good," Darla encouraged with a melodic cadence. He felt his wife's back against his, warm from the stretching. He did a little shimmy, and she giggled. "Raise your arms together." Darla demonstrated.

He followed, and with Eden's arms pressed against his, they lifted their arms like they were in a dance. Then, as one, they tipped side to side in the side-bend position.

Chris was feeling more coordinated now. He didn't even mind the camera's presence. Just knowing that Eden had him and would nudge him into the correct position if needed was enough that he could breathe into the poses as instructed by Darla.

"Now for the seated forward bend and backbend," Darla continued. "Eden, raise your arms and bend backward. Chris, you can support her by bending at the waist and reaching out your hands to the front of the mat."

Eden's weight increased as she bent back, but as he folded at the waist, Chris stiffened at the discomfort it caused. He wasn't as flexible as he'd thought. A groan threatened to escape his lips, but Eden eased. It was as if she knew he couldn't take much more, and while he still felt the deep stretch of the pose, the pressure against his back was a reminder that she'd been there all these years to push him and to make him better.

"Wonderful. Now Chris's turn," Darla prompted.

Knowing how challenging the stretch had been for him, Chris bent back slowly. Only then did it dawn on him that when it had been his turn earlier, Eden had known to stop stretching when Chris had resisted. It hearkened back to what Kit had challenged them to do on the first day of the retreat: to listen to one another.

At this moment, he and Eden were in tune, but how had he been the first four and a half years of their marriage? Had he listened to her? Had he listened to others when it came to Heart Resort?

Chris resolved that he would focus his stretch not on how far he could go but on how comfortable Eden was. He lengthened his body in increments, testing not only Eden but himself. And he tried to pick up any resistance, any objection.

But Eden was flexible; she was strong.

He knew that, of course. He'd known that all along, but in this intimate way where she was literally holding him up, he now wondered: Had he done the same? Had he been an equally solid partner?

He remembered their argument at the ropes course. He'd said to her that he couldn't read her mind, and she'd said *you should try*.

He slackened with regret; he eased his stretch. He thought back to all the years, all the rough times, like when he'd been mending his relationship with Brandon, or experiencing bouts of sadness when his parents had died.

How much had he placed upon Eden to shoulder because she was willing, and what kind of support had he been to her at the worst time of their marriage, when she'd had the ectopic pregnancy?

"Feel that stretch. Now ease back." Darla's soothing voice brought him back to the present. "Now, face one another, and remain cross-legged. Reach out for each other's forearms."

Facing Eden, Chris saw his wife with new eyes. With more appreciative eyes. His dad had once told him that he learned something new about his mother all the time, and Chris hadn't understood that. They'd been together almost thirty-five years and barely left each other's side.

I get it now, Dad.

With that simple stretch, Chris felt what Eden was to both families and to him: the rock, the glue. And he'd taken her for granted.

An apology was ready to leap from his tongue.

Eden winked at him, and it snapped him out of his thoughts. "You okay?" she mouthed.

He nodded sincerely. Now he was, with him properly schooled by yoga.

Eden reached forward and grasped his forearms. Her skin was soft against his. Her eyes fluttered upward to him, and a smile graced her lips.

"Eden, now lean back," Darla instructed.

Eden pulled Chris toward her, and he stretched forward. His first inclination was to resist. He'd been in this position just a few minutes before. He knew that he would come to a wall of discomfort. But just before he got there, Eden halted.

"Now, Chris, inhale, then exhale." Darla circled them. "That's it. Now, Eden, pull him deeper into the stretch. Yes. Trust her, Chris. She's got you."

Three words. *She's got you.* Tears pricked his eyelids, though he blinked them away. He didn't know where they had come from—a place that was deep seated and rarely traversed.

"Back to center now. Chris, it's your turn."

Chris pulled Eden gently, and this time, *this time*, Chris made it a point to listen even better. Like really listen. He pulled her and clued in to her breathing, to when it hitched, and that was when he stopped. He tightened his grip as she exhaled into the stretch.

He wouldn't let go, like she hadn't let go of him.

But they would have to soon, wouldn't they?

CHAPTER
TWENTY-TWO

Eden had needed another shower because couples yoga had stretched her emotional limits. And she hadn't really broken out into a sweat— she'd expended more energy writing three thousand words in a single day. But Darla's was a forty-minute session of learning, a yoga practice when every one of her hot buttons was pushed. Each pose had questioned the roller-coaster path of her life.

Because she was a *New York Times* bestseller. She was *there*, in the place where so many authors aspired to be. It was absolutely true that making lists didn't equate to success, nor did it guarantee that the book was any good, and yet . . . yet it was a pinnacle milestone.

Was Eden happy? Absolutely. She'd been moved to tears. The royalties alone. Every dollar counted for when she exited this phase in her life. But that was exactly it. Eden was living through a phase in her life—that included the bestselling status, the marriage, the connection—that was soon to end. And she wasn't sure now if that was something she wanted to happen. She'd come into this retreat hoping to ease this transition out of the marriage, and now, she wanted to fight for it.

She wiped condensation off the bathroom mirror, and her face came into a hazy view. Her skin was flushed from the shower, but in truth she'd been flushed since her rendezvous with Chris in their tent last night. And in true Eden fashion, above the bestseller stuff, a slideshow of images of her and Chris had kept replaying throughout the day, in full surround sound despite everything in her head.

The idea that a cold shower could smother a body's insatiable need? Totally a myth.

Eden decided on her plan: She was going to go out there and talk to Chris about last night. Earlier, she hadn't been ready, verklempt from the bestseller announcement. But she was ready now; she was going to ask him how he felt about her. She was going to put herself on the line as he'd done months before and hope that it wasn't too late.

And if she *was* too late . . .

She watched the blood drain from her face, and she sipped in a breath . . . then the original plan would continue. She'd move on with making an offer on the house, and she would be mature and walk away from the Puso family.

Eden looked around the bathroom and realized she'd forgotten to bring her clothes in. "Ugh."

She would have to walk out only in her towel. Though the cameras were off, the filming on hold until after dinnertime, her husband was out there, and she was fully naked underneath her towel.

With a hand on the doorknob, she took a breath. She stepped into the kitchen area to find it empty. "Chris?"

Eden was met with silence. She padded to the living room and looked up at the loft. "Hello?"

Still, nothing.

Curious. Chris hadn't said he was going anywhere. She turned to the kitchen table, where she'd left her clothes, and on it was a note in Chris's handwriting. *Check the closet and see you at 6 p.m.*

She opened the only closet in the house. Hanging from the rod was a long white dress with printed flowers at the skirt. She checked the tag, and sure enough: Beachy. The dress was her size.

Her heart trilled. What did he have planned? And when had he planned this? This was all so novel worthy.

She changed right there, on the spot. She dropped her towel and slipped into the dress. It was sumptuous on her skin. She looked at herself in the narrow closet mirror—the dress was a perfect fit.

Antsy at ten minutes before the hour, Eden grabbed her phone—now riddled with texts from her editor and her agent and congratulations from Josie and Paige. She could only imagine the notifications on social media, and on her real phone, that she would have to respond to soon.

Worry threatened to burst through at how much work was waiting for her at the end of this retreat. But she pushed it down, instead moving to text Beatrice.

Eden:

This dress is gorgeous

Beatrice:

????

Eden?

Eden:

Yep. Don't tell anyone that I have a phone

Beatrice:

OMG you two are unbelievable

Eden:

What?

Beatrice:

NVM. Don't thank me. Thank that husband of yours

He picked it out

Eden:

What is this about?

Beatrice:

I plead the fifth! It's a miracle that you're not wearing khakis right now

Eden:

Wait. What do you mean we're both unbelievable? Have you spoken to Chris?

Beatrice:

I can't with the both of you. Don't you need to be somewhere?

Buh-bye!

Love you.

Sure enough, it was five to six. Eden set down her phone, grabbed her sandals next to the door, and exited Tanggap.

She squinted against the sun, now casting a gorgeous golden hue all around the resort. It was breathtaking, and for a beat, what she felt was this familiar comfort of being home. She'd felt a tinge of it on the drive back from the campsite, rolling across the land bridge into Heart Resort.

Then as she blinked, the shape of her husband sharpened. Chris was walking her direction and came to a halt at the bottom of the stairs. "Wow," he gasped.

Her heart skittered headlong into what she knew showed up as a blush on her face.

"You're not so bad yourself," she said flippantly to brush off her nervousness. The man was so handsome it hurt, and when she walked down and took his hand, she felt lucky.

For so long she'd believed only in the power of will, in what she could do. How she could move things with hard work. She'd grown up since then, of course, and learned that family dynamics, societal expectations, and history had a great deal to do with what a person accomplished too.

But was there more at play? What if she hadn't taken that video call from her family and she hadn't found herself in the hallway inadvertently listening to Chris's conversation?

A million decisions and coincidences had led to this moment.

He held her hand as they walked along the sand, and the stroll felt especially intimate. She looked around; there was no sign of a camera or Gil or Jessie. This was . . . something. "We're alone."

"Are we?" He gave her the side-eye.

She peered at him. "What did you have to do to make this happen?"

"I told them we were turning in. And since they were so exhausted from the camping trip . . ."

Eden giggled.

"What?"

"I have a feeling they didn't mind having some personal time to themselves."

"Me too, but I'm trying not to think about it. One thing at a time."

His words took a double meaning, and Eden nodded. "So, where are we going?"

"Oh, I don't know, just thought it would be a great time for a walk." Mischief reflected in his eyes.

"Well, I love the dress. Thank you."

"I thought it would be fitting."

"For what?"

"To celebrate you." He gestured forward to Hapag's deck, which was lit up by lights. Instrumental music reached Eden's ears, and the tune transported her back to elementary school and singing at the top of her lungs as she daydreamed of the boy she was going to marry.

"Is that Boyz II Men?" She picked up her step, though it was useless in the sand. "What did you do?"

"Just a little something." He led her up the stairs to a lone table set up in the middle of the deck. A bottle chilled on a sideboard with two champagne flutes. And at one of the two place settings was a singular peony.

Her throat grew thick with nostalgia as she picked the flower up and brought it to her nose. He'd remembered. "Oh, Chris. You did all this? How?"

"Let's just say that you're not the only one who's resourceful."

She tilted her head as a belated thought came upon her, from her and Beatrice's conversation. "I don't know why I didn't think you'd have a burner phone too."

He gritted his teeth. "Are you mad?"

She didn't hesitate. "No. I'm not allowed to be mad. I did the same thing." There was more in her head, but she couldn't put a finger on it, and she didn't want to, honestly, right this second, with this perfect night.

She walked over to the railing to take in the deck view of the sound; it was her favorite. While others preferred the view from the north of the peninsula, where the pier was located, she liked to watch the lights of the traffic on Highway 12, across Bonner Bridge. She relished the idea that everyone had a life, had a motivation, had a story in them.

A warm hand grazed her back. Chris appeared from her right side. He fingered a lock of her hair, still damp from the shower, and trailed a hand down her shoulder, then took her hand. He kissed it, eyes rising to hers.

A rush of just everything started from her toes and filled her. It was the romantic setting, taken right out of her playbook of wishes. And with the sun reflecting off of Chris's dark-brown eyes, Eden wished that this moment would never end. That this was their reality. And that finally she would have her happily ever after.

She shut her eyes for a beat and committed the moment to memory—and pushed down the rising tide of doubt that had begun to creep up. In every story, there was a dark moment, the lowest point, and she wished that they were well past that. That they were on the long road of resolution before the final, beautiful epilogue.

The sound of a bell took her attention, and she turned to Chef Castillo pushing the cart with the chilling bottle. On a second cart, pushed by another Heart Resort employee, were plates of hors d'oeuvres.

"Thank you," she said to Chef, who returned a genuine smile before she headed back to the dining room.

Chris took the bottle out of the ice—it was nonalcoholic champagne—and shook it, aiming it toward the water. The cork popped; Eden giggled at the surprise and at Chris's rush to pour the drink into their glasses. He handed her a flute and raised his. "To your happily ever after."

She clicked her glass against it. "To the HEA."

And one day truly getting it, she finished in her head.

♡

Was it possible to be drunk without having a drop of alcohol in one's system? Because whatever Eden was feeling inside was as bubbly as the faux champagne. She was light on her toes as she and Chris walked back from their romantic dinner of tiny platters of her most favorite foods, miniature bowls of her cherished desserts, and a delicious cup of boba, all topped by an easy conversation under a star-filled night.

The mood was still festive as they burst into Tanggap. Chris opened the windows so the wind blew through, and the sound of the lively surf became their background music. And as true as they were to themselves, and to the long week they'd had, they both slumped into the couch at the same time.

Chris pretended to snore, and Eden snorted in laughter.

"What a day," he said.

"What a week." She turned to look at him and tucked her feet underneath her. "Ropes course, paddleboarding, hiking, overnight camping, and couples yoga in four days."

"Yeah. It's hard to fathom." He rubbed a hand behind his head.

"Back to reality, I guess." She opened her mouth to say more, because if there was a time to let him know how confused she felt, it would be now. Because everything about tonight had given her hope, as if they'd transcended their problems, even if they hadn't talked about them.

And they still needed to.

"This was an amazing night, Chris. All the details, from the dress, to the dinner—"

"Bea helped—"

"Still. It meant a lot." She reached for his hand. "And added to last night, I feel like we're going back down a road. So we do need to talk about *things*." She swallowed against the real words. *Pregnancy. Lost pregnancy.* Words that were still tough to say. "We can't make the mistake of jumping into something when we know the consequences."

"I know." He rubbed her hand with a thumb. "There's so much about that time that I wish I could take back. That I wish I could redo. That I wish I could have said back then."

"What do you mean?" This wasn't what she'd expected to hear from Chris. He oftentimes skirted tough personal topics, though she, too, had shied away. Sometimes that time in their lives had felt small and inconsequential; she hadn't been sure where to place the loss, especially in perspective of the Pusos' loss and even her mother's absence. But sometimes, their loss—the collective loss of the pregnancy and their intimacy—was the chasm that had kept her from softening to Chris all the way.

"That I'm so sorry, Eden. I'm so, so sorry. I didn't know how to help after the ectopic pregnancy. I didn't know how to feel, because I wanted to be strong for you. But I still left when I shouldn't have."

"I told you to go."

He shook his head. "When you said at the obstacle course a couple of days ago that I should have tried to read your mind, you were right. We knew each other well enough by then. There was no excuse. Instead, I dived into my head and made myself think that by taking you here to the resort, we would go back to normal, whatever that was. And when you finally returned to Heart Resort, you seemed it."

"I wasn't."

"I know that now. I wasn't either."

"You weren't either?" She peered at him. "You certainly didn't show it. It was back to work for you."

"It's sometimes the only thing I know how to do, because it's something I can do well. But I was sad too. I lost you. I lost us. But I didn't feel like I could say anything because I didn't know if I had the right. Because I should have been there for you, Eden. I shouldn't have come back. Most of all, I should have told you then, and well before you were pregnant, that you had become . . . the most important person in my life. When you said we were over—"

"I was scared, Chris. It had gone so well; we were in this happy place. It was friendship with benefits but with the freedom of not keeping it a secret, but when that pregnancy test turned up positive, I was faced with this truth that it wasn't in our plan. I didn't want you caught up in that when it wasn't what you signed up for."

"Eden." He halted her. "Our marriage might be of convenience, but it was never fake. I signed up for it all. I would have been there for you. I wanted to be there for you. I said I loved you. And I meant it."

"I know you meant it. And I loved you too. But the timing of that, Chris. It felt muddled. Babies should not be the reason to marry. In fact, I already knew that you would step up and be the best father our baby could have." She shook her head. This conversation was running away from her. "I want babies in the future. But this conversation isn't about babies. It's the fact that we hadn't talked about it as a possibility. Here we were, doing some real couple things, when we weren't one to begin with."

"How can you say that?"

"Can *you* honestly say that you can sort it out? We're so good at pretending that I can't tell my own feelings apart. We can't even get it together for one Couples Talk with Kit."

"I mean, Kit is pretty amazing. You can't put one over on Kit." Chris snorted.

"Honestly I want Kit's number after all of this, because I have never been this gratefully confused in all my life."

"We are a lot, right?"

"I could probably write a book about this. No, never mind. They always say never to write a plot that could be solved with one conversation."

"And yet." He winced.

She laughed. "If only we were as self-aware as book characters." But her laughter died in her throat. The truth of the matter was that they weren't done with this conversation. "Chris?"

"Yeah?"

"I don't want to make the same mistake twice, with us."

"Me either." He wrapped an arm around her shoulder, and she settled in. "But with all we've done, in this retreat, I want to ask you . . ."

She looked at him questioningly. "What?"

"Can we make this work?"

"And forget the contract?"

"Yes. Forget the contract. Tear it up. Stay married. Give this a real go."

"Really? But the house . . ." She knew it sounded silly, putting up the barely there possibility of a home against the realness of being with Chris, but it was the easiest to communicate. Her body had clenched, like the time when her editor had given her a nine-page editorial letter in single space when she'd thought that her draft was actually in good shape. There was work to be done between them. The mental shift alone . . . "And the way you're so stuck on work. My family, who I need to spend time with—"

"How about this? How about one step at a time." He gently swiped his thumb across her cheek, diminishing all her overwhelming feelings. It was so comforting, this act, that she snuggled closer. "Both parties will remove the contractual deadline from their speech and begin dating within the marriage."

"No contract," she whispered, the idea sinking in. "Both parties will become . . . a couple."

"The couple can do couple things."

"The couple can ignore PDA rules." Eden bit her lip at the possibility of intimacy being accessible. They could get back to the ease of touching, of lovemaking. She shifted on the sofa so she faced him fully. "We don't have to do that part slowly, do we?"

He grinned, eyes dropping to her lips and neckline as a hand gripped her waist. "Not unless you want to."

Chris was so close. She couldn't think, except to anticipate picking up where they had left off last night. "Multiple steps at once. I'm great at multitasking."

"That I know." Leaning forward, he caught her bottom lip in a kiss, a move so sensual her core temperature ratcheted up ten degrees, sure to melt the clothes she was wearing.

"I . . . I should take off this dress," she managed to say as he kissed the underside of her neck. "It's so pretty, and I'm hot and—"

"You undoubtedly are, and I agree you should take it off before I tear it off."

Oh gosh. Her body gave just a little. "I'll be back." Then, in a Herculean feat, she stood and made her way to the bathroom, first grabbing her clothes on the kitchen table.

Only for the zipper to stick when she tried to remove the dress.

"No." She struggled against the zipper, and as the seconds passed, trepidation settled around her.

Was the zipper telling her something? That perhaps she shouldn't be jumping into bed with Chris? That they were in over their heads, because they still had issues to work through?

She shook her head. *No. You're thinking too much.*

As seconds passed, it became clear that she needed Chris's help to get out of this dress. But before she opened the door, she took a moment, a breather, to lay her forehead against the wood.

The cool surface was a reprieve. She could do this. She could go out there and be with him, and enjoy him, and not fall into this world of angst.

She opened the door to her husband, who had changed out of his clothes and was now in his pajama bottoms and shirtless. His expression was wary. It touched Eden; apparently they were both going through their self-talk.

"Could you?" She turned. "My zipper's stuck. I can't seem to reach it."

Relief played across his features. "Oh, sure." He placed a hand against the dress, the pressure making her gasp. "The fabric's caught. Hold on." He started to perform what felt like surgery on the zipper, first lifting it up and then slowly working it down. "We're going to have to lodge a Beachy complaint," he remarked with sarcasm.

"You can be in charge of that."

He snorted. "I wouldn't dare." His voice softened. "Besides, you're stunning in it."

Eden bit her cheek at the compliment, at the possibility of soon being with this man. Impatience threatened to burst through, and she was seconds away from finding scissors so he could do the job already.

Finally, she heard him sigh. "There."

She felt the cool air against her exposed back, and goose bumps blossomed across her skin, but she didn't dare move away. She couldn't, with anticipation bursting from her ragged breath.

He didn't move either. As always, he was leaving it to her. So she looked over her shoulder and lowered one spaghetti strap. "Undress me, Chris. Put your hands on me."

"Yes, ma'am." He swept the right spaghetti strap off her shoulder, and the dress dropped, leaving her in her panties. Stepping closer, he cupped her breasts from behind and trailed a kiss from her ear down to her shoulder, sending delicious shivers throughout her body.

She pressed back against him and gasped at the evidence of his own excitement. And as his hand splayed across her abdomen, she became ravenous to complete what they had started the night before. Turning, she anticipated touching him too.

She pressed her lips against his warm chest. His heart was pounding at a fast clip, and it made her smile.

"Truth," he said, leaning down to nibble at her earlobe and kiss her behind the ear. "I think of you like this. All the time."

His voice was an aphrodisiac. She ran a thumb around the waist of his pj's, lowering it slightly. The temptation was so strong to shut him up by taking him in her hands—too strong—but Eden wanted to wait, to make it last. To savor it.

"Yeah?" She kissed his Adam's apple. "Tell me more."

"Before the camping trip, it had been almost a hundred and eighty days since we made love, and I yearned for it every day." His hands guided hers so that they both took off his bottoms, showing proof, indeed. "Even on the days when you're driving me up the wall. And especially on days when you were away, when I couldn't even see you." He led her up the stairs to the bed, fluffy with an extra comforter laid down.

With the lights on and the windows open, Eden's senses were on high. But in all the ways they'd pretended in their years of marriage, Eden wanted to have her eyes wide open. There would no longer be pretending; herein would begin their full accountability. This was a choice they were making. Good or bad.

CHAPTER TWENTY-THREE

People always wanted something from Chris. A day had yet to pass when someone hadn't needed advice, a favor, or to lodge a complaint. He was a transactional figure, the bad cop, the unfeeling, the logical. Never the one who needed support.

For most of his life, he'd accepted this image contentedly. To be seen as the strong one came with its advantages too. It gave him confidence when people complimented him, when they verbalized his competence, which fed into his image, creating this vicious cycle that was both a curse and a blessing.

Eden had always seen past the facade. It was in her empathy as an RT, as an author. And she never hesitated in pushing him. From the moment they had entered Heart Resort as man and wife, she hadn't stood for any of his crap.

But their contract had been a crutch. It had enabled him to run away when he shouldn't have. When he should no longer. What had he been so afraid of? He couldn't imagine a life without Eden by his side. He'd wanted exactly this: this intimacy, this closeness, kissing her, naked, with his emotions laid bare.

"Never again." He made love to her, savoring the friction of skin against skin. "We can never stop."

She gently bit on his shoulder, making him hiss.

"I mean it." He slowed, hips lifting and lowering. "This is it, Eden."

"Not yet," she whispered. "Wait." She flipped their positions so she could straddle him, and what had been a sincere moment flipped into lust. His brain took a back seat, with his body ramping up with anticipation.

Above him, she was so damn sexy that he forgot everything about anything else. He was woozy with desire.

Except he was lying. It wasn't lust and desire.

"Eden." He held her hips still before they resumed lovemaking so he could think, so he could say what he regretted not saying earlier. She looked down upon him in confusion, so he brushed her hair away from her face. "I love you."

"I know you love me."

Love was a word said without reservation in their family. When you lost people, you quickly learned how important it was to say it or hear it. There was no such thing as too much.

Saying it was also part of their ruse.

But this was different.

"No, I *love* you," he said softly. "And I want you, like this, everywhere, with me. It's why I sometimes get upset when you're away. Or when you give me the silent treatment. And how I need you when I don't have the right. I wish . . . I wish we had a shot at love without the contract, that we never had to think twice. Because what I feel is real."

Her eyes watered, and . . . something inside him tore. He had been going through this . . . transition, whatever it was, with a light touch. He'd known about the days counting down. The days were engrained. But he'd had to treat it that way. Business, right? Just business. But now, looking at Eden. His wife.

His.

Wife.

He'd said that term in his head. But did he in fact know what it meant? Because how much time had they wasted playing this game, denying their emotions?

"You mean it?" Her eyes glassed over with tears. "Me over work."

"Always." Chris was besieged with hope—it was that easy, wasn't it? They simply had to agree. "We're all about choice here at Heart Resort. I choose you." He kissed Eden's eyes to keep her tears at bay. "Do you choose me?"

"I choose you. I love you, Chris."

He kissed her fervently, now on a mission. He wanted to give her everything. Her happily ever after, especially in this bed. Spurred on by his need to satisfy her, and with the sound of the wind, he laid her on her back and kissed down her body, bringing her to climax. Then he tugged to spoon her, her most favorite thing, and they made love until he was absolutely sure that she would no longer have tears to shed.

CHAPTER
TWENTY-FOUR

Once Upon a Reality Show podcast
Season four, episode twenty-five

Welcome, everyone! On today's episode, we have who we consider *the* expert on reali-dramas, Sage Littleton. We're going to dissect our most favorite shows and find out when they turn the corner and take a nose-dive. But before we do, as promised, we wanted to keep you abreast of a new show coming up in exactly a week.

Is *Heart Resort Exposé* on your radar, dear friends? It's blowing up. The teasers they've posted are on fire, and the married couple, Chris and Eden, are exactly the flawed characters we're looking for.

Did you hear me say *married*? Yes, married. Forget hookup reali-drama, this show has higher stakes and definitely will be more delicious to watch. I've already set my alarm, and so should you. Word on the podcast airwaves is that this exposé was in response to another resort's dare. So it makes me wonder: What's up with these competing resorts, and is that where the conflict really lies?

Yes, friends, get your fingers working, and do your research, and I'll do mine. And in a week, make sure to tune in so we can discuss it all over a glass of wine or a pound of chocolate.

Subscribe to us if you haven't, and listen to us on your favorite podcatcher. And here we go to my conversation with Sage Littleton.

♡

91 days until Chan-Puso contract expiration
Word of the day: effulgent

Eden hadn't been able to stop looking at Chris. Not while getting dressed this morning or while making the bed from its chaotic previous state from their night's escapades or while packing up their things for home.

And especially not after he'd said that he wanted to put his feet in the water.

Eden watched her husband quietly from under the tent. She was wearing a new Beachy dress for this last day's activity, a final Couples Talk session with Kit. She wrapped her arms around herself despite the warm wind—she had goose bumps.

Because last night . . . last night they'd taken a step that carried both joy and risk.

Chris was standing at the water's edge. He was looking out into the horizon, so peaceful, like he was having a conversation with nature. Times like this, Eden thought that perhaps he was talking to his parents, or bargaining with the universe. There had been times when she'd found him up on the roof of the main house, when he couldn't be disturbed.

It had used to bother her. She'd feel rejected since he was normally gregarious and extroverted. Then she'd realized that she wasn't entitled to this moment. Just as he wasn't entitled to the moments when she was in the middle of a story—those were their happy places.

As if feeling her gaze, Chris turned to her. A smile grew on his face. It said, *That was us, last night.*

In her belly, the butterflies stirred, and she grinned back at him. *Yes, yes, that was definitely us.*

"You both have come a long way," said a woman, and Eden turned. Kit.

Eden wasn't sure what to say. Alone with Kit, she felt disrobed; the script that she and Chris had decided upon this morning—*We are so much better now; thank you. We're going to take what we can and do better*—fled her mind.

Because her logic had warned her as soon as she'd woken: it wouldn't be that easy. They could have all the intentions, but when it was time to face the real world and their everyday choices, would they endure?

"I think we still have a long way to go," she said, opting for truth in the most general sense.

"If you didn't acknowledge that, I would be inclined to think that you might not survive this. But perhaps you both will."

She looked at the woman's profile. "What is survival, anyway, in love? Does it mean giving up your ideals? Does it mean jumping in even if you know it's going to be hard?"

"Survival is having the ability to take another step. With the one you love, it means taking it together. To the same place, wherever that may be."

"That's the problem. Location."

An eyebrow lifted. "Actual or theoretical?"

"Both."

"Hmm . . . though it looks to me that it's here that he's stepping to." She gestured to Chris, who was walking toward them. "And he's certainly got his eyes on you."

Eden's cheeks warmed because the way he was looking at her was . . . Well, it was hot.

"Ready?" Kit said as Chris took Eden's side. "Final session."

Chris took Eden's hand and led her to their chairs. "What was that about? Looked pretty serious."

"We were just talking about how pretty it is today." She searched his face. "You okay?"

"Yeah," he said. "Much better today than I have been in a long time."

"Oh, good." Except, what she felt wasn't all good. There was a tinge of the foreboding. Because this retreat wasn't supposed to be the end of the story. They were just at the beginning. Which meant, technically, that the happily ever after was still a ways away.

She tried to keep focus as Kit asked them a set of questions. All easy. It was a wrap-up. And she and Chris had practiced for this. There would only be straightforward answers from their mouths to keep the session brief.

"So, did you get what you wanted from this experience?" Kit steepled her fingers together on her lap.

"Absolutely." Chris beamed. "I'm leaving understanding that the world doesn't revolve around me. That I need to be mindful about my everyday priorities. I want to make sure I listen to Eden's needs."

Eden didn't look at him and kept her eyes away from Kit's interrogating gaze. She had to have been seeing right through Chris's lighthearted tone.

"And how about you, Eden?"

She bit her lip. She wished she could ask Kit how she'd know when she and Chris would be okay. She wanted to discuss the fear of this next step. There was always the push and pull of priorities. Once they made it back to the real world, whose priorities would take the lead once more?

Still, she went by the plan.

"I realized that I need to cut Chris a little slack. That actually, we both want the same things. And I think this retreat is the start to something new, and something better. Right, babe?" She smiled for effect, aware that this would be the final footage of this exposé.

A shadow passed over Kit's eyes, but the timer rang. "That is the end of our session, and the end of this retreat. I wish you the best in this next step in your marriage." She stood and shook their hands and stepped out from under the tent. Jessie lowered the camera, and Gil came around to hug them both.

"We did it." Chris wrapped both arms around Eden and looked down at her face. He was smiling—smirking, really, with that double meaning.

She relished his tight hold, her mind still catching up from the last four days. "I'm going to miss her."

"Who?"

"Kit." She shrugged. "She had so many good things to say."

"*You* and *I* had so many good things to say to one another. We should focus on that."

From the house exited their family: Beatrice, Brandon and Geneva, and Izzy and Kitty.

Not all her family, because hers were still back in Texas.

He laughed. "*After* we deal with these jokers."

They were surrounded by congratulations and cowbells and noise-makers and hugs, but what came upon her was the feeling of loss as they were split apart and the knowledge that this was it. Their alone time was over.

Gil was laughing. "You guys were amazing. There's no doubt now that the program works."

"More importantly, there's no doubt that you guys are meant to be with one another," Geneva said, clutching on to Brandon. "They were just clips and pictures, but you could see it on your faces."

"Though it was kind of cringe seeing Kuya Chris all sweet." Brandon shivered.

"Hey. All I've got to say is that my plants better still be alive." Chris leveled him with a look.

"*Yes, Kuya*, they are."

Eden realized she had two extra appendages on her body and looked down to Kitty and Izzy hanging on her torso. As the adults continued to speak, Eden bent at the waist to give them her full attention. They had a handful of questions for her, and Eden, as usual, took her time to answer each and every one.

Clapping from above took her attention, and she stood.

"Puso family meeting inside," Beatrice announced and led the way.

Eden flashed Chris a look. "Family meeting?"

He shrugged but decidedly did not look innocent when he took her hand. She followed him into the house.

The lights were off when she entered, and a cake was lit up with one lone sparkler.

"This is your real celebration, Eden," Chris said. "Congratulations, *New York Times* bestseller."

"Oh, you guys." She was bowled over by the sight, at the clapping and the hooting, and tears sprang to her eyes. The cake was a beautiful creation, with blue-ombré icing that looked like waves. Orange sparks mimicked fireworks over a beach. "This is wonderful."

"Hold on right there. Let me take a pic for your Instagram."

Eden stilled for the photo, then heaved a breath.

Did congratulatory cakes constitute a wish? Because Eden was making one.

Eden hoped against hope that the trepidation she felt in her heart was nothing more than fleeting doubt and that it would be smooth sailing from here on out.

♡

The real meeting happened after the cake and ice cream and when they'd gotten the girls to bed that night. And this time, it was at the main house.

Eden was wearing sweats and fuzzy socks, legs tucked under her while sitting on the couch. The iPad was projecting the teaser videos onto the flat screen on the wall, though Eden could barely watch. Something about seeing herself on the screen brought a flush to her face. It was the same feeling she had when readers gushed over her books. But with these videos, she couldn't hide behind the Everly Heart name.

She was also eyeing the clock on the wall, her mind on her to-do list. She had a slew of author admin tasks to complete like her newsletter and her monthly website update, and a word count to fulfill. Now that she was back from the retreat, she was fully under deadline, down to five weeks before she had to turn in a book. She felt the pull of work grow with every minute that passed.

Tammy and the rest of the siblings were scattered or perched all around the office, with Chris standing in front of the flat screen with one hand on his hip and the other on his phone, his thumb perpetually scrolling. He was presumably checking on some of their social media and teaser videos. Which, admittedly, Eden had not peeked at. She couldn't allow herself to get caught up in it. The last time she had, she'd contributed to pulling the both of them into the exposé, and she'd learned her lesson.

"How are the optics?" Chris's voice was a clear indication that he was back to his serious self. The lines in between his eyebrows had reappeared as he'd watched.

"Willow Tree is virtually silent. Not a peep since we called their bluff," Gil said. "They wrangled that troll Ricci is what I guess."

"I don't think it's the last time we're going to hear from them." Chris glanced up for a beat. "Did the retreat translate to sales?"

"No, not as of yet, though we've had an uptick in all of our socials and website hits." Gil ran through the numbers.

"But," Tammy interrupted, "one thing that's not silent are media requests. We'll have to sit and schedule. Podcasts, interviews. That's sure to increase the resort's visibility."

Eden was starting to get that sick feeling in her belly. All the talk about numbers was stressing her out. Since the movie deal and the *NYT* announcement, her own numbers had begun to climb, and she had her own growth to think about. Josie must've been overwhelmed. "Guys, I think it's time for me to turn in," she said finally.

"What's wrong?" Beatrice asked. "You don't look so good."

"Yeah. I . . . just think that everything is catching up to me. I'm exhausted from the last five days. And I really should call my dad. We briefly texted after the retreat, and we need to catch up."

"Babe, let me walk you up. Everyone, hold your thoughts." Chris jogged to her while she padded down the hallway.

"You don't have to. I'm fine." All at once, she clamored for some alone time. "I've got work, and so do you."

He rubbed her shoulders. "I know it feels like a whirlwind coming back home. I feel it too."

She wrapped her arms around his waist and breathed him in. "There should be like a postretreat indoctrination."

"Truly. But I meant what I said, even if it was a planned speech. I'll do better." He walked out to the deck and up the stairs to the second level, to their apartment. At the door, he leaned an arm against it. "Wait up for me?" His smile was genuine, hopeful.

"Yes, of course."

He leaned down and kissed her, and she shut her eyes at the contact. There was a light in his eyes, of excitement.

But, of course, he was excited. He was back in his element. As soon as she was writing, then she would be back in hers too. She understood it well, and she couldn't hold it against him. But she wished . . .

She didn't know what she wished.

What she needed to do was finish her book. "Don't stay up too late."

He was bounding down the stairs, like a little kid being granted permission to play. "Later, babe."

She entered their apartment, which was strewn now with their dirty clothing, and she started up a load of laundry. She turned on her laptop, and the chime was the siren call of an old friend. She coaxed it by running a hand over the keys, and she stoked it back to life by pressing on the trackpad with her thumb.

Then finally, she opened up the file of her work in progress with the dismal word count. She transferred her dictation from that one night from her phone to the computer. Then she stared at the document and willed the words to magically appear on the screen, to no avail. Then she stood and stretched, a second later deciding that a short yoga session might wake her brain. Ten minutes later, instead of words came hunger, so it only made sense to make herself a grilled cheese sandwich. She ate it with gusto, sure that with the increased calories circulating in her bloodstream, inspiration would strike. And yet, when she sat down, nothing came.

Eden slammed the computer screen down and pressed her hands against her cheeks, panic running through her.

Why couldn't she do it? What was she doing wrong?

She was now a bestseller, and she couldn't write a book. She was a fraud.

Her phone, which was sitting on the couch at her side, lit up with her dad's photo. A wave of relief overcame her—he just knew when to call. He hadn't done it often, comfortable in waiting for his daughters to reach out first, but he had this uncanny ability to sense a crisis.

"Iha." His face materialized as video chat connected. "Finally. It's good to see your face. I mean, on the phone." He smirked. "Looks like you had an interesting time on the retreat."

She winced. "You saw."

"Yes, I saw. But I think I'm going to skip out on the full exposé."

Her cheeks burned. "Oh yeah, definitely—don't watch it. Josie will fill you in. There are some . . . sappy parts, Dad." She never talked to her dad about these things, about matters of the heart and, more so, matters of the body. And it wouldn't have been him to be embarrassed but her.

She shivered reflexively.

"I'm not concerned about the sappy stuff. But if I see your feelings hurt, I might come out to Heart Resort and give that Christopher Puso a talking-to. I like the guy, but you're my girl."

"Aw, Dad." That was it. That was the thing to cue her tears. She'd tried to remain strong around him, around everyone.

He frowned, and his face neared as if getting a better look. "Has something happened?"

"No . . . I . . . I'm just overwhelmed, with everything."

He paused. "Everything, meaning what?" At her hesitation, he raised a hand. "You don't have to say, iha. I know how private you are. But with everything you're feeling, you don't have to shoulder it all. We're here for you too. And we can't wait to see you. Josie said that you'll be coming home?"

"Yep. I'm buying tickets soon." She smiled; still, she felt the weight of responsibility, with the chief culprit her deadline. But she'd promised, and this trip was important to Josie. And maybe she'd find the rest of her book in Austin. She had her Realtor to speak to. But before then, she and Chris would need to make some definite plans of what their future looked like.

She shut her eyes at the increasing to-do list.

"We can't wait to see you. There's no more hole in the ceiling. And I want to cook for you."

"Thanks, Dad." She sniffed. Even if no one could write her book but her, the reminder that she wasn't alone allowed her lungs to take in a little more air. It was sometimes so easy to forget that she could say something. "I'd better go. The book calls."

And yet, what remained even after she'd hung up was the memory of the teaser vids of their knowing glances, their fights, their conversations. Kit's wise words.

It's interesting that the both of you did the same thing but with different motivations.

"Motivations," she said aloud, the word ringing a bell.

The room seemed to brighten as a victorious laugh escaped her throat.

Her characters' motivations were all wrong. That was why she was stuck.

Eden jumped off her couch and headed to the one and only desk in their apartment. It looked out onto the water, and on it was a laptop stand. She dug out her wireless keyboard and mouse from the drawer and connected her devices.

She clicked to find the right file: her outline and character descriptions.

Eden was what one called a *plantser*. The combination of a plotter, meaning that she charted an extensive outline, but also a pantser, or someone who wrote by the seat of their pants, because her characters never did what they were supposed to do or acted the way Eden had planned all along.

She scrolled to the character descriptions and rewrote their motivations. This time, she dug deep into why her characters came upon life the way they did. Just as the retreat had shown her that she was moved not only by the contract and her career but by having a mother who didn't live at home, her characters needed a deeper backstory.

Luckily, she could make it up.

Then she wrote actual real words and sentences and paragraphs. Her fingers flew on the keyboard. It was as if her heart had expelled an extensive sigh, and along with it came emotions: messy, complicated, and confusing. Because characters and people, too, were imperfect.

Her editor would be receiving a heck of a manuscript. But Eden also had the confidence that somewhere in the gush of words and the remnants of a plot was the start of a good book.

The document rose by one thousand words, then two, then three. Eden lost track of time, of what chapter she was on. She just kept writing until she crawled into bed for a short break that inadvertently became a nap.

When she startled awake at two in the morning, she was alone in the bedroom. Chris hadn't yet come up from the office.

CHAPTER
TWENTY-FIVE

To: Christopher Puso <HRCeo@Heartresort.com>
From: Max Aguilar <MaxAguilar@AguilarAssociates.com>

Chris,

Hey! Sorry for the delayed email but as usual the crap has hit the fan. Work, you know. I'm back in Philly, and Vanessa's here to meet the parents before she heads back home. I wanna make sure we see you, and of course I've got to show off the resort, and take the last couple of days with just the two of us. Do you have room at the inn? Last minute cancellations? LMK.

Great to hear about the contract. Burn the damn thing.

v/r
MA

♡

84 days until Chan-Puso contract expiration
Word of the day: promulgate

Chris peeked at Eden through the curtainless window from their apartment deck. She was at her desk, head cradled in her hands. It was the third time he'd come in to check on her today without going into their apartment, mindful of her need for silence and solitude. They'd been home a week, which gave her another four weeks before her book was due, and Chris was trying to give her space.

Which was hard. They'd had a media event every day.

Still, Chris couldn't help but miss Eden. They were sleeping in the same bed every night and making love, but their pressures were seeping in slowly. Life had certainly been simpler during their retreat, and now he'd begun to feel what felt like withdrawal, so closely akin to the times he'd gone cold turkey to quit smoking.

"Chris."

Chris jumped and spun. Tammy. "Dang, you scared me," he whispered.

She mouthed an *I'm sorry*. "I figured I'd remind you. About an hour until the exposé viewing. But looks to me you're doing your own right here." She peered into the window. "Serious business going on. More continuing education?"

"Yeah . . . she's catching up from not studying during the retreat. Let's hope it's all worth it. Time will tell if Willow Tree launches a smear campaign against us."

"They know we're not playing games. The exposé will prove it. But most of all, you and Eden survived it. Not to get too personal, but seeing you both up there gave hope for all of us."

"Us?"

"Your employees. You fought for the resort, and us indirectly. It also proved to us that the retreats mean something. That the retreat concept isn't just a gimmick. That time together, and therapy, could work."

He nodded, his mind on the staff and whether he'd done enough listening. "Are you happy working here, Tammy?"

Her eyes rounded. "What do you mean?"

"I don't mean to interrogate. And now is probably not the time to have this discussion. But I do think I need some kind of a sensing session. Get the feel of how our staff, from the part-timers to the directors, feel about working here and how I can make things better. Is that something you'd want to participate in?"

"Oh, yes." She stood straighter. "I would. I have some thoughts, with how we've expanded as a company."

He nodded decidedly. "Great. I'll set it up."

She beamed. "Well, I'd better get back. But oh"—she lifted a finger—"I also added a couple more events for next week. I hope that's okay."

"Thanks. I'll let Eden know."

As he entered his apartment, instrumental Jodeci greeted him, piped through the Bluetooth speakers. A glance at the kitchen countertop revealed several cups half-filled with coffee, because Eden grabbed a new cup of hot coffee when the current cup cooled. He followed the trail of papers, as if dropped midread, to their bedroom, to the nest of papers with his wife in the center.

She turned to him, eyelids heavy with exhaustion. With her hair in a bun, and in a T-shirt and pajama bottoms, he imagined that this was Eden in college, studying and writing, and his heart squeezed. He wished he'd known her then. He wished he hadn't spent all those years wasting his time with anyone else.

"How's the manuscript coming along?" He leaned against the desk, in a spot where he knew he wouldn't disrupt the process.

"It's going." Except her expression was pained. "Better than before, but every word is like pulling teeth. I'm in the saggy middle, so much that all my meatballs are going to bust through. And did you know that *circumlocution* means evasion in speech?"

"Oh . . . yeah." It was always best for Chris to go with the flow and agree. "What can I do for you?"

"Write my book?"

"I can guarantee you'd lose your contracts if I did."

"Then can I have a snuggle?"

"Uh . . . okay." This, this was new. Usually Eden was exasperated when disturbed. He offered his hand. "This must be bad."

"It is." She stood, and a page fluttered to the ground. He willfully ignored the sticky note attached to the hem of her shirt.

Chris led her to the bed. "How do you want me?"

"Just lay down."

He did what he was told, and Eden nestled her head in the crook of his neck. She slung her hand around his waist and then a leg over his. A body pillow—that was what he was, but he didn't care. Right now, she was letting him into her world, and he would take any bit of it. Her body fit exactly into his, like a key into a lock, their joints and muscles accommodating one another. His body exhaled minutely, just so he wouldn't disturb her but enough that the worries of the day left him.

"I miss you," she said finally. "I feel like since we've been home that things are going back to the way it used to be. Me at my desk, you at work."

"I'm trying to give you your space."

"I know but . . ." She shook her head. "I'm complaining. It's the manuscript. Because it's not jiving all the way, so everything feels like it's out of whack." She looked up at him through her long lashes, and it took everything out of him to not kiss her. To distract her the entire day. Forget the show; forget her book.

This probably also wasn't the best time to mention upcoming events.

She continued, "I haven't showered, still in pajamas. I haven't eaten anything healthy in a week. I don't know what day it is. Why am I even doing this? Why do I do this to myself? I could get a perfectly respectable and well-paying job taking care of real people. Real. Not made up."

Uh-oh. Eden was panicking. She'd always talked about panicking with every book—but had he been under a rock? Because this looked disconcerting. He objected with the first thing that came to mind. "But it wouldn't be you, would it?" And then he saw it, that smile of hers. It encouraged him to go on. "You're the Chosen One, Eden. This is your battle." He grinned.

He'd gotten good at the tropes.

"Battle, like, because I look like—" She patted her hair, which, while lying down, looked like a smooshed bun.

He pressed against her hand to keep her from doing so. "No, don't. I didn't say that for you to fix it. These are . . . signs of you winning."

Her cheeks darkened with a blush. "Or losing. What if I can't do this after all? I had moments of really good work the last week. But most of it, honestly, has been just like this . . . nothing."

"I have faith in you. You're the most amazing person I know, Eden."

"You're just saying that."

"I'm not." He caught her eyes, to make sure she understood. "In five years, I have seen you write your way into and out of books. I'm always in awe of how you can just make things up."

"Whatever made all that happen is nowhere to be found."

"It's in there, Eden. You're at the midpoint."

Then she wailed in desperation. "Still the midpoint!"

He growled, wishing he could snap his fingers and make a completed book appear. He brought her closer, hugged her tighter. Then he remembered. "Wait. Do you know what you need?"

She sniffed. "What?"

"Wait right here."

Eden was predictable with her deadline snacks, but maybe, maybe if he shook up the snacks, she'd snap out of her writing funk too. And who had the best snacks but Beatrice?

"Okay." Her voice wavered.

He kissed her on the lips. He'd meant for it to be chaste, but in tasting her, he wanted more. He hovered above her and supported himself with an arm and kissed her deeply, guiding her chin with a knuckle. She moaned into his mouth, hands finding their way under his shirt. Her fingernails dug into his back, and he groaned. "Eden."

"Mmm?"

"I can't believe I'm going to say this, but you have to write."

Her arms slacked. She whined. "I know."

"I'll be back with something perfect to get you out of that middle."

He ran up to the third floor and knocked on his sister's door, to no avail. Brandon and Geneva weren't in either. Chris could not show up empty handed, so he jogged back down to Gil's apartment. Gil, his healthy, clean-living brother.

He had to have a secret stash.

"What's your snack inventory look like?" Chris said without pretense when Gil answered the door.

He was met with a sardonic expression. "Why, hello, Kuya Chris, how are you today? It's a gorgeous afternoon, isn't it?"

"Ice cream? Candy? Chips?" he prompted.

He sighed. "Kombucha."

"A chocoholic without chocolate? I don't believe you." He marched straight to the freezer and pulled it open. "Aha!"

"Whoa, whoa, whoa!" Gil held up a hand. "Dude. My ice cream. You can't just—"

"It's for Eden. Deadline snack."

"Fine," Gil grumbled. "Anything for Eden."

It was then that Chris noticed his apartment was silent, without a niece tearing through. "Speaking of wives. I've been meaning to get you alone. You've been busy."

Gil rolled his eyes. "*Ex*-wife. And I've been busy because this exposé's taking up some time, especially with the editing. Jessie and I really want to do the both of you justice."

Chris noticed that at the mention of her name, his brother's gaze darted away. "About the both of you . . ."

"Not you too. Everyone's got their opinion . . ."

Chris lifted his hands in surrender. "Listen, I'm not casting an opinion at all. I'm not even going to judge—I'm the last to."

"Really?"

"Yeah, really. My wife and I just did a couples retreat. We are far from perfect." *If you only knew, dear brother.*

"Wow. Okay. Thanks, Kuya."

"I just want to know how to approach this situation with the both of you. You seem to have gotten close."

"Did Eden tell you?"

Chris raised his eyebrows. "She didn't say anything specific. But I guess something *did* happen."

"Busted." Gil's shoulders lowered by a smidge, and his voice lost its edge. "We are . . . trying to get along. For the girls. And this project has been good for us. It has been a vehicle for us to talk about things. I guess it's safer when you're watching someone else's problems." He winced. "No offense, Kuya."

"None taken."

"Can I say something, though? About you and Eden?"

"Of course."

"It's obvious to me, to Jess—and the rest of the world will see it too—that you both love each other . . ."

"But . . . ?" Chris coaxed. Gil was gentle, the mediator. And when it came to relationships, to marriage, he'd had the most experience, and right now, Chris wanted his opinion.

"Love alone doesn't make a marriage. I should know."

"And what does?"

"God, am I even qualified to dispense this kind of advice?" He laughed. He rested his hands on Chris's shoulders, grounding him. "I can only say that you should choose one another, actively. Every day. It's not passive. Mom and Dad made it look so easy, but I wonder if they kept that struggle away from us. Anyway." Gil tugged him into an embrace, and Chris melted into him, not having realized that he needed it. It was different to give a hug than to receive it, and especially from a brother, who Chris could pretend was his father for a moment.

"Thanks." Chris swallowed his thoughts and stepped back. "Can I admit something? On the DL."

"Of course."

"I'm glad it happened. Me and Eden, we needed the time together. It was long overdue. Though, now that we're back, I don't know if we're falling back to old habits. Then again, some movement is normal, right?"

"Only you can say what normal is, though if there's anyone that's sliding back . . ."

He raised an eyebrow at Gil, surprised at this turn in the conversation.

"Since we're being vulnerable." Gil cleared his throat.

Chris took stock of his brother. Last year, when Gil had signed his divorce papers, he'd gone through a period of depression. The only thing that had kept him going was his children. But recently, he'd looked better and better each day. He'd dug back into his closet of brand-name clothing. He'd begun to care about what was going into his body. He was back. "Okay?"

"I arranged this gig so that Jessie and I could try things out once more, that maybe . . ."

"Do you mean?" Chris started. "You were doing your version of the retreat too?"

Gil half laughed, resting a hand behind his neck. "It was a good opportunity to be together but not entirely alone . . . have I told you that she's got a place in town?"

"Yeah, I mean, it's where she's staying right now."

"It's more. It's *her* place."

He winced. "As in permanent? To try to work things out once more?"

"Yes. And I'd like your blessing . . . and your help to mediate with Beatrice."

Okay, now Chris had to sit. He went to the kitchen table and plopped down. His brother put the ice cream back in the freezer for the time being. "Who knows about this?"

"Bran. He hasn't told Geneva, though."

"Probably smart since Geneva and Beatrice are as thick as thieves. What did Bran say?"

"His reaction was same as yours, but I'm a kuya, so he knows he can't say much. You, though . . . you're like our dad, so . . ."

He rubbed his forehead. "What's your plan?"

"I actually don't know, except to bring her around more. Look, for all the bad, Jessie and I have to try, for ourselves. For the kids. Just as Eden went on with the retreat even if it's not her style. Whatever it takes."

Right then, he admired Gil. "But our sister . . ."

"Our sister doesn't have to like Jessie, but she has to respect her enough to be cordial. Jessie is still the mother of my children. And for someone who's got shady down to a science?"

"Shady?"

"Bea's never here. And sometimes she doesn't even sleep here on the resort. She takes Roxy and disappears days at a time. She doesn't have the right to ask me a million questions and to judge what I'm doing with my life."

Chris could only nod, making a mental note to keep an eye out. It was true; he hadn't seen that dog of hers lately either, but then again, he'd had so much on his plate. He stood, stunned. He accepted the box of ice cream. "I swear. It's never a dull moment." He put a hand on the front door but paused. "Thanks for the ice cream, Gil."

"Anytime."

When he reentered his apartment, Eden was where he'd left her, lying on her back on the bed. She was sprawled out like a starfish.

He approached her with the box of ice cream in his palms like it was an offering for a queen. "Not quite boba but—"

She responded by squealing and pulling Chris by the shoulders to kiss him in gratitude. And while it erased all the family drama Chris was entrenched with, Gil's words lingered. *You have to choose one another, actively. Every day.*

♡

The television clicked off, and Chris swung his eyes to Gil and Jessie standing at the front of the room.

To his right, Beatrice dabbed a tissue against her eyes. Brandon and Geneva were sharing a chair meant for one, bodies entwined. And Eden was curled at his side, arm threaded around his.

They'd just finished watching *Heart Resort Exposé*, an hour-long reel that gave the highlights of their week. It was a documentary of both good and bad; Gil and Jessie had captured their fights on camera but had also recorded their reconciliation.

"Well?" Gil asked. "Thoughts?"

"I . . ." Chris was still processing the video. "It's . . ."

"Beautiful. It was beautiful." Eden took over. "The editing was so . . . I don't know . . . kind. How did you do that?"

"It was all Jessie."

Gil stepped back, giving Jessie the floor. She exuded trepidation, fingers wringing together. She cleared her throat. "I think it worked out that we didn't have a formal setup or crew, so the footage felt more personal. And in editing, I just thought about what I would be willing to show, though still in the realm of authenticity. After all, the point was for people to believe in the both of you and in turn believe in the product, which is the resort. Thank you, by the way, for letting me in. It was an honor."

Finally, Chris grappled his thoughts. "I didn't know you were at our last dinner, at Hapag."

"I think that scene with the both of you alone on the deck had to be the most transformative. Don't you think, Gil?" Jessie looked to him. "There was so little said, but we could see everything in your expressions. It was clear that you wanted this to work out, and I found myself all in for the rest of the journey, for this resort."

Gil nodded. "I agree, the deck scene will be the clincher. I think that this entire thing will be a hit. And speaking of hit, it's scheduled to post in a few minutes. Then we wait to see feedback. I'm sure that Willow Tree will have a lot to say."

Willow Tree had been the catalyst, the reason why they had done the retreat in the first place, but now, they were the furthest from Chris's mind. His present, real worry was in what the video reflected. Had he represented himself, his marriage, and his family well?

"Kuya?" Gil prompted, snapping him into the present.

"Yeah?"

"Not that we can do any huge changes at this point, but is this a go?"

He looked to Eden. "Are you good with it?"

She took a breath. "I mean, it's going to be us out there, and we can't take that back. But I don't see anything about Everly Heart, and overall, the video's just gorgeous. I say yes."

"All right, then. Let's do it." He hefted himself to his feet, wanting air. The room felt stuffed with all his issues. Seeing himself from a third-person point of view was settling ever so slowly, like a seed's germination. "I'm going out to the garden. Keep me posted."

The warm sun on his face was a welcome relief, though he didn't relax until his lungs took in the smell of grass, of dirt, and of trees. The vegetable garden was on its way; the tufts of greenery from the carrots had burst from the ground. The tomato bushes were healthy and already starting to bear fruit.

He bent down to rub soil between his fingers, a soothing sensation that grounded him to that moment, literally.

"Hey, I was calling you." Eden was walking his direction.

"I needed to get out of there."

"Same. But also. We have to talk." Eden showed him her phone— her calendar app. "What is all this?"

"Oh, ah . . ."

"Two things tomorrow, another couple the next day. I didn't agree to this."

"It's promo."

"Promo. But for the resort." She looked off in the distance. "I've . . . I've got to get this book written."

"I know, but . . ."

She looked at Chris blankly, and guilt sliced through him.

"I know I should've asked before agreeing, but you were so focused, and I just forgot, especially after . . . you know." He slung an arm around her waist. "The ice cream."

She blushed; her reaction sent heat straight south. Chris tugged her so their torsos pressed together, and her face switched to mischief. "Aren't you tired?"

"Never." He pressed his forehead against hers. "And I'm sorry. I promise, no more additions to the calendar without your okay. But the timing of all this. This is all so good for the resort."

"You're right. I'm just stressed, I guess. I'll do them."

"See . . . this. This is why you're the best." He wrapped both arms around her and blew a raspberry into her cheek.

She giggled and gently pushed him away. "Seriously, Chris. Four weeks to my deadline."

"Yes, ma'am. Promise, no more events."

"Hey, you two!" Beatrice called from the porch. "It's uploaded. Let the games begin!"

CHAPTER TWENTY-SIX

Six and a half years ago
Munich, Germany
Word of the Day: contaminate

Chris had been prepared to be able to walk into a room of suits and strangers without a blip in his nervous system. But walking into this international-travel conference mixer felt a little out of his league. First of all, he was overdressed. As always, he was wearing his best—he'd anticipated that the keynotes, vendors, and industry leaders of travel and tourism would be there. He wanted to make a good impression. He, after all, was looking to make partnerships, to network. Most of all, he was seeking a mentor. When he'd lost his dad, he'd also lost his advisor and the only person he could trust when it came to investments. It had been his father who'd intuited that the tech stocks would explode and, under everyone's nose, invested wisely to Chris's and his siblings' advantage.

But most everyone at this conference was wearing short sleeves, open collars, comfortable shoes, and something that delineated their brand. He took note of the logos and the colors, and his mind ran with insecurity and with ideas. And he started to sweat.

He texted his best friend, Max: I'm in over my head

It was dawn in DC, but he was sure Max was awake. That, or he'd respond anyway, because he was as attached to his phone as Chris was.

Max:

You're good

Chris:

No, I'm not. It was a mistake buying that island

Max:

Technically bro, it's a peninsula

Anyway, you've got this. Go in there, find someone in your category, and meet them

Chris:

It's like sharks in the water except they're dressed like dolphins

They look chill, but they're not. I can feel the competition

Max:

And you're?

Chris:

Dressed like a dang shark

Feeling like a dolphin

Max:

Own it.

Find out everything you can

Chris took a breath. He should have really brought one of his siblings. He'd insisted on doing this on his own, not wanting to seem ignorant. Second, well, they just couldn't afford it. Last-minute tickets cost a dime. And the dang island—er, Heart Resort—took too much out of his inheritance, more than the rest of his siblings'.

"You're gonna go in there." He nodded, more to himself, and after hanging up with Max, stepped into the conference room.

He immediately grabbed a beer from one of the servers, then regretted not paying attention. After chasing the server down to return the drink, he asked for and received a bottle of water. Then he circled the room.

Groups were huddled around counter-height bar tables. Raucous laughter emanated from the occasional group, but he knew from the participants' intense stares and assertive body language that the conversations were more shop than social, and in a variety of languages. He picked up German and French, Mandarin, and Japanese.

He trained his ears to pick up the English language. For Tagalog too. Something familiar from a group that he could gravitate to.

He had never been so glad to see a bunch of loud Americans. They had taken up a corner of the conference room, a group of twenty, all surrounding one imposing man. He was White American, built like a tank, his voice booming. He looked old enough to be Chris's father, and he had the crowd.

"Here's the deal, y'all," he said. "I didn't name our company Willow Tree for no reason. We sway with the wind. We're resilient. We've been in business since the sixties, the era of summer family resorts. Right now we're expanding and making our way back to the Outer Banks, slow but sure."

Chris noted the name: Willow Tree. He hadn't even heard of them; then again he hadn't exactly done his standard recon before he'd bought the peninsula. Beatrice had had one of her feelings about the piece of land when it had come up for sale, and for the first time in his life,

Chris had gone with his gut. Not his gut and research and experience. Just gut and gut alone.

A guy next to him crossed his arms and nodded as this Willow Tree person continued to speak.

"Who is he anyway?" Chris asked.

"That? That is Dillon McCauley the third. He's got about three resorts spread apart in the US and is going to take over the resort space—you watch."

Chris watched him throughout the duration of the mixer and kept him at his periphery. He seemed to be congenial—he was approachable. To another sputtering and nervous attendee, Dillon had even said, "Here's my card. Drop me a note. I'm always willing to share knowledge. A rising tide lifts all boats."

Hope flared in Chris's chest. Those were words of a mentor. Already he began to imagine their connection. After all, everyone stood on the shoulders of giants.

This man, this McCauley, was a giant.

So Chris skirted around him and, ten minutes before the end of the mixer, approached the man. He offered a hand. "Hi, I overheard that you have three resorts all across the United States. So impressive."

McCauley shook it. "Thank you. It took a lot of work. A lot of work, a lot of strategizing, and the right people working for me."

Chris was taking notes in his head: he needed experts. He'd already hired Sal Medina for security and Mike Strauss for maintenance. But he was still in the recruitment process. "If you could say one thing to an up-and-coming entrepreneur in this field, what would it be?"

"That's a good question . . . what's your name?"

"Christopher."

"Christopher. The one thing I would say is to be vicious."

Surprised, Chris took a sip of his water to process the man's answer.

"We might be working in a field that brings people joy, but behind it? It's all about who'll survive. By the way you're looking at me, you're taken aback by that, and that's okay. Let me give you a personal example. Willow Tree is trying to maneuver our way back to our home state of North Carolina. We almost got there, but we lost a sale of land by literally a week. My son, God bless him, lost track, lost focus, and another business swooped in. I'm still mad about it."

Chris kept his face still as he listened to him describe the heart-shaped piece of land, though his insides began to stir in warning.

"But I'm not giving up. I tell you, vicious is what makes you survive. You don't get through years of hurricanes and storms in the Outer Banks without a few layers of skin, hear me? And you can't get ahead of legacy, of roots. Willow Tree's roots are what everyone else stands on."

Chris's earlier hope flipped to anger that simmered just under his smile. He had to get out of there. "Well . . . thanks. Great." He started to back away.

"Oh." Dillon produced a card, and he twirled it in his fingers. The light caught the shine of the cardstock when he presented it with a flourish. "If you ever need anything, hit me up. What's your name again?"

Chris could have slunk away, then ditched the card. But he couldn't allow McCauley to get away with what he'd said. So he puffed out his chest and refused the card with a wave. "Christopher. Christopher Puso of Heart Resort. Outer Banks."

He watched the facts settle into Dillon's head, and it worked its way into his expression. When he knew that Dillon understood, he added, "Thanks for your advice."

He spun on his heel and exited the conference with only three things on his mind: He would never allow Dillon to lay his meaty paws on Heart Resort, and he wouldn't take what the man had said for granted. Finally, Chris couldn't let his guard down for one second.

CHAPTER
TWENTY-SEVEN

Reddit

Posted by LoveStigator 1 day ago

Has anyone watched Heart Resort Exposé? <u>Here's the link</u>. Listen, maybe I'm looking too closely, but I think this person is Everly Heart. Okay, so I'm a fangirl of this author, and I've been trying to figure out who she is. <u>Here's her Instagram</u>. Check out the clues <u>here</u> and <u>here</u> and <u>here</u>. Is it just me? Am I too excited?

Posted by BookLover 1 day ago

<u>This person</u> on Twitter noticed that Eden quoted Everly Heart's book.

Posted by IDontCare 1 day ago

Yeah, I don't really care.

Posted by LoveStigator 1 day ago

For those people who do care, this might be the smoking gun. Look at <u>Everly heart's profile</u>. Then check out this <u>screen shot</u>. It looks just like her, right? This is the hottest news to hit since Nicholas Sparks and his divorce.

♡

83 days until Chan-Puso contract expiration
Word of the day: impresario

Eden pried her eyes open after a late night writing and squinted at the phone lit up with a text from Josie: Call when you can so we can talk about your feed. Some stuff seems to be happening.

Eden checked the time. It was ten in the morning. She texted back: What kind of stuff?

Josie:

> Hard to explain. But I think people are trying to figure out who you are.

Eden sat ramrod straight and dialed up her sister, and Josie answered without preamble. "Have you been watching your feed?"

"No. I'm on deadline. I've just kept everything off." Last night, much like Chris, she'd vowed to stay off the net, her work taking priority. Now at 48,245 words—and that included the title page because everything counted, darn it—she was so close to a first draft that she could taste it.

Eden clicked on her socials. Her notifications were off the charts from thousands of new followers. "Oh gosh. Is this all from the exposé?"

"Yes. But click on your tagged photos."

Eden did as she was told. She'd been tagged in screenshot pictures of the retreat. One in her Beachy dress on Hapag's deck, with Chris popping the nonalcoholic champagne. The photo was gorgeous, backlit by the sunset.

Her breath hitched as she read the captions as well as the comments under the photos.

Is this Everly Heart?
All this time, this is where she's been!
So is it love after all?
"Oh God."

"This is what we want, right?" Anticipation laced Josie's voice. "Didn't you say that you wanted to go public with your identity? This just did it for you. No more scenic pics. Now you can do selfies and TikToks and other things. This could be really fun."

"Yeah . . ." Was she thankful that people were interested in her? Absolutely. All she'd wanted was to be read, and it had been inevitable that she would be known and recognized too. But it felt thrust upon her, when she was simply trying to do the minimum of her work, which was to make her deadline.

She rubbed her forehead. She thought of who she would need to speak to today: her agent, maybe her editor, her critique partners? Just to keep them abreast.

As her to-do list twisted in her head, a Twitter notification buzzed in.

@ColeRicci—Would you read a romance writer who had their own marital problems? Isn't that like buying snake oil? @EverlyHeart

Eden leapt on her husband and shook him awake.

CHAPTER
TWENTY-EIGHT

Travel Magazine
Spring 2022
Top three resorts in the United States (click through photos)

1. Heart Resort—The best of both worlds. Beachfront and relaxed atmosphere but with custom amenities and novel programming in the Outer Banks.
2. The Charlemagne—A castle in the Catskills. For the couple that wants to feel like royalty with a custom, avant-garde experience.
3. Mountain View Retreats—Glamping on overdrive. Set over the sprawling red rocks of Sedona, Arizona, where couples can experience an intimate outdoor setting.

♡

80 days until Chan-Puso contract expiration
Word of the day: clandestine

In less than forty-eight hours, Heart Resort had been inundated with unprecedented online attention. Eden's identity had been researched and stalked meticulously by very observant folks who had traced the lines in her books to the resort photos. Both the resort and Eden had been tagged by countless people. The discovery of her identity and her participation in the Heart Resort Exposé was discussed in various online media outlets, though no one in the resort had given an official statement to anyone.

As far as Chris was concerned, despite Cole Ricci's one disparaging tweet, all this exposure was good. Finally, they'd been named as *number one*. Hell, he wondered why he hadn't thought of asking Eden to disclose her identity sooner.

And Chris believed that they should take advantage of the buzz.

Chris was currently trying to convince Eden that there were positives in the admittedly chaotic situation, though Eden was ignoring him. They were in their apartment; Chris was perched on their bed, holding an iPad with the *Travel Magazine* article on the screen while Eden sat at her desk. Her eyes were on the computer screen, so focused on her book.

"Eden, I'd like your thoughts, please."

She shook her head while peering at the screen. Her fingers tapped on the keyboard. "About what?"

"About taking advantage of the buzz. A few videos here and there. Some day-in-the-life stuff. There's so much opportunity here—"

"No more videos for me." She heaved a breath. Her pointer finger now impatiently tapped on one single key, in the right-hand corner—was that the Delete key?

Chris shook his head of the thought, refocusing on his mission. "They won't be like the exposé. It'll be planned. It'll be good for both the retreat and your pen name, won't it?"

"No. What would be good for my pen name is to finish this book." She spun in her chair. Dissatisfaction was written on her face. "And we're too busy. We've got Max coming with his fiancée today, which will require us to entertain for the time he's here. One evening's taken up by my virtual event—that entire day will be shot for sure—and then my visit to Texas. I don't usually write on travel days. If you add all those days up—"

Chris frowned, and he felt himself fall into the same frustrated thoughts of what he'd assumed they'd fixed. "Texas? You hadn't said anything about Texas."

"I'm telling you now." She blew out a breath. "Look, I must have forgotten with everything going on. I bought tickets the other day. You know I've been planning to go since before the retreat. My calendar was free, so I scheduled a long weekend with my sister."

At the reminder of the retreat, Chris eased his voice. They'd come so far, and he couldn't push her. "But do you really think this is the right time?"

She half laughed. "Ah, so I've got to be mindful for my time if it's my family but have to move mountains for these events that you're attempting to guilt me into doing." She sighed audibly and turned around so she was once more facing her computer, which apparently meant that the discussion was over.

"Don't turn your back on me, Eden."

"Then don't put me in a situation where I have to make a choice. I need to go to Texas."

"But we have events this week and next."

"Surely you can handle it on your own. And you have an entire staff at your disposal. I have a family I haven't seen."

"But we're trying to build something here."

His voice echoed, too loud, and he regretted his tone. His words had taken on a completely different meaning. As the room settled into a painful and enormous silence, he took a deep breath. He couldn't let this spiral.

His phone buzzed in his pocket, and Eden snickered. "You wanna talk about building something? That's rich. Go ahead; I know you want to check your texts. Work calls, as usual."

Dammit.

And yet, he did exactly that. Because he was the boss.

Mike:

More WT information. Free? At the pier

Chris:

I'll be there in five.

"I've . . . I've got to go." He stuffed his phone back in his pocket.

"Of course you do. We're all on your schedule. Give me a buzz when Max gets here. I want to make sure I'm ready. We wouldn't want him to think that anything's amiss in the number one couples resort in the United States."

He caught the sarcastic tone in her voice. "Eden." But when she didn't answer, he added, "We're not done talking."

The golf cart ride to the north side of the peninsula was bumpy, and the skies were gray as Chris mulled over his conversation with Eden, but the ocean air had eased his thoughts by the time he jogged up the pier to the gazebo.

Willow Tree had continued to be silent the last couple of weeks. And today's *Travel Magazine* article, despite Eden's remark, had been a milestone triumph. They'd done it.

Mike was hunched over, hammering away at a loose board, and he stood. "Hey, boss."

"What's up, Mike?"

Mike sat on the bench, face contorted into seriousness. "McCauley's got secrets."

"Okay?" Chris took the opposite bench and girded himself.

"This is big." Mike paused. "McCauley had another woman."

"Wait. What?"

"He has a kid. I mean he's not a *kid* kid. Like he's a grown man. But illegitimate."

"How do you know?"

"My sister."

"Wow." Chris's mind spun. This information, whether or not it was true, was something. The personal nature of it alone was a weapon, much like the one that had been launched at their family. "This is . . . something."

"What do you think you're going to do?"

At the prompt, he talked it out to sort through how he felt, because suddenly, the information didn't affect him as it would have in the past. "This could really turn them all upside down. While it wouldn't discredit Willow Tree as a business, going public with it could take them off their game. It would shut them up for a while. They'd deserve it with all they tried to instigate."

"It could really piss them off." Mike winced.

"It would. It was exactly the info I would have jumped on even just a couple of weeks ago. But honestly"—Chris looked up at him, a moment's peace settling in—"I don't think I care now, especially with everything happening to Eden. Look, I want to thank you for helping me out. I know I put you in a tough spot."

"The McCauleys might be my in-laws, but it doesn't mean that I agree with what they're doing. You hired me at my lowest point. I was down on my luck, and you trusted me."

"You don't owe me anything."

"Maybe not, but it doesn't mean I don't want to do right by you. All of you are like a second family to me, and my loyalties are to you, so I think it's worth the risk, even if it ends up pissing my sister off."

Discomfort ran up his spine. At Mike's mention of the word *loyalty*, he was instantly remorseful of his conversation with Eden. He shouldn't have told her not to go to Texas. He should have supported her. Chris had a tendency to do this—he pitted the idea of loyalty against actions—and Mike was an example that the decision to side with someone came with consequences.

His phone buzzed him out of his thoughts. Sal, at the front reception area: Mr. Aguilar is here

Chris:

Thank you, Sal

"Mike, I've got to run. See you soon?"

"Yup." Mike performed a relaxed salute. "Almost done here. Then I'm off to Miss Beatrice's apartment."

"Oh? What for?"

"Her oven light bulb's out. I guess she left it on a few days straight."

Weird. His sister was never one to forget an oven light. And a few days straight?

Chris was still thinking about that when he arrived at the reception area. Since the exposé, they'd installed an arm gate, just as a precaution. He'd also required Sal to stop all nonguests or workers at reception to be escorted in.

When he entered the air-conditioned space, he was greeted by multiple voices in different states of bickering.

The first person he spotted was Max, dressed in a short-sleeve tropical shirt and shorts. The sight of him brought relief from what felt like a long, tedious decade. "Took you long enough to get here, man."

Max turned. His skin was a deep golden brown—must have been from his Italian getaway. His arms lifted in prep for a hug. "Chris!"

He muscled him in. "So glad you're finally here."

"Thanks for putting us up for a couple of days." He stepped aside and introduced the woman next to him. She was blonde, with a tan, and she wrapped her arms around his waist. "This is Vanessa. Vanessa, this is Chris."

She shook his hand. "I've heard so much about you."

"It's nice to meet you too. I . . ." Chris remembered that he'd forgotten to text Eden about their arrival. "I'll have Eden meet us at the beach house. Where've you been placed?"

"Halik." Vanessa turned to Max and kissed him, with obvious admiration. "The most perfect name. And yes, please take us away before Max gets into a fight."

"Fight with who?"

From behind him, the doors opened, and Eden walked in. She stuttered to a stop upon seeing Max.

For a beat, Chris was confused. "Hey, babe, I forgot to text. How did you know to come?"

"I called her," said a voice from behind Max.

Paige stepped up to the foreground with a scowl. Next to another woman.

Max dipped to whisper in Chris's ear. "I thought the contract was null. Because that woman next to Paige is Ann Allred. She went to my alma mater. Not to mention—her picture was plastered all over the billboards on the drive down here. She's a divorce attorney."

CHAPTER TWENTY-NINE

Here was the thing about being an unwilling participant in a social media storm: it upended your entire life. Though nothing that had been said about Eden was scathing—in her mostly obscure author life, she'd maintained a neutral presence, with what she considered the requisite promo—the idea of being scrutinized had a jarring effect.

Being tagged had made Eden want to click. And when she had, she couldn't help but read. And then she'd had no choice but to internalize their comments.

What had been a harmonious online life separate from her real life now was one big mush.

So when Chris had wanted to talk logistics and events earlier, Eden hadn't been in the mood. More than that—she was upset. Upset and disappointed that less than two weeks after coming back from what she'd thought was a relationship-changing retreat, she and Chris were back to where they'd started, with her feelings torn once more and him clearly not understanding her priorities.

Now, seeing Max and Paige in the same room, which stirred up memories of her and Chris's wedding day, Eden froze. What was this chaos of her life?

Paige's hug woke her from her thoughts.

"What are you doing here?" Eden managed to say.

"You haven't texted me back in days."

"I'm sorry. I've been bombarded."

"I figured, but since I was headed down to Hatteras, I thought I might as well stop by." She stepped back. "Though I had no idea that *Max* was going to be here. Hi, Chris." Her eyes slid over to Eden's right, to her husband.

"Paige." He nodded.

Max stepped in, pressing a kiss against Eden's cheek. "Eden, this is Vanessa."

It was jarring, with too many people speaking at once, but Eden focused and shook Vanessa's hand.

"And who are you?" Chris added, looking beyond Paige's shoulder to a woman Eden didn't recognize. It brought the group to silence.

"This is my dearest friend, Ann Allred," Paige said.

"Nice to meet you." Eden shook her hand, but the familiarity of her name was like the sound of wind chimes, subtle, but a warning. Then the doors of the reception building opened, bringing in the warm air and the chatter of Geneva, Brandon, and Gil. The room became a chaos of noise as more introductions and hugs took place, but Eden couldn't kick the feeling that something was amiss.

Before she could think about it much more, Chris pulled her gently by the hand. "We need to talk."

She toddled after him outside, and they turned the corner of the building, down the grass path that overlooked the sound, and in that time Eden pieced together the name, the situation, and the misunderstanding. The fresh air also woke up all the feelings that she'd kept to herself earlier this afternoon. As soon as they stopped, and she caught her breath, she said, "I didn't call Ann Allred, Chris. I considered calling her, even up to the middle of the retreat."

"Then what is she doing here?"

"I don't know. I can't help it if Paige still thought we were following through with the divorce."

"But why would Paige think we were getting a divorce if you had told her otherwise? And why would you have her bring an outsider into our business without telling me?"

You need to take care of yourself.

"I totally forgot, okay." She barked a laugh. "Because I've been too busy, oh yes, writing a book. And because I've been outed and am dealing with that, and we're doing these events when I should be writing a book." She forced her heart to settle and steadied her voice; it had started to become shrill. "Looking back, yes, perhaps it wasn't a good idea. But it's obvious no one is advocating for me but me."

"Advocating for what?"

"For me. For what I want." Eden hedged at this pain in her heart, at the truth that was squarely in front of her. She'd been skirting around it like a conflict point in her book that she didn't want to explore. Because it was painful, and to admit it would mean failure—and this time, in public. "Because this isn't working out." She held on to his hands, knowing right then what she had to do.

"What do you mean it's not working out?"

"I mean we're back to where we were before."

"Then we keep trying."

"Chris, no." She squeezed his hands to focus him. "I'm taking my trip to Texas early."

"No. You can't leave. We can't work things out when you're not around."

She shook her head, intent now. "I'm burned out. This is why I can't finish my book. And especially now, now with everyone knowing who I am. Now with all these requirements. Look at me. Writing has always been my love, and I can't do it. And I don't think it's just about the writing itself. You need to be with someone who can be here for you

297

one hundred percent, who can keep up with your speed and what you want, and that's not me."

"I don't need to be with anyone else. You're my wife, Eden. We need to figure out how to meet in the middle."

"That's the thing." Her eyes welled with tears. "What I know from experience is that the middle is a farce. It's a flux, Chris, and I'm always coming to you. And here . . . I'm suffocating."

As she spoke, Chris's expression hardened. It was matched by the change of his grip, now at the edge of her fingers. "That's not fair. I *have* been here for you. Don't make me the bad guy. I love you, and I'm willing, Eden. But are you?"

Eden bit her cheek, belatedly hearing the mistake in her words. "I'm sorry. I know you have. But right now, being here is not helping me."

She let his hands go and walked back up the path.

$$\heartsuit$$

Eden still wasn't left alone. Up to the security checkpoint of Norfolk International Airport the next day, she was trailed by Paige, Geneva, and Beatrice.

Paige hadn't stopped apologizing. "I feel horrible. I didn't mean—"

"I know you didn't. But maybe it was a good thing. Because I said what needed to be said. I have to find a way to breathe."

After Eden had told Chris she was leaving, they had been met by their family, watching them on the sly from the resort's windows. They'd brought them back to Heart Resort headquarters, where Chris and Eden had come out with the truth—about their contract and that something had evolved from their marriage of convenience. That there was love.

But love wasn't everything. It was a start, but it wasn't the finish. Love didn't solve the issue they continued to face: the acceptance of each other's expectations.

That family meeting had been probably the most functional thing that she and Chris could have ever done. It was also the most painful.

Still, Eden couldn't cry, not here, with these three women—sisters—who loved both her and Chris. She didn't want them to take sides.

"Heart Resort can be a lot." Beatrice nodded. "I just wish that your home wasn't a four-hour plane ride. And that Kuya Chris wasn't so clueless sometimes. He has these big ideas and grand gestures when all he had to do was listen."

Eden's maternal instinct, as well as her tendency to protect Chris, kicked in. "Your brother is the best that he can be. No one is perfect. I'm certainly not. It's just that we all have our limits." She turned to Geneva. "Your vows . . ."

Geneva was verklempt, and she swiped at her tears. "Don't worry about that."

"Of course I'm going to worry, but maybe, maybe I'm not the one to write it. It has to come from your heart. Trust that you know what to say."

"When do you think you'll be back?" Beatrice asked.

"I don't know, quite honestly." Eden shook her head. She had to take it a day at a time.

"For the record," Geneva added, "I support you. Sometimes it takes leaving to know where you belong."

"That's true, Geneva, but I'm looking at it a different way. I'm not leaving here. I'm going, for me."

The three women converged on Eden for a final hug, and she shut her eyes against their strong hold. She committed them to memory.

She let herself cry only when she entered the passenger tunnel into the plane's entrance, when she knew that there was no choice but to move forward and there would be no temptation to turn around. Because the fact of the matter was she wasn't sure if she'd made a mistake after all.

CHAPTER THIRTY

To: Christopher Puso <HRCeo@Heartresort.com>
From: Kyle Mortimer <KMortimer@KyleMortimerEsq.com>

Mr. Puso,

I've attached a screenshot of an article from Celeb Insider, indicating that Mrs. Eden Puso is residing in Austin, Texas permanently due to a separation. Not one to give credence to tabloids, we wanted to confirm your marital status as it pertains to your trust. You can reach us at any of the phone numbers below.

Sincerely,
Kyle Mortimer

♡

64 days until Chan-Puso contract expiration
Word of the day: apologia

Chris stood from the windowsill, tore his eyes away from his garden, and turned to face a roomful of his staff. Faces stared at him expectedly.

"Chris?" Tammy said. "Did you hear us?"

He squinted at her and looked for clues as to what she had asked. His eyes meandered to the television, which had a frozen picture of him in front of the beach. Without Eden.

Right. He was reviewing the footage to go up for their socials tomorrow.

"Yep," he croaked out and infused conviction in his voice. "Thank you. The video looks good. I approve."

Gil stood. "All right, meeting's over. Thanks, everyone." He shuffled everyone out of the room, leaving Brandon with them.

Chris couldn't even bother to care. He went to the couch and slouched into it and kicked off his shoes.

Brandon's eyebrows lifted. "This has gone too far. We let it go too far, Kuya Gil." He took a seat across from Chris on the ottoman. He bent and rested his elbows on his knees. "Kuya Chris, are you okay?"

"No. I'm not okay." He snorted, picking up from his last thought at the windowsill. "What's wrong with me? Why didn't I listen? Why did I push?"

"I think I've heard myself say a version of those words once upon a time."

"Me too," Gil said. "And if our sister was here—though of course she's not, but this isn't about her—she would say the same thing too. We *need* people. We hang on. Which makes us clingy and protective and stubborn."

Brandon nodded. "My therapist agrees with me that it's because we lost Mom and Dad. But with the right people, it's not such a bad thing to be so loyal."

"What's not great about this is that you aren't trying to figure out how to get her back. Mortimer's been emailing," Gil said.

"Mortimer's been emailing?" Chris had admittedly been distracted. Since Eden had left, he'd barely been able to get himself into the shower every day. He'd started to resent his phone. With every buzz he was reminded of Eden's disdain for it, and his compulsion to work. "I didn't notice."

"It's all right. Kuya Gil's been running the place," Brandon said. "I took on some things too."

"You have?" Brandon was a home-building consultant with his best friend, Garrett. "How about P&C Homes?"

He shrugged. "I can do more than one thing at a time, Kuya."

"Thank you, Bran." Then, to Gil, Chris said, "And Mortimer can email all he wants. I don't care about the damn money."

Gil's jaw slackened. "You really don't care about the money."

"I mean, of course I care. This business takes care of a lot of people. But I don't want to do this, any of this, without Eden. We can find the money elsewhere if we have to, but I'm done pretending."

"Then you're ready." Gil crossed his arms, grinning.

"Ready for what?"

"To get her back."

Brandon snorted. "Though he surely can't go with that shirt." He gestured to the ketchup stain on Chris's collar.

"It's from my fries," Chis said, just as an FYI. But as he said it, he registered their expressions, their worry. Had they ever looked at him that way? The reversal of roles woke him up, and he took stock of his clothing. Sure enough, both his shirt and his pants were wrinkled. He was wearing mismatched socks. He ran his fingers through his hair and noted how long his sideburns had gotten. "Anyway, I *have* thought about begging her to come back. Hell, I thought about buying a beach house for her family. Bring them all here."

"No. Not a beach house. Nothing big or grand. Just reach out." Brandon smiled. "You remember that Ate Eden was my resident advisor my freshman year."

"Yeah."

"She loved making care packages for each of her residents, for finals. She'd go out of her way. A banana, a bagel, and a granola bar in a bag. She cares. And showing her you care means knowing what she cares about."

"I don't even know where to start. Hell, I don't even know what she's up to."

Gil tossed him his phone. "You're such an old head sometimes, Kuya Chris. Check her freaking socials."

CHAPTER
THIRTY-ONE

SmashingBooks.com
Upcoming Events

Smashing Books presents a night with Everly Heart in her long-awaited and rescheduled first virtual and in-person conversation. This is a ticketed event with a giveaway. The highly anticipated event with this New York Times *Bestseller will feature her rom-com* One Plus One Equals Me and You, *which was recently optioned for film.*
Click here to register today.

♡

Austin, Texas
32 days until Chan-Puso contract expiration
Word of the day: advocate

The End.

With bleary eyes, Eden typed the final two words on her manuscript. She'd been working all night, and it was six in the morning. Her body was going to hate her in a couple of days, but right now, this was a triumph.

Was it a readable first draft? Far from it, but it was a shell, and that was all she needed. Something to work with, something to mold. And especially something to turn in to her editor, though late. Because what she had thought would happen hadn't. Leaving Heart Resort hadn't unblocked her. In fact, in addition to being blocked, she'd missed her husband.

But she'd made her decision. And she had to live with it, at least until she completed her event, which was set for tonight, and she could think about what her next step would be.

It was always anticlimactic finishing up a book. The planning, the writing, the revisions, and the lamenting. And just as with all her books, as she typed those final two words, all she wanted was a nap. A nap and some healthy food to reverse all the junk food she'd consumed, to get out in the sun because she'd turned into a vampire.

It had been Chris who'd always wanted to celebrate.

Eden felt herself soften at the thought of him. He would have pulled her out of her chair and rounded up the troops for a dinner at Salt & Sugar or a trip to Nags Head for ice cream.

On Eden's childhood bed, Josie roused from sleep. She was still in clothes from the day before; she had read chapters as Eden had completed them. She'd been a trooper, and Eden's thoughts trailed back to Chris, who had been her very first reader since she'd become Everly Heart. Knowing this book would be the first that he didn't read before she turned it in felt like a strange milestone.

Her phone buzzed on her desk with a text. She smiled at the sender.

Dad:

Did you finish?

Eden:

Yes.

A knock sounded on the door; she giggled. "Come in, Dad."

Paul walked in, a cup of coffee in hand, with a doughnut perched on top. "Congratulations, iha."

He was freshly shaved, and he smelled like toothpaste and deodorant. Eden was acutely aware that perhaps she did not. Still, her heart melted at the treats. "Aw, thanks." She immediately took a bite of the doughnut and plopped down on her bed, because she was probably hypoglycemic. Dehydrated too. Light streamed into the room when her father pulled the miniblinds cord. "Oh my God, that's bright," Eden said with a full mouth. "I'm melting."

Josie flip-flopped on the bed with a frown, and they both giggled. Her dad took her chair. "Did you sleep? At all?"

"No. And no time to nap. I've got dress shopping with Josie and then the event tonight. If I sleep, I might never wake up."

"Are you ready for your event?"

She shrugged. "The bookstore said that the location sold out, and there's a hefty amount of folks registered virtually. What if I won't match up to their expectation of Everly Heart?"

"It's pressure, for sure." He smiled. "But you can only be you. And you're pretty great."

Her father always knew what to say. And he knew how to say it, with this even and sincere tone, using very few words. She trusted his words and his messages, his intentions. It was the opposite of her mother, who was verbose. At the thought of her, she asked, "Do you ever get mad at Mom? About leaving?"

"Not mad. A little sad. Regretful, maybe. It's very hard to be angry when the other choice is family. I always imagine how hard it is for her, to live away from you and Josie."

"I get mad sometimes."

He nodded. "It's because you've had to take her place—and probably at times when it should have been me."

Eden realized what she might have implied. "I didn't mean . . ."

"Iha, you're the matriarch of this house. It's no secret. And I allowed it to happen. You have such good instincts. Not only do you care, but you also act. And even after you married, and you continued to come home, I didn't stop you." He paused. "But this trip home feels different. It worries me. Not for anything else but that I want you to be okay."

Eden was on the verge of saying *I'm okay* but thought otherwise, because at the heart of it, she wasn't. She felt incomplete.

"Do you still want to be married to him?"

She nodded.

"Then why are you here?"

"I needed space."

"I understand that. And we're here. But it's hard to make a marriage work from hundreds of miles away."

"Chris said that too."

"He's a good man, Eden. But for the record, when I talk about those miles, it doesn't mean that it's you that has to traverse them. He has to meet you somewhere on the path too."

♡

Eden ran a hand down the silky navy-blue fabric, fluffing the skirt of a potential prom dress before looking up at her sister's reflection in the mirror. "Is this it?"

"I love it," Josie answered, almost breathless.

"It's a perfect fit. The color, the brocade on the skirt."

"Everything would be perfect if you didn't look grumpy."

"I'm not grumpy." She tore her eyes away from her sister and bent down. "I'm just nervous about my event." But it was more. Her father's words had dug deep. Add it to the lack of sleep, and Eden was down-right impatient. Because she had to do something about Chris.

It's a flux, Chris, and I'm always coming to you. Guilt settled in with what she'd said before she'd left. It was hurtful; it erased all the things he'd done for her. She would need to fix this, somehow.

"I think we need to hem at least a couple of inches. And I saw a pair of shoes at DSW that would be perfect. Silver and strappy. Three inches," Josie declared.

"Okay to hemming, but one-inch heels."

"Two."

Eden heaved a breath. "Fine. Two."

"Can you pop down the zipper so I can change out?"

"Yep."

Minutes later, Eden paid for the dress, and they walked out of the store with the wrapped-up dress draped across Josie's arm.

"Perfect timing." Eden said as they climbed into the car parked outside the door.

Josie's phone buzzed, and she texted as Eden backed out of the space. Her sister hardly looked up on the drive to Smashing Books. If Eden hadn't been used to it, she would have been offended.

Smashing Books was located in a busy strip mall—though judging from the parking lot, half of the state was there. It took a couple of rounds to find an empty spot.

The bookstore itself had a crowd. Madeline, the event coordinator, a spritely pale-skinned woman with auburn hair, led them to the back room that would act as a greenroom and set Eden up with books to sign. Josie assisted and took photos.

As Eden finished up signing the last of the books, and with the start time of the event nearing, she whispered to her sister, "I'm super thirsty."

"I'll grab something for you. There's boba two doors down." Josie passed down her phone. "But take a look at your socials; some have already arrived for the event."

"Don't take too long." Eden's voice shook with the start of nervousness.

"I won't."

Eden had ten minutes before the event started, and the bookstore staff had vacated the back room to take care of customers and to close the shop to those not attending the event. She logged on to her socials.

Her Instagram account had dozens of notifications. She gawked at her follower count. Curious, she clicked to see who'd tagged her, and one profile name rang familiar.

@themrheart

She thumbed on the profile, and front and center was her husband's face as the first photo.

Hi there. This is Mr. Heart, yes, @EverlyHeart's main squeeze. You've heard a little about me, so I thought, why not get to Everly through my eyes. Every hour, on the hour, I'm going to post a picture of our family.

"What the heck?"

The second picture was of Eden with her nieces, taken from the back. She remembered this moment. They were sitting on the front steps of Puso, cloud watching. She hadn't realized he'd captured it.

She's a fun tita. That's auntie in Tagalog. She hardly ever says no to her nieces, and if the beach is involved, there's no stopping them from playing hooky.

The third photo was of her sitting next to Brandon. Looking at the hair, at the sadness in their faces, and at her arm around Brandon, along with the decorations in the background, it had to be New Year's Eve.

This was a rough night for our family. But this is your Everly at her best, with an arm around for support.

"What is this?" She looked up to Josie, who'd entered the room with two plastic cups of boba.

Josie leaned in and nodded approvingly and without the least bit of surprise. "He picked the right picture."

"You knew?"

"I mean, yeah. This has all been up for hours now. At least half the day." She sipped her drink. "Keep going, though," Josie encouraged.

The next picture was a candid of her and Chris from weeks ago, an outtake from their magazine photo shoot that didn't make it to the feature. She was fixing his shirt collar; he was tucking her hair behind her ear. This, she didn't remember at all, probably because this was them in their normal state. Taking care of one another.

Because she loved him.

They knew each other by heart. And they loved each other still.

She's my rock. And I hope I can always show how much I love and appreciate her.

Her face warmed with the start of tears, and she looked up to Josie smiling at her. "I'm going to text him."

"Everly, two minutes." Madeline peeked into the room.

"Okay." But before she stood, she clicked on her message chain with Chris. Aside from a text to confirm that she'd arrived in Austin, she hadn't responded to any of his messages. At first it had been to let Chris know that she needed her space. But over time she had realized she needed these boundaries as much as Chris. That what happened between them wasn't all Chris's doing.

She thought of the only word that she knew would matter between them. It had been their home for five days. It meant *acceptance*, an active word.

Eden:

Tanggap

♡

"Do I look okay?" Eden set her boba down on the stage floor next to her feet. She was sitting on a velvet wing chair. Opposite was a similar chair, with Madeline sitting in it as her host.

"You look amazing. Happy." Josie kissed her on the cheek one last time. "Good luck. In the middle of the event, I'll refill your boba. You'll need the sugar."

"Okay." Was she really doing this? *Oh my God.*

It was standing room only. Josie made her way to the back, near the entrance, and gave her a thumbs-up. Then she pointed to her cheeks— she wanted Eden to smile. And Eden followed suit, hoping that she didn't look like she was grimacing.

Madeline explained the night's events. A camera was set up on the side for their virtual attendees, who could be seen on the projector screen in the back. She'd be taking questions from both virtual and in-person guests. There was more, but all Eden could focus on was the sweat building under her arms and the buzzing in her ears, along with the fear that she would say something wrong.

"Thirty seconds and we're on," Madeline added.

Then, the lights dimmed, and the projector turned on. Boxes appeared like tiles, and those boxes turned to heads.

Madeline spoke into the microphone. "We're so excited to host Everly Heart here at Smashing Books, where we promise a smashing good time. A reminder to virtual attendees that you are welcome to log in your questions in the comment field. We will now mute all of your microphones. And we can get started with the interview."

Eden scanned the faces of the in-person audience and then the virtual guests on the screen; she found that watching the screen felt less intimidating, so she took her time looking at each individual guest. One person was wearing a top hat, which she thought was strange. Then she spotted another person with a top hat, then a third, and then more. And then she realized. The Pusos. They were all there. Chris, Gil, Beatrice,

Geneva. Her heart seized with gratitude, finding even Jessie with the two girls on one screen. And Mom.

Mom. It was dawn in the Philippines. And the idea that she was there . . .

Madeline began the interview, and Eden answered as best she could, though stumbling every few words. Most of the questions were easy: What was her process? Did she outline? Who did she want to cast for her movie? What book was she reading? Who was the author who gave her the most inspiration?

She answered honestly, and soon she was settled comfortably in her seat. A couple of times she felt calm enough to take a drink of her boba. Josie slipped in from behind with a second cup.

It didn't quite feel real to Eden that people wanted to speak to her. That real people were reading her books. That they cared.

It humbled her.

"We have another ten or so minutes left before this conversation ends, so I'm going to take the last couple of questions. Everly, Janice C. in Dayton, Ohio, asks, 'You have such a loving relationship with your husband. We saw that in the documentary. What hints would you give to people who are new in their relationships?'"

Eden paused in order to frame her relationship with Chris correctly in her head. She had to be careful here. Because a triple-digit number of people were watching, and they were taking her experience to heart. And what if she gave them the wrong advice? No one knew what happened behind their closed doors.

She shut her eyes and spoke her truth. No more pretending. "I . . . I don't know if I'm qualified to give advice. My marriage to Mr. Heart, Chris to me, is young—in my opinion, in its infancy. But if I were to give it, it would be what was given to me: find out what *you* want, and start there."

I want him. Her conscience answered without hesitation.

A microphone was being passed to a person in the audience. In the lull, Eden reached down to her new cup of boba. It was frigid against her fingers, a relief. She was parched.

But when she brought the drink to her lips, she noted writing on the side of the cup.

She was deciphering the words when the microphone squeaked, and a woman stood. "Hi, I'm Leslie Singh. I'm such a huge fan. If you had a dream nuptial ceremony, what would it be?"

"Hmm." She thought of how magnificent and beautiful her wedding had been, even though it had been thrown together so quickly as part of a transaction. She remembered having the jitters and how she'd declared that she had a choice. And her choice was marriage.

"My choice . . ." She looked down at the cup once more. She made out the letters T . . . a . . . n . . . g . . .

Tanggap.

She twisted the cup to the boba shop's logo. "How did this name get here?" she asked aloud.

Leslie raised her eyebrows in question.

Eden looked up at the screen, at the tiled boxes. The Pusos seemed to all have a similar dark background. She found Chris, gaze steady across the screen. Presumably at her.

Behind him was the dark background.

And she had a cup of boba with the word she had texted to him.

"Your choice?" Madeline prompted.

"Choice . . . ," Eden started once more, though her thoughts were still on Tanggap. "Leslie, I already had my dream nuptials with all the bells and whistles. But for my vow renewal, I want it to be at Heart Resort, with our dearest families. Flowers in my hair, sand at my feet. My nieces blowing bubbles for our procession. Because it's about the marriage, isn't it? Not the ceremony, not the pomp and circumstance. I loved my fancy wedding. Every person who wants one should get one. But for this next ceremony, I want it to be simply about me and my husband. And I want it for real and forever. Now, will you please excuse me." Eden handed Madeline the microphone. "I'll be . . . I'll be right back." To her guests she said, "Don't go anywhere."

Then Eden walked down the center aisle and out the door. She was going to get her husband.

CHAPTER
THIRTY-TWO

"Wait, did you hear that? She said *vow renewal*," Beatrice squealed in Chris's ear. "She totally *Notting Hill*'d you. She's a romance writer through and through."

They—the whole family except Jessie and the girls, including Paul Chan—were sitting in a quiet corner of Big Shot Boba, slack jawed. Chris stared at the video-chat screen, where Eden had left the stage. He leapt to his feet. "Did she read it?" He looked down at his family.

"I read it," came a voice from a few feet away. *Eden.* After a beat of silence, she said, "You're here."

"I didn't want to miss it." Chris didn't know what to do with himself. It had been weeks since he'd seen her, and while part of him wanted to speak to her privately, he understood that this had to be done here, in front of their families. There would be no more pretending.

"Nice hat." She grinned. A good sign.

Chris took off the plastic top hat from his head and shrugged, cheeks warm. "Izzy's idea. She wanted us to have party hats, but the party supply store had shut down, and these were the only ones available at the grocery store . . ." He was rambling, so he tossed Brandon the hat and stuffed his hands in his pockets. He needed to snap out of it; he couldn't just stand there. So he approached Eden and took her hand in his.

His hand shook; he was more nervous than he'd been at any boardroom meeting, but it was because he had more at risk. Eden was his wife; she was family. She was the love of his life. And she'd written enough declarations of love to know when one sucked.

So he spoke from his heart. "It was wrong for me to make you choose. I was afraid of losing you, and I put my foot down instead of listening. You gave me all the opportunities, but I was too wrapped up with work. I was selfish. And I know this seems like a grand gesture, with everyone here, but I swear, they insisted on coming."

"We did," Brandon said in the background.

Eden laughed softly. Another good sign, and it encouraged Chris to go on.

"You have always been first, Eden, but I failed at showing it. Like it took me too long to come here. I know it's a lesson I'm going to need to keep learning. I've made plans to add assistants, hiring more people. Gil is helping me to restructure. So I can step away. For me, for us. So I can step off the resort, so you never have to choose, and I can show you that you are the most important person in my life."

Eden was unmoving, and silence permeated the shop.

Chris's tummy twisted. "I'm too late. Oh God."

She leaned up to kiss Chris, and her lips halted his runaway words, causing him to shut his eyes. When he refocused, she said, "You're not too late. I've missed you so much, and it's been awful without you.

"I don't regret taking the time out, Chris. But in leaving, I know I never want to do that again. I'm sorry I blamed you for my writer's block. I used our relationship as an excuse because I was scared. I was scared to be dependent, and then to be left behind. But I'm not willing to let us go. I want to work for this, for us. We're going to need help. At least I know I do, to create boundaries, to learn to say what I want. To say no if I have to and not feel like I have to be everything to everyone.

Kit might get a phone call from me soon." Her lips curled into a smile. "But I'm willing to fight for us. Because I love you. And I want to be married. For real."

"Thank God." He choked out a cry; he palmed her cheek, swiping away her tears. "So we're doing this?"

She was smiling, and she pulled him down by the shirt. "Yes."

And Chris kissed the hell out of his wife.

Then Chris got down on one knee to a collective gasp in the room. He presented a velvet box containing another inheritance from his parents. In it was a platinum eternity band his mother had worn. "Eden Puso, will you marry me again?"

She looked into Chris's eyes and said, "Again."

CHAPTER THIRTY-THREE

Heart Resort, North Carolina
Word of the day: de novo

"I'm nervous," Chris said, for about the millionth time that morning.

"Yeah, you are," Max said. He adjusted Chris's shirt and pulled a stray speck of lint from the white fabric. "But you shouldn't be. This is old hat to you."

"But this is different."

"It'll be better."

Chris peered at his friend. "Who are you, and what did you do to my best friend?"

"It's called love, brother."

"I mean, I knew you loved me."

"Har har," Max said. "But smile; it's not a business meeting, man. It's your vow renewal."

Chris pursed his lips and blew out a breath. It was ridiculous how he was feeling. There wasn't a cloud in the sky. The wind was cooperating. Everyone was in their right spots, and most of all, he had not a single doubt in his mind that five years to the day of their first wedding, they were finally doing this right.

He wanted to get this right. For Eden. For him.

Music sounded from the distance, and Chris turned toward Tanggap. And finally, after the longest minutes of his life (he knew he was really nervous by how hyperbolic he was being), his nieces came out wearing white sundresses and ribbons in their hair, blowing bubbles as they came up the aisle.

Then, from the door, emerged Eden, his wife, in a long flowing dress with thin shoulder straps. Hair loose, lips a glossy pink, shoulders bearing a bit of a sunburn from her days on the beach. She was barefoot and was seemingly floating through the sand, and with the sun shining from behind her, she looked like an angel.

Chris never thought he'd be a hero in a romance novel, yet there he was, from a marriage of convenience to a marriage of love. But this was better.

Because this was real.

ACKNOWLEDGMENTS

This book. This book. Throughout the writing of Chris and Eden's story, these two words were on replay in my head.

This book.

This book is special in so many ways that cannot really be condensed into the acknowledgments section. What I *can* do is thank all the wonderful people who helped bring this book into the world.

Montlake editor Lauren Plude—you gave Chris and Eden the ability to *go there*, to get to the root of what made them tick. Your enthusiasm for their story pushed me to give them the HEA they deserved. Agent Rachel Brooks, my unyielding cheerleader, thank you! Deepest thanks to the team at Montlake, especially Jillian Cline, Cheryl Weisman, Mindi Machart, Ashley Vanicek, Morgan Doremus, and Susan Stokes. Cover magicians Hang Le and Regina Wamba. The Amazing Kristin Dwyer of LeoPR, who is always at the ready. Melissa Panio-Petersen for coming into my author life at the most perfect time. #girlswritenight April Asher, who read a super early copy of this book, along with Annie Rains, Rachel Lacey, and Jeanette Escudero. #Batsignal Mia Sosa, Tracey Livesay, Nina Crespo, Priscilla Oliveras, and Michele Arris. Tall Poppy Writers, especially Amy Impellizzeri and Sonali Dev. Teri Wilson. #5amwritersclub, especially Ralph Walker for his special intervention on those critical days when I was wrangling my draft into submission. My home support crew, Greggy, Cooper, Ella, and Anna, who endure deadline season on the regular. And my husband of twenty-four years, Greg, who talked through Chris and Eden's marriage with me with as much investment as I had for them.

None—absolutely none—of this would be possible without my generous author friends, readers, influencers, booksellers, and librarians who have shouted my books from the rooftops and who are always willing to go on another roller-coaster story. From the bottom of my heart, thank you.

ABOUT THE AUTHOR

Photo © 2020 Sarandipity Photography

Tif Marcelo is a veteran US Army nurse who holds a BS in nursing and a master's in public administration. She believes in and writes about the strength of families, the endurance of friendship, and the beauty of heartfelt romance—and she's inspired daily by her own military hero husband and four children. She hosts the Stories to Love podcast, and she is also the *USA Today* bestselling author of *In a Book Club Far Away*, *Once Upon a Sunset*, *The Key to Happily Ever After*, and the Journey to the Heart series. Sign up for her newsletter at www.TifMarcelo.com.